The Garden Path

The Garden Path

A Novel

KITTY BURNS FLOREY

Copyright © 1983 by Kitty Burns Florey

Cover design by Neil Alexander Heacox

ISBN: 978-1-4976-9359-3

Distributed by Open Road Distribution
345 Hudson Street
New York, NY 10014
www.openroadmedia.com

For Dan Wickenden

The Garden Path

Chapter One

A Wind from the West

Rosie Mortimer's garden, the one that has been seen and admired on television by millions, was as bleak as anyone else's in the middle of January. Rosie looked out the window at it that cold morning, as she did every morning before doing anything else. In spite of the weather-stripping Barney had installed on all the windows, a thin gust of the cold got to her, and she pulled her old wool bathrobe tighter as she stood there. She didn't enjoy getting out of bed at seven in the morning in the dead of winter. Who does? thought Rosie, trying for some kind of kinship with those who had no choice. She had set her alarm so she could get to work on the book she was supposed to be writing: *Rosie Mortimer's Garden Book.* She hadn't had much luck in the afternoons or evenings, so she thought she must be an early-morning writer. She was beginning to be afraid she wasn't any kind of a writer at all, and her morale was low as she stood there and shivered.

The sight of her backyard, dearly though she loved it, didn't help. It was an untidy pattern of browns: brown earth, dead-brown trees, shrubs and bushes in dull khakis and tans, brown leaves in loose piles thrown by the wind against the compost fence. Six stubborn hydrangea snowballs, bleached beige, still clung to their branches. The few bits of color—purply red holly-grape leaves, periwinkle still green under the burlapped rose bushes, scarlet berries on the euonymus— were overwhelmed by the drabness, and so, nearly, was Rosie. It took a gardener's imagination to see the garden as alive and potent, full of change and slow growth, with juices running in its chilled veins. And that was the way she did see it; part of her did, anyway, the most ancient and basic part, and the professional side as well. She made her living by such observations. "Rosie Mortimer's Garden"—check your local listing for time and channel.

One of her most well-received programs was the tour of her January garden—not this one, but two Januarys ago, when she had demonstrated to her faithful viewers evidence of life and renewal designed to chase away the winter doldrums: forsythia buds, snow-drop tips, leaflets on the azaleas, and scaly tufts on the pussywillow. "In the Midst of Death" was the gloomy title Janice, her producer, had given that show. "Nature doesn't hibernate in winter along with the bears," Rosie informed her audience—tartly, as usual. Tartness was her trademark—not tartiness, which her producer firmly suppressed. All attempts at ribald humor were considered out of place in the bosom of Mother Nature, who was seen by the folks at WEZL–TV as a bit of a prude. All off-color remarks were deleted, and if on a summer day Rosie should wear a shirt that exposed even one millimeter of cleav-age, on went the old canvas gardening apron along with the makeup and the hidden mike. So she came across all brisk and hearty, and she said things like, "Nature doesn't hibernate in winter along with the bears. It's only the gardener who does that, for want of a better occupa-tion. Hibernates with the seed catalogs, that is," and she twinkled her eyes at the cameras and they followed her indoors to her fireside, the pot of tea, the plate of scones and jam, the pile of seed catalogs on the old trestle table. Her producer had provided the nice new pot—one of those fat brown ones that scream England—and the scones and the jam. Jampot, too. The seed catalogs were Rosie's, though, and she had made the fire because no one else understood her fireplace.

But in spite of all the cheery, upbeat gardening talk for the cam-eras, January always depressed her, and she thought, as she stood there looking at the scene and shivering, that it was nice, it was reassuring, it was even quite beautiful, really, that Nature was so busy with her fecund underground life; but what showed when you looked out the window was simply winter, the weary brown look of it. The garden was like an empty house before the movers come with the furniture and pictures—better yet, like an unattractive pregnant woman. She was pleased with that last image. She looked around for a pen and paper to write it down for her book, found nothing, closed her eyes and said it over three times to imprint it on her brain. By the third time it sounded far less clever. When she opened her eyes it was snowing, and she stood and watched as the snow slowly, silently covered the dull garden browns with nets of snowflakes, softening and cleansing, getting heavier and quicker and more substantial, until the primroses were covered, the brick borders, the hay mulch on the strawberry bed. Even the lower shrubs threatened to be lost as snow gathered on their bare branches and piled up on the cold earth around them.

But enough. Rosie dressed quickly, in old jeans and a red sweater, and went downstairs to get herself some hot breakfast: instant oatmeal, one of the great advances of our time, and only a hundred calories if you don't count the butter and the brown sugar.

She was outside knocking the snow off the conifers with the broom when her son Peter telephoned, and he drove over to see why she hadn't answered the phone.

"You were worried about me," Rosie accused, after she hugged him and kissed him. She was aware that she had been, perhaps, an excessively fond mother to her son, but it was too late to do anything about it now.

"I wasn't." He sat there in his favorite chair, handsome and blandly smiling. Rosie's son looked like her father—not like his own father, her ex-husband. This made her happy every time she looked at him, even at that particular moment, when he was irritating her.

"You were. You'd think I was *elderly*. You'd think I was helpless and decrepit. I am not quite fifty years old, Peter. I'll be forty-nine until May. I had a complete physical last month. I am in perfect health. Just because I don't answer my phone is no reason you have to drive twenty-five miles to check up on me." Her voice, meant to be humorously reprimanding, came out fretful and fussy—overemphatic.

"Oh, Ma," he said, responding to her tone, waving one hand around aimlessly and slouching down in his chair. For years those words and that gesture had meant *let's drop it.*

Rosie was willing. She looked out the window. The snow had stopped; there were a few wan rays of sunshine. The backyard was blue-white. The shrubs she had cleaned off were blackish against the snow. "This will thaw before evening," she predicted. "Won't amount to a row of pins, as Grandma used to say."

"I had a letter from Susannah."

Rosie looked from the backyard to Peter. "I beg your pardon. You had what?"

"A letter from my sweet sister Sue. After all these long, peaceful years. That's why I called you."

He was slouched so low in the rose-patterned wing chair that he was almost flat, his head propped at an angle that gave him a double chin. She wanted to tell him to sit up, then realized that wasn't the proper response to what he had said. She stayed silent.

"She and her hubby are moving back East."

Rosie knew he was watching her, and she made herself look out the window again, gazing hard at the snow, the side of the garage, a chickadee in the feeder. "Where East?" she asked.

"Chiswick. Practically the old home turf."

She clenched her fist and banged it down on her knee. "Damnation," she said, glaring at him. "And will you please sit up straight? You look deformed."

He sat up. "Don't get mad at me. I didn't invite them here. She and Vladimir or Nikolai or whatever his name is are going into business."

"Ivan. What kind of business, may I ask?" Rosie tried to imagine—her coldhearted, hippie daughter and her son-in-law the expriest. What business? Penny arcade. Massage parlor. Crackpot church. Hypnosis/acupuncture/meditation center.

"Are you ready for this one?"

Rosie wasn't. She wasn't ready for the fact of their arrival, much less for the harebrained project that was bringing them. "Tell me," she said, wearily but not without interest.

"Health food restaurant. They've rented a place on the Post Road, right near Dunkin' Donuts, with some friend of theirs who lives near here. Remember that bookstore that closed up a couple of months ago? In there."

"Damnation," Rosie said again, but absently, thinking hard. She was trying to imagine her daughter, who used to scatter candy wrappers behind her like falling leaves and who couldn't, Rosie believed, have much more business sense than a cat, running a health food restaurant in a location partnered by fast-food chains, auto body shops, a roller dome. Another thought struck her. "Why here, Peter? Why so close to me and to you? Did she tell you that?"

"No, she didn't, but it ain't nostalgia. I'll give you one guess."

Rosie stood up and went around the corner into the kitchen to hide her agitation. "Well, they certainly won't get one cent out of me." She filled the kettle and put it on to boil, and stayed in the kitchen to wait for it. She needed to be alone to compose herself; the anger that gripped her at Peter's announcement was a complete surprise. She had thought her daughter's life had long ceased to affect or involve her, and here was her heart thumping loudly and her pulse beating audibly in her left ear and her breath coming short. What if I die? she thought. What if the news kills me? She imagined Peter hearing her fall, finding her in a heap on the kitchen floor, stretching her out, trying the CPR techniques he had learned in a class at the Y, in vain, and then blaming Susannah for it, and Susannah . . . Rosie saw her daughter's triumphant smile and pressed her hands to her heart, forced herself to breathe deeply, to relax. She looked out the kitchen window. There—the sun was out properly, shining yellow on the snow. Brown patches showed already on top of the stone wall. The triumph of the sun, she thought. The idea rubbed away the image of Susannah's smile and cheered her. The phrase might do for her book. A chapter title? For a chapter about what? She must at least do an outline today—this afternoon, before Barney came.

"You making tea?"

"Yes."

"Ah—good old Mum."

Dear Peter. The thought of Susannah prompted the sentiment, though it was never far from her mind. The dear boy. Except for the fact that his sexual preferences precluded grandchildren, he was a perfect son—a daughterly son who dropped in for tea and gossip. And as for her daughter, who at the age of ten had rejected her mother and chosen to live with her deplorable father, Rosie hadn't seen her in seventeen years, except for one disastrous incident. But there were her letters. The first one had arrived when Susannah was in college, an attempt at mollification with a plea for money at the end of it. Rosie burned the letter, then regretted it. It was an unbeatable specimen of sheer gall, and she wished she had it to read over periodically as a reminder of the depths to which human nature could sink. And though she didn't answer it, more letters came, erratically, maybe two a year on the average. They got subtler as Susannah got older. One or two didn't mention money at all, or did so only obliquely, with statements like, "It's dreadfully expensive living in San Francisco, and Dad is so busy sometimes he seems to forget I exist." This sort of thing failed to touch Rosie's heart; her heart, alas, had become untouchable from that particular quarter. She did pay off Susannah's last college loan, though, not because of Susannah's plea but because of Peter's, after he saw his sister on a trip out there and said she was unemployed, undernourished and unhappy. But Rosie gave the money to Peter and made him pay it off in his own name, and directly to the Financial Aid Office, not to Susannah. Lord knows what she would have done with it—or what heights her begging letters would have reached if she'd known who was her fairy godmother. Shortly after the loan was paid, Rosie got a letter from her, reproachful in tone, in praise of Peter's generosity and, by implication, lamenting her mother's lack of same.

During the first few years after Edwin and Rosie split up, when he and Susannah were living in New Mexico and then California and she heard from them only via child support payments and their occasional letters and cards to Peter, Rosie's feelings toward her daughter had been composed, she admitted readily, as much of hurt pride as of dislike. If Susannah had chosen to stay with her and Peter, Rosie could still have viewed her as a troublesome but salvageable brat. At least Edwin would have been out of the way, unable to spoil the child and make excuses for her behavior. But with the coming of the letters, active animosity entered Rosie's heart and expanded there until the day she had come face to face with Susannah, three summers ago, and made the scene that became family history. After it, the letters ceased. And now the wretched child was on her way to Connecticut, to settle with her hippie husband and her insane business in the next town.

I'll go to Florida, she thought wildly, knowing she wouldn't. Her friends the Sheffields were there for the winter. A pelican had stolen Kiki Sheffield's handbag when she set it down to snap the bird's picture—just picked it up in his bill and dropped it out in the ocean somewhere, with her pills and two hundred dollars and three exposed rolls of film in it. The Sheffields sent postcards of garish tropical vegetation. "Azalea blossoms the size of grapefruits," they wrote. "Grapefruits the size of basketballs. Avocados in our backyard. Roses in January. Wish you were here. Love, Jim and Kiki."

No thanks, Rosie always thought when the postcards came. *They can have it.* She knew she wouldn't change her mind, even with Susannah and her husband in the vicinity. Even if war was declared, she would stand her ground. Let them back off if anyone did. I was here first, she thought, knowing she was being childish and not caring a damn.

The kettle boiled, and Peter and Rosie sat by the fire with their mugs of tea. Rosie saw them there, in imagination, with the eyes of someone looking in through the dirty weather-stripped window: a woman in jeans, busty and big-bottomed, with her hair gone scraggly, needing a cut; and her fashionable—foppish?—son in a toast-colored sweater patterned across the chest with a row of red hens, his mustache waxed upward at the corners, and his brown eyes—like hers, like his grandfather's—soft with sympathy.

"I don't mean to jump to conclusions," he said. "She may not have money on her mind at all. She says they're both sick to death of California. They're homesick for *weather*, she says." The fire's fangs gnashed at the logs, and Rosie held her cold hands toward the blaze. Peter sipped his tea and smiled at her. "Poor Ma. What do you do if you meet her on the street?"

"Just what I always do! Go on about my business. And Dunkin' Donuts is not an establishment I frequent. Neither are health food restaurants." This was said in her best tart TV manner, but the scene entered her imagination for a painful second: herself versus Susannah on the street, in a store, thrown into inescapable proximity on line, in a waiting room, at a restaurant. What then? Rosie's mind numbed and went blank, and she shivered. The fire failed to warm her.

"Knowing Susannah, she'll be going down to McDonald's for her lunch break," Peter said. "I don't see her going the bean curd route. Though I suppose California could do it to anyone."

"I'm sure I won't run into them."

"They just might look you up."

"She wouldn't have the nerve."

"Don't underestimate her."

Florida, Rosie thought desperately, hugging her tea mug with cold hands. Her pulse pounded in her ear like the surf. It was true—Susannah had the nerve of a pelican. Just because her mother had slapped her and insulted her and cursed her in public, it didn't mean she would stop trying. Edwin, never very generous anyway, was, last anyone had heard, in Mexico with his new popsie, who was younger than his daughter. And not too long ago, *Peopl* e magazine had spilled the beans about what kind of money Rosie was making from her television show. She should have expected to hear from Susannah.

"Well, they won't be here until spring," Peter said. "And who knows if it'll come off, anyway? I don't get the impression she and Dmitri are the world's most stable individuals."

"Ivan," she said, trying to remember what her son-in-law, the expriest turned painter, looked like. Ivan Cord, his name was—short for something unpronounceably Slavic, probably. She had seen him just once, and she had a vague recollection of a large and hairy man with a pale, sullen face and thick lips. "He looks like something from a monster movie, if I recall," she said to Peter. "*The Creature from the Black Lagoon*, or *White Pongo*. I'm sure he's some kind of an addict."

"I don't think so," said Peter. "He's not so bad, really. Probably better than Susannah deserves." Peter's derogatory remarks about his sister were halfhearted, automatic, designed to please, and almost without any connection to the real Susannah, who had achieved, with the two of them, the hazy status of myth, she'd been gone so long. "He's not my type, of course," Peter added, looking at Rosie for reaction. Such remarks were still fairly daring: he'd confessed his homosexuality to her only a little over a year ago—for Christmas. "Too macho."

"Hmm," was all Rosie said.

"Or yours, either," said Peter. "Too counterculture."

"Please, Peter." Sometimes he went too far. "What amazes me," she said, maliciously, "is that he and Susannah are still together. What is it—four years since the wedding we were so kindly not invited to? He must be a dreadful man." In the midst of anger and dismay, Rosie felt curiosity creep up.

Peter refused lunch. It was a Friday, and he always spent Friday afternoons in the computer center at the university. Rosie wasn't sure why a dissertation on Dante required the assistance of a computer, but Friday had been Peter's computer day for so long she no longer questioned it, or even thought about it—just as she took it for granted that Barney Macrae got up from her warm bed to go to church on Sunday mornings.

"Mr. Chips coming for the weekend?" Unlike Peter's sex life, hers had been common ground between them for years. "You two going to sit around the fire in your shawls talking about the good old days before there were Cuisinarts and indoor plumbing?"

"Something like that," she said, regarding him fondly as he put on his camel-hair coat, his plaid muffler, his red earmuffs. There was always a campy touch, like the earmuffs, or a satin tie with palm trees on it, or a Dumbo watch.

"Really, Ma—can an old guy like Barney still cut the mustard?"

"Old guy indeed! You should be in such good shape when you're fifty-five. And it's none of your damned business." She kissed him and patted the knot of his muffler. "Have fun with your little machines, dearie."

He picked his way down the slushy front walk, and Rosie watched him from the door until he got into his Volkswagen and drove off, honking. The sun was gone, the sky flat gray, and it looked like snow again; it was as if the dark shadow of Susannah was already blighting the weather, putting any sunny predictions out of whack. Rosie slammed the door and returned, shivering, to the fire to think about her daughter.

It's not that she hadn't been a good mother. She was dedicated to Peter from the start, from the minute he was handed to her by a perky nurse, his eight pounds swaddled in blue flannel, his eyes shut and his mouth open, and his red fingers, with their tiny ragged nails, opening and closing in a way that seemed to Rosie heartbreaking. She fastened him to her breast as if he were a little lost thing in a storm and she the Saint Bernard with the cask of brandy, and felt a pang of unprecedented joy—symbolized, she always felt, by the pinching pains that tugged at her uterus whenever the baby nursed. The organs tightening up again, the doctor told her, getting ready for the next one, heh heh heh. But Rosie knew better—they were the bittersweet pains of motherhood, and she welcomed them.

She tended him gladly, restless while he slept, running to the crib at his first waking cry to change him, nurse him, cuddle him, exchange baby talk—anything. She was a mother before all else; when her baby was asleep it was as if she ceased to exist. She bragged, like any mother, about what a good baby Peter was—meaning he slept a lot, slept through the night after a couple of weeks, took long naps—but she would have actually preferred him colicky or high-strung or just plain active, so long as he was awake.

"I don't know anyone who's such good company," she used to say to people, especially the other mothers she met on the Common. While they complained about night feedings and diaper rash, Rosie confounded them with her unbroken serenity, and she must have disgusted them with her smugness. She was unpopular, but she didn't care. She had Peter, after all—her snugglewumps, her baby bunny, her muffin, her piggywig.

She was twenty years old when Peter was born. She had been married to Edwin for a year and already things were going badly. Peter was her refuge, and though she had a glimpse now of how unhealthy that was, then it saved her from certain despair. She left Edwin out completely, deliberately, laughing at his disgust when he came upon her cooing and making silly noises at the baby. "Oh, Edwin, you old prune," she used to say, smiling a little as if she were joking.

"You're spoiling him with all that attention," Edwin would say, and Rosie would turn to Peter. "Was oo a spoiled muffin? Was oo?" watching Edwin's disapproval from the corner of her eye.

He was five years older than she, just out of law school, working in the legal department of a big Boston insurance company. They lived in a dark, grubby building on Marlborough Street, in a third floor apartment at the back. Rosie had been plucked from her parents' vast green acres— Liliano's Garden Center, on Route 1 near Westerly, R.I.—and transplanted to the barren wastes of the city, where the only garden she had was a row of houseplants that grew in the one window of the apartment that didn't face north. During that first year, before Peter was born, she used to walk not only in the Common and in the Public Garden with its bright formal beds of annuals, but out as far as the Fenway where there were wildflowers, and vegetable plots grown by city dwellers, and one gorgeous rose garden tended by an old Scotsman in knickers and a cap. She had wondered how one went about getting a plot there, and always meant to ask Mr. McPherson, but she never did because then Peter was born and she no longer needed a garden. Peter was her plot, her lovely, lush flowerbed, and she was his Mr. McPherson; she was little Mary Lennox, and he was her secret garden.

Rosie was a gardener, of course, the daughter and granddaughter of gardeners. It was in her blood—green veins run in the family, her father used to say. Rosie's father was Peter Liliano—named for the owner of the estate in southern England where her grandfather, Massimo Liliano, had worked as a gardener. He had been imported from Italy for the purpose in 1896 when Peter Elliot-Casson, a wealthy young fellow on the Grand Tour, admired the work he was doing at a villa near Naples and decided the gardens at Silvergate needed restoring. He had a vision, he said, at the Villa Bianca, on the steps that swept down to the goldfish pond bordered with box and camellias, of the way life should be—green and verdant and full of flowers. He offered Rosie's grandfather a job on the spot, and Massimo and his wife, Anna, arrived in England less than a month later, in August. Silvergate was a wreck. The following summer it had become a promising wreck, a year later a charming wreck, and by the time the century turned it was on its way to being a showplace.

The Lilianos emigrated enthusiastically to England, and like typical converts they became more English than most Englishmen. Times had been hard in Italy; their *padrone* was mean and stingy—so tight he squeaked, as Massimo learned to say when he got to England. A real skinflint, Anna would add, but you had to know her well to catch the words through the maze of Italian inflections they were lost in. They both learned English quickly, but they never lost their accents—Rosie's grandmother especially, who always called her Rose in three elongated syllables. No one else, Rosie was sure, had ever spoken her name so beautifully.

Rosie was born at Silvergate in 1931, and she always thought her grandparents' story was better than a story in a book: the two simple young Italians brought by a great lord to the ruined estate, to turn its brambly wastes into a place of beauty, and succeeding beyond anyone's dreams, and founding their modest dynasty there. Anna and Massimo had three boys, all given English names—Frank and James and finally Peter, named after their new padrone. All of them became gardeners at Silvergate, all three married English girls, and all three—in the late thirties, when old Sir Peter was dead, Massimo was dead, Anna was an old woman gone blind, Silvergate belonged to the National Trust, and war was on the way even to the gardens of Kent—all three emigrated to America. Peter was the last. He had hoped to stay at Silvergate forever, but he didn't get on with the caretaker the National Trust had installed to oversee the place, Mr. Horace Hogg, who called Italians "Eye-ties" and wrote a monograph for tourists stating that Sir Peter Elliott-Casson had designed the gardens himself and carried out his plans "with the help of imported peasant labor." No mention of Massimo Liliano, whose genius had cleared away the decades of brambles and brush and neglect and put in their place the roses, the delphinium borders, the lily pond, the clipped box hedge that people traveled to Kent especially to see. Peter Liliano took his mother and wife and daughter, his copy of Gertrude Jekyll's *Wood and Garden* and his back issues of *The Countryman*, and sailed to New England to work in the garden center where his brother Frank was manager. In three years he had his own place—Liliano's Garden Center, as famous in its way as Silvergate had been. Where else could you buy Bramshill lilies and the double bloodroot?

Rosie was six years old when she arrived in Rhode Island with her Italian father and her English mother, and she already knew about rose blight, and bone meal for bulbs, and the proper pruning time for japonica. Her knees were usually dirty or greenish, crisscrossed with the print of grass blades or stuck with tiny stones, and her hair was so often matted with dirt and leaves that her mother cut it short. None of them cared about such things. What the Lilianos liked was getting out in the garden and digging in it. Rosie was given *The Secret Garden* one Christmas. She was sure it was *her* book, written for her pleasure, and she knew much of it by heart, including the parts in Yorkshire dialect. She used to amuse her parents by asking, plaintively, "Might I have a bit of earth?" in an accent so thick as to be, like her Nonna Anna's Italian one, nearly incomprehensible. She always had a bit of earth, too—even at age five she had a six-by-six patch behind the gardener's cottage, between her mother's grape arbor and her father's rose bed, where she grew, in neat rows, daffodils, cosmos, coral bells, sweet peas, and strawberries—so that at nearly fifty she could say, "I've grown strawberries since I was five years old," leaving out the seven years on Marlborough Street where nothing grew but geraniums and spider plants in the one sunny window. And babies.

And her dislike of Edwin. During the first year of marriage, Rosie had declined from being madly in love with him to disliking him profoundly. It seems a short time for such an enormous change, but it happened, and it was, Rosie insisted, Edwin's fault, though she was sure he blamed her. But he was the coldest man she had ever met; any warmth in him was faked, and temporary. They never discussed their problems. Both of them sensed they were insoluble, not really problems at all but simply the results of a mating error—two different species coming together by hazard in a monstrous union that no amount of discussion could ever put right. They despised each other quietly for twelve and a half years, and then one day, after two wild, bitter, violent months of arguing, Rosie threw him out. At that point she stopped hating him and seldom, in fact, thought about Edwin any more at all, considering him, when she did allow him to enter her consciousness, faintly disgusting—an old guy pushing sixty living his warped conception of the good life, last heard of in Mexico with a twenty-year-old chippie who he really believed loved him for his fine mind and his gorgeous body and not for his bank account. Poor old Edwin.

Susannah was his idea. She was born when Peter was two years old. Rosie had suspected that Edwin wanted a second child, from his sudden unwelcome ardor after Peter's first birthday and his denunciation of rubbers as unnatural. She didn't mind having another baby. Edwin wanted it, she was sure, so he'd have a child on his side as she had Peter on hers, and she looked forward to the sheer fun of getting the second one in her camp too, imagining Edwin's dismay when he found himself on the short side of a 3–1 score.

But Rosie didn't take to Susannah as she had to Peter, especially after the child passed out of the purely helpless stage. She was a difficult child, unresponsive to cuddling, and nothing like the good sport Peter had been. And she resembled Edwin, especially when she was getting ready to cry and the closed-in, stubborn look turned her face an angry red.

Rosie was shocked at herself when she realized that she wasn't warming up to her troublesome new baby, but she blamed it all on Edwin. He'd forced this second child on her before she was ready, and she spent her days in a blur of exhaustion that he did hardly anything to ease. She felt they were in league against her, Edwin and Susannah, to wear her out, to turn her into a shrew; and the more Rosie looked at Susannah's petulant little face the more the child resembled not only Edwin but Edwin's mother. *She's not mine*, Rosie thought to herself almost from the beginning, both sickened and fascinated by the way the thought persisted. And it was as if Susannah shared her conviction. She would look up at Rosie with her hard blue eyes antagonistic and knowing, unimpressed by Rosie's attempts at mother-love, and the expression on her face said *I'm not yours*.

Rosie used to walk both children laboriously down to the Public Garden, Susannah in her carriage, Peter toddling haltingly along Commonwealth Avenue at her side. Now Rosie joined the other mothers in complaint, and understood the solace to be derived from communal bitching. The mothers in the park were mostly a new bunch. No one remembered Rosie's old boasts about Peter's charms, though she had no doubt they were appalled by her blatant favoring of Peter over his whiny sister, and gossiped about it, predicting woe for the gallant little lad. But Rosie always told herself, with conscious liberality and a touch of defiance, that if Peter's homosexuality flowered from her love for the boy, then homosexuality must not be such a bad thing.

Peter used to wobble over to his sister's crib and look at her in wonder as she lay there squalling. "Baby cry," he would say, looking puzzled.

"I know," Rosie would answer, weary from her efforts to comfort and placate. "Baby cry all the time."

And Edwin would stalk over, put the baby up on his shoulder, and cuddle her magically into silence, glaring at wife and son over Susannah's red, bald head.

When, at the age of ten, Susannah said, "I don't want to live with you any more—I want to go to New Mexico with Dad," that must have been the sort of thing she remembered: her father coming angrily to her defense, her brother looking on calmly, secure in his good behavior, her mother turning away with a sigh. Or so Rosie thought, helplessly, in later years, when all the harm had been irrevocably done.

They moved out of Boston, finally, when the children were still small. Edwin was transferred to the Hartford office of his company, and he commuted there from the town where they finally bought a house, after much looking, that suited their needs.

Rosie's needs were simple—she wanted a place where she could garden. And so were Edwin's—he wanted something more impressive than his brother Art's house on Long Island. They agreed, without discussing it, that a long commute wasn't a drawback. When they were looking in East Chiswick and the real estate agent, dubious, pointed out that it was a good hour away from Hartford, Edwin and Rosie looked at each other briefly, then away, and said, in unison, "That's no problem."

They both knew that the less time they spent together the better they got along. In fact, as years went by and their marriage was increasingly revealed as a disastrous mistake, they admitted it—not openly, because, from the first, little with them was ever honest and open, but by a series of tacit machinations that struck Rosie later as absurd, even crazy. If she told Edwin, for instance, that she and Peter would be spending Saturday afternoon baking cookies for the first grade Halloween party, then he'd volunteer to take Susannah to the park. He was capable of pushing her on the swing there for an hour or more at a time, and she was capable of sitting there just as long, going down and up, down and up, her skinny little legs dangling, making no effort to push herself. Or they would go for long, pointless bike rides, racking up the miles on their odometers. Or they would drive to the other end of the state to see a dog show, or a planetarium show they had already seen three times. But Rosie was glad they had their diversions, just as they were no doubt glad she and Peter had theirs. She could think of only a few things the Mortimers did *en famille*—the circus, once, at which both children cried when the lion-tamer flicked his whip at the animals. Things like Thanksgiving dinners, of course, with one or the other set of grandparents and in-laws. Now and then the beach, which Rosie hated but the rest of them loved—and she wouldn't let Peter go with Edwin and Susannah alone for fear Edwin wouldn't watch him closely enough and he would drown. She used to picture the police coming to the door, her son's bloated, wet body dripping seaweed, and her hands around Edwin's throat, squeezing and squeezing, her nails digging in. So she would put on her bathing suit, pack a lunch, and sit grimly on the blanket in the sun getting a headache from trying to distinguish Peter's wet bobbing head from a hundred others while Edwin, a strong swimmer, swam back and forth along the ropes, steady and determined, his elbows going up like fins, his head swiveling from side to side—and anyone who failed to get out of his way was out of luck.

So they bought the house in East Chiswick, a tiny town attached to Chiswick like a nose to a face. The shopping centers were in Chiswick, and the auto body shops, the McDonald's, the Dunkin' Donuts; East Chiswick had an old wooden-floored Woolworth's, two antique shops, a florist, a greengrocer, a butcher, a French restaurant, and a store called Trade Winds that sold imported china. All this appealed to Edwin. It's a well-known fact that to be able to afford to live in a sleepy, simple little hamlet like East Chiswick you have to have plenty of money. It pleased Edwin to advertise the fact that he had moved up in the legal department of his company with a rapidity that startled even his mother, who thought he was a genius and who had told Rosie on her wedding day that her son was quite a catch and she hoped Rosie could live up to the responsibility of being married to him. And this is how naive Rosie had been—she said she would try; she even took Mrs. Mortimer's fat hand and squeezed it.

The house itself was too small for them. "Buy the community, not the house," the real estate man told them. "Better a three-room shack in East Chiswick than a palace in someplace like Middletown or Danbury." So they ended up with not quite a three-room shack but a small, tidy Cape Cod on a dead-end street with an acre of land. The acre was what sold Rosie. Edwin liked the land, too, because Art had only half an acre, but what finally sold Edwin was Susannah's discovery of a shed that had been converted to a playhouse, complete with window boxes and a doorknocker. "Buy this one, Daddy," she pleaded in the imperious way that Edwin found so winning. "If you buy this house, you get two—one for me and one for you." She gave Peter and her mother an excluding frown and pulled on Edwin's arm with both hands. "Please, Daddy, please, please." He grinned down at her and ruffled her blonde hair. "Well," he said, and then he looked at Rosie and pretended to become serious and businesslike. "It does have a nice kitchen, Rose. Two bathrooms. Good yard. Just about what we need."

"Only three bedrooms," she pointed out. "And don't forget it needs a new roof."

"Still . . ." Susannah tugged at his arm. "I don't know. Let's make an offer on it. I don't think we can do better."

"Daddy! Daddy! Daddy!" Susannah yelled, and streaked off toward the playhouse, Peter following her and trying to look nonchalant.

"I don't seem to have much choice, do I?" Rosie said with a shrug and a facial expression she had mastered over the years—a magnanimous but pained smile, as if the goodness of her heart forced her to squeeze it out against terrible odds. "We might as well take it. I suppose we're all sick of looking." Her lukewarm approval, hiding the fact that she had fallen in love with the place as quickly as Susannah had, was meant to ruin any pleasure Edwin might find in the purchase. Oh yes, she was a terrible bitch, but she felt she had to pay him back for tricking her into marriage.

Edwin had tricked her into marriage, when she was nineteen and he twenty-four, by pretending to be interesting. He kept it up for an entire year, from the day they met until the wedding. By the time they were married he was thin and tired and nervous and unable to go on with it—the pretense. It crumbled on their Caribbean honeymoon, when he spent long hours simply lying in the sun, and stopped talking to her in restaurants while they waited for their crayfish and their mango pie and their exotic rum drinks served in hollowed-out pineapples, and while the steel band played with a black intensity that made Rosie sad. She thought Edwin was tired of her already, that she had begun to bore him, and she cried into her pillow every night after they made love and he went to sleep. She thought he had decided she was good for only one thing. It took her months to discover that he was simply tired of being fascinating—of taking her to the theater and the opera, of telling her funny stories from his college days, of asking intelligent questions about gardening, of promising to take her to see the gardens of England and France and Italy, of devouring *Newsweek* and the Sunday *Times* so he could wow her with his knowledge of the world. He settled, as if with a grunt, into the cold dullness that was natural to him. The repetitive acts that she came to associate with him—the back and forth swimming, the long sessions pushing Susannah on the swing, the tolerance for those daily drives up and down Route 91, even his incredible but, in the end, tedious endurance in bed—were, she decided, his way of winding himself up for life. He was always in danger of running down. He was a taciturn, introverted, selfish, incurious man who wanted most of all to be left alone. If she had a meatball for every time he said that all he asked was a little peace and quiet she could open a restaurant.

She must have been, at nineteen, just the kind of wife Edwin wanted—young, pathetically naive, and upwardly mobile. She loved her parents dearly, and she loved her old Nonna Anna, who was still living with them, blind and arthritic but funny and full of beans. She was fond of Liliano's Garden Center, too, and she was perfectly con-

20

tent to work there on weekends all through high school and, when she graduated, to work full-time, either behind the cash register or outside taking care of the plants and shrubs. But she didn't want to spend her life there. She had grand ideas, vaguely incorporating an estate not unlike Silvergate. She wanted to be the grande dame ordering the viburnum and the wisteria, not the person who delivered them and sent the bill. At this utterly inane period in her life, she met Edwin. Edwin was a clerk in a law firm in Providence that summer. He was in his last year of law school at Harvard. He used to drive his fat and patronizing mother to Liliano's to pick out flats of boring annuals, or he used to stop by for bags of fertilizer and grass seed. Mrs. Mortimer fancied herself a gardener because every spring she had her favorite son, dear Edwin, plant the perimeter of her lawns with lavish borders of red and white petunias and impatiens and salvia, outlined in blue ageratum for a patriotic effect. By the end of the summer, these garishly florabundant plots, cultivated and fertilized and pinched back every weekend by dutiful Edwin—who gardened in bathing trunks so he would tan—were undeniably an impressive sight. So, incidentally, was Edwin.

"You should see my mother's garden," he said to Rosie one day when she was selling him a length of garden hose. He was in his bathing trunks and a T-shirt. His legs were long and golden-haired.

"I'd love to," she said.

"Hop in the car. I'll take you over."

She admired the red, white and blue extravaganza, then—sensing she hadn't gone far enough—gushed heartily. Mrs. Mortimer, after all, was a good customer. She beamed at Rosie when she finally hit the proper level of enthusiasm and offered her a lemonade. It was hot out on the lawn, and she accepted. Rosie discoursed on the benefits of planting perennials rather than annuals: the financial saving, the greater variety, the satisfaction of watching something grow from year to year. Edwin, pretending to be interested, asked intelligent questions. His mother nodded patiently for a while, then quit listening and smirked with satisfaction at her petunias. Rosie had a second glass of lemonade and a tuna sandwich. While Mrs. Mortimer was inside fetching the food, Edwin asked Rosie to go to the movies with him. She accepted. They went to see *High Noon*, and Edwin impressed her profoundly by comparing it to the *Iliad*. She assumed later that he lifted the comparison from a movie review he had read, but at the time she was limp with admiration—a 24-year-old Harvard law student with intellectual leanings and a passionate curiosity about perennials was a far cry from Roger Mitchell, the boy she'd been dating, a freshman at the University of Rhode Island whose favorite activities were bowling and drinking beer. Rosie would never forgive herself for being taken in by Edwin, and often thought she'd have done better to stick with Roger, a good-hearted boy without a phony bone in his body. But a year later, dazzled by his ersatz culture, Rosie married Edwin Mortimer, who carried within him the seed that sparked Susannah.

Barney was due for dinner. Their weekends were unvarying—on Friday nights Rosie cooked for him, on Saturdays he took her out to eat. In between, they watched TV, played Scrabble, made love, and—weather permitting—worked in the yard. They were pleasant weekends. Neither of them wanted to elongate them into marriage.

So after Peter left, and Rosie had brooded a while over another cup of tea and a peanut butter sandwich, she put together the makings of a beef stew and set it to simmer. And then, she decided, it was time to get to work on her book.

She had signed the contract for *Rosie Mortimer's Garden Book* in the fall, soon after they finished taping the shows for the new season. She was scheduled to take two years off from television in order to, as her producer Janice put it, "have a fling at the print media." The deal was arranged between WEZL and Rosie's publisher, which were owned by the same vast conglomerate. So far no one had said anything about a major motion picture, but there were pots of money involved. All she needed to do was write the book. So far, she had the title, a thick pile of pages from Janice containing the transcripts of the shows, and an uneasy feeling that writers are born, not made, and that the fairies had failed to sprinkle the proper dust over her wicker cradle in the gardener's cottage at Silvergate.

Barney kept saying that any intelligent person could write a book. He was writing one about his twenty years as an elementary school principal, to be called *Giant Among Pygmies*. It was pretty good, too—a nice mix of theory, advice, and anecdote, which was exactly what Rosie wanted to do in her garden book. But so far, every time she sat down to work on it, she turned in a performance something like Jane Fonda's portrayal of Lillian Hellman in *Julia:* she had an overflowing wastebasket, the urge to throw the typewriter out the window and the need for a stiff drink.

She was at that point when Barney arrived. He was early, and Rosie was glad. If the Muse wouldn't visit her, at least she could count on Barney Macrae. School had let out early, he said, so the kids could be taken to a performance of *The Pirates of Penzance* given by the Drama Club of the local high school, a treat Barney had bowed out of. "I decided I'd rather pull your knickers down," he said, drinking Scotch and warming his feet at Rosie's fire. The snow had ceased, but so had the sunshine, and the weather appeared to be settling in for a freeze.

Barney was lovable the way Bertie Wooster would be lovable if he had a sex drive. He had a corny sense of humor, with a strong silly streak, and he had very strange tastes. He once gave Rosie a silver lamé hostess apron, and he steadily lavished on her a supply of filmy nightgowns so sexy they were comical. On the other hand, he always sent her a singing telegram on her birthday, and one February when she had the flu he brought over a huge bouquet of violets and a teddy bear. He had been born in Georgia and had a sweet Southern accent that was, probably, what had won Rosie when she first met him, four years before.

She had needed some children for one of her programs, "A Child's Garden," and she made an appointment at the Helen Palmer Elementary School in Chiswick. When she arrived, Mr. Bernard Macrae, the principal, was playing chess in his office with a skinny black boy of about ten. He waited while the boy completed his move, looked at it a minute, and then introduced him to Rosie (as "Scott Garnett, the chess king of Palmer School"), sent him back to his classroom, and motioned her to a chair.

"I'm glad you showed up," he said. "That kid was killing me. This'll give me until tomorrow to come up with a move." He looked dubiously down at the pieces, and sighed. On his desk-top, besides the chess board, were a small, smooth white stone, a piece of a two-by-four, a photograph of what appeared to be a girls' baseball team, and a miniature taxicab with one wheel gone. He toyed with one of the chess pieces, a knight—picked it up, put it down, tapped the board with it.

"You play every day?" Rosie asked, to remind him she was there.

"It depends." He put down the knight and picked up the piece of wood. He balanced it between his palms, then twiddled it between his fingers. He always had to have something in his hands. If nothing else was around, he'd crack his knuckles. "The kid is flunking everything except gym," he went on. "But you put him in front of a chessboard and he's a genius. I'm trying to get him to transfer some of that concentration from chess to schoolwork."

"How do you do that?"

"I play him a game every time he passes a math test."

"Bribery!"

"Sure—that's what teaching kids is all about—didn't you know?" He grinned, put down the piece of wood, and reached across the desk to shake her hand. "I'm glad to meet you," he said. "I'm a real admirer of your show, but you look even better in person."

He was wearing rimless glasses and a denim shirt with a frayed collar. His frizzy brown hair was both graying and receding, and it stuck out in all directions as if he'd clutched at it in despair during the chess game. He was tall and relaxed, and as skinny as Scott Garnett, and quite obviously a true, unaware eccentric.

For the show, Barney supplied Rosie with a boy named Jonathan, who brought a hockey stick to the taping and accidentally whacked Janice with it; another boy, named Arthur, who wore thick glasses, asked too many questions, and was generally a caricature of the Class Brain; and two giggly girls named Jennifer and Amanda, who squealed when they saw a worm and picked most of the early golden Dayspring lilies for their mothers. Nevertheless, the show was such a huge success it was repeated every year. After the first one, when they'd finished filming the kids pigging out on Rosie's strawberries, and Janice and the film crew had gone back to New York, she and Barney sat in the garden drinking gin and tonics and telling each other the stories of their lives. The next night he came back with a bottle of champagne and a pepperoni pizza, and stayed until morning, when he kissed her good-bye and went off to Sunday mass. They had been—what could you call it? Lovers? They'd been lovers ever since, though lovers didn't seem exactly the right word. Barney was too nutty, too easygoing and famil-iar and, Rosie supposed, too unexciting to qualify as a lover. He liked to call himself, facetiously, her fancy man, her ravisher; she tended to refer to him publicly as her boyfriend, a word which still carried for her an indelible image of herself and Roger Mitchell in the back seat of his 1949 Ford. But what Barney was, mainly, was a friend.

After they had their Scotch, they went up to bed, another of their unvarying routines. Barney was always ready, always, it seemed, look-ing at her expectantly, poised to leap to her side at the tiniest hint of desire, to—as he put it—pull her knickers down. To tell the truth, she wasn't as interested in it as he was. He knew that, and he had various ways of wearing down her resistance—pitiful complaints of his midlife crisis, pleas to her humanity, her nobility of soul, her heart of gold. Or he would smirk like a teenager and say, shuffling his feet, "I kinda thought you owed me sumpin after I spent all that money on our date." Or he would read her passages from D. H. Lawrence: "'She traced with her hands the line of his loins and thighs, at the back, and a living fire ran through her,'" he would intone, breathing heavily. Or he would bring her yet another funny black nightgown.

And, God knows, most of this succeeded. They spent plenty of time in bed. What Rosie objected to about it all was that the payoff didn't justify the energy expenditure involved; she was sure there was some economic principle that covered the case—the Law of Dimin-ishing Something-or-other. She used to lie there with Barney, black nylon up around her neck or tossed in a heap on the floor, her fists pressing against his lean backbone, and her cheek rasped by his five o'clock shadow, and gradually, while he was still enthusiastically mak-ing love to her, she would have the sensation of shrinking back and away and down, of getting smaller and colder and harder until she was a stone. Barney above her would seem both very large and very distant. She would look over his shoulder at the window shades, at the frosted-pink lighting fixture on the ceiling. She would stretch her arm above him and look at her knobby wrist and stubby fingers. She would make her hand into a claw. She would conduct imaginary music. She would think how she really should replace that ugly lighting fixture. She would wait for it to be over. And because she was so fond of him, she would—when he had collapsed on her and then rolled quickly off so as not to hurt her—stroke his neck and his whiskery chin and his wild hair and smile at him in the dim light. And he, unaware, would tweak her nose and say, "Nothing like copulation for working up an appetite. What's for dinner?" And she would shower while he switched on the radio and listened to "All Things Considered" or "Kammermusik," and then he would shower while she went down to get dinner going. It was the same every weekend, right down to his singing "Second Hand Rose" in the shower.

It was the same that evening, except that when she began to detach herself from the action and shrink to a stone, there in her mind was Susannah; not so much her face or any specific memories of her but the dull knowledge that she was on her way from her cold, hard little planet to Rosie's—Susannah Mortimer Cord, her daughter, her failure, her discontent, and her blue devil of guilt.

Rosie's mental disengagement was so extreme that Barney noticed. "Is anything wrong?" he asked when he was done. His face was buried in her armpit, and he spoke in a deliberately casual mumble, but she knew his worry was genuine. He was continually afraid that she would tire of him—and this not because of any disaffection he spotted in her but because of his fears for himself. His midlife crisis was no idle joke.

"I'm getting a cold," she said, trying to sound nasal.

"Bullshit," he replied.

"I'll tell you over dinner."

He raised his head in alarm. "You're going to become a nun. I knew it would come to this."

He always joked when he was serious, and she laughed and kissed him. "It's nothing to do with us—nothing to do with me. There's a small family crisis."

"You're not throwing me over for some duke?"

"Nope."

"Ballplayer?"

"Nope."

26

"Rock star?"

"Nope."

"International terrorist? Dress designer? Avant-garde filmmaker?"

Rosie kissed him again. "Come and take a shower with me," she said to reassure him. Normally she was not the reassuring sort; she was bad at mollification, and she never had much tact. But she didn't see why Barney should suffer because she and Edwin Mortimer had once unhappily combined to produce the serpent's tooth that was Susannah, so she invited him to share her shower. This was a logical sequence Rosie rather liked, but she didn't much like the idea of showering with Barney. He always got amorous all over again, and he had tried and tried to find a way to do it standing up in the tub, but this had never been a success, and they always ended up on the bath mat on the hard tile floor. Well, no, she couldn't say she didn't like it; at the time she always, reluctantly, rather enjoyed it. It usually either went fast or involved interesting variations—soap was handy, and so was hand lotion. She didn't usually shrink to a stone—there wasn't time. But, when it was done, she still couldn't help feeling it was an absurd series of actions, more trouble than it was worth, and time that could be better spent. And it worried her that she felt that way. The words "past your prime" darted around in her head. She would be fifty in May, and she knew she was scared to death of that birthday.

"Well?" he asked as they sat down to their stew.

It wasn't Barney's way to plunge directly in—he was more of a meanderer—so she knew he was still worried, in spite of what had just taken place on the bath mat. "Susannah is coming back," she said without preliminaries.

"Susannah your daughter?"

"My ex-daughter, I prefer to say."

"Coming back from California? To bedevil you, or for some other purpose?"

She told him what she knew. She had long ago told him, of course, the outlines of her life, and had filled in most of it since, as people do when they know each other well, but she had said little about Susannah. There wasn't a lot to say beyond the fact of their estrangement. She had a daughter, never got along with her very well, and lost her at ten to her father—not a loss she ever allowed herself to spend much time mourning.

"Let's run away together," Barney said. It was something he often proposed, enjoying the absurdity of the suggestion, the idea that two middle-aged single people without ties should flee like star-crossed lovers. One of Barney's gifts to her had been a large map of North America, mounted and framed. It hung in the nook off the kitchen where they always ate dinner, and they looked at it that night as they sat eating their stew and drinking cheap Bardolino.

"We could go to Montana," Barney said. "Or we could go out to Vancouver." Barney was a Far West buff who had never been west of Ohio, and Rosie was a travel buff who had hardly ever traveled. He was afraid to fly, and she was reluctant to leave her garden in the summer. But they were always planning theoretical trips that would accommodate both their hang-ups—winter trips by train, chiefly. They had a lovely one picked out, to Santa Fe via Amtrak. Or they considered sailing to England, at off-season bargain rates, on the QEII, paying a quick trip to Silvergate (admission £2), and then taking the train to the Riviera. Or a January cruise through the blue Aegean, stopping at Delos, Mykonos, Thíra. . . .

They looked at the map together. All Rosie could see was the imaginary line, like some monstrous leftover umbilical cord, connecting her to Susannah. There was nothing between them but Nevada, Utah, Colorado, Kansas, Missouri, Illinois, Indiana, Ohio, Pennsylvania, and New York.

"Look," said Barney. "We could take the train to Grand Central, and from there we can get the Lakeshore Limited to Chicago, then in Chicago we change to the Empire Builder, and in three days we're in Vancouver."

"I don't really want to go to Vancouver, Barney."

"How about Montana? We could get off in Butte."

"I don't want to go anywhere. I just want to stay here in peace and Susannah to stay in California where she belongs."

She said this with a vehemence that, even to her, sounded excessive. Barney put his hand over hers. "Don't get hung up on it, Rosie. Don't let it throw you."

She looked at the map with tears in her eyes, and all the pink and blue and green states blurred together. "I don't like her, Barney. Isn't that terrible? She's my own daughter, and I just can't stand her."

Rosie got less hung up, less thrown, as January went on. But every now and then she would recall, involuntarily, the last time she had seen Susannah, and her fevered dislike, with its attendant pangs of guilt, would return. The occasion had been her mother's funeral.

Why Susannah showed up at all, Rosie didn't really know. She did know Peter called Susannah in California and told her her grandmother was dead. But what prompted the child, on hearing this news of a relative she hadn't seen in fourteen years, to hop with her husband on a plane and to attend the funeral? Expectations from the will, Rosie always assumed—and, indeed, Susannah had been left a little money from her grandmother's dwindled estate. Enough, maybe, to pay off some of their bills, including the airfare, which—Peter informed Rosie—they had Master Charged. She pictured them hugging each other in glee all the way back to Los Angeles, Susannah triumphant—she had managed, by dint of occasional Christmas cards and school photos, to worm her way into the old lady's will. Furthermore, she had faced down her hostile family, and she had even succeeded in reducing her mother to a screaming shrew who lost control of herself in public. Oh yes, their monstrous euphoria would have filled the plane. She imagined them plotting the spree they'd have on their expected wealth, just like rotten-to-the-core heirs in Victorian novels.

Rosie loved her mother. Both her parents, in fact, kept their light, tight parental hold on her until they died. She may have had her failings as a parent, but she was a model daughter. She adored them both as unreservedly at forty as she did at four.

Her mother was English, born May Dennison in the town of Shepton Mallet on the second of May, 1906. (Rosie was born twenty-five years later, on her birthday.) May was the daughter of a naturalist, John Dennison, who made a small name for himself with a book called *Somerset Nature Rambles* illustrated with watercolors by Nora, his wife. Both of them died when May was in her early teens; all Rosie knew of those two grandparents was their book, the two headstones in a Somerset churchyard, and her mother's stories about them, which always ended in tears. May was taken in by her father's sister, Aunt Charlotte Dennison, a grim spinster in a little cap, who made her niece memorize a poem every Sunday. To her death, May remembered bits of poetry and came out with them at appropriate moments. "'The hounds of spring are on winter's traces,'" she would call out cheerfully on a March morning to get Rosie out of bed. "'Hail, blithe spirit—bird thou never wert,'" she would say to her husband when he came in for dinner. He used to laugh, flap his arms and squawk, and then kiss her. Rosie always envied them, their marriage. They were both blithe spirits.

May used to make "clouted cream" as her mother had taught her to (with mace soaking in it, strung on a thread), and she kept a bird life-list as her father had. She held on to her English accent until the end— it even intensified in her later years, as her mother-in-law's Italian one did—and Rosie had inherited a thread of it. Barney pointed out to her once that she pronounced the "t" in "Mortimer" as a "t" instead of a slurred "d." Watching one of her old television shows one night, he said, "There's the secret of your charm," pointing to her bedraggled TV self holding some iris she had just uprooted. "You look so earthy and Italian, and you sound like an English schoolmarm." Rosie took this for a compliment from Barney, especially as spoken in his own sexy Georgia accent, with his wandering arm around her.

After Rosie's father died, her mother declined. When she set her apron on fire, severely burning her left arm and shoulder—the skin delicately pink and translucent when it healed, like puckered mother-of-pearl—Rosie brought her from the old stone house in Westerly to a nursing home just outside Hartford. She visited her almost daily, doing Edwin's old commute, for the three and a half years it took May to fade out of life. She died, finally, of nothing her doctor could pinpoint. Old age, he said, though she was barely seventy-two. She just pined away. "I miss him so," was one of the last coherent things she said. Rosie brought her a cake on her last birthday, but she had no appetite for it. She smiled her sweet smile, holding her daughter's hand, and said "I miss him so" with tears in her eyes. A couple of weeks later she stopped making sense. She looked out the window once and said to

Rosie, "Look at the frost on the lawn, Sandra." It was July, and Rosie wasn't Sandra—she had no idea who was. The last thing May said to Rosie, with a giggle, was "Goblins." She died that night in her sleep.

And then the funeral, three days later. Rosie had finished her crying by then, and was talking to her Uncle Jim, her father's remaining brother, in the vestibule of St. Terence's Episcopal Church in Hartford, when Susannah walked in. Rosie could remember it all with perfect clarity.

"I believe she had a happy death," she had been saying, and her old uncle nodded and nodded, his brown eyes mournful. His hair was thick and white, and his big white mustache was yellowed at the corners. He put his hand on her arm. "Rosie," he began, and was about to say something. She took her arm away with what must have seemed rudeness. "Excuse me," she said, and walked over to Susannah.

"What are you doing here?" she demanded. Susannah stood there looking at her mother. Rosie hadn't seen her since she was ten, but she would have known the girl anywhere. She looked exactly like Edwin, though her coarse blonde hair had darkened slightly and she'd lost her baby fat. She had Edwin's big white teeth and his long thin nose and his air of fatuous assurance.

"I wanted to come and pay my respects to Grandma." She looked around at the family—Peter, Uncle Jim, his wife Thelma, the cousins and their families—and she gave the smirky smile Rosie recalled so well from her daughter's childhood, the smile designed solely to ingratiate, and said, "I wanted to see the family, too, of course. It's been so long," and pulled forward the hairy man who stood behind her like a footman. "This is my husband, everyone. Ivan Cord." She waved her skinny hands around like a parody of someone with social graces. "Ivan, this is my Uncle Frank, I think . . . Uncle Jim? My brother Peter. This must be Aunt Thelma—"

Rosie grabbed Susannah's arm and turned her around. Though Rosie looked murderous, Susannah kept her smile, as if she was just about to introduce her mother, unctuously, to her husband, maybe even attempt a daughterly embrace. She was all bland affability, and she reminded Rosie at that moment of Edwin's mother, old Mrs. Mortimer, whose self-satisfaction thinly disguised as goodwill hung

31

around her like smog. Rosie said, "You don't belong here. This isn't your family any more. And don't call her *Grandma*, you little bitch," words that entered the family annals for keeps.

In some part of her, Rosie was horrified to hear herself speak these words. Some tender little fold in her mind wanted her to hug Susannah, to forget everything and resolve to love her. She had just lost her own mother, and here she was driving her daughter away. And part of her also was appalled at the listening silence. She saw her cousin Deborah, with whom she had never gotten along, nudge her paunchy husband and roll her blue-shadowed eyes. Peter touched her shoulder—just a touch, as if to remind his mother. But she went on, and it was unfortunately true that while parts of her were dismayed, most of her thoroughly enjoyed the scene. She said things she hadn't been able to say when Susannah was a child of ten.

"You have no right to be here. She wasn't your grandmother. I'm not your mother. I want nothing to do with you. This isn't your family any more than it's his." Rosie gestured toward Susannah's silent, glowering mate, the ex-priest. "You get out of here, damn you, both of you. I won't have you contaminating my last memories of my mother."

Susannah's face was red, her smile had slipped away, but she stood there and defied Rosie, just as she used to at seven, eight, ten. "I loved her too, you know," she said softly. "She was my Grandma, and I loved her."

That was when Rosie slapped her. "Get out of here before I strangle you with my bare hands," she said. Her voice rose, then lowered to a snarl. "Get out, get out, get out." Rosie could hear it still, could see it as if it were all on film: her hand raised, the palm hitting Susannah's cheek, the girl's head spinning to the side, and her twisted mouth, the low chant of "Get out, get out . . ." Susannah looked at Rosie in an odd way. She was angry, of course, and indignant, and stunned, but she also looked, in an instant, teary and woebegone—a poor-little-matchgirl look that might have gone to her mother's heart if she hadn't hardened it so thoroughly for so long.

Then Susannah's husband took her by the arm, supporting her with his other hand around her waist, and led her out, both of them strangely silent, unresisting, looking at no one. They went out the open door and down the steps, heads bowed, his arm supporting her. Rosie noticed what thin legs she had and how inappropriately she had dressed, in a garish nylon print wrap-dress with long, hot sleeves. Then they disappeared around the corner to the parking lot.

There was silence for a moment in the church, and no one moved. Then Rosie's Aunt Thelma said, "Well," and a buzz of conversation started. Peter put his hand back on her shoulder and said, "Ma," but whether in compassion or in reproach Rosie couldn't tell. Then the rector came in, and Barney, who was late, and the service began, during which she wept and wept, with Barney on one side of her and Peter on the other. She knew perfectly well she was weeping for her daughter as well as for her mother.

Rosie hoped, desperately, that that was the last of Susannah, but she and Ivan apparently went straight from the church to Uncle Jim's house, where they waited for him and Aunt Thelma to return from the funeral. They waited a good long time, too, because everyone went out for lunch afterward, and Uncle Jim had too many gin and tonics. It was late afternoon when they arrived home, but Susannah got out of him the name of her grandmother's lawyer, and went to the reading of the will a few days later—she and Ivan staying in the meantime with some hippie friend of theirs in New Haven. Rosie could just picture the place: incense, waterbed, astrological charts, marijuana, roaches. She didn't attend the will-reading, but Peter did, and he told her they left for California right after. "Tell Mom I said good-bye," Susannah said to Peter, with stupefying chutzpah. Peter and Ivan had a talk about the Red Sox. Susannah spoke to Russ O'Dell, the lawyer, about how long they'd have to wait for the money. Not that they got much. The bulk of it went to Rosie, of course, with Peter's small legacy and Susannah's tiny one and a few to old friends and contributions to the National Trust and the New England Federation of Garden Clubs. But to a pair of California ne'er-do-wells it must have seemed like a fortune. Neither of them, they told Peter, was employed "at the moment." The moment, Rosie suspected, was a long, persistent, improvident one, cushioned with food stamps, sweetened now with Grandma's legacy. Rosie never reproached her mother for anything in her life, but after her death she clenched her fists and asked her mother's memory: "Why? Why leave her anything? How could you?" And her mother's sweet fairness, her blithe spirit, reached back from the grave in reproach.

Peter came to Rosie's for dinner on a snowy Tuesday evening. Rosie hadn't seen him for a week or two, and her first impression of him when he came in and shook the snow off his camel-hair coat was *something is different*. He looked, somehow, not himself. Was he thinner? tired? What it was didn't come to her until he was sitting in his favorite chair with a drink in his hand and the light from the fire illuminating one side of his face.

"So how's it going, Ma?" he asked her, and she saw then that he was unhappy, the idle, affectionate question forced, his natural ebullience gone flat. And the ends of his mustache, unwaxed, drooped.

"Peter dear, what is it?"

He looked at her, startled, smiling, but Rosie knew she wasn't mistaken; the smile was dredged up from murky depths. "What's what?"

She backtracked. It didn't seem that many years ago that he and she had passed through his touchy, protracted adolescence. The wounds were barely healed. And yet, she remembered, even in the throes of teenage anguish—anguish that, in her son's case, was made even more poignant by his then-unresolved sexual crisis—even in the midst of the sulks and late hours and slammed doors and mumbled apologies that characterized those difficult years, there had been a fizziness about Peter, an ability to enjoy life even when it went bad, that was now, Rosie realized with a shock, missing.

"You must be tired," she said, giving him that for an out—the legendary fatigue of the graduate student working against time.

To his credit, he didn't take the out. He looked at her steadily, the strained smile gradually slipping away, and she felt a surge of joy. *I've brought him up well*, was how she would have articulated that surge if she hadn't been so involved in the moment. He refused to pretend, he insisted on truth, he would tell her his trouble. How she hated it when people pretended there was nothing the matter, as Edwin had insisted on doing for so many years. The stiff upper lip had never appealed to her: in this she was more Italian than English—though her English mother was, to the end, as honest and open in her quiet way as her flamboyant father, who wept without shame, even as an old man, when something moved him. And Peter, the dear boy, sat before her in the rose-patterned wing chair, with wet eyes.

"I am tired," he said after a sip of sherry. "I'm not sleeping very well." She didn't ask why not; she waited, sipping her own drink but keeping her gaze on him. "Hollis left me," he said finally.

"Oh, my dear." Rosie moved forward to touch his knee, then stopped. It wasn't a mother's touch he wanted. "When was this, Peter? And why?"

He and his friend Hollis had seemed settled for keeps. In fact, it was the permanence of his relationship with Hollis that had made Peter decide to confess to his mother, formally, a year ago December, his preference for his own sex—the only secret he had ever kept from her for long. "Is it like a marriage, then?" she had asked him, saying any old thing to disguise the initial shock that wasn't really a shock but the jolt that comes with confirmed suspicions, and with a sort of relief that it was all out in the open, and that it could have been so much worse. A long-term relationship instead of barhopping and diseases and absence of love.

"It's better than any marriage I've ever seen," he had told her, his face shining with such delight that she couldn't take his words as a reproach. And how, when a sexual preference she considered incomprehensible provided her son with such joy and contentment, could she disapprove?

And when Rosie met Hollis, she loved him too. They were like twins, those boys—both of them dark and handsome and clever. Hollis, an architect, was also a gifted painter and cartoonist; Peter was a superannuated graduate student in Italian literature. What they had in common was no less than everything—Dante and Robert Venturi and Shaker furniture and traveling and scuba diving and English murder mysteries. They were perfectly matched, even wore the same shoe size, had identical soft brown mustaches, hated beets. They never touched each other in her presence. Their tact was immense. They could have been two brothers who'd grown up close, sharing the same jokes, the same tastes. In fact, when the three of them were together, they concentrated their attention on Rosie, teasing and flattering her as if they were her young lovers instead of each other's. But the affection between them was obvious. It had warmed her, and she would miss it. She would miss the teasing, and the flattery too, and the absurd cartoons Hollis used to send her in the mail, and all the fun the three of them had had for so long.

"When?" Peter repeated after her. "Last Saturday night at ten-thirty precisely. He took all his stuff. I helped him pack."

"Oh, my dear." She could see the tears run down his cheeks, and she could see, too, what she'd never really noticed before: the lines in his face, the wrinkles around his eyes. Peter was twenty-nine years old. Rosie thought fleetingly that his thirtieth birthday, coming up in eight months, would be as big an event for him as her fiftieth would be for her. "Peter, honey," she said.

"And as for *why*," he went on, his steady voice incongruous with his tears, "he left to get married. He's gone to Vermont. He's got a job there and everything."

"You mean—*married*?"

"To a girl—excuse me, a *woman* he met at his sister's place last summer. He's been—"

There his voice choked and stopped, but Rosie had no trouble filling in: Hollis had been seeing her, corresponding with her, wooing her, bedding her, all this time. Rosie closed her eyes. It was unbelievable. "The little bastard," she said. "Leading a stinking double life. Oh, *Peter*." She opened her eyes. Incredibly, he was grinning at her through his tears with a touch of his old humor.

"Ma," he said. "You're terrific. Pissed off at Hollis because he's straight."

"I'd kill the little bastard if I could," she said. "I'd tear his heart out with my bare hands."

They laughed together, probably a touch too loud and long, and after dinner and a bottle of wine she did hug him while he wept, briefly. Then they sat by the fire and talked about Hollis, and Rosie was again proud of Peter; he didn't vilify Hollis, didn't bring up his tendency to drink too much and make an ass of himself, or his dreadful Italian accent. She would have cackled over these things, gladly—her hatred for Hollis was pure and bright and shining—but Peter wanted to talk about the good times. He'd passed through the bitchy stage on his own. He confessed that he'd gathered up all of Hollis's funny cartoons, ripped them to bits, and burned them. And that he'd stuffed Hollis's favorite sweater, left behind in a pile for the cleaners, into the trash. And that he spent two days drunk, tossing his glass after every couple of drinks into the fireplace so that he had a pile of shards to clean up when he recovered. But the anger seemed to have passed, leaving behind a resigned, sad tenderness that wrung Rosie's heart. He wished he had the cartoons back.

"Tell me the truth, Ma," he said as he was leaving. "You wish it had been me, don't you, going off into the sunset with a woman to have babies?"

Rosie tucked his red scarf around his neck and shook her head firmly. "No, I don't," she said. "I don't care who you love, Peter, as long as you're happy. I really mean that. No jokes. I want you to be happy."

"Thanks," he said, and kissed her on the cheek.

She shrugged. "I'm your mother."

He hesitated, looking at her there in the front hall. "Then let me ask you this," he said, paused again, then went on. "You're Susannah's mother, too."

Rosie stiffened immediately, and dropped his hand that she'd been holding. "So?"

"Well, I think she's been unhappy, too. I think she'd like to have your—"

"Hmm?"

"Your support."

"My support."

"Just a word, to say you welcome her back East, that bygones will be bygones."

"Bygones never will be bygones, Peter." She felt her heart begin to thump again, her pulse pound. The anger she'd had to suppress all evening, against Hollis, for Peter's sake, brimmed over toward Susannah. "She left her mother of her own free will, and she was brought up by her father to be a despicable human being. I haven't got a reason in the world to give her my damned *support*."

"You're her mother."

"I'm *not* her mother! I've disowned her, and I want nothing to do with her, whether she's in California or on my doorstep. I don't even want to talk about her, much less give her my *support*."

He looked at her unhappily. "She's been calling me."

"She's been calling you."

"She called me a couple of weeks ago."

"Collect, I assume."

"Well, yes, but then she called me again direct. She talked for a long time, about—well, the family, about you, about Dad."

"She did."

"She really seems to be sincere. I mean, about wanting to make it up with you. I feel bad that I was so snide about her. I don't think she's trying to get anything out of you, except—"

"Support," Rosie said sarcastically. "In every sense of the word."

"Ma . . ."

"Go along, now, Peter," she said, opening the door. It was snowing, very gently. She had never kicked him out before, but she was sick of it—his pleas for Susannah, the way he'd let the girl get to him, her own pounding anger that was beginning to appear ridiculous but which she couldn't, wouldn't, couldn't shake. "And please drive carefully. And I'll call you tomorrow, maybe. Do you want to go to a movie one of these nights?"

He sighed. He drew on his gloves—red woolen ones, with leather palms—and kissed her again, lightly. "Sure," he said. "Let's go to a movie. You pick." And then, just before he left, he said, "You're going to have to face her, sooner or later."

She didn't even answer. She just pushed him out the door, and then watched him go down the walk to his car, get the brush out of the trunk, clean off the windshield. *Do the back window, too*, she said silently to him, and was relieved when he walked around to do so. He got in the car and drove off—*drive carefully*, she said to his taillights—leaving her with her anger. It didn't go away but intensified as she sat by the fire having a last glass of sherry before bed, remembering for some reason how Susannah had abandoned her playhouse after that first summer, declared it was dirty and full of bugs and spiders, cried when Rosie told her she was spoiled, and gone to Edwin for the approval he

38

was quick to give. "Kids outgrow things," he had said to Rosie, who hadn't deigned to answer. She had turned the playhouse into a garden shed, and always felt warmly toward the spiders who built their webs in the corners and scurried over the pots.

When she finished the sherry, she threw the glass at the fireplace, where it shattered, and she felt better. She even chuckled a little, imagining Peter's pile of smashed glass. But when she went to bed, tired though she was from the late hour, the sherry, the angry bumping of her heart, she couldn't sleep for thinking of her children. And lest she dwell on Susannah—her tantrums, her school troubles, the fistful of squash she threw at the dining room curtains, the time she rode her bicycle into the box hedge; all this was waiting just outside Rosie's consciousness for her fury to pounce on—and lest she dwell on it, she thought of Peter, remembering.

When Edwin left, followed soon by stony-faced Susannah with her three suitcases and a huge plastic bag full of stuffed animals she should have outgrown, and Peter and Rosie were left alone in the house, she felt happiness settle into her and into all the rooms. It was the feeling she remembered from childhood at the start of summer vacation, of infinite possibility, of blessed release. The house, which had for so many years been blighted with the growing enmity between herself and Edwin, between herself and Susannah, between Peter and Edwin, and Peter and Susannah, was blown clean and healthy again by their exit.

With glee—yes, it was glee, there wasn't a shred of sadness in her (though for months she couldn't bring herself to enter Susannah's room)—with glee she tossed out the old mattress she and Edwin had avoided each other on for so long and bought a new one, hard the way she liked it. She also got rid of the scratchy white muslin sheets Edwin's mother had given them, which he had always, perversely, claimed to prefer, and bought herself sheets patterned with roses. Edwin had been scornful, after that brief courting period when he'd faked tolerant benevolence, of the roses she surrounded herself with, not only in the garden but in the house. It was something her parents started—roses for their Rose.

She remembered coming home from school one day when she

was eight years old to find her bedroom transformed: rose-colored walls, roses on the curtains, a bedspread to match, roses glowing on the lampshade, the two framed Redouté prints moved from the living room to the wall over her desk, and on the desk a little box whose cover was a full-blown porcelain rose. She was overcome, not least that her parents—garden people, not house people—had done this for her. The rest of the house was a comfortable shambles; her room was a palace, though what her mother called it sometimes, shyly, fearing to be corny, was "Rose's Secret Garden." Now, all these years later, if Rosie had burst into that long-gone rosy room, where even the sun coming in the windows had a pinkish tint, she might have found it garish and tacky—all but the Redouté prints, which she still had. But then it was a heavenly place that summed up all the bliss of her early years.

And when she and Edwin bought the house in East Chiswick she did it up in roses—not a bower, just here and there a touch, a nosegay. She slipcovered the old wing chair, she hung rose-patterned drapes in the dining room (it was these Susannah hurled the blob of acorn squash at, leaving a stain), she put down a rose-strewn runner in the upstairs hall, she hung the Redoutés and bought a large watercolor still life of roses lying, cut, on a table with secateurs and a pair of old gardening gloves. Something about the way the cut roses, fresh and hopeful but with sharp brown thorns, waited there for the vase and water that don't appear in the picture appealed to her. Would it be too much to say they reminded her of her waiting, thirsty self? Edwin never liked the picture, thought all her roses were a silly affectation, and even disliked the ones in the garden.

When he left she overdid it, rosifying the house (as Peter, a smart-aleck twelve, put it) to a perhaps absurd degree.

"It looks weird, Ma," he said, *weird* being the word of the moment.

"I'm asserting my own personality, Peter," Rosie told him with a touch of self-consciousness.

He understood what she was needing to do, of course. He treated the flowered sheets and rosy towels with affectionate amusement. She heard him, one day, apologize to his friend Ronnie, "See, my mother's name is Rose, so she gets everything with *roses* on it."

"Neat," Ronnie said, and Peter groaned.

40

But then, once, he told her, "It's not the kind of thing a *boy* wants to live with," looking, himself, at thirteen or fourteen, not unlike a dark, graceful blossom of some exotic kind. And though then she scoffed, pointing out that he had his room—a sparsely dressed brown confusion—and the basement rec room with pool table and bare white walls in which to assert his personality, and that the house was hers, dammit, his words affected her, and gradually she "derosified" things a bit, sensing, perhaps, as she let the roses fade, that there were many reasons for Peter's discomfort with the aggressive femininity of a rose bower.

But roses aside, they were happy together in their newly roomy, purged house. Peter was a bright, eager, lighthearted boy, a good companion to her always during the lonely parts of those years. Not that he hadn't his difficult moments, but they were *moments*—he wasn't like Susannah, whose sourness was continual, who refused to settle with the world on any terms. Rose didn't hear from Edwin and Susannah, though her parents occasionally did. She knew they were in New Mexico, where Edwin managed to get himself a company transfer when the divorce became final. She knew when his mother's money came to him, and she assumed, from the swaggering reports of life deluxe that Susannah's scrawled communiqués contained, that he had used that money to make more money. But Rosie and her son seldom thought about either of them.

Was this, as her cousin Deborah used to say, "a shame"? Was it really "too bad" that they hadn't all parted friends as Debbie's sister-in-law and *her* ex-husband had? "A real pity" that they didn't spend at least Christmas together for the sake of the children? Rosie tried sometimes, though the attempt always either bored or infuriated her, to explain to Debbie that it wasn't any of those things, that it wasn't abnormal or sinful or even particularly sad (not to mention none of her business) for the members of a family to dislike each other and want nothing to do with each other. She and Peter, Rosie insisted, were *happy* without Edwin and Susannah. "Then you're cold fish," said her cousin. Rosie turned away with a shrug. "Not to even want to spend Christmas together," Debbie persisted.

Rosie could remember Christmases past, and she imagined Christmases present suffused with the malice and discontent of Susannah, with the dullness and pettiness of Edwin—and with the meanness that grew in her own heart in their company—and she said to Debbie, "No, thanks. Peter and I are going to Aruba with Larry for Christmas."

Debbie gasped, disapproval turning her face red under heavy makeup. "To Aruba!" She always gasped; everything confounded the poor girl.

That was 1968, when Peter was sixteen. Rosie was seeing a tweedy lawyer named Larry Bruner. The Christmas trip to Aruba which so shocked her cousin was in fact Rosie and Larry's last attempt to love each other enough to marry. The venture wasn't a total washout, compared, say, to that tropical honeymoon with Edwin, a comparison Rosie inevitably made and which endeared to her Larry's garrulous good humor and constant attention. The three of them were charmed by the gentle blue-green beauties of the place, by sun and sea and tangles of bright flowers, and Christmas presents opened on a terrace under an umbrella. But Larry didn't like the bond, viewed at close range, between Peter and Rosie. That's how he put it: "I don't *like* it," meaning he considered it in some way unhealthy but not wanting to say so, even when she pressed him. And she did press him, wanting to hear the words that would part them, knowing they were there to be spoken. But he kept hedging and hinting, telling her meaningful anecdotes from his own life. He himself at sixteen had been hard at work battling his parents at every turn. He couldn't comprehend a teenage son who was openly fond of his mother, who kissed her not only good night but good morning, and who had no interest in joining the group of noisy, flirting teenagers who gathered nightly on the hotel terrace while their parents crowded into the bar. And he resented her allowing Peter to sit up with them until all hours. She didn't tell Larry she permitted such liberties—liberties that certainly did sabotage their romance—because she had already decided she and Larry had no future. She preferred Peter's company to Larry's—though, when Peter did go to his room at night, what she and Larry did in the privacy of theirs continued to be ingenious and gratifying. Sometimes, lying in bed with Barney or digging in the garden pondering her lost youth, Rosie missed Larry Bruner. But on New Year's Day she bid him farewell forever, because—this is what it came down to—he didn't like her son.

There were other men, of course. She preferred reasonably long, temporarily permanent relationships, the kind in which they installed a toothbrush in her bathroom but still called before coming over. Peter was initially suspicious of each of her beaux. Having learned the vocabulary of the age, he was always afraid they were using her, that she was being taken advantage of simply because she slept with them, that "serial monogamy," as he called it, was an unhealthy, dangerous lifestyle. But Rosie was lucky in love—up to a point, the point being one just short of remarriage—because she had an instinct for nice men. She had used up all her bad judgment and gullibility on Edwin. After the divorce, she was canny. She developed a nose for phonies, and for the smell of dullness. Her life, during the years of her thirties and her forties, was busy with men, full of delights for both the spirit and the flesh, with here and there a sad parting thrown in for drama.

Peter got used to his mother's liaisons and began to have some of his own, the nature of which Rosie had no inkling of at the time. Or very little inkling. He had girlfriends, too. He told her, all those years later, with tears in his eyes, how he had tried to want to do with his girlfriends what the guys at school boasted they did with theirs, and how he had failed. He had taken Nancy Kirkpatrick to the senior prom. Nancy Kirkpatrick had had an aggressive and highly visible crush on Peter all through high school. Rosie could never understand why he didn't like her—a bright, pretty girl who knew something about gardening. Ideal daughter-in-law material.

"I couldn't stand her lipstick," Peter told Rosie during his Christmas night confession. "She laid it on with a palette knife."

"But, Peter, a *lot* of men don't like heavy lipstick," she said.

He gave her a reproachful look she'd never forgotten. "Ma," he said gently, and she blushed. "I'm telling you how I am," he went on. "You're not going to talk me out of it. It's not just a matter of lipstick."

She apologized. She swore to herself that from that moment she would accept it. She became by an act of will the tolerant, large-minded mother Peter was so proud of and so amused by, and gradually she became that way naturally, genuinely, wishing for her son exactly what she'd told him she wished—happiness.

As Rosie lay awake that night, imagining the soft snow falling outside on her garden, she despaired of it, of happiness for Peter. She could think of him only with woe. What would become of him? She wondered whether Hollis had come to hate Peter as she had hated Edwin, had looked on his face as he slept with loathing, had cringed at picking up an article of his clothing or sitting on a chair still warm from his bottom, had come to dread the sound of his voice. . . . Oh, it was unimaginable. She remembered the sweetness of the two of them together. She half considered getting in touch with Hollis and begging him to go back to Peter, offering him money, weeping on her knees—finding a certain pleasurable disgust in picturing this grotesque scene. It was preferable, at least, to the scene Peter's last words had conjured up. "You're going to have to face her sooner or later," he had said. It was, of course, true, and it edged closer and closer to her imagination until she got out of bed, put on the lights, and went downstairs to her pile of seed catalogs. *Susannah hath murdered sleep*, she said to herself, making tea and a peanut butter sandwich.

But sitting down to the catalogs was a treat she'd been saving up all month, holding off until she had them all, leafing through them as they came but waiting for the right moment to actually get down to business, make charts and lists and diagrams and decide what to order. She put on her reading glasses and let the catalogs console her, their thin pages crowded with color photos showing improbable lushness, unattainable perfection, staggering beauty. Rosie got out the paper plots she had made of her garden in spring, summer, fall, to see where the gaps were and what had died or failed or been a mistake, and how she could fill them in. They wouldn't be taping this year, so this wouldn't be a television garden, and she could afford to experiment a bit. Should she try a rock garden again? Hers had always failed—hadn't, at least, equaled the one she remembered at Silvergate that her grandfather had made, with its green and white and blue and purple clusters of tiny Alpine flowers, looking as if nature had done it all by accident. The one Rosie attempted had looked studied and rather silly, and she had eventually ripped out all the plants and let it revert to a rock pile where the Sheffields' cat sunned herself. But she was tempted by her memory. Or sweet peas: she'd never grown nice sweet peas, though she had dug them deep, mulched with peat moss, watered like mad, and provided expensive "weatherized trellis netting" for them to climb on; and yet she remembered the Painted Ladies and Queen Alexandras that had flourished so easily in the garden in England. And Japanese iris, of course, which she could never get to thrive properly in her yard.

She sat for hours with catalogs from Park's and Wayside and Harris and Johnny's and Weston's and the New England Rootstock Association and Thompson and Morgan. There was a stack of letters, too, from nurseries and seed companies and manufacturers of garden implements, asking her to endorse their products or accept free samples. She looked through these, to see what temptations she was so nobly rejecting, and then threw them in the fire. She never gave in to such blandishments; she hated being beholden. What she liked, in spite of any small fame she had acquired, was to sit down with the catalogs like a typical suburban gardener, and paw through them. She picked out a new hybrid primrose, decided to skip the rock garden, took a chance on a perennial bush strawberry and some yellow raspberries, and ordered more vegetable seeds than she could ever use.

"Rosie Mortimer's Garden," perforce, contained plenty of veggie lore. Unlike the English, whose flowers come first, Americans tend to grow vegetables.

"If I can't eat it I don't grow it," Kathy Andrews always said. She was Rosie's across-the-street neighbor, whose backyard plot produced a stand of corn every summer that could serve as a set for *Oklahoma!* And Jim and Kiki Sheffield, next door, grew tomatoes; their garden was a wilderness of red fruit, green foliage, and yellow beetle traps, and they put up hundreds of quarts of tomato sauce over Labor Day weekend every year. "What do you do with it all?" Rosie asked once when they brought over her annual gift of a half a dozen jars. "I put tomato sauce in *everything*," Kiki said. And it was true that whenever Rosie ate dinner there they had something red and Italian.

So she did vegetables for her fans. If she concentrated chiefly on flowers, her great love, she'd be briskly canceled. But she had nothing against veggies, and she happily grew plenty of them herself, though she drew the line at corn. For one show, she invited the cameras across the street and introduced Kathy, her picturesque family, and her corn-patch onto WEZL–TV (and that segment was expanded by the genius of Janice into a series they called "My Neighbors' Gardens").

Rosie was unable to decide about the iris and left that order for another sleepless night or peaceful afternoon. Wandering among flowers and shrubs and rows of vegetables—even on paper, in imagination, in memory—soothed her and made her, toward dawn, comfortably sleepy, so that she slept at last with gardens in her dreams instead of children.

It snowed all that night, and by morning there were several inches. The plows hadn't yet come when Rosie got up at ten. Schools were closed; the Andrews children, in red and blue hats, were out in their yard making a snowman. There was the hushed, clanky rasp of shoveling. A dog woofed excitedly over someone's lawn. Precarious rims of snow outlined the branches of the trees, and the sun shone on everything, laying distinct angles of black across the white.

Rosie awoke utterly refreshed. Looking out on the purity of the day, she felt as if the snow had fallen on her own hot soul, cooling and cleaning it, leaving it new. After she had her oatmeal, she put on her boots and mittens and down jacket and knitted cap and, after shoveling a path, she went for a walk. The streets were quiet; even the Post Road, where the plowed snow was gradually turning to slush and leaving bare spots, was nearly deserted, and she walked along it, liking the way the soles of her boots met the fresh snow, the merest pull as the snow grabbed on, the slight difficulty as she lifted her foot again. It was "good packing weather," as Peter and his pals used to say, and she made a snowball now and then and threw it at the side of a building or a parked car. It was a beautiful day, so beautiful that even the tawdry stores—Big B's Discount Haven, The Liquor Supermarket, Galetti's Drug, E-Z-Do Laundromat, Alexander's Hair Works—seemed purified in the snow and the sun.

She walked west, into Chiswick. Her objective as she stated it to herself was to see if Zakrzeski's was open—the Polish bakery where she sometimes bought *poteca*—a fresh, yeasty hunk of poteca being just the thing to munch on when she returned. But as she walked she realized, with a furtive and unexpected sense of adventure, that she was heading for the vacant storefront in Chiswick that Susannah and her husband had rented. She would see if it was true; she would spy on them, anonymous in her cap and her heavy clothes. She imagined peeking in a window and seeing Susannah languid in a chair eating a candy bar while her poor husband huffed and puffed over packing cases full of ginseng and soybeans.

She passed Zakrzeski's—yes, they were open, she'd stop on the way back—and headed quite deliberately past McDonald's, Arnie's Auto Body, the Glitter City Roller Dome, Fosdick Body Works, Shoe City, Dunkin' Donuts, Chiswick Princess Beauty Supply Shop, and finally the site of the failed bookstore, in a mini-shopping center between Wendell's Tropical Fish Paradise and the Post Road Liquor Boutique.

Rosie trudged across the pristine parking lot. Only the Liquor Boutique was open. In Wendell's, there was the purple gloom of rows of dimly lit fish tanks. The plate glass window of the empty store was dusty and bare—no hand-painted sign announcing the imminent opening of SUE'S NATURAL EATS or IVAN'S GOURMET HEALTH EMPORIUM or whatever absurd and probably inaccurate label they planned to tack on their place. She peered cautiously in through the grime, ready to pull her collar up and her hat down at any threat of recognition. But there was no one inside. The store was still lined with bookshelves, one of which had fallen over. There was a counter. There was a filthy black and white tile floor. There were empty-looking card-board cartons in a corner. That was all, just those bleak innards staring out at her indifferently. Rosie felt a vague disappointment—she had liked the idea of spying. She also felt a pang of pity for her daughter, for her ugly, taciturn husband, for the anonymous local friend who had talked the two of them into this nonsensical step or who had let them talk him into it. Doomed crazy hippies who would never grow up. Irresponsible flower babies who hoped to push tofu burgers in this wonderland of exhaust fumes and Big Macs and sweet pink wine and hair spray. It all looked, to say the least, unpromising. The view in that dusty window, Rosie decided, was one of the most depressing sights she'd ever seen.

And, perhaps unreasonably, she took it as an emblem of her daughter, the empty store killing off her good mood just as definitively as Susannah used to. There had been that same drowsy indifference, that deadness at the center, about Susannah—about Edwin, too, as if they'd abandoned their souls and left them to moulder away. They had flat, light blue eyes that seemed good for nothing but to see with—mere sense organs, like ears, with no depth or mystery, no revelations lurking there.

The memories of the years she spent with them returned to her painfully, like headaches, as she stood there in the snow. There, stabbing behind the left eye, was the recollection of Susannah turning away from a hug, a kind word, a smile—right up until the last time, when she was leaving. She stood in the front hall, in sunlight, her hair clean for once, a large leather purse tucked absurdly beneath her ten-year-old arm, her three suitcases stowed away in the cab and the cab-driver waiting to take her to the airport. She was meeting Edwin in New York. She and Rosie stood in the hall. Susannah looked petulant, she had set her mouth in a line and made her eyes go hard, but Rosie thought she detected beneath this a glimmer of regret, or at least of the childish sadness you'd expect from a ten-year-old kid about to leave her mother for the first time and forever.

"You can still stay, Susannah," she said. "You can still have a home here with Peter and me."

Any glimmer she saw there disappeared, or had been imaginary in the first place, the culmination of years of disappointment from her daughter. "No, thank you," Susannah said. That was all—a simple negative, with the uncharacteristic polite tag at the end, for emphasis.

Partly to see what she'd say, Rosie went further: "Sure you don't want me to drive you to the airport?"

She was only ten years old, she had never been on a plane, she was about to leave home forever, and she didn't answer. She picked up her bag of stuffed animals and walked out the door to the taxi while Rosie stood gaping in the hall. By being silent, she got the last word.

All Rosie's little memory-headaches were variations on that scene: love offered, love rejected. Perhaps Susannah's memories were similar. Who rejected whom first? Could such a tangle ever be sorted out?

It was true that in babyhood Susannah had often cried when Rosie held her and quieted down for Edwin; was it instinctive distaste, or the apprehension of some tenseness or roughness that Rosie wasn't aware of? It was certainly true, also, that Rosie had seen Edwin's features in Susannah's, and had recoiled from the resemblance. But Rosie had painful memories of a sullen, whiny, unloving daughter; Susannah's may have been of a flinty, distant mother who playacted affection from time to time. Both of them, no doubt, remembered accurately.

Rosie stood there looking through the dusty window until her toes began to freeze, and then she went into the Liquor Boutique for a bottle of sherry.

"Planning to get snowed in in style?" the proprietor asked as he bagged it. He was a fat man dressed gangster-style in a dark shirt and light tie.

She snickered dutifully.

"Tell me the truth," he said. "Is this stuff really worth the extra money? Is it really that much better than the stuff from California?"

"I think it is."

"I really want to know," he pursued. "I'm serious. Now I'm not a sherry drinker. Do I look like one?" He roared with laughter; whether he referred to his weight or his masculinity or some other quality Rosie didn't know, but she snickered again. "So level with me," he said. "Is it really better?"

"I think it's good," she said obligingly. "Nice and dry."

"Worth the extra dough? Tell me the truth."

"Definitely worth it," she said again, and held out the money. Time to ask her question and scram. It may have been laughable, at her age, to worry about men trying to pick her up, but they still did, often enough, and she could see the look in this one's eye.

"Seventy-eight, eighty, ninety, seven dollars, eight, nine, ten," he said, counting the change into her hand and touching her palm with each number. His tie was ivory-yellow brocade with an unpleasant glint to it.

She pocketed the change quickly and put her mittens on again. "Tell me," she said, stepping away from the counter. "What's going in there next door to you?"

He made a face. "Health food, from what I hear."

"Ah," she said.

He made another face. "Kids. Opening in March." He laughed and said, "Tell you what," placing his huge palms flat on the counter and leaning toward her. "You come in when it opens and I'll take you over and buy you a cup of dandelion tea." He guffawed and wet his lips. "With a little snort of something in it."

Rosie smiled, even chuckled a bit, and left. Gad! Did she look like the kind of woman that kind of man wanted to get friendly with? She thought about that all the way to Zakrzeski's, and it wasn't until she was walking home with her *poteca* that she comprehended what the Liquor Boutique man had told her. It was true, then, all of it: the restaurant, the tofu burgers, Susannah, Ivan. And it was soon, less than two months away. They weren't in residence yet, but they would be next time she looked.

She squared her shoulders, with a bundle in each arm hoisted up like twin babies, and walked fast. *They won't get a thing out of me:* her steps marked time to the words. It was colder on the trip back, the wind in her face instead of behind her. She was tired, she felt her age, and suddenly she wanted to be home in her warm house eating sweet bread and butter and maybe having a little sherry to thaw her out. And she would call Peter to see if he got home all right and ask him if, weather permitting, he'd like to go to the movies that night.

He would, and they did, and then it was the weekend again, and Barney. Thus the winter went on, cold rather than snowy, as Connecticut winters had tended to be lately. Rosie watched Peter's spirits rise, sink, rise again, and finally stabilize at a point just short of depression. He informed her in March that he'd finished his computer work on Dante—some sort of textual analysis involving word order in the *Paradiso* versus that in the *Purgatorio*—and was ready to finish up the writing of his dissertation. But he'd lost heart, and the family case of writer's block became a full-blown disease. He and Rosie sat around comparing symptoms, the chief one being a sudden pressing need to do something else the minute one sat down to write. Peter was eternally dashing off to the library or his advisor's office; Rosie tended to paw through the seed catalogs—ordering, after all, a few rock garden plants, deciding on another miniature rose, a tool for turning compost, a last-minute packet of yellow tomato seeds.

At one point, she took the train down to New York, where she was put up for the night at the St. Moritz and fattened at Lutèce and at The Coach House by Janice, her producer, and Joyce, her editor. They discussed her book. When they asked, "How's it going?" Rosie grinned and replied, "Slowly, slowly," and they laughed maternally (both of them young enough to be her daughters) as if they knew all about it, that's what writers always say. Rosie didn't dare tell them the book was, so far, only a title on a legal document. She gave them, instead, gardening stories, reminiscences of Silvergate and its acres, tales of letters she received—fan and otherwise—from her public (she got regular marriage proposals, usually from elderly, widowed men who grew roses), and anecdotes about gardeners she knew. "I hope you're going to put that in your book," Janice and Joyce kept saying, and "It's going to be a super book, a really *fine* book, Rosie," and "Honey, if you write *half* as well as you *talk*!"

If, indeed. Back home in Connecticut, the large notebook she had bought stayed empty except for doodles and a few notes she'd made so long ago they were now incomprehensible.

The winter seemed long; it always did. Like the bulbs and tubers that slept underground in the cold, Rosie was in a state of anticipation. She always felt in some way pregnant as winter slogged on to its end, waiting for her own rebirth along with that of her garden. The waiting was difficult. Every morning, as always, she looked out her window at the garden, sometimes bare and brown, sometimes softened by a snowfall, sometimes promisingly wet with thaw. She felt explosive with waiting, irritable, useless. Every morning she looked at her own face in the mirror, and even there winter stared back at her, lined and gray and tired out. She would be fifty in four months, in three months, in two and a half. There were days she couldn't bear to look at her face until she'd slapped a little makeup on it, but though it helped it didn't, of course, change anything. Her face, unlike her garden, remained a landscape to which spring would never come again.

Chapter Two

Cloud House

The last thing Susannah did before she left California was to visit her father at St. Theodore's Hospice in Newport Beach and promise him that she and Ivan would, after all, have a child. As a consequence, the day they moved out of the Dimmick Street apartment, she tossed her diaphragm into a bag of trash, with the feeling that there should be some ritual to accompany this act beyond twisting the bag shut with a little wire gizmo and hauling it out to the curb. And then, all the way across the country, in the van with the three cats, they tried to make Susannah pregnant, making love repeatedly when they stopped for the night—making love frantically, dutifully, hoping to connect, lying there afterward (the cats hesitantly creeping back to their places on the bed) willing the sperm to hook up with the egg, willing the egg to be there waiting, willing one little hustler to penetrate it and start something—a kid with the name Louisiana or Arizona.

She was, she supposed, ready for it. She had resisted the idea, always, but that had been an automatic response, a vow she took years and years ago: *I will never never never produce a child*, an article of faith that crumbled away, easy as wood ash, at her father's request. "We will, Dad, we'll try," she said with a promptness—a *rightness*—that made it obvious she was ready, and merely waiting for the push that would knock her over. Of course—a child—why on earth not?

Ivan, of course, had always been ready, had all these years been subtly pressuring her, not in ways she could reproach him for, but simply by being so blatantly the earth father, flaunting his bountiful, life-embracing vitality which was supposed, in his scheme of things, to encompass a large brood of children—mainly daughters—climbing over him, pulling at his beard and snuggling in his lap and twining their chubby arms around his neck, adoring him.

Susannah's father cried at her promise; at least, his eyes became wet and his mouth twisted up. It consoled him for her abandoning California, abandoning him—consolation that he needed even though it was he who insisted they leave and get on with their lives instead of waiting around for an old man to die, sentiments that sounded like the conventional, martyred, false mumblings of old age. *Don't worry about me, I'm not long for this world anyway*, words that fluttered in the air at St. Theodore's like a plague of moths, along with *they don't care, they'd just as soon I died tomorrow*, and all the rest of it, those ancient resentments, perenially green and vital, that the staff at the Hospice was trained to cope with; to turn, sometimes, to good use by giving the old folks something to live for—the "I'll show *them*" syndrome, one of the nurses called it.

But it wasn't like that with Susannah's father; he meant what he said, and when he told her, in effect, "Go, with my blessing," she knew he wanted her to go, and she did. During all his hard-lived years, he'd learned to tell the truth, if nothing else—or so he'd said to his daughter, more than once, and she believed him, she could see he *was* telling the truth, that he wished as he always had to spare her pain if he could. Go, he said, but promise me—and Susannah promised, and he cried, and then smiled his rare smile, and the creases in his cheeks deepened. While he didn't, wouldn't, say *Now I can die in peace*, she sensed the words forming in his head. Hoping, despite what the doctors said, that he would live long enough to know his grandchild, she squeezed his hand and left him for good.

Susannah and Ivan Cord came east for a number of reasons, some of them mutual: they were sick of California; they missed New England, where Susannah hadn't been, except for one brief visit, since she was a child and Ivan since he left the seminary; they had what sounded like a good opportunity to go into business with Ivan's old buddy, Duke; they needed a change.

But they also, both of them, had private reasons, secret ones. Susannah wanted to improve their marriage, and had the idea that if she took Ivan east he would stop screwing around. Ivan wanted to get Susannah away from her father—who, even dying, he considered a bad influence on her—and to look up Rosie, her mother, in Connecticut. He didn't tell Susannah this, but she knew it; it was part of an old story. He had told her, many times, that she had made the wrong choice when she had elected to follow her father out west, where, once he inherited his mother's money, he rapidly ceased to be the model of propriety Susannah had so sorely needed. Instead he gave up the responsible position he had once been proud of, as one of the chief legal counsels of a large insurance company, and began to devote his life to women and booze, severely shortening that life in the process and leaving his daughter largely to her own devices—or to the devices of a series of far-out schools where she learned to make goat cheese and tie-dyed saris and to act out her feelings in role-playing sessions, but was never taught to discipline herself.

Susannah's version of her biography was simpler. "He loved me, Ivan," she always told him. "And my mother didn't."

"Susie, was it love to let you rattle around by yourself in that house for weeks at a time?"

"I wasn't alone, there was always a housekeeper." Her voice was sulky; he called her *Susie* only when he felt she was being unreasonable, and she hated it.

"Was it love, then," Ivan started over patiently, "to leave you alone with a Mexican housekeeper—a succession of Mexican housekeepers, who couldn't even speak English—"

"Some of them could, and some of them were nice."

"—to ignore you, to let you bring yourself up, practically, or stash you away in some rotten school for problem children to get you off his conscience, not that he ever had a conscience, and then forget to pay the bills."

"You're distorting everything," she said, hopelessly. She never won these arguments, and they left her depressed, doubting, confused: was she then so simple, so weak, so deluded? But she went on doggedly. "That's not the way it was, at all. He loved me, no matter what. I always knew that, Ivan, and that's what was important."

"May I ask *how* you knew?" he said sarcastically. "You'd have to be damned subtle, it seems to me, to figure it out from the evidence."

"Maybe I *am* damned subtle, Ivan," she said. "You just *know* when someone loves you." Just as you know when someone doesn't, she might have added, but she stayed silent.

She hated those conversations about her parents—and there were many of them, especially when she and Ivan were newly married, conversations that often took place when they were high. She hated having to summon up her wits at such times to defend her father, particularly since, as Ivan was always pointing out, she was incapable of a logical defense—not, said Ivan, that one was possible. F. Lee Bailey couldn't get her father off; Clarence Darrow couldn't have done it. Edwin was a terrible father, and yet Susannah hung in there, defending him anyway. No, he wasn't like other fathers, neither like the good old reliable daddies who took their kids to ball games and hovered over their homework (the kind Ivan would be), nor like the wealthy, neglectful, California caricature fathers who gave their spoiled offspring everything but love and a value system (as Ivan was sure Edwin had been). He was, it was true, a careless, sad, destructive man—doomed, Susannah thought, a doomed man—but one who communicated such love, such simple, wholehearted acceptance of all that Susannah was, that there had never been a time, she told Ivan, when she hadn't felt secure, bound together with her father against anything, everything, the world.

"You must see how unhealthy that was, Susie," he would say, gently, and hand her a fresh, neat joint, made by him for her, as if to help her see, since she refused to see it on her own, the unhealthiness of her relationship with her father. She knew Ivan had come to consider himself her savior, a kind of substitute for her sensible eastern mother and an antidote to her profligate western father who was now dying, painfully, of what Ivan no doubt considered his just desserts—cancer of the spine—and was still doted on, in spite of everything, by Susannah. And she and Ivan were traveling east, away from him and toward Rosie Mortimer—toward her mother.

It was always hard for Susannah to think of her—and she thought of her often—as *my mother*. The words embarrassed her, as if they were shameful, denoting a curse on the family instead of a mere biological fact. To herself, she had begun to think of her mother as *Rosie* because that's what she was on her television show, which Susannah and Ivan watched faithfully. Susannah once referred to her as *Dad's first wife*, a circumlocution that caused Ivan to yell at her to grow up.

He had repeatedly tried to make Susannah get in touch with Rosie, to write to her, call her, smooth things over with a fan letter (wouldn't that be a gas?). Or let *him* call, write a letter—a telegram? He loved "Rosie Mortimer's Garden." He thought Rosie was amazing for her age, couldn't believe she must be nearly as old as poor Edwin (who was only fifty-five when they left him, but prematurely aged by booze, painkillers, pain), and held her up as an example to her daughter. *Now* there's *a woman who takes care of herself, who* cares *about herself,* he used to say—and he should have known Susannah better than to think such comparisons would inspire her to greater heights of fastidiousness or chic. Instead, when Ivan got on one of his reform kicks, she sank deeper into sloth and slackness, refused to wash her hair, lost weight, wore an old pair of baggy cotton pajamas around the house, and sat up in bed with the cats all day, reading and writing stories, her glasses slipping down her narrow nose—behavior which sent Ivan out to look for a California girl with clean blonde hair and tanned hairless legs with roller skates at the ends of them and earphones on her head. Or so Susannah imagined his women to be, simply because women like that were so plentiful in California, as ripe for the plucking as the fruit on the trees in their backyard.

In Connecticut, she thought, there wouldn't be so much opportunity, and they'd be working together where she could keep an eye on him—and then, if little Louisiana did come along, that would keep him busy. Just as she had once vowed never to have a child, she had also promised herself never to marry. After Ivan sent that promise scuttling away, she made herself another—never to let her marriage break up. Susannah's life had been hemmed in by these *nevers*, these melodramatic resolutions, and then complicated by the breaking of them. She was always starting over, determining to mend her ways, trying to burn her bridges behind her and failing. As a consequence her life had always seemed to her chaotic and pointless, the endless abandoned good intentions only making matters worse. But she was beginning, belatedly, at the age of twenty-seven, to accept that pattern as hers. Must every good life, every well-lived life, be as orderly and groomed as her mother's appeared to be? She was also descended from her father. She told this to Ivan once when he was preaching at her, and he called her hopeless and stomped out to find some tidy roller skater. But he came back, as always; and she was, as always, glad. Ivan's comings and goings were part of the disarray she welcomed in her life, and her failings were part of the missionary zeal he required in his.

It had excited her, when she met him, that Ivan used to be a priest. She wasn't a Catholic, never had been. Even her Italian grandfather hadn't been, though her great-grandmother had practiced her own brand of Catholicism, which required her to go to mass on special occasions: on Christmas, Easter, Palm Sunday, and Ash Wednesday, on the feast of St. Blaise (February 3) so she could get her throat blessed, and on her name day—the feast of St. Anne on July the 26th. Susannah had been raised without any religious trappings except the old crèche, with its chipped plaster sheep and golden-haired angels and smiling infant, made in Italy and brought from England by her grandparents in the Thirties, that was set up beneath the Christmas tree every year. She didn't count the Quaker school she had attended for six months when she was twelve, or the Episcopalian boarding school she finally graduated from, though she had sung hymns in the choir for two years.

Ivan's history was part of what attracted her to him, aside from his good looks and his interest in her. Those two things would have been enough; his years in the priesthood were something extra, something secret and special and forbidden. Sleeping with an ex-priest just suited the rebelliousness she cultivated; their affair, and the first spaced-out years of their marriage, were the dregs of the brattiness that had been part of her, it seemed, since birth.

During the years before their watershed trip east for her grand-mother's funeral, Ivan had been, like Susannah, a drifter, pill-popper, odd-jobber, welfare case, pothead, but once they returned to California, buoyed by the promise of Susannah's legacy and by the glimpse of normal life they had seen in Duke and Margie and their babies, things changed. Susannah steadied herself against Ivan's new incarnation as solid citizen, she let him save her, she settled down to be a wife—though she had as singular a version of settling down as her great-grandmother had of Catholicism and Ivan had of fidelity.

In Los Angeles, Ivan worked at a place called Ancestral Heritage, Inc., where he put his meticulous, accomplished, unimaginative painting style to good use doing portraits of imaginary forebears for social-climbing Californians. Ivan specialized in faking a stiff, primitive, early-eighteenth-century style that was much in demand. Working from a photograph of the customer—usually some *arriviste* from Manhattan Beach or the Marina—he would play around with the features, shortening a nose, raising a forehead, thinning a mouth, until he had a face that might have been an ancestor: Great-Great-Great-Grandfather Ephraim (see the resemblance around the eyes? the twist of the lips?); or Grandmother's old Aunt Amelia (they say she married a full-blooded Chock-taw, and isn't she the image of our Tiffany? Look at the chin). Then he transferred it to canvas and put a waistcoat and a cravat on it, or a dress with prim neck-ruffles and a cap, and then it was passed on to someone else at the studio to be "antiqued," and then framed in "distressed" wood, and then delivered to the delighted descendants of bogus Aunt Amelia and mounted on the fashionably stark-white moldingless walls of their waterfront condo, there to speak eloquently of roots, values, and money.

It wasn't a bad living, faking ancestors. The job supported the two of them, which was fortunate because, after a disastrous and mercifully brief attempt to work in an office in downtown Los Angeles, Susannah stayed at home with the cats and wrote stories. Ivan never begrudged her this privilege, even before she began to sell her stuff; he believed in her talent—blindly, since he seldom read what she wrote, having no taste for the fantastic, but never hesitating to put himself and her into separate art camps, the phony and the real. "Real artists are always slobs," he said in his generous moods, but it was obvious that he wished, since Susannah was home all day, that she'd keep the place cleaner, maybe work in the garden a little (look at your mother!), fix herself up more, make an *effort*. Shave her legs, at least.

Susannah wished she did, too. She promised herself she would reform, and sometimes she did for a while. There was a time, not long after her father got sick and entered St. Theodore's, when she rose early every morning, showered, put on a sundress which she had washed and ironed herself, and spent the day cooking, cleaning, poking through cookbooks she got from the library, weeding the vegetable garden Ivan put in (he was always putting in vegetable gardens, and he would weed and water them himself for a while, then—inevitably— turn them over to Susannah, and they would first turn into jungles and then, slowly, sadly, wither and die). She was very happy during that month, making lentil soup and banana bread and nice fruit salads. She used to drive up to see Edwin nearly every afternoon and come home on the freeway during rush hour, completely unruffled either by the heat or the press of traffic or her father's deterioration, which was, from day to day, horribly apparent. During those drives, those hours in the kitchen, those scrubbings in the shower, she never had a thought in her head.

She got over it, though. Her slovenliness, partly the result of years of living with Edwin—who had never cared how she looked, who approved of or ignored everything she did, who hired people to clean up after her—and partly a response to Ivan's grumbling and Ivan's infidelities and Ivan's prissiness, was deeply ingrained, as much a part of her as her long nose and her blue eyes—and what Ivan would call her artistic temperament.

The walls of their apartment (the second floor of a ramshackle frame building on Dimmick Street, with a weaving studio downstairs and a skeletal macrobiotic couple upstairs) were filled with Ivan's paintings—not of ancestors but of domestic landscapes, quaint solitary little gingerbread cottages set in deep woods, beautifully painted, with a sound grasp of color and design, but looking always in the end like greeting card art, or children's book illustrations. Gnome homes, fairy huts, little houses in the big woods.

He was self-taught, having taken up painting when being a priest began to go wrong for him, and considering how short a time he'd been at it his technical abilities were truly remarkable. But he was always modest about his work, aware that for all its proficiency it lacked even a flicker of greatness, and that prettiness was his stumbling block. The paintings, worked on sporadically but, when the mood hit him, obsessively, were the oil and canvas equivalents of his California girls, just as clean and tidy and empty.

There was one Susannah liked, though. He had attempted for a while to break out of his mold by adding a touch of fantasy, and one such experiment was a painting of a hut that seemed to be emerging from a chaos of sunset clouds, an elusive little structure seemingly constructed of vapors in the process of solidifying. The twilight, rose-gray colors were lovely, and the indistinctness of the scene intrigued Susannah, but what she liked best about it was the hint of someone, something, watching out the windows—a rarity for Ivan, who, except for his ancestor portraits, never painted people. They hung the painting in their bedroom, and it was a constant source of inspiration to Susannah—not the actual scene, but the potentiality of it, the sense of infinite possibilities beyond those clouds, behind those windows. Ivan liked the painting, too, but it seemed to puzzle him; he grinned at it when it was first hung and said, "Did I do that?" He was very happy to think it inspired Susannah, and that she saw it as the auspicious start of a new, more mature style. And yet it never led anywhere; he went back to banal prettiness, and the painting itself, which he called "Cloud House," was really, taken alone and not seen in relation to his other things, no more than a superior sort of decorative art—hopeful and important and inspiring, Susannah supposed, only to herself.

She used to sit on the bed for hours and hours, with the shades drawn, and Ivan's painting glowing faintly, mistily on the wall, and imagine things: people, usually, and bits of conversation and ways to describe faces, voices, gestures. Tags of poetry ran through her head, fitfully remembered from her college courses: "Fled is that music, fled is that music. . . ." The line rang and rang through the long afternoons, and so did "I fall upon the thorns of life, I bleed," and certain words she liked—intercontinental ballistic missile, duenna, martello tower, Sri Lanka—and colors from Ivan's paintings—vermilion, rose madder, heliotrope. . . . The words had powers to create landscapes around themselves, strange places she had never seen, except maybe as marijuana dreams in her spacier days: underwater vistas with pale plants whose fronds reached wispy fingers out at slippery fish and faceless swimmers; or rocky, dry, hot stellar landscapes, sometimes with a figure—who? what?—lurking, waiting; or desert places where sand blows, and banks itself against the base of a mountain, and then on the horizon after millions of years of nothing but sand, something moves.

These visions, colors, skeins of words got themselves transformed, eventually, into science-fiction stories, a term Susannah rejected as not descriptive of her work but the one editors used whether she liked it or not. She wrote very slowly, and only after weeks of sitting, like a hen on eggs, in her darkened room, watching the quality of the light subtly change around the sides of the window shades, thinking of nothing but that light. Not even thinking of it, just taking it in, her brain purposely emptied out, but differently from the emptiness of that dutiful domestic month—empty so it could fill. She sat caught fast in her stories where the drudgy details of daily life never intruded, where no one ever washed dishes or ironed a shirt or pulled weeds. She forgot to eat, forgot Ivan would be coming home and she would have to slap dinner together, idly petting Keats or Byron or Shelley, whichever of the three cats had achieved the place of honor on her lap during that day's feline power struggle, maybe reading a little but not in any sustained way, opening books at random, mostly poetry or the long Victorian novels she was partial to; and after a couple of weeks of this she would rise one morning and hatch four sentences, a paragraph, and spend the rest of the day reading and sitting and thinking. And the next morning her paragraph would lead to another, by some lovely and unfailing principle of incubation and growth that always astonished her, so that she might end that day with a page, even two. And by these tiny increments, like sand blowing against the base of a mountain, something in the end got built, and she gave it to her friend Carla to type, and then to Ivan to mail, and it always, now, was sold. The stories didn't interest her once they left her keeping. The checks, of course, were nice; they went for luxuries, things she couldn't afford because she and Ivan were hoarding every bit of spare cash—books, dinners out, little presents for Ivan and Edwin and Carla and Carla's little son. But the real reason she wrote stories was for the odd white, or yellow, or greenish light that filled her room, and the visions that came with it. And because she didn't want to work in an office.

One place she liked to imagine, but which had nothing to do with her stories—for some days, while she sat there with the cats in the pleasant gloom, she pondered not her visions but her life—was Silvergate, the estate in England where Rosie was born, and where Rosie's father and grandfather had been gardeners. Susannah remembered, with effort, concentrating so hard she got headaches, what she had learned about the place when she was little. There wasn't much to recall—mainly conversations she had overheard between Rosie and Peter, cozy chats about Rosie's childhood that used to infuriate Susannah with their intimacy, their exclusiveness.

Not that she ever so much as hinted at her desire to be part of them, or let on that she was listening. She would be deep in a book in one room while Peter and her mother chattered in another, but she had picked up certain things, and over the years she retrieved them from the back of her mind: Silvergate, in Kent, which was in the south of England, and her brother Peter was named after her grandfather who was named after the old man—the earl? baronet?—who inherited the place in the 1890s; and the gardens were beautiful, and vast, and designed by her grandfather's father Massimo Liliano—what a wonderful name!—who was cheated of the credit for it; and there was a famous hedge clipped into fancy shapes, and a lily pond, and every kind of flower, and a huge patterned rose bed; and there were sheep whose wool used to catch in the wooden fence supports they scratched their backs against, and little Rosie used to collect it into soft, oily, dirty balls, and she had her own strawberry bed, where the berries tasted better than anything—*anything*—even the ones she grew out behind the house; and Nonna Anna (who died when Susannah was eight) wasn't blind then, and she used to make yellow pasta, hanging it in strands to dry all over the kitchen, on ropes strung across the room and on broom handles propped between two chairbacks; and this was in the gardener's cottage where Rosie was born in the back bedroom, delivered by Nonna Anna because it happened so suddenly, on the birthday of Rosie's mother, whose name was May after the month, and who said to her husband when he came rushing in from the garden to find his baby girl already born, safely flannel-wrapped in a wicker cradle, asleep, before he or the doctor or the midwife could get there, and his wife and his mother beaming and laughing, proud of what they'd accomplished all on their own, "Thank you for my birthday present, Peter!" and they named her Rose.

That was all—not much, though for a long time it was enough. Susannah used to ponder it, feeling a furtive happiness and trying to fill in the blanks, picturing it all in her head with the help of bits of England gleaned from movies and television and books. When she came across Pemberley, Darcy's Derbyshire mansion, in *Pride and Prejudice*, her excitement was so intense that, gripping the book in both hands, she split it halfway down its paperback spine.

On the long trip East, Susannah and Ivan made love once, twice, three times every night, bombarding her womb with possibilities. Ivan was full of ideas about how to manage it a third, a fourth time, how to assist the little fellows—as he called, affectionately, his sperm—on their epic journey. He jammed pillows under her pelvis, massaged her belly, proposed standing her on her head, made her assume fanciful positions that sent them both into giggling fits. Susannah became sore and tired (*tired*? Ivan seized on it, hopefully, as a pregnancy symptom), but their forced lovemaking could still ignite her sometimes. Unbelievably, there they'd be, going through the familiar motions at two in the morning, at a campsite in, say, Ozona, Texas, for the second or third time, and it would suddenly be good, better than ever. She and Ivan would gasp with joy and kiss hungrily and fiercely, and then move slowly, very slowly and carefully, making it last, before the little fellows exploded inside her, and she and Ivan rocked together, ground their bodies together in uncomplicated ecstasy on the narrow bed, while the cats waited politely, whisker-washing on the floor until they were done.

"There," Ivan would say, stretching out beside her. "That must have done it. Don't move, don't move, let the little fellows swim, quietly, quietly, come on, guys. . . ." It gave their lovemaking, Ivan said, a whole new dimension, a sane, determined, purposeful quality. "Grown-up lovemaking," he called it, and when she accused him of being an unregenerate Catholic he protested, and explained to her with great seriousness that his ex-religion had nothing to do with anything, that in fact there could be no greater blasphemy than an ex-priest making babies—*don't move, Susannah, lie still*—that it was the life force he was talking about, primitive nature in the raw struggling to perpetuate the species. That's what he liked—not to mention the immediate, tangible result of grown-up lovemaking, i.e. the possibility of little Virginia or little Louisiana, of diapers and rubber duckies and solace in their old age.

They progressed steadily in straight lines, screwing their way across the country, aiming to see a bit of it. But they never stopped, except to eat and sleep and buy gas, letting everything go by: strange and wonderful vistas, mountains, and flat, flat stretches of dirt, promises of interesting sights advertised along the roads, state capitols and art museums and parks and hiking trails. They preferred to make haste slowly, so that each day was like the one before it: rise, let the cats out, breakfast in the van on thick slices of the whole-grain bread they brought along (getting staler and staler as they progressed east but made palatable with peanut butter and honey and gulps of herb tea); then collect the cats and get on the highway, drive until late afternoon (lunching en route on fruit and nuts); find a gas station and a campsite and, their resolves to stay pure and healthy broken down under the stresses of boredom and cold weather, tracking down a McDonald's or a Pizza Hut for dinner. And then Susannah would, maybe, write for a while, or peacefully daydream, while Ivan went out to talk to people or listened to the radio. And then baby-making, and then sleep, with the cats curled around and between them.

Susannah had plenty of time to think and daydream. Those twelve days on the road were themselves like a long dream, a strange dislocated period of time for her, during which they moved steadily east, never still, and the days blurred together and even the hours, so that she was surprised, at times, to find the sun setting, the day's destination reached, the van pulling into a campsite, and Ivan saying, "I sure could use a pizza or something."

She would think back later on the trip and remember sex, highways, and the story she was writing, but there was much more to it, of course, than that. Ivan seldom let her drive, and during the long hours on the road, while she sat beside him in the van, they sometimes sang old songs in two-part harmony. They were good at it: "Juanita" and "Moonlight Bay" and "Shine On, Harvest Moon." But mostly they talked—he talked, while Susannah chewed her cuticles and looked out the window at distant skylines, mountains, storm clouds. What Ivan talked about was the future—the restaurant and what it would lead to, the importance of self-sufficiency in this day and age, the fun of the reunion with Duke. He didn't mention the reunion with Rosie, but she knew he had that in mind. He ruminated endlessly on the restaurant, manipulating the money, designing menus in his head, assigning roles as if they were playing a kids' game: *I'll be the manager, Duke'll be the cook, you'll be the waitress—until, of course, you become the Mommy.* Ivan seldom had a past tense; he didn't talk to her any more about his life before they met, or about their first year together when they'd been groping through their experiments with drugs, clinging to each other in confusion. Only her childhood interested him; she knew very little about his. She had a feeling he used hers to cancel his own, but that was unconfirmable. On the road he spoke only of the future, and Susannah wondered if that was good or not—it was fine to be hopeful and optimistic and full of plans, but was he staking too much on this move? Would they be better off back home on Dimmick Street with a steady income and better weather, and her dimly lit room which she missed sorely, and her father dying just a few miles away?

Sometimes, she stopped listening to Ivan's monologues and just looked at him. There were times when she couldn't stop looking at him and appreciating not only his head and profile silhouetted against various kinds of sky and landscape but his optimistic soul, his steady, good-humored voice going on and on, his rambunctious affability. *Ivan.* At such times, she would feel light-headed with love for him, with gratitude for the odd fortune that had given him to her. She never wanted to lose him, and not only because she loathed change and upset—she loved him. She would put out her hand and touch his flannel-shirted sleeve with one finger, as if testing his reality, and he would look at her, still talking, and smile, and turn back to the road. He was a conscientious driver, keeping his eyes alternately on the speedometer—they went a steady fifty—and on the road, gazing with a small frown out the wide tinted windows that he wiped clean every time they stopped.

When they drove through towns, searching out restaurants and gas stations, Susannah looked with interest at the people on the streets, hungry for faces after the long hours of highway and scenery. Some of the people she saw would, she knew, stay with her a long time, maybe turn up in a story. There was a cat-faced black man in front of a restaurant where they had corned beef sandwiches one night, who said, "Howdy, folks" to them; fleetingly, Susannah thought it would be fun to know him, even be his girlfriend; she liked his mad look, his funny chuckle and wide-open eyes. And in a knot of women coming out of a store there was one about her age in a red head-scarf and an old raincoat, with an intelligent, humorous face, and Susannah thought, I would like to be her friend. And a nice waitress in Mississippi; and a middle-aged couple, look-alikes, with cropped gray hair and sensible shoes, who camped next to them at a place in Tennessee; and a boy of about fourteen with a pale, beautiful face and hair dyed pale green and brushed straight up like spiky grass, who filled their gas tank in a little Virginia town. Susannah devoured their faces, and other faces, missing her friend Carla and the long walks she used to take from her apartment to Carla's where she sat listening to gossip about people she didn't know—Carla's landlady, her son's nursery school teacher, her sister, her sister's friend Diana who worked as a jockey, her old college roommate who had become a nun. Carla loved to talk, Susannah loved to listen. When she left, after pots and pots of tea, she would walk home watching the people she passed and pondering Carla's tales, all of whose characters were as real to her as her own friends, or the people in the stories she wrote.

But she wasn't bored, alone in the van with Ivan all those long, changeless days, and they never quarreled. Susannah wondered whether she would come to look on that trip as an idyllic time, when Ivan didn't nag at her or deceive her or tell her to grow up.

Once, when they were crossing the interminable space of Texas, Susannah looked out at the setting sun: pure brilliant orange fading to pink (*rose madder, mallow pink, ocher, helianthin*) with the distinct black of a row of trees outlined against it.

"Death," she said to Ivan, speaking before she thought. It was not a word he liked, not a word it was easy to associate with him. He always seemed to her to represent life; even the way his dark hair sprang from his brow, the way his beard curled crisply around his chin, so eager and healthy, spoke of life. He looked, she had always thought, especially in the mornings when he liked to prowl around naked until it was time to get ready for work, like a god.

"What?" He took his eyes from the road to look at the sunset. "Did you say death? Why *death*?"

"I was thinking of my father, I suppose," she said apologetically. "And I read somewhere, I can't remember where"—*you can never remember where*, he sometimes said, but this time he was silent—"that the souls of the dead are held captive in natural objects like trees until, I forget, there's some way we can release them—"

"Your father's got a long time yet, Susannah."

She looked from the black trees to his profile. "No, he doesn't, Ivan. He could go any minute."

"Well. At least he's getting the best possible care."

"And then I read, I think some Indian tribe has this belief, that the dead live only as long as they're remembered. That as long as there's a living soul to remember them they never truly die."

"He's lucky he can afford a place like St. Theodore's," Ivan said. He always followed his own train of thought, and laid it out patiently until her mind veered to meet it. "Your Dad couldn't be in better hands." He reached over and patted hers, clasped tight in her lap around Keats, who slept there in a neat furry ball. "Quit worrying about your Dad. Think about the coming generation." They left the black trees behind;

buildings and a low-lying hill blocked the sunset. "Concentrate on getting pregnant," Ivan went on. "I'm convinced it helps." He grinned. "The power of pregnant thinking."

She was grateful to him for trying to cheer her up. He was always either cheering her up or getting impatient with her when it didn't work. He couldn't believe she was, in fact, contented enough most of the time without his efforts. It's because I don't make jokes, Susannah thought. She had never learned to be funny, though she could laugh at other people's jokes. She turned her hand to clasp his and looked at his forehead, nose, beard, the planes of his cheeks against the sunset colors. "Do you think that's why people have children, Ivan? Because of death?"

He merely frowned straight ahead at the highway. A little later he said, after a silence, "Don't be so morbid, Susannah," and she was sorry she had brought up the subject. She felt she had ruined the sunset for Ivan. But when they stopped for the night and went out for a spaghetti dinner he was as jolly and talkative as ever, and teased her about getting tomato sauce all over her chin.

They were traveling the southern route because it was February, but they ran into snow in Arizona and a blizzard in New Mexico (where they were stranded for two days at a deserted campsite, dozing and listening to the radio in the van, with the heater on full blast and in the distance reddish mountains rising from black evergreens). There was sleet and freezing rain in San Antonio, the city immobilized while they, old New Englanders, scoffed at its inability to cope—no plows, no sanders, no snow tires—and holed up in the van another two days, until the temperature rose, miraculously, overnight, into the fifties, and foiled the ice, turning the roads black and wet, with streams of melt running urgently in the gutters. They also encountered a heatwave in Baton Rouge, hurricane warnings in Mobile, and violent rains in Knoxville, where they had to pull over for three hours and wait it out, munching on granola and reading. "All we saw of the country was the weather," Susannah said afterward to Duke.

And superhighways: Route 10 out of Los Angeles through Arizona, New Mexico, Texas, Louisiana, and Mississippi, where they started climbing north, through Alabama, nicking the northwest corner of Georgia, and picked up Route 81 in Tennessee, following it through Virginia and Pennsylvania, and then east on Route 84 to Connecticut. Up north, it was a fairly snowless winter—Pennsylvania and New Jersey surprised them by having no snow cover at all—but it was cold. Toward the end of the trip, to prevent having to sleep in the van (where despite the cats and the heater and their strenuous sex life they woke with toes and noses totally numb, too cold to pee, too cold to talk), they drove longer and longer each day, not stopping until dinner time; and once, through Pennsylvania, driving in shifts all night, so that Connecticut loomed, after the leisurely southern leg of their journey, frighteningly close all of a sudden. They were in New York late one afternoon, they were crossing the Hudson, they were in Danbury by rush hour, and they pushed on and arrived in Chiswick for dinner—Connecticut, where, even longer ago than Susannah had taken her vow to remain childless, she had sworn never to return. Well, vows are meant to be broken, as Ivan always said (referring to his leaving the priesthood), sounding as he sometimes did like a popular song from the fifties. But it was probably true. If people change, and change, shedding skin after skin throughout their lives—and Susannah believed they did—it becomes necessary to review such matters as vows. Particularly those taken in early youth, like hers, which she made at ten, after she traveled in a taxicab at a terrifying speed down the Connecticut turnpike to the New Haven Airport where she got on an American Airlines plane, clasping the bag of stuffed animals she'd been collecting since she was a baby, her talismans against airplanes, homesickness, terror, whatever demons awaited, vowing never to come back, *never never never.* As the plane soared into the air, she turned to the nice stewardess, who had come to sit buckled in beside her because she was young and upset; Susannah's face was filled with such misery and anger that the stewardess recoiled in shock and then put her arms around her and let her cry on her trim bosom, and when that was done brought her a lemonade and a ham sandwich. By that time, Connecticut was lost beneath the clouds—forever, thought Susannah, not having yet learned about the fragility of vows.

But there they were, at Duke's place in Chiswick—a big shingled house, painted red, with a wide stone-pillared porch and a view of barns, hills, and not too far off in the distance a plant that manufactured creosoted railroad ties.

When they arrived, finally, after twelve days on the road, Susannah was travel-tired and downhearted, overwhelmed simply at being there, of being jerked back into the present tense in a cold Connecticut house on a dark rural road. Ivan was full of energy after all those days cooped up in the van. While he and Duke went out into the cold dark with a flashlight, for a look around the place (woodpile, orchard, frozen pond, all the paraphernalia of self-sufficiency that Susannah, eventually, would become so fond of), Susannah called her father—called, at any rate, the number of St. Theodore's, hoping they'd hook her up to her father out there and not to Dr. Strauss or Mrs. Campbell or Mrs. Panza, which would mean she was too late and he had died while she was reading a road map in Virginia or screwing Ivan in Mississippi.

But they put him on the phone. "Susannah?" he said, his voice so weak and distant it was as if he were talking from the fictional star settlement she'd been writing about all the way across the continent.

"Dad, Dad, we're here, we're in Connecticut. How *are* you?"

There was a pause, and it sounded as if someone was propping him up on the pillows; she heard him grunt, heard a voice—Mrs. Panza, it sounded like—and then he said, more strongly, "What say, honey?"

"How *are* you? How are you *doing*?"

"Where are you now, Susannah? Did you get there? Are you all right?"

"Yes, we're here, in Connecticut. But how are *you*?"

"You know how I am, Susannah." Neither of them spoke; he was being hoisted up again, and drank a little water. She heard a glass tap against the mouthpiece. Duke's phone was on the stair landing, and she sat on the step and leaned her head against the grimy brown wallpaper; it was ice cold. "There," he said, not to her. Then, "Susannah?"

"Yes, Dad."

"You don't need to call me, you know. I meant what I said. I can do this alone." These words came through clearly.

"I know, Dad, but I need to know. I'm sorry, I just can't let you *go* like that."

"Susannah? I don't want you to cry." If she'd heard those words once from him she'd heard them a thousand times.

"I won't," she said, crying anyway. "But don't say I can't *call*, Dad."

There was another pause. She could hear him breathe, in, out, in— was he asleep? Where was Mrs. Panza? She imagined his pale, lipless mouth open in sleep like a slot, his caved-in cheeks. Then he said, "No," and she waited. "No," he said again. "You call, honey. You call if you want to. I like to hear your voice."

His voice at that point faded away, and Mrs. Panza came on. "Mrs. Cord? How are you? It's Mrs. Panza. Your father has had his medication and is just about to drop off for a little nap before suppertime."

"How is he, Mrs. Panza?" A motherly woman, on whose shoulder Susannah had wept, out in the hall, more than once.

"Doing pretty well today," she said. "He's holding his own." There was a smile in her voice, and Susannah could imagine her looking fondly at Edwin as she spoke—her baby. There was a low mumble, and she added, "He says for you not to worry." Another mumble, pro-longed. "He says be good and be happy and not to worry."

"I'll call tomorrow, Mrs. Panza. Is that okay? Does it do him any good?"

"It certainly does him no harm, Mrs. Cord," she said carefully. "You call as often as you wish. Even if he can't take the call someone will give you an update."

Susannah carried a suitcase up to the room she and Ivan would sleep in. The cats followed her, the three of them skulking low and wary up the stairs, practically on their bellies. "Think of this as your home," she said to them; it was what Duke had said to her when he kissed her hello. "For however long," he had said.

She thought of it as her dark, cold home. It would be dark, she could tell, even in daylight. The windows were small and sparse, with dark green shades pulled down over them. All the light bulbs seemed to be forty-watt energy-savers. There were two woodstoves going, one in the huge and drafty kitchen, one in the toy-littered front room, but the house was still cold. Tiny, invisible gusts of frigid air whisked from behind walls and moldings and window-frames and cut through her jeans, her thin sweater. She unpacked Ivan's flannel shirt and put it on, and a second pair of heavy socks. From the room next door she could hear voices: the two little girls, aged five, talking in bed, sleepy murmurs with long pauses in between. She lifted up a shade and looked out at the night. She couldn't see much, but as she stood looking Duke's flashlight came into view from behind a grove of trees, and she could make out, just, Duke and Ivan behind it, Ivan with his hands in his jacket pockets. They'd have to buy some heavy gloves; neither of them had any. While she watched, he removed one hand and gestured with it. What's he telling Duke, she wondered—about his women? about Edwin? about the baby they were trying to make? about her? Anything—it could be anything, from what they had for lunch to what they did in bed. Ivan had no secrets except from his wife.

She let the shade fall and surveyed the room. It was what one would expect: stained wallpaper, an old sewing stand, an oak bow-front dresser, a strip of dingy carpet, a sagging double bed covered in a chenille bedspread with a pile of blankets folded at the foot, and the three cats under it. She squatted down to talk to them; three pairs of eyes gleamed; the three cats sat in perfect stillness. She stood up. Creaking floorboards. One wobbly brass floor lamp beside the bed, with the usual dim bulb. Could she write there? Well, why not? The room wasn't much different, except in temperature, from the bedroom they had left behind on Dimmick Street. Cleaner, maybe. She would hang Ivan's painting there—the only one they had brought with them, "Cloud House."

She heard Duke and Ivan come in, and went down to join them. They had supper in the kitchen, sitting on rocking chairs pulled up to the blazing stove. It was the kind with glass doors in front, and they could see the flames licking the crossed logs. There was hot vegetable soup with barley in it, hunks of bread, and cold beer. They held the bowls in their hands, and Duke ladled in the soup. Steam rose from it, along with the smell of tomato and some pungent herb. Duke's hands were scarred with burn marks—long purplish welts and, across the back of one, a delicate white streak, healed.

"What've you been doing to yourself?" Susannah asked him.

"Just handling the stoves," he grinned. "I've never had a really bad burn."

Ivan was silent, eating his soup with single-minded concentration. It was the most substantial, and surely the most delicious, meal they'd had in many days, but a few spoonfuls made Susannah warm and full, and she stopped eating to ask Duke questions.

"Aren't the twins cold up there? There's no heat upstairs."

He grinned at her again, enjoying his role of hardy New Englander against hers of California naif. "They've got thermal trapdoor sleepers on over long johns, and a bed full of quilts, and furthermore they sleep together. I go in to get them up in the mornings for school and they're cuddled together like kittens."

"School?"

"Kindergarten. Palmer Elementary School, on the other side of Chiswick. They take the school bus." He relished imparting this information. Susannah could see that his daughters enchanted him—just the fact of their existence, their presence in his life, their trap-door sleepers, the name of their school. "Is that where you went, Susannah? Palmer School?"

"No—mine was just called Chiswick Elementary School. Though I suppose it could be the same building. I don't know where it'd be from here. I've lost my bearings."

But she remembered Mrs. Garmer, and rows of inky desks, and dusty hardwood floors, and her friend Ellen Moffat, who also had a terrible mother. Ellen's threw tantrums and had weeping fits; thinking back, Susannah realized Mrs. Moffat must have been alcoholic, like her own father; she dimly recalled the smell of booze, a blurred look in her eyes. Mrs. Garmer was the fifth-grade teacher, she had pimples and a crown of braids. Susannah was always in trouble, the principal (Miss Clelland?) calling her mother, and Rosie giving Susannah the silent treatment.

"And who looks after them, Duke? I mean, when they get home from school?"

"I do," he said, surprised. He was stocky and handsome, a little shorter than Susannah, with a neat pointed nose, mild no-color eyes, a cherubic face with long, turned-down lips, and thinning hair hanging to the middle of his ears. He had neat, aristocratic wrists and ankles, and quick, square hands. His wife, Margie, had been a tiny woman, curly-haired, competent, with gold stars in her pierced ears. She wore a light blue nurse's uniform, and that summer when the Cords came to Connecticut for the funeral and stayed with Duke and Margie, when Susannah had been so sick and desperate, she used to look at Margie—a nurse with gold stars twinkling at her ears—and think *Help me, save me*. And she and Ivan were, of course, helped and saved, by luck and money, and it was Margie who was lost—killed not long after in a car crash on Route 95.

"The bus doesn't get them home until four o'clock, and I'm here by then," Duke said. "If I'm not, Ginger looks after them—that's my neighbor, in the white house across the road and down. They love Ginger."

Susannah wondered: *will they love me*? "I'm afraid of children," she said to Duke, and Ivan stopped eating and said, "For Christ's sake, Susannah, that's what I *mean*," as if he were continuing an old conversation. As indeed he was. "Pull yourself together, for Christ's sake."

When Duke said, "You'll love the twins, Susannah, and I know they'll love you. I don't want you to worry while you're here, I want you to throw yourself heart and soul into your new life and get a little *happy*," and whacked his warm hand down on hers, she knew what Ivan had been gesturing about out there in the dark.

Duke and Ivan talked about the restaurant: about money, about the lease, about ordering equipment, about quantity cooking. Most of what Ivan had speculated about on the road was proving to be wrong-headed; Duke knew all about it, it would be all his doing, all his ideas. They had the money—her grandmother's legacy, expanded through some lucky investing—but Duke had the experience, and the head for practicalities. He had managed a health food store for five years, he'd cooked for two years in a vegetarian restaurant and another two years in an Italian restaurant in New Haven, and if his soup was any indication, he was a good cook, sure enough.

Susannah felt as they sat there that they were in the hands of a wise doctor, or guru, or shrink—that as things stood Duke would be a father figure not only to her but to Ivan, and she wondered how and where Ivan would gain the upper hand, for she knew he'd have to have it in some aspect of their new communal life. Maybe by becoming a father? Surely a proud new daddy doesn't need a father figure?

She didn't know Duke very well. He was an old college buddy and fellow seminarian of Ivan's. Duke, though, had left the seminary after a year, while Ivan went on to be ordained, to batter at the walls of the priesthood in a slum parish in Buffalo, New York, and finally to leave not only the priesthood but the church, split for California, and hook up with—among others—Susannah. He and Duke had kept in touch via occasional and expensive phone calls, one visit from Duke to California, their trip east three years back, and an annual Christmas card from them to Duke. From what Susannah had observed of Ivan's friendship with Duke, it seemed to be composed of equal parts rivalry, affection, and a set of vague shared aspirations—toward *what* it would be hard to say precisely, but what it came down to was an aspiration toward whatever they didn't have at the moment: first holiness, then freedom, then mainstream respectability, now Yankee self-sufficiency. And there they all were, breaking wholesome bread around their woodstove, with the aspirations of Duke and Ivan rising in the air around them.

Susannah decided to share them, however vague. She believed in Ivan (she must believe in Ivan; what other choice had she?). She would believe in Duke, too. And most of all she believed in the holiness of the heart's affections. Where had that phrase come from? what poem? She couldn't recall, but she said it to herself as she sat in the stove's heat, listening to Ivan's travel stories, listening to Duke's plans for the restaurant. "You name it, Susannah. You're the writer," Duke said. "Come up with something poetic." It would be real, then; it would have a name; it would materialize in a happy confusion of pots and pans, and tables and chairs, and the smell of cooking. She had been unaware, until that stove-lit moment of certainty, that she had ever been dubious about the project.

She settled down easily at the house on Perkins Road. After the first shock of its dark draftiness, she began to like it. The hugeness of the place pleased her—the high ceilings, the maze of unheated rooms, the vast empty attic, the clutter of outbuildings, the calendar-scene view behind the house, to the west, of a red barn on a hill, a white farmhouse, cows. Even the red-flagged mailbox, shiny black against the white snow, filled her with delight when she trekked out in her boots for the mail. And from the front porch, Duke said, the factory would be nearly invisible in summer when the trees leafed out. From her bedroom window she could see Duke's six apple trees, gnarled as witches, and the frozen pond surrounded by stiff brown weeds.

They did little for the first few days but talk, eat, and drink beer, sitting around the kitchen stove in heavy sweaters and wool socks. Susannah listened, chewing her cuticles, while Duke and Ivan reminisced about their college days and the seminary. All their stories were absurd, designed to make themselves look as silly as possible; they liked looking back from their thirties at their frivolous and misguided youth, and there was an unspoken satisfaction between them with how well, after all, they'd turned out.

Susannah and Ivan told Duke about California, where he'd been just that once and was reluctant to travel to again. He was scared of earthquakes—afraid, since Margie's death, of disasters in general, cautious about cars, protective of his daughters. Susannah told him about the time she and Carla had taken Carla's little boy skiing at Big Bear, outside Los Angeles.

"We had to rent him a snowsuit—can you imagine? Southern California kids don't own them."

They all looked at the hooks by the kitchen door crowded with the twins' well-worn and grubby collection of snowpants and down jackets, the pile of mittens and wool hats in a basket on the floor, the tangle of boots left on newspapers to drip, and Duke laughed. "Sounds like paradise, right about now. Sometimes I think if I have to zip another boot or hunt up one more lost mitten I'll just flip out, and the little men will have to cart me off to L.A." He looked at Susannah in belated surprise. "You *ski*?"

"Oh no," she said. "I sat in the clubhouse and watched."

"Just watched? All afternoon?" Duke look amused.

"I read old magazines. *People* magazine, and *Time*. I learned a lot."

"Normally, Susannah is sort of out of touch," Ivan said, waggling his eyebrows as if to say: understatement of the year.

"I thought writers had to have their fingers on the pulse of the world."

"My writing is strictly other-worldly," said Susannah, smiling at them both, wondering how soon she could stop being sociable— a *guest*—and get to work. Her half-formed story pulled at her; even as she sat talking, bits of it wandered into her head, fanciful fragments mixed up with Duke's striped socks, cold beer, Ivan's laugh. In the evenings, the twins played in the front room and the three adults, sitting in the kitchen, could hear tags of their conversation. Everything they said made Duke chuckle, or smile secretly to himself with pride. His mouth turned down at the corners when he smiled, giving him a rueful look. Susannah wondered whether it tormented him that his little girls, with their tiny hands and feet, and their light, curly hair, looked so much like his dead wife, or whether it consoled him. She tried to imagine herself, Ivan dead and gone, with her baby grown to a miniature version of its father, but she didn't linger on the thought; it horrified her, and she looked with great respect at Duke, who was able to enjoy his children, and to enjoy life in spite of what it had inflicted on him.

She wished she could make friends with the twins. She suspected she would, in time, but for the moment she couldn't think of anything to say to them, couldn't talk to them and tease them as Ivan did. She merely observed them, with wary interest, as if they were extraterrestrial beings, or some new and intelligent breed of cat—alien creatures. Their conversation fascinated her; they could, often, be one person talking, so closely did their twin thoughts connect. Once Susannah heard them jointly telling a story to the cats:

"So they went down the dark, dark path."

"And it got darker and darker, like a tunnel."

"All the bushes and plants closed in."

"And the flowers."

"And they walked and walked until they came to a cave. And what do you think was in it?"

"It was a beautiful princess with long silver hair."

"And she said, 'Won't you come in and play with my cats?'"

"They seem very precocious," she said to Duke, and he smiled his turned-down smile and blushed.

Sometimes it snowed, lightly, never lasting. Large wet flakes drifted dreamily down, letting the wind bat them around before they settled and melted. Once there was a snow day, and the twins were home from school, exuberant at the holiday. Susannah, shyly, played a game called Sleepy Time with them. You had to match pairs of pajamaed animals and tuck them into little cardboard beds. She had a feeling they let her win. She made them cocoa, and they sang "Oh Susannah" to her. She liked the way they fussed over the cats, who bore all their attentions, except being dressed in doll clothes, with surprising aplomb.

"Why do they have those names?" Mary Claire asked her.

"They're named after poets," Susannah said. "I took a course in college once, and read their poems, and liked them. They were all three friends," she added, wondering if she was remembering right.

"I like Shelley best."

"The *name*, you mean," said Mary Grace.

"Oh, yes—the name—I like all the cats," Mary Claire said, and the twins petted each cat in turn, scrupulously refusing to have favorites lest they hurt feelings.

She found she could relax with the twins by the process of recalling herself at that age—five going on six. She could remember the long blissful excursions with her father—bike rides or car trips, neither of them caring where they went as long as they could go far enough to wipe away for a while the hard silences of home. Susannah would tell Edwin about school, her teacher, her friend Ellen, her feuds with the other girls, her difficulties with numbers, her joy in learning to read. He always listened carefully, asking questions—not too many, and all the right ones, so that you knew he really cared about the answers. Their conversations were keepsakes to put away and treasure, and at night, in bed before sleep, she used to clutch her old plush tiger or her floppy-eared dog in her arms and go over and over them, committing them to memory just in case, just in case. . . . She always knew—so did Peter—that her parents would split up, and she had dreaded losing her father. She could still recall with precision the sensation of scared joy that filled her when they did separate and she was allowed, after all, to go west with Edwin.

She telephoned Peter one night after the twins were in bed and Duke and Ivan were drinking beer in the kitchen. She sat on the landing wrapped in a blanket and dialed Peter's number. She had talked to him twice from California, feeling he should know about Edwin's condition, and then about her migration back to Connecticut. They were, in a way, friends, and always had been, though they had often hated each other and had fought, bitterly, as children—little caricatures of their parents—and whenever Susannah heard Peter's voice, or had a letter from him, it was as if something that had been pinching her was eased and made comfortable, some weight removed, a missing piece clicked into place. *My brother*, she thought—and just as the words *my mother* seemed so strange and unwieldy that she sometimes stammered over them, *my brother* sounded right. She loved to say to people: my brother in Connecticut, my brother Peter who's in graduate school at Yale, my brother back east. . . .

"Peter? It's me—Susannah. We're here."

The stair landing seemed to be at the center of all four winds. Susannah got colder and colder as they talked about the trip, the restaurant, movies, Peter's writer's block, Edwin, the weather. She loved talking to Peter, she could have sat there forever discussing the new Woody Allen film if she hadn't been freezing. She pulled the blanket tighter around her feet, tucking them in.

"I've got to hang up in a second, Peter, this phone is in the coldest spot in the house—"

"Call me back in the spring."

She chuckled and said, "I just want to ask you, though, about—I mean, does she know we were coming?"

"Mom? *Oh*, yes."

"You told her?"

"I told her." He sighed, and she waited for him to go on but he said nothing.

"I assume she's not exactly overjoyed," Susannah said finally.

"It was a surprise to her."

"Did you tell her about Dad?"

79

"Oh, no—no. I never do mention him to her."

"No, I suppose not." Susannah sighed herself, wondering what had happened to their pleasant conversation. "Well . . . I suppose I'd better go thaw out my feet."

"Okay. I suppose I'd better go and do some damn thing."

"Peter, are you all right? You seem sort of glum all of a sudden."

"No, I'm fine, I just wish you and Mom would . . . I guess I mean that I wish she wasn't so—"

"What?"

"Touchy. Close-minded. I don't know."

"O God, why did we ever come here?" Susannah hit her frozen feet with her closed fist; it hurt, and she rubbed first one foot, then the other. Tears tickled her nose.

"She'll get over it, Susannah. You know how she is. And *I'm* glad you're here. I'm sorry if that hasn't been coming across, honey pie." Susannah smiled and wiped her eyes—honey pie. "I've been having kind of a hard time myself with this damned dissertation, and with other things." He snorted, meaning it for a laugh. "Too numerous to mention."

"Oh, Peter."

"Don't worry. I just want you to know I'm glad you're here, and I think it'll work out with Mom. She can be terrific, Susannah, but I don't deny she can be a bitch, too. And she's getting *old*. Set in her ways."

"Well, I didn't move here for the purpose of reconciling with her, Peter. I'm not all that keen on it myself. It's Ivan who thinks it would be so neat."

"Maybe it will be. Who knows?"

Susannah shook her head. "It doesn't sound neat, Peter, it sounds damned messy. Oh, why can't I just have a regular, supportive mother, who'd welcome me and back me up a little? She's always—" A flare of anger, with tears behind it, rose and then subsided. She sighed again. Who was she angry at, anyway? A face on the television, a woman she hadn't seen—except for a few dazed, painful moments—in seventeen years.

"Don't worry, Susannah. I'm pretty sure it'll work out."

"I don't intend to worry. Now tell me when you're coming to see us."

They arranged that he would—hesitantly, it had been so long, and they didn't make it soon, but Susannah looked forward to it happily, with a catch of excitement she knew Peter shared. After she hung up she sat on the landing a while longer in spite of the cold, rubbing her feet through the blanket, wondering what Peter's problems were, wondering what ways her mother was set in. She tried to recall Rosie smiling—in person, not her black-and-white television smile (even that was rare enough)—but all she could remember was the disapproving frown she had seen so often, and always, dimly, that horrible memory of their last encounter, and the force of Rosie's palm striking her cheek, and the hard strength that had seemed to flow out of her to Susannah, sweeping her away like a dead leaf.

Duke came out to see if she was off the phone; he had to make a call.

"I was talking to my brother," she said, painfully getting up. "I invited him to come out and see us one of these days."

"He's in New Haven?"

She nodded. "He has writer's block."

"What's he writing?"

"A dissertation on Dante."

"You're a family of other-worldly writers, I see," Duke said with a laugh. "And you look like you're freezing, Susannah. Get in there by the stove."

She moved aside for him to pass her on the stairs, and he smiled his upside-down smile. "You're sure you don't mind that we're here, Duke?" she asked him.

"Mind?" He stopped a step above her and looked down. Normally she was a fraction taller than he, and it seemed odd to look up at him. "Do I *mind*? Susannah, I love having you two here. Don't you think I've been lonely?"

She reached up, squeezed his hand quickly, and released it. The backs of his fingers were rough, as if they'd been sandpapered. "It's good of you all the same, Duke, to take us in."

"It's good of you to come all the way east to be taken in," he said.

81

They stood a moment smiling at each other before she made her way downstairs, wrapped in her blanket, to the stove.

Ivan sat making sketches at the kitchen table. The cats lay curled in a heap. "I just talked to Peter," she said.

He looked up. "Oh. How's old Peter?"

"Ivan, I don't want you to get in touch with my mother. Please. Promise me you won't."

"Well, not right away, Susie. In time."

"No." She sat down in a rocking chair and let her blanket fall away. She wore a denim skirt and black woolen tights with a hole in the knee, and she pinched the sides of the hole together over her skin. "I don't want to get friendly with her, Ivan. She doesn't want me here— she doesn't want to be friends. And I don't either."

"How do you know she doesn't?"

"Peter."

"Oh, *Peter*. Of *course* Peter's trying to keep you two apart," he said, as if this was an obvious, reasonable, and long-held conviction. "He doesn't want to share his precious mama."

"Why do you say that, Ivan?" He bent over the table again, laid ruler against paper, and carefully, in silence, drew a short black line. "What on earth makes you think that's true?" she asked.

"Oh, come on, Susannah." He looked up irritably. "Same reason you never tried to bring Edwin and Peter together. Remember when Peter came out to see you? Did you engineer a reunion?"

"Dad was in Mexico, Ivan. I never even thought of it, and neither did Peter."

"You think he wouldn't have skipped going to Mexico if you'd told him his son was in town and wanted to see him?"

"But Peter *didn't*."

"That's what I'm saying, Susannah. It takes two to work things out, and they sometimes need a third party to arrange them. You know that perfectly well. And you never made an attempt. So don't be surprised if your brother doesn't, either."

She didn't reply. She pulled at her tights with the fingers of one hand while she bit the cuticles of the other. There was silence in the room except for a rasp when Ivan erased something. Duke was talking softly on the landing. She wondered whom he had called; there hadn't, so far, been the hint of a girlfriend. Byron extricated himself from the other two cats, stretched and yawned, and leapt to Susannah's lap. She sat scratching him behind the ears and resenting Ivan, with his glib analyses of other people's business, and his know-it-all tone of voice, his *instructor* voice that must, she thought, have driven his Buffalo parishioners up the wall. "Father Cord," she imagined them saying to each other with a grimace. "Yack yack yack, he's got an answer for everything." The idea amused her—Ivan in his cassock (had he worn a cassock?) hammering home tedious doctrine to a sea of irritated Sunday-morning faces. They kept looking at their watches and nudging each other, rolling their eyes. She wondered if he drove anyone out of the church with his smug lectures, and she cheered up, imagining a stream of people marching out of St. Lucy's to a Lutheran or Baptist church down the street, mumbling, "I can't take it any more, that Father Cord. . . ."

Duke returned to find her smiling. "What's so funny?" he asked, and Ivan looked up from his work, curious.

But she said nothing, just shook her head and smiled on. As always, it was her own thoughts that consoled her—that delighted her, amused her, and reconciled her to the thorns of life, and the blood.

Ivan and Duke applied themselves to their project, the still unchristened restaurant. They began interviewing contractors and pricing supplies. Ivan, who enjoyed manual labor, kept saying, "I can hardly wait to get my hands on *lumber*." They were planning to do much of the renovation work themselves, and the talk around the woodstove in the cold evenings was all of two-by-fours and floor tile. There was a great debate over ceramic tile versus vinyl—Ivan wanted earth-brown ceramic, Duke wanted black and white checkerboard vinyl. Duke called Ivan extravagant, Ivan called Duke middle class—-joking exchanges with grains of sincerity embedded in them. Susannah suggested bare wooden floors, plain plywood, simple and rustic.

"The Board of Health wouldn't approve," said Duke.

"Tacky, anyway," said Ivan. "Too California."

His calm good nature began to worry Susannah, not because it was uncharacteristic (Ivan was renowned for his amiability; only with his wife did it ever slip) but because in this case it seemed forced: his smiles were too quick, his silences loaded, his gaze wandering off into the distance while his fingers drummed on a tabletop. He might fool Duke, but he didn't fool Susannah, who was used to scrutinizing Ivan's words, Ivan's moods, for concealed dangers. She had a feeling these conversations made him boiling mad, and not only at her for her ignorant suggestions—predictable spinoffs from her general uselessness in the real world—but at Duke for his infernal practical streak, which Ivan knew would prevail. The cheap black and white vinyl was as good as laid.

Still, he persisted, while Susannah watched and listened with apprehension. "Sure it's cheaper, Duke, but you want durability you go with ceramic," Ivan would say, making Susannah smile in spite of herself at the ease with which Ivan had picked up the vocabulary and the inflections of the workmen they talked to, the men at the wholesale lumber supply, the plumbers and carpenters. She wondered, too, if her apprehensions about the collaboration weren't a trifle absurd, as so many of her worries proved to be. Ivan was always telling her she took life too seriously—on the days when he wasn't telling her she didn't take it seriously enough—and she knew that sometimes she did. Maybe Ivan's anger didn't go deep; maybe it was at least half show, maybe it was a private, affectionate signal between him and Duke— Ivan's way of saying to his old friend: I'm so fond of you I can even put up with this *damned bullying*. Duke smiled at Susannah sometimes, over Ivan's head, a friendly, even intimate smile that she felt vaguely disloyal returning. She wondered if Duke found Ivan funny, if he also had visions of Father Cord and his grumbling flock.

She hadn't, after all, gotten pregnant in the van. "You'll get pregnant here, then," Ivan told her confidently when they'd been at Duke's a week. "Back home in good old Connecticut where you were born. And we'll call the kid Chiswick."

"I was born in Boston, Ivan."

"Well, *raised*," he said, looking annoyed.

She laughed at him. "We could take a trip to Boston if you insist on seeing this so mystically. We could make love on Marlborough Street where I was conceived."

She felt his smile against her cheek. They were lying in bed; his palm was spread out on her flat stomach. "I know people have babies every day," he said. "But it seems so staggering to actually do it, ourselves. I can really understand all those primitive fertility rites. It's so *important*." He peered at her in the dark. "Do you feel comfortable here? In this house? Do you feel as if it *could* happen?"

"Oh, yes," she said drowsily, and snuggled against him. If they were very still she could sometimes hear the old house creak. "I feel more *home* here than I did back in L.A."

"You seem to like the kids."

"I love the kids. I love the way they enjoy their lives. That's something I can't remember doing, not really—I was so ornery at that age."

"Not scared of them any more?" he teased her. He must have been drowsy because he didn't pursue the reference to her childhood. She wondered if he'd been in touch with Rosie. She was sure he hadn't, but Ivan was an expert dissembler, and *sure* was the wrong word. She was never sure; for all she knew he already had a girl.

"I'm not scared of anything but Dad dying," she said.

"Susannah." He removed his hand from her stomach; he was wide awake. She sensed his exasperation in the dark, and she was sorry for having caused it. She knew why she had brought up her father just then—as a foil to Ivan, to her mother, to Ivan's girls. As a specter of death to set against Ivan with all his life. She was ashamed of herself.

"Sh," she said. "Never mind, I'm sorry, I know it's best this way, Ivan, and I'm glad we're here. I just miss him, I can't help it. But I know we've done the right thing." She could feel how tensely he was lying beside her. "Don't be angry, Ivan."

"You call him often enough."

"I know," she said, and lay quietly, wondering if it would be a relief to her, after all, when she called one day and Mrs. Panza or Dr. Strauss told her it was over. "Maybe it will be a sort of relief when he dies, Ivan," she said after a while. "I won't be so torn."

"Mmm," he said. He was asleep. She turned over, he snuggled

against her back, and she thought to herself, *it's not true, I don't want to be there watching him die, I want to be here.* A scene came into her mind, an improbable one out of old movies—herself telling Ivan they were going to have a baby, and his tender, solicitous astonishment. She smiled. The way Ivan monitored her menstrual cycle and her fertile days and their lovemaking, he'd probably know before she did. How funny it must have been, back in the days—had there been such days? really?—when women's bodies were mysterious temples to their husbands. Could men have been so ignorant? And was it now, this very minute, happening deep inside her, sperm and egg uniting in their vital embrace, and their baby, even now, beginning to grow? The thought rubbed away the guilt she inevitably felt whenever she admitted to herself that she preferred cold Connecticut, where life was, to her father's slow dying in California.

She lay curled against Ivan, listening to the sound of the wind whipping past outside their window, and the cats purring themselves to sleep at her feet. She had never stopped being grateful for silence to sleep by—this kind of silence. For a long time after she and Edwin had moved out to New Mexico, Susannah had fallen asleep to the echoes, from the depths and crannies of her mind, of her parents arguing. They had begun to argue, with brutal suddenness, one summer evening, and hadn't stopped until Edwin left the house for good in the autumn—a couple of hard months that had finally brought her together with Peter in fearful horror. Their parents had never argued, all those years—had long since, in fact, stopped speaking to each other. The children had become used to the cold silence in their house—had become part of it, so that when the noisy fights began, on hot summer nights after they had gone up to bed, they hadn't known what to do. Susannah sometimes crept into Peter's room, and they sat in the dim light staring at each other, wordless and frightened, listening to the long, noisy, heedless battles downstairs, the angry words bouncing off the walls. The words had struck Susannah and her brother with their violence, their ugliness, like actual blows, her mother's shrill voice going on and on, her father's hard and strained, as if saved up for the long, almost guttural speeches that hit and hit and hit until her mother's protest came. And now and then a blow, or something thrown. And then a horrible silence out of which Susannah and Peter would try to salvage sleep.

Sleep came easily to her now, and had for years—but never, she thought as she drifted off, never so easily as it did in this old, cold Connecticut house. She sank into it thankfully, receptive to any and all dreams, ready to examine each of those that remained in her memory when she awoke, in case there was anything there to learn.

February became March; the weather stayed cold. While Duke and Ivan worked on the restaurant, Susannah worked on her story. It had changed drastically from the form it had been taking back in California and on the road. It no longer involved a star settlement; it had somehow located itself inside Ivan's painting and she had titled it "Cloud House" in acknowledgment. It was funny how different the painting, with its colored mists and vague presences, looked in their bedroom here. Maybe it was the cold. Could it be the cold? Susannah pondered the question, trying to be rational. What on earth could *cold* do to a painting to change its appearance—no, its *aura*. She winced at the California word, wished it weren't so accurate. *Pull yourself together, Susannah.* It was the light, not the temperature, that made the difference, surely. The light here was so much less intense. And yet she couldn't help feeling some urgency, to get the story done before the weather warmed up and the painting lost its—what? Its mysterious cold thrilling *chill*. And with it the muse that inspired her—some new muse, for the story was better and more moving than anything she had done before.

It frightened her. Calling it "Cloud House" frightened her, as if she were stealing from Ivan, though she knew he would be delighted and flattered. But mostly it was the fact that the twins had somehow got into her story, first on the fringes, then as the inhabitants of the mysterious house of mist. She had never put anyone real into her stories—just, sometimes, strangers glimpsed and given life in her imagination. But she felt a large, peaceful conviction that Mary Claire and Mary Grace had to be in "Cloud House," and whenever she contemplated the little girls in her story, in that shivery space where its events took place, she was happy; in the midst of her panic she was secure in the knowledge that it was right. She wondered whether her happiness was artistic or personal. She had vowed to be happy here, had been exhorted to, had sensed she would be, and she was. Her happiness grew from a fine tangle of causes: being in Connecticut, whose hard brown and white winters she remembered with pleased surprise; her father's continuing to hang on; Ivan's fidelity apparently a fact, at least for the moment; Duke invariably kind; the continual possibility that she might be pregnant; the growing friendship with the little twins; and her story taking this strange, exhilarating turn.

She was downstairs early every morning, in spite of the cold. The cold, she sometimes thought, got her going as the more languid California air never could. Or maybe it was the morning routine with Ivan, their own private fertility rites: the taking of her temperature while she lay flat on her back, still half asleep; the graphing of her fertile days; the pacing of their sex life to the workings of her body. When the time was right, they made love sleepily, warming their cold skin when they embraced, curling their toes together and murmuring softly while everyone else slept. They dozed off, still entwined, until Susannah heard the twins' alarm clock go off next door and slipped out of bed and downstairs, followed by the gentle footsteps of the cats. The house was freezing, but in the kitchen, where Duke already had the stove going, it was almost too hot. Once fed, the cats clustered around it— "stove worship," Duke called their invariable early-morning gathering at its feet—and the children dressed there while Susannah made oatmeal or pancakes and Duke prepared sandwiches and cut apples into slices for the lunchboxes. The radio station Duke listened to always began with bird song at seven, followed by Baroque music. The announcer's slow, gravelly reading of the news, the trills and twitters of birds, the trumpets and violins of Vivaldi mingled pleasantly with the voices of the twins as they dressed. Susannah and Duke did their tasks in silence, smiling now and then at the chatter, watching the two identical little bodies pull on overalls, turtlenecks, wool socks, boots, leaving their long underwear and sleepers on the floor in a pile that Susannah would take upstairs later, and then they watched them eat, Mary Claire daintily, Mary Grace with gusto, both of them ending up with milk mustaches.

That early hour belonged to the children, Susannah thought. She and Duke were half-awake, bemused by the radio, the heat from the stove, the sun that poured in without warmth through the east-facing window (with its paper cutout snowflakes taped on). They moved slowly, like animals coming out of hibernation. The twins by contrast were quick, noisy, full of energy. They loved school, loved Miss Ralston, their teacher, loved Monday because it was show-and-tell day, loved Wednesday because it was music day, loved riding the yellow bus, and leapt up when they heard its horn, wiping off the milk on their upper lips or leaving it, grabbing jackets and lunchboxes, and kissing not only Duke but the cats and Susannah good-bye—quick messy kisses that often brought tears to her eyes. And the house would seem instantly bigger, and empty, and she and Duke would sit down to coffee, and Ivan would come downstairs wet-haired from the shower, and they would eat breakfast, and the day would begin, with its talk of tile and lumber.

During those first weeks, nearly every day, Ivan and Duke went off to price supplies or oversee their delivery, or to work on the renovations. Susannah went with them twice, once out of curiosity, the second time dutifully. They drove here and there in the van; there were interminable waits. Ivan and Duke stuck their hands in their pockets and looked down at their shoes and held long conversations with men who did the same, conversations in which pipes and stoves could suddenly, inexplicably turn female: "She'll never go under there, Duke— you're going to have to knock off a couple inches," Ivan might say, and Duke would reply, "You're right, old buddy—she's bigger than she looks."

The empty restaurant, squashed between a liquor store and a tropical fish store, was dingy, unimaginable as an inviting place where people might come and eat. Susannah stood around, sat on an empty packing case, went to fetch pastries at a Polish bakery she discovered down the road, drove to a hardware store for a retractable measuring tape, waited alone in the empty store in case the stove was delivered, while Ivan and Duke went to check out an ad in the paper for cut-rate ceramic tile.

The man from the liquor store came over. "Health food, eh?" he asked, glancing around skeptically: fattish, oldish, with greasy strands of hair combed over a bald spot—glued down? Susannah wondered. "Doesn't look all that healthy right now." He kicked at a swept-together pile of debris. They didn't have a dustpan yet.

"It'll take a few months," Susannah said reluctantly. "One of these days it'll be all green and white and wood, with plants and good cooking. But there's a lot to do."

"Sure is." His shiny pants were tight across stomach and crotch. He had dashed over without a coat, and he rubbed his cold hands together. "Well, good luck with it. I'm Eliot Stang. All the merchants here are pretty friendly. You get tired of peppermint tea, come on over and have a quick one with me. All natural ingredients," he said with a big grin. When he jerked his head in the direction of his shop a few strands of hair broke loose and flopped on his scalp. "And tell your boyfriends, too."

"My husband," Susannah said quickly. "I mean, one of them is my husband, the other is an old friend of ours."

"Well, whatever," he said, looking dubious, and after a last survey of the place he left, shaking his head and whistling tunelessly. In the window of his store there was a mechanical liquor sign—a metallic pink heart with a bottle shot through it like an arrow, pouring brown stuff into a glass: a leftover from Valentine's Day.

After those first couple of days, Susannah stayed home when Duke and Ivan went out to measure and negotiate and compare prices and argue tile. "I'm not much help," she said apologetically.

"There's not a lot you can do at this stage," Duke said, beaming at her through his glasses as if he was sure the time would come, and soon, when she would be their mainstay, their rallying point.

"We could use someone to run errands," Ivan said.

"We're so well organized we aren't going to have any errands." Duke laughed. "I'll tell you. If Susannah will stay home and keep the stoves going I'll gladly go get my own coffee—and yours too, you lazy bastard. It'll be nice to come home to a warm house."

"And dinner," said Ivan.

"Sure," Susannah said. "I'll get dinner. Of course." Only she and Ivan knew what a momentous statement this was. "And I'd be here when the twins come in," she added defiantly. "You wouldn't have to rush back."

"That would be great," Duke said sincerely.

"Watch it with the stoves," said Ivan. "I hope you've got smoke alarms, Duke."

"Three of them," Duke assured him. Susannah knew Ivan would check them later to see if they worked. "And don't worry, Ivan. You're worse than my mother. I've lived here for three years, and she's still sending me clippings about woodstove safety."

"But your hands, Duke," said Susannah, looking at the pink and purple scars.

"I don't even feel them—that's why I keep burning myself. But you wear gloves, Susannah. The ones hanging on the hook next to the stove. Promise?"

"I mean it, Susie. Be careful," Ivan said in the morning when they left her alone. "Watch out for sparks." He looked from her to the stove, as if calculating her chances of burning the place down. "And wear the gloves," he added, shaking his head; his calculations obviously hadn't come out well.

Duke instructed her in the stove's use, the most efficient placement of the logs, when to open the vents and when to shut them down, how to use the tongs.

"I'll be fine," she insisted.

She couldn't wait, most days, for them to leave. As soon as they did she went upstairs to the bedroom and huddled with her notebook under a quilt, leaving the stove to keep the kitchen cozy, to subside, to dwindle to coals, then to ashes, and grow cold, unless she remembered to go down and fill it up. Sometimes she did, often she didn't. Loading the stove both scared and excited her—the way it ate up the logs, reducing them in no time to a pile of bright coals, filled her with awe. She liked to toss into the stove the shriveled leaves that came in with the wood, and watch the fire expose their ribs and then consume them in a gulp—or bits of paper, junk mail, brown bags, so that the fire fluttered high, teasing them before it chewed them to bits.

But usually Susannah forgot the stove until it was nearly time for the twins to arrive—some sixth sense keeping her alert to four o'clock—and then with newspapers and twigs and gingerly manipulation of the vents and the judicious placement of small logs she got it roaring again, ending up flushed and hot and out of breath. Duke and Ivan caught her in delinquency only once, when they arrived home early to find the house stone cold and Susannah upstairs correcting her typescript, her hand cramped and sore, her teeth chattering.

"Susannah, for heaven's sake—"

She smiled a dazed smile. "I'm done, Ivan. I've finished it."

So that was all right. He was proud of her dedication. Duke was impressed by it, that she could fail to notice the cold because she was so involved with her work.

"That's really something," Duke said with respect.

Susannah laughed. "Read the story, Duke," she said, coming out from under her quilt. "Then decide if it's really something."

"Can I? Read it?"

It surprised her. "I guess so," she said, and didn't know what to think when he held out his hand for it and took it downstairs to read then and there.

"The typing isn't very good," she said, following him. "I've never done my own typing before. I haven't even finished proofreading it, really."

"That's okay," said Duke. He was sitting in the rocking chair by the stove, eating an apple while he read, taking large distracted bites. "It's fine."

Susannah watched him while Ivan built a fire. It was the twins' late day; they stayed after school for gymnastics and were brought home by the mother of a friend. The big red thermometer on the wall said fifty-eight degrees. Duke read steadily through the sheaf of white typed pages. Once he paused, stopped chewing, and sat motionless for half a page while Susannah held her breath before, in slow motion, his jaws began to move again and the rocking chair to creak. Ivan puttered around the kitchen, poking the fire, putting the kettle on, sweeping ashes from the floor around the stove and depositing them tidily in the ash bucket. What a dear domestic creature he is, Susannah thought, only half taking it in; her other half watched Duke. No one ever read her stories in her presence. Ivan had, once or twice, when they were first married, but they seemed to embarrass him—he didn't like their strangeness, Susannah knew, and didn't know how to say so tactfully—and he'd soon stopped. Carla had, of course, when she typed them, but she had never commented much. Susannah couldn't even bring herself to read them over once they were typed. And now here was a complete stranger, nearly, who never, so far as Susannah had observed, read anything but *Prevention* and books with titles like *The Complete Guide to Solar Energy* and *Cooking With Whole Grains*. She didn't know if she was more scared or exhilarated—it was like making the fire.

Duke looked up, finally, after Ivan had set a pot of herb tea on the table with a plate of oatmeal cookies; he smiled at Susannah, stacked the pages neatly against the tabletop, and handed them back to her. "Quite a story," he said.

"What does that mean, old buddy? Quite a story?" Ivan asked, sitting down and slapping one hand possessively on the pile of pages.

"I've never read anything like it," Duke said, looking at Susannah with his stunned smile. He pulled the teapot toward him and poured himself a cup, doing everything slowly, speaking slowly, as if he were still thinking. "It's the most unusual piece of work—"

"But did you like it, Duke?" Susannah asked desperately. "Did you think it was *good*?"

He blinked at her. "Good? My God, of course it's *good*, whatever that means. Susannah, you must *know* it's good. But it's much more than just good."

She sat there smiling at him, on the verge of tears. "It's so strange, you know," she said. "To have someone read it and say something like that about it. It means a lot to me—the story does, and what you said."

Ivan picked it up and looked at the first page. "You named it after my painting," he said, and looked at Duke. "That sappy piece of crap Susannah always hangs in our bedroom."

"The story came out of the painting," Susannah said. "I can't really say how." She bent her smile over toward Ivan.

"I'll have to go up and look at it again," said Duke, but absently, his mind obviously still on the story. "I love the way you blend the real and the impossible, Susannah. And the way you describe things—crystal clear. And the kids, and the shock ending—no, not really a *shock*, but . . ." He sipped at his tea, set the mug down, and grinned widely at Susannah. "I'm going to have to look at you differently now—now that I know you're capable of something like this. I don't know what I thought you were doing up there. Ivan never prepared me for something like this. He said you *wrote*, but I thought you were some kind of dilettante, or . . ." He made a gesture with one hand, holding his palm out flat. The light from the hanging lamp glinted off his glasses, hiding his eyes until he ducked his head a little and chuckled. "Why didn't you *tell* me about this woman, Ivan?" Ivan didn't smile; he was looking at Susannah.

Susannah mailed her story away, as usual, to the editor who paid her the most. March went on, and warmed. Lavender crocuses appeared by the front steps. Early in April there was a freak blizzard; when it had melted away, Susannah went out into the muddy backyard with the twins, and cut forsythia to put into a jar where, two days later, it sprang into yellow bloom. Her story done, Susannah spent occasional afternoons at the restaurant, painting woodwork and washing windows and fetching pastry from Zakrzeski's Bakery. A gray-haired carpenter named John Dow built a partition between the cooking and dining areas, and two aging brothers, the Guarinis, put in a stainless steel sink and a tidy little bathroom. The stove was delayed at the factory, and then delayed again.

"You've got to have this particular stove, Duke?" Ivan asked finally. The black and white tile was down, he had even admitted it looked nice, but the stove exasperated him. "We could go down to Sears and get a goddamned stove."

But Duke insisted on a large black restaurant stove like the one he had cooked on in his last job, and they were made only at a place in Michigan that was having labor troubles at the plant. Ivan grumbled but gave in, while Susannah silently pondered his acquiescence.

She found she liked being at the restaurant, and went there more and more frequently as spring advanced. They had made friends with Wendell, who ran the tropical fish store, and his wife Harriet—vegetarians who were thrilled at the prospect of the restaurant. And they got used to Mr. Stang's gloomy skepticism. Susannah had a letter from

Carla—she missed them, her son had lost a tooth, her new boyfriend was a very caring person, she sent her recipe for zucchini cake in case they could use it. Susannah read the letter to Ivan.

"California," she said, folding the crinkly pages when she was done. "It seems like another existence."

"One of our many," Ivan said. He was screwing shelf supports into the wall, and he grunted, giving the screwdriver two last turns. "I wish you'd come up with a name for this place, Susannah, before we have to call it something like The Carrot Connection." He fished another screw from the pocket of the little tool apron he wore. "We've got to get a sign up in the window so people will know we're coming."

"I'm working on it," she said, and she was, but she could think of nothing that satisfied her. She wanted the name to express everything she felt about her move east—hope, fear, delight, even the flickers of nostalgia that surprised her whenever she recognized a place she used to know well. Palmer Elementary School, for example, turned out after all to be her old school with a new name, new playground equipment, new desks, new principal; she had joined the gymnastics car pool, and she had driven there twice to pick up the twins after school before she recognized the dark red brick and the sloping schoolyard.

"Work on it harder," said Ivan.

"I will," she promised, and it was on one of those afternoons at the restaurant, while she was drinking tea and watching the spring sun shine in through the clean window, thinking of her childhood, of this stretch of Route One as it was in those days—what was on this spot? a field? houses? she would ask Mr. Stang from the liquor store—thinking of the old playhouse and her mother's flowers, when the perfect name for the restaurant came to her. She printed it in block letters on a piece of posterboard—THE SILVERGATE CAFÉ—and held it up to Ivan and Duke to see.

"How about this? What do you think?"

Duke nodded immediately. "It's good, Susannah. For one thing, it gives us options—it could be anything from a coffeehouse to a night-club."

Susannah smiled at him—Duke, she knew, had ambitions for the place beyond vegetarian lunches—but it was Ivan's response she was waiting for. He was up on a ladder, his face pushed into the squint-eyed grimace that meant he was deliberating. When he finally said, "I like it," a stab of grateful relief startled her so much that when Ivan laughed and said, "The old homestead, eh?" she didn't, for a moment, know what he was talking about.

Chapter Three

In the Garden

Rosie saw the first signs of spring that year in Barney. During cold weather, his lechery always died down a bit—not entirely, of course, but now and then he'd burrow against her, shivering, in bed, and say, "It's just too cold." By the time the bed warmed up he'd be snoring. "Cold weather makes me sleepy," he said, needlessly apologetic. "It's my Southern blood." Barney attributed everything to his Southern blood—laziness, booziness, braininess, restlessness, as well as both desire and the lack of it.

But as February gave way to March, and the little gusts that sneaked their way through the bedroom windows became less icy, Barney expanded like a flower. He couldn't get enough. And it was more than just his usual randiness, more than the desperate lust of a midlife crisis or the deep stirrings of his Southern blood. The quality of his love-making, even the quality of his voice and the look on his face, had subtly changed, and one day Rosie realized, when she opened her eyes to see him propped on one elbow gazing at her with goofy tenderness, that he was in love with her.

Oh, no, she thought, and he said, "I can't get over how beautiful you are, Rosie. I could look at you forever." He stroked her cheek with one fingertip. "Ah Rosie, Rosie," he said, and buried his face in her shoulder, kissing her neck, and she knew they were ready for another go-round.

She didn't know what to do with this kind of romantic passion. She hoped it would remain undeclared. She loved Barney dearly, but she wasn't in love with him. She didn't wish to marry him, or even to see any more of him than Friday night and Saturday. She didn't mind at all that he left on Sunday morning for church and didn't appear again until the next weekend. This arrangement just suited her. She had no qualms about living alone; she liked it, in fact, and though her house may have been a bit large for one person, she had never wavered from the idea, since Peter left, that it would be too small for two. It gave her the same thing she got from the old gray sweatpants she sometimes gardened in (the castoff of a large, athletic, long-gone lover named Dennis)—a feeling of spaciousness, room to maneuver, freedom. A permanent Barney would make the comfortable old house a tight fit.

And yet the way he was looking at her implied marriage. *Wife*, she could see him thinking as he stroked her cheek or took her hand on impulse and kissed it. He was thinking of seven-day-a-week availability, of coming home from a long day playing Good Shepherd to his flock not to an empty bachelor pad but to a smiling wife and a good dinner. He was thinking of pooled pensions and long train trips in their old age when the Helen Palmer Elementary School said, "Goodbye, Mr. Chips," and Rosie was too decrepit to garden. She could see it all, and in order to forestall the declaration she dreaded, she instinctively became, at times, aloof from him. She'd be busy in the kitchen instead of snuggling by the fire; occasionally she failed to laugh at his jokes, and once she even pleaded flu symptoms too severe and probably contagious for lovemaking.

Meanwhile, spring invaded her garden, withdrew, changed briefly to winter, returned in force, and settled in. The backyard went through the usual steps: snowdrops, crocuses, the first red shoots of peony and bleeding heart, the pale green spikes of daffodil and tulip leaves, the delicate blue and white of hyacinth and scilla. The silver pussy willows furred, the early purple iris blossomed, the magnolia buds swelled, everything greened. Rosie checked her previous year's garden calendar; things were earlier this spring, the Emperor tulips by two days, her beautiful Geranium narcissi by a full week. She sowed peas, lettuce and radishes, and put in onion sets and shallots. The dahlia tubers were rooting, the snapdragon seeds sown in their little pots. The tomato and pepper and eggplant and herb seeds, in flats out in the greenhouse, sent up their green beginnings. Mother Nature kept her promises, as she always did.

Rosie was busy and happy, working hard, digging in compost, pruning the exuberant red shoots the rosebushes sprouted, fertilizing them and also the hydrangeas, liming the lilacs. The smell of the earth—rich and wet, clinging in the creases of her fingers and under her nails—excited her. She didn't think to look in the mirror so much.

"It's wonderful to see you, Rosie," Barney said to her. "You're like a spring blossom." She smiled; she even kissed him. At her age, she was grateful for such flattery, but she was apprehensive hearing it from him, with that look on his face.

It was Barney who spotted the sign on the empty shop. He burst in one Friday with the news, and he drove Rosie out on the Post Road to Chiswick to see it. Roller Dome, Shoe City, Dunkin' Donuts, then the Liquor Boutique and Wendell's and in between them a washed window and a sign painted on a white paper banner:

COMING SOON
THE SILVERGATE CAFÉ
NATURAL FOODS

with a smiling bunch of cartoon carrots down in one corner.

"Cute," Barney said.

"Cute," she repeated. "Cute."

She began to tremble with anger, a phenomenon she had read about and never believed in or experienced. But there was a fluttery buzz in her stomach and chest that made its way to her fists when she clenched them and even to her teeth, which began to chatter. "Damn the child," she stuttered out. "Damn her. Damn, damn, damn."

"Hey," Barney said, taking one of her hands to uncoil the fist. "Hey. Calm down. This is your *daughter*. What's the matter, Rosie? Leave the kid alone."

They sat there in the car, motor running, with that blasphemous sign smirking at them, while Barney tried to soothe her. He didn't succeed—she would never, never, never be soothed, she vowed—but he stopped her trembling, and she reminded him of the Silvergate she'd been born in, how Susannah had filched the name of her sleazy dump from a dear memory that she had no part in, and whose adoption by her was a deliberate provocation, a slap at the family, a call to arms.

Barney held her hands. "Rosie," he said every time she paused. "Rosie, Rosie." And when she stopped he began to defend Susannah. "First of all, why do you call it a sleazy dump? She may be a first-rate businesswoman and a first-rate cook—just like her mama." He smiled at her, shook her hands up and down a little and squeezed them. Rosie glared at him. "And then the name of the place," he went on. "Couldn't it just as well be a gesture of friendship to you? A little nostalgic feeler for you to grab on to, Rosie? Hm? Come on, honey. Give the girl a chance."

"You don't understand, Barney," she said, wearily, pulling her hands away. *I will never marry this man*, she said to herself. "But why should you understand, anyway? Let's go home, let's have dinner." She took one last look at the sign, the idiotic carrots, the window. There was a light on inside. If she'd had a rock, and was within aiming distance, she would have thrown it.

"They must be in the back room," Barney said, craning forward in the dusk to peer through the windshield. He grinned at her. "Sure you don't want to go in and say hello? Disarm the opposition? Fire the first shot?"

"I do *not*," she said. "How you can be so insensitive as to suggest such a thing I don't know. Let's get *out* of here."

"Aw, come on, Rosie, don't get mad at me," said Barney, and put the car in gear, looking pleadingly, fondly, part impishly at her. But she was angry. She was livid, she was furious—at him, at the sign in the window, at life, at herself. Her heart knocked frighteningly in her chest. That girl will kill me yet, she thought. She breathed deeply all the way home to calm herself, and had an extra Scotch before dinner to cheer herself up.

"I'm sorry," she said to Barney. "If I've been bad company lately. Tonight. I hate having what's past and done with pop up again, things I've worked out for myself and put in their place and gotten to terms with coming back to haunt me."

It was a cold early April night. Dinner was overcooking in the oven. They were sitting on the floor by the fireplace, drinking, and Barney had his hand companionably under her skirt, on her stockinged thigh. "I like my life to be settled," she said.

She felt Barney's hand tense, then relax. His thumb went back and forth, back and forth. "So do I," he said, in a voice full of meaning. He took her drink from her with his free hand and set it at a distance, and then he applied both hands to various parts of her body, pinning her down on the hearth rug. "Rosie, Rosie," he said with his lips against her ear. "Marry me, Rosie. I love you, honey," he said, and the hand on her thigh moved up, wiggled under her pantyhose and down again, and he sighed happily as he got to work. "Marry me, Rosie," he said. "I love you so much, baby."

She didn't need to answer just then. In a second they were both busy with buttons and zippers. Rosie didn't know what it was, but she hadn't felt such need in years. Maybe it was simply knowing that sooner or later—and sex on the floor in the firelight would make it later—she'd have to say no to his proposal. Whatever the reason, she wanted him frantically, and she tore at his belt, his pants, his shirt, she whipped out of her clothes and sat astride him, lowering her breasts to his mouth while she rode him slowly up and down—a fairly awkward procedure but one that made him grip her bottom hard with his two hands and moan with pleasure. "Ah, Rosie, Rosie," he mumbled and sighed, but it wasn't marriage he was thinking of by then. She prolonged everything, keeping it all slow and dreamlike, while the *coq au vin* dried out in the oven and the fire burned down to coals. She waited for the old detachment to take her over, as if it were some powerful force watching and waiting to turn her to stone in the midst of her pleasure, to say: you shall not enjoy yourself with this dear man. But it kept back, it let her be, and she fell on Barney and rocked him against her with a cry and nearly wept into his shoulder with happiness when they were done.

But the reckoning came. You can't make love on the hearth rug forever. They dozed a bit, woke, felt chilled, kissed and hugged, poked the fire, threw on a log, dressed, and sat down to their ruined dinner. Barney looked at her across the table, his electric hair rumpled and his eyes still bemused from the hearth rug.

"What about it, Rosie? You going to marry me?" His Georgia voice was slow and calm. She could hear him cracking his knuckles under the table.

The words *you'd be crazy to say no* crossed her mind, and in the same instant she said no. "I can't, Barney," was what she actually said. "I don't want to be married."

"Why not?"

"I've tried it. I don't like it."

"Honey, I'm not Edwin. We're happy together, Rosie."

"We wouldn't be if we were married."

"We would."

She put down her fork and leaned across the table. "*I* wouldn't be, then," she said with great distinctness. They stared at each other a while before she sat back and resumed eating. The chicken was practically melted, falling off its bones at the touch of a fork, bits of bones wandering around in the sauce. "Don't ruin things, Barney," she said. "It's so nice the way it is."

"I want a wife, Rosie," Barney said, looking forlorn. She didn't pity him, though. He had a good life. You can't have everything.

"Then you don't want me," she said.

"I *do*."

"But I'm not a wife, and I don't intend to be."

"I'm getting old, Rosie, dammit. I want to settle down, preferably with you."

She still refused to pity him, though she could see that he was pitiable, also lovable, also—probably—right. She should have said yes. Who was she, at her age, to take offense at "preferably with you"? But she did. She said, "Ah, I see. Preferably with me. In other words, it's some abstract notion of a wife you're looking for. It's not me you love, it's wifiness. And if I don't choose to settle down with you, you'll find someone who will. Some *wife*. Right?"

"Aw, come off it, Rosie," he said, pushing bones around on his plate. "Am I right?"

He stood up and whacked his fork on the table. "You're a hell of a woman, Rosie, but you're no spring chicken, either, and one of these days you're going to find yourself all alone and you're not going to like it."

"Yes, I am," she said perversely, though of course that wasn't true. It wasn't that she hadn't thought of solitary old age and a life narrowed to the TV, a doggie, her own cold flesh, and too much drink. "Why don't you sit down and eat, Barney? We can still be friends. You can still come over and pull my knickers down while you look for a wife."

It took him a few seconds, but he laughed and sat back down, and they finished dinner. He even stayed the night, and the next, as always. They played Scrabble, drank, watched Vincent Price in *The Fly* on the late movie, took a long walk—not toward Chiswick—on which Rosie told him more about Silvergate, the real Silvergate, the sacred one. When they got back she showed him, again, the National Trust booklet, with its color photographs of the box hedge, the lily pond, and the pinkish brick manor house topped with the octagonal cupola. They no longer plotted to sail to England some day, but he let her talk, and he had the tact not to try any more to persuade her of Susannah's admirable motives.

It was a normal weekend in every way, except that they were unusually considerate of each other. They were retreating, warily, from each other's province; even their friendly, intimate talks were no more than a smoke screen thrown up to disguise and soften the split. And there was no more lovemaking, except for a Sunday morning before-church quickie, and that was Rosie's idea. She felt bad, because she knew she had hurt him, and because their time together was up, and so she seduced him—a laughably easy task, as ever—and sent him off to mass. They smiled ruefully at each other at the door, and kissed lightly, formally, with a certain reluctance, and then she let him go. She was sorry—even, once he was safely out of sight, weepy—and though she knew she'd feel, before too long, a kind of ultimate gladness, like a long sigh of relief, she knew she'd miss him too, probably forever, as she continued to miss Larry Bruner, and Dennis of the sweatpants, and a man named Dan Powers whom she almost married when she was on the verge of forty, and vulnerable.

Jim and Kiki Sheffield, tanned and wrinkled, returned from Florida, and filled some of Rosie's Friday nights with Scrabble tournaments. Besides her, they invited two other couples and Jim's older brother, Ralph, a hard-smoking bachelor of sixty or so who wore suspenders and did magic tricks. He used to reach across the Scrabble board and pull little plastic bunnies out of Rosie's ears—a nice man, good at Scrabble and crossword puzzles and checkers and bridge, with a store of funny anecdotes from his days as a television newscaster in Boston, but so patently designed for her by the Sheffields that Rosie obstinately considered him a buffoon and nothing more.

"What do you think of Ralphie?" Kiki asked her one day, girl to girl, over tea.

"He's a real card, Kiki," she said. "Har de har har."

"Really, Rose," said Kiki, disappointed, looking down into her cup: a matchmaker thwarted, but a smile twitching at her lips because she knew what Rosie meant.

They were pals, Rosie and Kiki—or as palsy as it was possible for a divorcée and a devoted wife to be. In Rosie's opinion, there were always limits in those friendships—territories in each other's lives they hesitated to enter because they were alien or threatening or downright impenetrable. Kiki didn't like to hear, for example, about Rosie's beaux. She had married Jim at twenty-one, after a two-year engagement, and had never known another man; not that Jim wasn't a perfectly nice chap—a more dignified Ralphie—but Rosie had a feeling Kiki didn't want to think about what she had missed. Nor did Kiki dwell on her own domestic felicity, for the same reason, but reversed. And they carefully disguised their mild disapproval of each other's way of life—Kiki having to dash home to get Jim's dinner, Rosie having to dash home to primp for a date—disapproval in which there was always a smattering of envy.

Rosie had never told Kiki much about Susannah and Edwin, beyond the bare facts. When Kiki mentioned, one day when the two women were outside sighing over a late dusting of snow covering their gardens, that there was a health food restaurant opening up in Chiswick, Rosie said, "My daughter and her husband are running it. Don't eat there."

"*What?*"

"My estranged daughter, from California. And her husband—an ex-priest." Rosie piled it on, keeping her voice even and her face straight.

"Your *daughter?*"

"My estranged daughter. We don't get along."

"But, *Rosie.*"

She was so flabbergasted and, when she realized Rosie wasn't kidding or exaggerating, so horrified on her behalf—Kiki had two daughters and two sons, all of whom she was selflessly devoted to—that Rosie invited her in for tea and told her the rest of it.

"You *must* go see her," she said when the story was done. Rosie could detect in her face something of what she'd seen in Barney's—the desire to be the instrument of reconciliation.

"Nope," she said. "Not a chance."

"Well . . ." Kiki hesitated over her words, treading carefully. She was dressed in a navy blue wrap skirt printed with green whales, a matching green jersey with her monogram on it, and blue knee socks. Her knees were as brown and bony as a monkey's, and Rosie stared at them while she waited for Kiki to go on. "I'm sure she'll come to you, Rosie, but perhaps she's afraid to . . . you know . . . she may be a little . . . but if you approached her, Rosie, it . . . she would . . ."

Rosie said, as gently as she could, "This is hard for you to believe, I know, Kiki, but I don't want to make it up with her."

"Oh, Rosie."

"I mean it. I don't know what *your* method of dealing with unpleasantness is, but mine is to face up to it and then *eject it from my life.*" She was no longer speaking gently, but it wasn't Kiki she was scolding.

"You're her mother," Kiki said, bringing one brown hand to her cheek as if a tooth ached, *mother* being one of her sacred words, like *marriage*.

"That girl hurt me to the depths of my soul, Kiki," Rosie said, not wanting to. "Over and over. I don't feel like her mother any more."

They dropped it. Kiki, it was clear, could say no more. Rosie was her friend, she liked her, they'd known each other for years; and yet her friend had spit on the floor of Kiki's favorite temple. She was shocked. Her eyes damp with puzzled sympathy, she went home to fix Jim's dinner.

Rosie avoided the Post Road into Chiswick. She didn't want to see the progress of the Silvergate Café. She imagined it plenty, picturing not so much the roomful of tables, the water-spotted silverware, the inevitable scrawled blackboard menu, as her daughter: tall, pale, sharp-nosed, sloppy, lank-haired Susannah, in an apron, yawning without covering her mouth while she took orders for tofu burgers. Now that she was actually in town, Rosie couldn't help fancying that Susannah was inching closer to her, like plague germs or a cold front, and that it was, as Peter said, only a matter of time until they met. She tried to contemplate this prospect calmly, tried for resignation, for indifference, for maternal tenderness, for detached amusement, but all she felt was an irritable dread.

"It's just that you don't know her, Ma," was Peter's opinion. He gave it one lovely April night when he came over to have dinner with Rosie. He was leaving the next morning for a friend's cottage on the Cape. He hoped to surmount his writer's block there. Who the friend was, he didn't say, so Rosie didn't ask. She wondered, though. She also wondered if he had gone to see Susannah. She couldn't believe he would keep it from her if he had, but he kept saying Rosie should give her a chance, get to know her, then decide whether to go on with what he had begun to call "this absurd family feud."

"It's the strangeness and the awkwardness you're afraid of," he lectured her. "Right now you see her as an ogre. Once you actually meet her and talk to her, she'll be just like anyone else. I'm not saying you two will become soul mates, Ma, but you might not find it that hard to be civil to each other."

She looked at him. He sat across from her at the table in the kitchen-nook, calmly spooning up his soup, slurping a bit, half-smiling at her while he ate. No doubt about it, he had lost his dapper *joie de vivre*. He was dressed in a blue work shirt and khakis—a bad sign. She didn't even know he possessed such clothes, and she wondered whether he had bought a whole new wardrobe to go with his new mood.

"Have you seen her, Peter?"

He flushed a little, and stopped his spoon halfway to his mouth. "No, but she calls me."

"Still?"

"Yeah."

"For what, may I ask? Still trying to get my support? Or have you two become soul mates?"

"She's all right, Ma. Really." He spooned in more soup. "She's not so bad."

"Peter?"

He looked from his soup to Rosie, smiling. "She's family, Ma. For years that didn't mean anything to me, but now it does. Maybe I'm getting old, I don't know."

His smile was pleading, a sad smile. She sighed. How could she deny him a sister when he had just lost a lover? "Tell me about her," she said cooperatively, keeping her mind in a narrow groove that didn't admit that impudent sign in the window, or even any sour memories. She would think of Susannah as a stranger, someone she didn't know very well. "What do you mean, she's *all right*?"

He considered, glad to be asked. "Well, she's twenty-seven years old. She's an adult, after all."

"That makes her *all right*? Adults are somehow more all right than children?"

He reached over and smoothed her hair. "Don't be cantankerous, Ma," he said. "I just mean she seems to have grown up."

Rosie didn't answer. She merely looked. Of course, she felt betrayed, but her feelings as she gazed over at Peter in his work shirt were more complex than mere pique at his going over to the enemy. She was invaded by the sure knowledge, filling her all of a sudden, that not only would she indeed be seeing Susannah, but that some sort of reconciliation would no doubt take place, that the long years of resentment and anger and dislike were coming to an end. She could see that all this was inevitable, that only an unnatural, unreasonable bitch would oppose it, and—clearest of all—that Peter wished it.

"I haven't seen her or Ivan," he said, speaking the name of Susannah's husband with awkward casualness, as if his familiarity with it was thorough but recent. "But when I get back from the Cape I'm going there for dinner. Two weeks from Sunday. At their house, I mean, not at the restaurant. It's opening Tuesday, by the way, this coming week, but only for lunches at first. If it does well they'll start serving dinners, too."

"You know all about it."

"Well, she calls me."

Rosie tapped her fingers on the table. She would have liked to take her knife and dig it into the tabletop, hard, putting gouges into the pine. But she sipped soup from her spoon for a while in silence—oxtail soup, her mother's recipe, a nuisance to make but one of Peter's favorites. Peter sipped, too, and buttered bread and dunked it in and ate it dripping. The absurd thought passed through Rosie's mind: *I'll lose him to Susannah.* She realized as she thought it that it had no basis in reality, that it was a pathetic grasping after a new grudge to take the place of the old imminently crumbling ones, that it said more about her state of mind than about reality, and that she was perhaps becoming a bit nutty on the subject of her children. So she said, conversationally, to Peter, "Did you say they have a house?" Just your average Mom and Sonny discussing good old Sis.

"In Chiswick, up on Perkins Road," he replied. She could tell it made him happy, this attempt at normal chattiness. "They share a house with this guy Duke, the chef—the one they're running the restaurant with."

"The chef." What did *chef* mean to people like Susannah and Ivan? What did *sharing a house* imply?

"He's had a lot of restaurant experience, Susannah says."

But she didn't want to hear about Duke the chef. "Peter, tell me truthfully. Has Susannah said anything about money from me?"

"Not a word." He said it eagerly, his eyes bright; he sensed capitulation.

"Implied it, then. What about all this *support* stuff?"

"I think she means moral support, Ma. Emotional support. She tends to use the word supportive. You know, she thanks me for being so supportive, she wishes you'd be more supportive—"

"She does."

"Well, yes. She does." Was there defiance in his face? Was it really absurd to think she'd lose him to Susannah if she didn't knuckle under to family feeling? Was this blackmail?

"What about her father?" Rosie asked, still reasonable. "Is he being supportive?"

"I think he gave her some money," he said, and there was something evasive in the way he looked into his soup.

She sniffed it, as surely as Ann Landers would—emotional blackmail. "Dear Ann Landers: My daughter has managed to extort cash for a business venture out of my ex-husband. Through my son, she's trying to get money out of me by holding her father up as a sterling example of parenthood. Should I give in? Signed, Bewildered." "Dear Bewildered: Wake up and smell the coffee, honey. This is a classic case of emotional blackmail."

"Good," she said. "So she's all set in the money department."

Peter shrugged. "We haven't really discussed her finances, Ma."

Rosie had another question, but she saved it until they had finished dinner and were having coffee, and she asked it with reluctance. She was sick of the whole matter. She felt weary and bruised by all that Peter had told her and all she had deduced, and by the vista she saw stretching ahead, of awkward family gatherings with the old grudges lurking behind everyone like shadows, like lashing tails. But she had to ask it. "Why did she choose to call it that, Peter? The Silvergate Café?"

Peter grimaced. "I knew you wouldn't like it. She thought you would, but I couldn't convince her. You know how she is."

"I thought she wasn't any more."

"She can still be pretty stubborn," he said, smiling apologetically. "Maybe it's inherited," he added in a stage whisper.

She ignored that. "So she thought I'd like it. It's supposed to touch my heart."

"I told her it would have just the opposite effect."

"Did you," she said, and finished her coffee. "Well, you're right. It does indeed."

"And then she says it's an allusion to San Francisco—Golden Gate, Silvergate. She likes San Francisco. She used to live there." He stood up and took her cup. "Let's not talk about it any more. I'll get you some more coffee. Tell me what happened to Mr. Chips." Diplomatic change of subject, transfer of emotional emphasis. Rosie seized it gladly, but she got depressed telling him about Barney. She missed him, she realized—good old Barney, dear Barney. She looked into the fire and could remember only their lovemaking on the hearth rug.

She and Peter had more coffee and cake, and they talked a little about Hollis, whom Peter still mourned. Before he left, he asked, "When are you going to settle down, Ma? With some nice man?"

"When are you?" she could have countered, but she said, "I am settled down, Peter. Without some nice man."

But it wasn't the truth. She didn't feel settled down; she felt shaken up, and in the weeks that followed she found herself searching for a sign, an indication of what she should do. She had reached the point where she was willing, though not happy, to bow to the inevitable, but she didn't know how to do it, how far to go, what to give in to and what to preserve. And try as she might—and she did try, for Peter's sake if nothing else—to get out from under her ancient burden of anger, she felt sometimes that the reason she was giving in to the necessity of seeing Susannah face to face was to pick a fight with her that would lead to a new, more profound and permanent rupture. She had never been so bedeviled by her own motives, so confused—not, at least, since the months before she actually split with Edwin.

She'd been hemming and hawing that summer, afraid to be on her own with (as she thought then) two young children. At that time, she had a thrice-weekly fifteen-minute gardening program on a local radio show produced by Jim Sheffield in Hartford, and it brought her perhaps enough income to support a small dog on—not a family of three. As it turned out, when Edwin did leave, she boldly asked Jim if she could expand to half an hour. What eventually happened, after days of talk and weeks of negotiation and months of ironing out the wrinkles and getting out the bugs (and here Janice, her producer, appeared in

Rosie's life with her steam iron and spray gun) and a couple of pilot films, was that she got a show on the station's television affiliate that was, before too long, picked up by public television, and "Rosie Mortimer's Garden" was born. Rosie came along, it seemed, at precisely the right time. "Americans are turning back to the soil in droves," as Janice put it back in those early days. Rosie pictured long grim lines of citizens armed with trowels and seed packets, marching over vast tracts of Roto-tilled earth. But Janice was right, of course, and the show took hold like ivy on a brick wall, and became an institution, and made Rosie rich.

But that hot, miserable summer when she made the decision to break up her marriage, all this was in the future, and she was scared and uncertain. So she performed a test. She stood on the back step, took off her wedding ring, and threw it as hard as she could out into the tangle of the back garden. She closed her eyes so that she wouldn't see it flash through the air and land, and she said to herself, *If Fate wills that I find it, I'll stick with Edwin.* Then she went inside to get dinner. And found the ring the next morning, in the strawberry bed, when she went out early to pick off Japanese beetles. And cried and cried, slipping the slightly gritty ring back on her finger.

But she wasn't a very good fatalist; she was a manipulator. She had her astrological chart done once, and spent a great deal of time grouchily and defiantly circumventing the pattern it laid down for her (she would have another child, she would lose a large sum of money, she would change her residence), much as the hero of a detective novel ducks into alleys and takes false turns to shake off the sinister characters who tail him. So she tried the ring trick again not long after—shut her eyes, drew back her strong right arm, and threw the ring out, out into the garden, knowing she would do so again and again until Nature swallowed it. But she never found the ring—Fate, she decided, must have been on her side, to be manipulated so easily—and as the days and then weeks went by she slept more peacefully than she had in years, and went through the days smiling. She hummed as she worked, and fixed Edwin's dinner with extra care, knowing her ring was buried in the dirt by a squirrel, or woven into some trinket-loving bird's nest, leaving her free.

She remembered the ring that lovely April when Susannah was about to invade her life, and she looked for a sign—afraid, almost, to encounter one because she didn't trust her deepest wishes. She might manipulate Fate again, with who knew what results? Not she. Personally, she was stumped by Rosie Mortimer. And then she alternately inspected her feelings and shrank from inspecting them and sickened of it all; she tried again and again to get to work on her book, while she sought solace in the garden and at the Sheffields' Scrabble parties (where she and Ralphie won so consistently as partners that they were separated and Rosie was matched with a man named Gene Swan, whose wife viewed her with transparent suspicion); and while spring was thrusting its way toward summer, and the lilacs blossomed and the wisteria hung its purple clusters on the stone wall, and the roses set their tight green buds—she had a visit, one day, from her son-in-law, Ivan Cord.

Rosie was out in the back garden. It was mid-May, and warm, and she was staking the peonies—restaking them, actually. She had tried out some new metal stakes she'd seen advertised, and they hadn't worked. The heavy, swollen blossoms were the size of peaches, and the stakes wouldn't support them. They were all bent over. Damned flimsy things, she thought, pulling them out and putting in the old, ugly, reliable wooden stakes. She'd send the new ones back, and, furthermore, on some future show she'd warn her audience against them.

She became aware of a noise behind her, and when she turned there was a young man coming toward her down the path. She stood up quickly, with one of the wooden stakes in her hand, and faced him. She wasn't suspicious or unfriendly by nature, but she was aware that you don't welcome strange, strapping, bearded young men into your yard with open arms—you gird yourself with the nearest weapon, you try to look fearless, and you imply, somehow, by your stance or the look on your face, that your wrestler-husband is weeding the rose bed just over there behind those trees.

"Yes? What is it?" she said as he advanced. He didn't look at all familiar; if asked, she would have sworn without hesitation that she'd never seen him before in her life.

"Rosie Mortimer?" he asked, extending a large hand.

She relaxed a little, dropped her weapon but didn't hold out a hand. "Yes," she said warily.

He put on a grin she could only describe as joyful—a kid's grin. "I'm Ivan Cord," he said. "I'm Susannah's husband. I'm your son-in-law." The grin intensified until, with his last words, it became a laugh, and he picked up her limp hand in its dirty gardening glove and shook it, chuckling happily. "I'm glad to meet you," he said, and squeezed her glove once and let it go, wiping the dirt on his pant leg.

"Well," she said. "I guess I'm glad to meet you, too." She looked behind him for the sight of Susannah following languidly around the side of the house—with dread, and yet with a lick of excitement, too: *all right, this is it, let's get it over.* But he seemed to be alone. "What brings you here?" she asked inhospitably. She didn't really mean to be rude; she was taken by surprise. She had imagined, from time to time, her meeting with Susannah and what she would say, but she hadn't ever predicted that her son-in-law would come creeping up on her in her garden. Nor was she prepared for his disconcerting appearance. She remembered him as a sullen, hulking, silent hippie brute, and here was Kris Kristofferson, grinning at her like a puppy. Could she, actually, have impaled him on a peony stake? And would that poor piece of wood have had any effect on this giant?

"I just wanted to meet my mother-in-law, darn it," he said—and, somehow, she'd untied her gardening apron and left it and her gloves by the peonies, and they were walking together toward the house. "I'm not much of a feuder. I hate arguments, and I like family, and Susannah and I don't have so much of it that we can afford to let any of it get away. At least, that's my feeling." He held the screen door for Rosie and followed her into the kitchen. "I don't mind telling you that Susannah has been just a little reluctant to come over and see you. It's certainly not my place to make any judgments or say who's in the wrong, and I'm not going to do it. But I decided I'm not going to just sit back and let this thing accumulate any further, not if I can help it. So I said to myself, I'm going over there and see that mother-in-law of mine. I'm going to get some friendliness into this family if my wife murders me for it. Oh—thanks," he said, accepting the can of beer she held out to him.

They sat down at the table, and his presence seemed to fill her kitchen. He was an amazing creature—older, she saw, than Susannah, but full of all the vitality her daughter, as Rosie recalled her, had so comprehensively lacked. She could barely take it in, that this was her husband, and she wondered what on earth had drawn them together— or, more accurately, what had drawn him to her. She had no trouble imagining Susannah wanting to latch on to Ivan—any woman would. Rosie found herself warming to him, amazed at the transformation he had undergone since his brief appearance at her mother's funeral. Was it simply a matter of a haircut, a trimmed beard, a puppydog smile?

It wasn't, she found out soon enough. "I feel I ought to apologize, just about, for that other time I met you," he said. His grin disappeared, and he ran his fingers through his beard, looking pensive. "It was a pretty bad time in my life. Susannah and I were at our wit's end. We were jobless, moneyless. We were hopeless. Literally. We didn't have a hope in the world." He drank a huge swallow of beer, keeping his eyes on Rosie; they were, unexpectedly, blue eyes, almond-shaped above high, ruddy cheekbones. "We were taking pills. Amphetamines. I still can't believe how low we'd sunk, what depths we—" He leaned forward across the table to look at her close up. "I was a different person, Rosie," he said. "And I know I didn't ask you if I could call you Rosie, but I'm asking you now, and I hope you won't mind."

"No," she said. "Of course I don't. Ivan," she added.

"Rosie," he said, smiling again and then going somber as he resumed his story. "Anyway, we were taking these damn things, and then we decided to come east for Susannah's grandmother's funeral. That was my idea, mostly, I suppose. God, I hated California—still do, always did. I'm a New Englander myself—from Maine, way up at the cold end of it, and I jumped at the chance to get back east for a couple of days. I'm probably the only person on earth who hates the West Coast. Hates it! So we got on the plane, and Susannah forgot to pack the damn pills. We realized it just before Chicago. There we were, a thousand miles from home, and we clutched each other, and we *wept*. Rosie, I'm telling you the truth. We cried our eyes out. That's the condition we were in."

He paused, and Rosie got a beer for herself. She could feel him watch her as she went to the refrigerator and returned. He had a steady gaze that never seemed to blink. She wondered, suddenly, if he was Susannah's emissary, sent to break the ice.

"I was a priest for eight years," Ivan said. "Can you believe that? I was at a parish in Buffalo for the last five of them. And I was miserable there. Miserable. But while I was sitting in that jet at O'Hare airport waiting to take off again, I was twice as miserable, ten times, a hundred times as miserable as I'd ever been up in Buffalo. I knew I'd hit bottom, and I was sick with the knowledge of it. I spent a good portion of that trip in the john, just throwing up and crying. I can't forget it, either. A grown man, thirty-three years old I was then, puking in the bathroom of a jet plane because my wife had forgotten to pack a little bottle of brown pills. I can't get it out of my mind."

Rosie hadn't, so far, spoken, and she continued not to speak. She was speechless with—she didn't know what. Shock, but more than shock. Some kind of release, relief, the consciousness of her life flowing through her body.

"So," said Ivan, and took a swallow of beer, "so by the time we saw you at the church we were in bad, bad shape, and Susannah—my wife—" He paused, shook his head, fingered his beard. "She didn't handle it right. I can't blame you for getting mad. We just barged in. Oh God, it was awful. Wasn't it? Awful?"

His narrow eyes widened, deepened. They looked wet, the thick black lashes around them stuck together in points. "Yes," Rosie said. "It was. Awful."

He let out a sigh as if he'd been holding his breath. "And then we got the money, and it changed our lives. God bless your mother, Rosie. I just wish I'd known her. God rest her soul."

Yes, she could imagine him a priest, those long, hairy-knuckled fingers holding up bread and wine, that urgent voice raised in prayer, those arms stretched out in blessing. She could imagine him a priest with far more ease than she could imagine him mated with Susannah.

"What did you do with it? How did it, the money—" She stopped, because he had leaned toward her again, and this time he took her hand.

"Do you really want to hear this, Rosie? I hope you do, because

115

it gives me a lot of satisfaction to tell it." His eyes were blue, but not cold. Blue eyes normally made her uneasy—the flat, insipid light blue of Susannah's and Edwin's eyes, like those that look so eerie on Siberian huskies. Ivan's eyes were different, warmer, a darker blue, with depths. They were like the ocean, like certain flowers, they were—he was—she hadn't even realized it until then, she'd merely thought there was something unusual about him, she couldn't think what it was, but when he took her hand she recognized that the oddity about him was that he was the most attractive man she'd ever been close to.

"Yes," she said, and removed her hand from his. "I do want to hear it. Ivan."

He smiled at her. His hand had been warm and rough. She looked at it, curled around his beer can, the long fingers splayed out. There was a bowl of purple and white lilacs on the table between them, and as she watched he touched a blossom with his fingers, caressed the tiny petals, and then picked a floweret and rolled it thoughtfully between his thumb and forefinger. "It wasn't just the money that changed things," he said. "It was the visit, the trip east, the whole thing. First of all, I said to Susannah that first night—we were staying with Duke. He's our chef. He was working in New Haven then, and he and his wife had a big apartment where they kindly let us stay. Duke's an old college buddy of mine, and his wife is dead now, poor bastard. But that's another story. So I said to Susannah, now's our chance to kick the habit, those goddam California *pills*. It was providence, I said, that made you forget them. It gives us a *chance*. At first she was going to get Duke, or Margie, Duke's wife—she was a nurse—to get some for us, but I talked her out of it. Sick as we were, we sat on our bed that night after we saw Susannah's Uncle Jim, and we talked it out, and we made the decision: *no more*. And we decided something else. We'd go back to California, and we'd wait, and plan, and save, and when we could manage it we'd come back east, for good. And here we are," he added triumphantly. He tipped up his beer can and drank, and she watched him. She looked at his short, soft beard, and at the black, curlier hair brushed back from his forehead, and at his arms tanned golden beneath their tangle of hair, and she became conscious of a desire to touch him.

He went on, cheerfully. "So we *invested* the money we inherited. It took months to come. Hell, I don't think we got it until around Christmas, and when we got the check we took it to a broker. I'm serious, now, we went to a regular stockbroker on Wilshire Boulevard. Can you imagine this? Believe me, we're not the type, but there we were. Ronald and Nancy Reagan. Mr. and Mrs. Filthy Capitalist System, handing our cash over to the money boys. We invested in one of those budget motel chains, a little one called Happy Nights. I don't think they've come east yet, but they will. They're a hell of an outfit, and we tripled our money in two years. Can you believe it? We just sat back and watched that stock shoot up like wildflowers. And then, the summer before we left, just before we were going to sell it—when we got the chance to go in with Duke on a restaurant—the goddamn stock *split*. This is the *truth*, Rosie. It split, and we sat on it, and we cleaned up, and we headed for Connecticut with our pockets lined with gold." He sat back, chuckling. She laughed with him, and then they sat, smiling comfortably at each other.

"I talk a lot," he said. "But I have a lot to tell you. It's not every day you meet a long-lost mother-in-law. I don't mind telling you I've admired you for years. I used to love that TV show. I'd sit there and think, this terrific-looking lady is *family*."

It was late afternoon, a glorious May day, and sun was streaming in the kitchen window. The room was filled with a golden glow, with heat, with the scent of the lilacs. Rosie wiped a rim of sweat from her upper lip and pushed her hair off her face. She was wishing she could go upstairs and wash—she'd been in the garden since lunch—and put on some makeup and brush her hair, but she was afraid if she excused herself he'd be gone when she returned. He was a large, sturdy, staggeringly tangible person, but she thought of him as fragile—he'd come into her life so unexpectedly, so whimsically, she feared he'd disappear from it the same way if she didn't keep an eye on him.

She offered him another beer. He crushed his empty can in one hand, considering the idea, and said, "I'll tell you what. I've got a lot more to say, Rosie, and if you're not scheduled for something more interesting tonight I'd like to cook dinner for you. Here in your kitchen, if you don't mind. Susannah and Duke and the kids went to

Mystic for the day. They're going to the Aquarium, and then Duke knows someone over there who wants to sell one of those antique cash registers, cheap. We open in a week, you know—or maybe you don't. We've had to push back that date about ten times. You'd think it'd be a simple operation, getting the place ready—I mean, it's not as if we're doing anything fancy, it's not exactly the Four Seasons! But the details, the waiting, the red tape!" He stood up. "So let's do this. You go on up and shower or whatever; I know how you feel after working in the garden on a hot day, I've done enough of it—and do you know there's dirt on your face? There." He pointed to her left cheek. She thought for a second he was going to touch it, and she drew back and rubbed at it. "Nope," he said, laughing. "You're going to have to wash it. So while you're doing that I'll go to that posh little market in town and get the ingredients for the best dinner you've ever had. How does that sound?"

He stood over her. The sun poured in the window behind him, and looking up at him, she thought, *Here's the sign I was waiting for—Ivan.* But what he signified, she had no idea.

"What kids?" she asked. She took in the word belatedly, and her heart jumped.

"Kids? Oh—kids. Duke's two girls—twins. Mary Claire and Mary Grace. Duke let them stay out of school today so they could see the Aquarium. Cute kids, but holy terrors. See?" He grinned at her. "I told you I had a lot to tell you. I've got a thousand things you've got to know. What do you say? Can I make you dinner?"

"Well . . . yes, of course," she said, standing up. "But you don't have to go to the store, we could—" She gestured around the kitchen, trying to recall what food was on hand.

"Nope—I insist. This has got to be my dinner, and I only know two recipes. No substitutions." He took car keys from his pocket—he wore jeans, a red polo shirt, and sneakers—and jingled them. "I'll be back before you're out of the shower. Leave the door open."

He was gone—out the back door, down the steps, around the side to the front. She could hear his footsteps, hear him whistle—what was it? an old Beatles song she couldn't place—hear him slam a car door, start the motor, drive off. She sat at the table and finished her beer.

Her heart pounded. No, Susannah hadn't sent him, she was sure of it. He had come to see her out of curiosity and simple friendliness. Ivan.

The silence and the beer and the sun lulled her, nearly put her to sleep. All she could think were two things: would he come back? and what was she getting into?

She roused herself and went upstairs to shower. She threw her sweaty gardening clothes in a heap and stood naked, wondering what to wear. What did you wear to entertain the husband of your estranged daughter? She shivered in spite of the heat. She remembered, suddenly, Barney and herself in the shower, on the bath mat, and she was shocked at the longing, the loss she felt.

When she looked in the mirror after her shower, her face was pink and glowing, she thought, even without makeup. She looked unexpectedly girlish, and she smiled, for once, at her reflection. Ridiculous, she thought, smiling. But Barney had said she was beautiful. *Barney's a fifty-five-year-old man*, some baleful echo answered. She ignored it. She shook her hair forward, bent from the waist, and blew it dry—or nearly dry. It was thick and heavy, and held water like wool, and she was in a hurry: what if he came back, found her not ready, and left? She turned off the dryer, listening for a car, a whistle, footsteps. What she wanted was to be dressed, downstairs, at ease in the cool living room with a drink when he returned. He had come to see *her*, because he had always admired her. He'd just wanted to meet his mother-in-law, darn it. Rosie smiled, and her heart pounded hard in her chest. This visit, this dinner, the bearded god who'd invaded her garden had nothing to do with Susannah. Ivan would be *her* friend.

Briefly, for a space of seconds, she was conscious of disappointment, that it was Ivan, and not Susannah, who was offering a hand to her. But she didn't let it last. Of course it was a bizarre situation. Kiki Sheffield would be horrified. Her cousin Debbie would swoon with disapproval. But when had she ever done the conventional thing? And why should she be a conventional mother-in-law?

She put on some makeup and dressed, quickly, in clean jeans and a T-shirt, and looked in the mirror—too gardeny, too tailored, too *masculine*, for God's sake: *he* was wearing jeans and a T-shirt. She changed into a dress, a black flowered cotton with a flounce around the hem, and looked into the mirror again: too la di da? too self-consciously feminine? too contrived? or—God forbid—too juvenile? too much the last gasp? the aging sexpot? But she left it on because it had a low neck and showed off her smallish waist (her hips she ignored) and there wasn't time to change again. She began to feel frantic; he'd be back any minute—but *would* he come back? *would he*? She brushed her damp hair, leaving it to hang around her face in waves, then—no, pulling it loosely back with a barrette, then braiding it and twisting it into a loose knot. Too messy, too wet. She ran back to the bathroom, dried it some more, listening—a whistle? a step?—and pulled it off her neck, finally, into a neater knot, leaving it loose in front, unstudied. Messy? Mirror—it would have to do. Did she still look girlish, still pink and pretty? A little more blusher—not much (thinking of old women with a spot of rouge on each cheek)—and earrings. Gold hoops? Too ethnic? No. Fine. Hoops.

And ran downstairs, hearing a car door slam. But it was the Sheffields, unloading bags of peat moss and a new garden hose. Rosie looked at the clock; she had been upstairs exactly fifteen minutes.

Well. She pressed both hands to her chest, breathing deeply: *calm down, old girl.* Her heart still pounded, and the question pounded in her head: *will he come back*? She poured herself a little sherry—not beer, or she'd be running to the bathroom every half-hour—and stood by the window, in the sun, watching Jim and Kiki. She considered going out to talk to them, so he'd find her, if he did come back, chatting casually with the neighbors, absorbed, indifferent—"Oh, *there* you are! Back already? Jim, Kiki, meet my son-in-law, Ivan Cord." But no—she could imagine friendly Ivan inviting the Sheffields over to dinner, and the evening turning into a Scrabble tournament, with the Sheffields telling him how Rosie really should get down to Florida in the winter, and Jim talking about his arthritis and how Frank Sinatra might look like an overweight businessman but he still had his voice, God bless him.

The Sheffields went inside. She continued to stand by the window—barefoot, she realized, and went to find sandals, and returned to her post. She was watching, she thought to herself with disgust, with delight, like a teenager waiting for her date—watching for a car she wouldn't recognize, one with California plates, most likely, to pull up in front, and Ivan to jump out, whistling. She looked at the clock. He'd been gone twenty minutes. Five minutes into town, ten in the store, five back, he could be here by now if Clyde's wasn't crowded. Ten minutes more at the most. If he wasn't back in ten minutes he wasn't coming, and she'd go next door and invite Jim and Kiki for drinks.

She poured herself another sherry—*will he come back? and what am I getting myself into?*—and, to demonstrate to herself how truly nonchalant she could be, she began to straighten up the living room, brushing crumbs off a table, stacking up books, fluffing pillows, and she began to hum the song Ivan had been whistling. What was it? Surely an old Beatles tune. Dee dee dee *da* da, dee dee dee *da*—it came to her, with a jolt. "When I'm Sixty-Four." That's what it was. *And he won't come back, he won't. You're ridiculous, ridiculous, in your little dress, your earrings—*

And a door slammed. She ran to the window. A large blue van had pulled up, and there was Ivan hopping out of it, with a bag of groceries, whistling "Tea for Two."

It was as if Susannah was the *carte de visite* that had brought them together and could now be discarded. Her name didn't come up again, and most of the things Ivan had promised to tell Rosie were never mentioned—Susannah-centered stories that both of them, in some unspoken agreement that had stretched from shower to market, had decided to omit from their evening. Ivan made leathery green pepper omelets, hush puppies that burned in the pan, and something he called "Green Bean Rondo" with onions and pimentos. They ate their dinner, and Ivan drank the Mexican beer he had brought, on the back porch. Rosie wished she had suggested the kitchen, even if it was hot and smelled of burned cornmeal. She wanted to keep Ivan to herself; she didn't want the Sheffields to hear his hearty laughter, his loud baritone. She wished his van wasn't so large, so visible, so blue—such a *youthful* vehicle to be parked out in front of her house for so long, obviously not belonging to Peter, or to Rosie's sober, middle-aged-businessmen

beaux. She wondered if the Sheffields would notice, if out in the garden next day Kiki would ask her, with a watchful smile, who was the
bearded god with the fancy van.

They talked about gardening, about California, about Rosie's television show. She dragged out her store of funny anecdotes, and Ivan's
noisy laugh floated out over the garden. She thought to herself—but
only once—that Susannah's presence was all the more real between
them for having been avoided: Ivan might have lived in California
alone, and traveled east with only the cats for company; Rosie might
be a childless widow, a swinging single. Would it be better, she wondered, if they talked about Susannah openly, if Ivan confided in Rosie
the failure of his marriage, the daily misery of life with her daughter?
But gradually she forgot Susannah—truly, totally, if temporarily, forgot that the delightful man who had cooked her such a wretched meal
was her son-in-law.

He didn't stay late. They finished eating; she made coffee; they
drank a little Kahlua. Their laughter together had moments of tentative affection, as if they had begun what would be a long process of
knowing each other well. Their chairs had been pulled closer together.
Their knees occasionally touched and were moved, without haste,
away. They sat without a light, and the moonlit garden outside the
screens was full of black and green mystery. The sky changed from
light blue to dark blue, the stars appeared, the three-quarter moon
brightened over the garage roof, and Ivan said he'd better get along.

Rosie didn't press him to stay. In amiable silence, she saw him to
the door, where he kissed her gently on the cheek. *My reward*, she
thought to herself, surprised, reminded of movies she had seen, books
read, about people who tamed wild beasts or befriended shy primitive
peoples: there were setbacks, slow stalking, patient waiting, and suddenly an unexpected breakthrough that drastically advanced matters.
Ivan's kiss—cool lips against hot cheek—was such an event, and after
it Rosie said, "Come to dinner again, and I'll cook for you."

"A week from tonight?"

His face was still close to hers, and she felt dizzy. Events went much
speedier with Ivan than with lion cubs or aborigines. "Why not?" she
asked, her heart racing and the sweat coming out on her upper lip.

"Same time, same channel," said Ivan. Another kiss bounced off her cheek, and he was gone. The van roared away while she leaned weakly on the door.

Next day, and the days thereafter, she took to the garden, refusing to think or expect or do what she really wanted to do, which was to pick their evening apart bit by bit as she would a tangle of dahlia tubers. She concentrated instead on the flower beds, digging out the early bloomers, separating them, hauling huge loads of compost, replanting—getting her hands filthy, her knees stiff, and her back sore. It kept her mind off what had taken place, and what might come of it. To ponder it would be to jinx it.

When it was too wet or too dark, during that interminable waiting week, to work in the garden, or when she got so tired out she was good for nothing but a bath, a drink, and a comfortable chair, Rosie got out her father's collection of his favorite magazine, *The Countryman*. She had a suitcase full of the old green volumes, faded and tattered, much thumbed. Her father, with his big black mustache, curly hair, soft brown eyes, and Anglo-Italian accent, had revered all things English, and had dragged his collection—with its articles bearing titles like "How Birds Sleep," "Poacher Turned Gamekeeper," "Lupins in Drought"—across the sea in the old leather suitcase with the rotted strap, where they were still stored. Toward the end of his life they were his only amusement besides the soft voice of his wife, the visits from Rosie and Peter, and old Alastair Sim movies on TV.

Rosie had developed a fondness for the little volumes, and had even based one of her programs on them. What she liked best—besides the excellent gardening advice—were the advertisements. *Adverts*, both her parents used to call them. She sat back in her rose-patterned chair, with her feet up on an old velvet ottoman, and dug in, picking a volume at random. "Euthymol Tooth Paste," she read.

> A good horse and an eager pack; a wily fox and a long chase; the blue sky above and the grass beneath; the English countryside in all its fresh beauty. Could anything be more thrilling and exhilarating? Unhappily, too few of us are able to join in the thrills of the chase. Yet every morn-

ing and evening brings a pleasurable thrill to Euthymol users. For Euthymol not only cleans the teeth but kills dental decay germs within 30 seconds . . .

She loved it. It tickled her, and she sipped her Scotch and smiled, thinking of her father. She turned the pages slowly. Lost times, lost places. And the oddest products! "Energen," she read. "Unlike other breads. Keeps indefinitely. Entirely British." She tried to recall whether Energen had been served at the gardener's cottage at Silvergate, but could remember only her grandmother's hard-crusted *focaccia* and her mother's wholemeal loaves. And had they used Euthymol? She recalled something called Kolynos. "Pan Yan Pickle," the next page said. "Good AS a salad, good WITH a salad." Rosie smiled, but her mind wandered to the garden at Silvergate where she had helped her mother stake the lilies, where she had watched her strawberries run wild over their little plot, where their cat, Mossy, had loved to roll in the dirt. *I should go back to England*, she thought, as she had many times. *I should go now, when we're not filming, I should go over there and write this damned book.* And then the fluttery feeling came into her chest and she realized she couldn't, couldn't possibly go now, not this year, not at this particular time.

What am I getting into? What do I think I'm doing? Her fiftieth birthday had sailed over her while she was out in the garden, too absorbed to mark it properly, but that didn't mean it hadn't come, and gone, and set her on the road to the next, and the next. *You're a pathetic old woman*, she told herself, but the flutter in her chest didn't go away, and what she felt, chiefly, was the kind of thrilled, rapturous hope that hadn't come to her in years. She leaned back in her chair, stretched her arms over her head, and felt young, young.

Every day, she spent hours in the garden—proud of her ability to do so. Kiki, four years older than she, used to straighten up, press her hand to her lower back, and grimace—Rosie watched her covertly from her rose bed or her pea patch—and then go inside, where, Rosie knew, she would take her nap before she showered and did her hair to be ready, when Jim arrived home from work, with a cool drink and a warm smile. Rosie kept smugly on, moving from bed to bed, from perennial border to vegetable garden, ignoring her own back, her stiff fingers, her headaches from the sun. The good weather held, the yard looked wonderful, the notebook she was keeping in preparation for her book was thick with jottings, and when she had put in a day long enough to satisfy her she curled up with *The Countryman*. She dreamed of going to England with the distinguished middle-aged man in the Chilprufe Underwear ad, lighting his Balkan Sobranie cigarettes for him, taking a cruise with him on the Orient Line ("Designed for Sunshine") to Australia and back for £140, brushing her teeth each night with Euthymol Tooth Paste, and taking Eno's Fruit Salt every morning with breakfast.

> If poisoned by congested foodways, the human system cannot sustain healthy exercise. Make the morning draught of Eno's Fruit Salt a golden rule. Pleasantly, safely working in Nature's way, Eno ensures the punctual dismissal of the body's waste . . .

But she knew that what she really liked was exactly where she was, in this place and this time, with the gasping feeling of infinite possibility rising in her chest.

But he wouldn't come. He'd forget—wasn't the restaurant supposed to open? What had he said? And why *should* he remember, anyway? She looked long and critically into the mirror, wary of its deceptions, experimenting with makeup and hairdos as she hadn't done since the first heady weeks after Edwin left. She should get a haircut, she decided; then she rejected the idea. She went shopping and bought another dress with a low neck and a flounce, this one a soft blue with lace on the sleeves, and then she came home and hung it way in the back of her closet, embarrassed by its sexy exuberance. Her energy was inexhaustible. She couldn't leave the garden alone, she invented unnecessary tasks, she hovered over transplanted seedlings and the tender buds on the geraniums as if by breathing on them she could hasten their growth. In fact, that had been somebody's theory a few years back, that human presence—voice, breath, touch—encouraged plants to thrive. She had conscientiously tested it on her begonias and a flat of dianthus and had found it to be, as she reported to her viewers, claptrap. Of course, she had acknowledged, it was good for the *gardener* to hover, to coddle, to get close to growing things, to take comfort from them, and strength. And yet—she had never said so on her program but she thought to herself as she dug manure into the strawberry bed—gardening was in a way a gloomy activity, if you considered the wanton rankness of plants' flourishing, with or without your help, of the way they would, if you lay down and died in their midst, creep over you and cover you and take life from your remains without a trace of gratitude. Or if you thought about the speed with which things grow, flowers blossom, time passes. . . .

When she ran out of gardening chores, she got down on her knees and spent a couple of hours laboriously picking bits of roofing tile from behind the rhododendrons in front of her house, a chore she'd been postponing since the new roof was put on two years ago. She washed all the windows in the greenhouse. When Kiki hailed her over the fence and invited her for Scrabble, she declined, cheerfully pleading exhaustion; what if Ivan should call?

Kiki had said nothing about the van or the visitor with the young, long-distance laugh, but Rosie sensed a tenseness in Kiki's smile, disapproval in the way she admired how the Gudoshnik tulips had lasted. Or was she imagining it? She had a giddy thought that made her clutch a trowel to her chest in silent laughter: what if she'd imagined the whole thing, from Ivan's van to Kiki's disapproval? What if the pressures of her unwritten book and approaching senior citizenhood had unhinged her, and Ivan with his beard and his blue eyes and his strong tanned arms was a dream of her early dotage? But there was the hopelessly burned and crusted frying pan out in the trash.

Would he come? On the sixth day she abandoned her chores and planned a menu. Nothing heavy, nothing that might not set well on her butterfly stomach, nothing gassy, nothing that looked awkward to eat (no artichokes or lobster or spaghetti) and nothing that required strenuous cutting or chewing or—she closed her eyes and thought, *Yes, I'm going insane, truly*, but nevertheless she came up with a menu that met her specifications. Baked chicken, rice with mushrooms, asparagus from her garden. At the little Town Market, where she tried to imagine Ivan trundling one of the tiny shopping carts up and down the congested aisles buying his pimentos and cornmeal, it came to her as she stood musing over the display of chicken parts: *what if he's a vegetarian*? she remembered the tough omelets, and stood for several long moments in a sweaty panic. What to do? The image of the baked chicken on its platter sat firmly before her; she couldn't dislodge it. Barney had loved her chicken; she remembered his greasy fingers, greasy smile. "Excuse me," said a woman with a loaded shopping cart who wanted to push by, and Rosie moved on, calmed, toward the fish department. All vegetarians eat fish. She would substitute some nice filets. It was simple, no need to sweat, no need to clench her stomach muscles together until she felt sick.

Standing at the fish counter, she laughed at herself, and reflected that she always seemed, lately, to be laughing at herself. Rueful laughter had become her trademark, it was the price one had to pay for, for, for . . . what? There was no acceptable way to think about Ivan, to think about how much she wanted him to like her and be her friend. *Hers.* She stared glassily at the sole filets until the fish man asked her, for the second time, if he could help her.

Ivan showed up that evening, while Rosie was sitting in her chair chuckling over *The Countryman*, October 1933. "Munch," she read. "The perfect cereal in biscuit form. It is neither indigestible nor filling. The flavour is unique and irresistible to old and young alike, while the . . ."

She heard the sound of the van—*could* it be the van? O Lord—and dashed to the window to see him swing out of the front seat and up the path, whistling, looking for her at the door. She panicked, then calmed. She was in her bathrobe, just out of the tub, her hair in a knot on top of her head, her face not made up, her new dress still in the back of her closet—disaster! And yet *he was here*, and evidently meant to stay because he had a six-pack with him, and a package. She hugged herself with happiness and ran to the door to let him in.

He whistled when he saw her, whether in amazement at her getup or as a compliment, she didn't know. "Don't tell me—I'm a day early. Right?" He grinned and stepped inside from sunshine to dimness, and his teeth gleamed. "Darn it, I was afraid of that. I thought it was tomorrow, and then I said to myself, you couldn't have made it for the night of the day the restaurant opens—could you?" He ran one hand through his hair and shook his head. "But I guess I did."

"It's quite all right," Rosie said. His loud, sunny presence overwhelmed her anew. "Have a beer, make yourself at home, and I'll go up and get dressed. I won't be two seconds."

She was hardly more than that, and when she came back down with her heart beating fast, and her face made up and her new dress on, but barefoot and with her hair still in its loose knot, there he was, leafing through *The Countryman* and drinking Mexican beer out of the can.

"I like your house," he said. "You did a show by this fireplace once. Am I right? And are you going to give me a tour of the garden this time?"

"If you like," she said, delighted. Oh, he was perfect, perfect—handsomer than ever there in her living room, too big for the elegant chair, his hair tousled, his blue chambray shirt the color of his eyes. She'd thought she'd had him memorized, but there were new surprises, like the sprinkle of freckles across his cheekbones, and his neatly trimmed nails with their large half-moons. She wondered what excuse he'd used to get away, or if he'd told the truth, or if the relationship with Susannah was so deteriorated that he needed neither excuses nor truth. She pictured the two of them doggedly not communicating, like Edwin and herself; a fleeting sadness accompanied this thought, a thin chime of pity for Susannah and her ugly inheritance. Then Ivan stood up, with his brilliant smile, and they went through the kitchen to the backyard. He had brought her a pan to replace the one he'd burned.

"You didn't need to," she said. It was a cheap pan, and smaller. She put it away hastily in a cupboard and poured herself some sherry.

"That's a great dress," Ivan said, looking at it in a way that made her blush. Maybe the neck was too low, she thought, ever watchful for absurdity.

"Just an old sundress," she smiled. Would she ever be able to drop this spurious nonchalance, to say frankly: I bought it because of you, because I thought you'd like it, like *me*. . . .

She did show him the garden, after they had a drink together on the porch. Drink affected her oddly when she was with Ivan; one glass of sherry made her head light, her feet slow; she moved languorously, with a dreamy smile, and leading Ivan into the garden she had the odd sensation that she had no need to show it to him—the fading iris, the scarlet and gold Rembrandt tulips, the white azaleas and spirea against the old fence, the trillium in the grass. She felt that he was part of it, he looked as natural in the garden as a stone statue of a god. She moved with him through its green-gold light, with hints of pink sunset just beginning in the west, as if the Sheffields next door and the Andrews across the street had ceased to exist, and there was only Rosie and Ivan in the garden. She forgot, even, to laugh at herself and to stay alert for unbecoming absurdity. They sat on the bench under the flowering dogwood, by the tightly budded roses, and she drank her second sherry while he sipped beer and told her about the incredible greenness of downtown Los Angeles.

"I know it's hard to believe," he said. "All anybody thinks about is smog and traffic and movie stars when it comes to L.A. There—you can tell I'm not a native and don't even *like* the place, or I'd never call it L.A. But it's beautiful, all right, some of it." He turned and looked at her, with a bemused smile like her own. "I dream about it sometimes, or I did during the winter, on cold nights. I'd just dream I was walking down some street, some little nothing street out there, on my way to work, say, and it would be lined with flowers, and the sun would pour down." Under the beard he seemed to have dimples, his mouth was pink and swollen-looking, his blue eyes were narrowed slightly against the low sun. "You should take a trip out there, Rosie. I mean, as a gardener. Every gardener should see California, just to see what lushness really is. Go to the Palisades, Rosie. Go to Bel Air. You could even do a couple of shows out there, just for fun. Get old Janice to set it up. take the cameras into some of those fabulous gardens, show these poor New Englanders freezing by their woodstoves what it looks like to have an orange grove in the backyard." He grinned at her. "I've seen all your shows, some of them twice. I always thought you were terrific, Rosie—a nice, earthy broad." He laughed. "Literally! You always had dirt on your hands, you were always wiping your hands off on that apron."

"I was always afraid of looking too eccentric," she said, pleased. "Too much absorbed in my own messiness. But Janice said I was the Julia Child of the garden—that should be my image, so involved in what I was doing that I didn't notice if my hair came down or my face got smudged."

"The agony in the garden," Ivan said, and laughed again. She remembered that he was a renegade priest—unfrocked? or one of those who left voluntarily? She'd never been told. Well, whatever the case, he could now make gentle little jokes against his church. "Your *image*, Rosie," he went on. Yes—a dimple appeared on one side when he smiled. She longed to press her fingers against his face where the hollow was; she recalled the softness of his beard brushing her cheek when he kissed her. "What a way to look at it—as *image*, as if you were Nixon, when it was obvious that it was all real, that it would have been impossible for you to be any other way."

She didn't tell him it was partly cultivated, that manner, that naturalness before the cameras. "You can't garden neatly," she said. "I mean, in order to keep the garden relatively neat you have to forget about keeping yourself that way." What a boring conversation, she thought, he must be bored to death and wishing he hadn't come. But in the middle of this thought, while she still smiled brightly at him, she recognized, with a jolt, just what kind of a conversation it was that they were having. She hadn't had one in years, not since her first meeting with Barney. It was a—what could you call it?—a seduction conversation, its purpose only to fill a certain amount of time with words, to set up a decorous interlude before . . .

And—she caught her breath—they were in it together. He was talking about a vegetable garden he'd had in Buffalo, in the rectory backyard, but it was a skimming kind of story, not meant to settle them down into a real talk, but something to fill the time, a warm-up exercise before the real event.

She listened carefully, she prolonged it, just to make sure. Her head cleared; she must be very slow, very certain. The possibilities for absurdity were enormous, were staggering. But she knew the signs well, she could tell by the way he looked at her while he sipped his beer, by the amount of space between them on the bench, by the number of times he called her by name—oh, there were dozens of signals, there could be no mistake. She felt breathless, tense with hope, ready to burst into bloom like the swollen heads of the peonies over by the toolshed.

When they stood up and began to walk slowly toward the house, close together but not quite touching, the familiarity of it all made her want to laugh, and she knew that if she did laugh it would be a harsh, abandoned sound, near to hysteria. Her heart ticked faster as they went up the path, and when they paused by the back porch, well screened by the rhododendrons and the latticework fence, and looked at each other, she understood that he depended on her to act, to break the spell or cast a new one; so she moved close to him and, with her fingertips lightly on his cheek, she turned his face so that his lips came down readily, firmly, warmly on hers.

Chapter Four

Rapunzel

"I should become a vegetarian," Susannah said. "I love animals so much. Every time I eat a hamburger I have to brace myself against the idea that it used to be a cow. Big brown eyes. Pink nose. Moos."

She and Duke were sitting in the empty restaurant on an April morning, drinking tea. The sun shone through the paper banner in the window:

COMING SOON
THE SILVERGATE CAFÉ
NATURAL FOODS

The tables were set up, in two rows of four each, birch tops sanded smooth by Duke and Ivan, coated with polyurethane, and set on metal bases. The sturdy old oak chairs, with their calico cushions, were pulled up neatly. The serving counter in back had been covered in white formica, and a latticework screen surrounded it, hiding the kitchen and harboring plants. The kitchen was ready to spring into action except for the gap between the wooden counter-tops where the stove was to go.

"And I remember at one of my schools we had to learn to farm, and we had three milk cows, and we had calves." She sighed. "Sickening sentimentality. I know, don't tell me."

"It doesn't strike me that way," Duke said. "Margie and I didn't eat meat for years, until I got the job at Luigi's. The pepperoni pizzas did me in. But if we're going to run a vegetarian restaurant we ought to go all the way. What about it? You want to?"

Susannah sighed again and looked around the pristine room, a place that should smell of cheese and eggplant and oranges but stank instead of fresh paint. It looked like a stage set. "Ivan says I worry too much."

"What's more important—what you think or what Ivan thinks of what you think?"

She smiled wryly at him, and he got up and went to the front window to peer out. Whenever Ivan's name came up lately, in her conversations with Duke, it seemed charged and dangerous, enclosing volumes of explosive words left unsaid. Susannah watched Duke wipe an imaginary smudge off the window with his sleeve.

"Dammit," he said, returning to the table. "I wish that blasted stove would get here."

"We couldn't just open anyhow, and serve salads?"

"No!" They'd had this exchange before; their conversations had begun to meander in circles. "We can't even boil water," Duke said. "We can't even—" He broke off, shaking his head and smiling at her so she'd know he wasn't really angry—just mildly frustrated, as usual. "How can I show off my cooking without a stove? I want to lure people in here with my black bean soup, my stir-fried veggies, my pizzas."

"Duke Foster's Famous Goat-Cheese Pizza." Susannah smiled back. That's what it said on the menu, along with Lentil Salad Susannah and Mushroom Caviare Ivanovitch.

"And we can't serve it *cold*," he said, getting up again. He paced around the room, straightening a chair, picking a sick leaf off a plant. His hair needed cutting—he was waiting until just before they opened—and it hung in wisps over his collar. "Oh, hell, let's become vegetarians, Susannah, instead of wishy-washy *almost*-vegetarians who don't approve of veal and don't eat *much* meat and go around saying big old roasts of beef oozing blood make them sick and any kind of killing is unacceptable violence."

"I don't say any of that," Susannah replied. "I just say sentimental platitudes about how much I love animals."

"Well." He disappeared around the partition to the kitchen where the hot plate was. "I assume you want some more tea," he called.

"Sure." What else have we got to do? she refrained from adding. She didn't really mind the inactivity. She liked sitting around drinking tea, talking, playing with the twins, reading. She was teaching herself to bake bread, from a book. She especially liked sitting in the empty restaurant. Not that she didn't look forward to their opening; now that her story was done and sent away, she felt herself more a part of the place. It was she who had washed the inside of the front window until it sparkled, and she who had patiently given the table tops their three gleaming coats of polyurethane. But she liked the empty neatness of the place, the expectancy of it. And how could it fail if it never opened?

But Duke and Ivan were restless. They'd begun to bicker, mostly about the recalcitrant stove, but there were spin-offs: they argued over the menu, over the sign for the front, over where and how to advertise, even over the best way to fix a wobbly chair leg. And once the chair leg was fixed, the menu at the printer's (without the cute bunch of carrots Ivan had envisioned as part of the logo), the advertising contract signed with the newspapers, they argued over money. It tormented Ivan that they were living off savings—off, specifically, a check from Edwin and the money they'd made from Susannah's legacy—and that the stove delay would mean doing so for that much longer.

"Let's not forget whose fucking money is financing this stupid delay," he had said the last time he'd stormed out, and Duke had jumped up and gone to the door to shout, "Don't get so goddamn self-righteous you forget it's your wife's money!" to which Ivan had replied, "Just leave my wife out of it, you son of a bitch," and roared away in the van.

"There's nothing like a couple of ex-priests for foul language," Susannah had said to Duke. He had laughed and apologized, and when Ivan came home late that night, they had entangled themselves in a welter of apologies that finally reduced them all to embarrassed laughter. That had been the last; *no more of this*, they had sworn, and had gone to bed full of good will, except for Susannah, who had lain awake wondering where Ivan had been all those hours.

The bitterness between the two men lingered, though. Duke was snappish and defensive, his easy good humor continually on the verge of collapse. Ivan was becoming smug, detached, mocking—it wasn't *his* insistence on a Rimrock Excelsior Restaurant Model Cookstove imported from Flint, Michigan, that was the source of all their troubles. Duke knew it, but he wouldn't give in.

"If you're going to do something you do it right," he insisted, refusing to look up when Ivan said, "Well, I can't sit around here all day feeling sorry for myself," and left.

Days off, he called his nameless excursions. "Where do you go, Ivan, on your days off?" Susannah asked him once, lightly.

"I just drive around, getting the feel of the place." Back in California, he used to say, "I'm just going out to see what's happening," standing at the door with his hands in his pockets, bouncing on his heels and grinning innocently at her. It all came down to the same thing— she had known what was happening there, she knew what he was getting the feel of here. She gave up on her notion that Ivan could be domesticated. Coming east—as if New England was full of starched, prim, tight-buttoned ladies like the ones Ivan used to paint. *I've got to accept it*, she said to herself, adding sometimes, when acceptance seemed not only impossible but vaguely immoral, and anger gripped her: *or leave him*. But they were still trying to make a baby.

"Oh, sometimes I don't know what I'm doing," Susannah said when Duke came back with the tea. "I don't see why life has to be so complex. Sometimes it's worse than a Henry James novel, only not so interesting."

"Let's go vegetarian," Duke said. He set a white earthenware mug in front of her. Ivan had won that round; Duke claimed earthenware was false economy, it chipped too easily, but Ivan had begun to balk at expense, and refused to finance anything else. Every mug of tea Susannah drank recalled harsh words and stony silences. "Let's," said Duke. "That will simplify things."

She shook her head. "No, it won't." Ivan was capable of making her life miserable over such an issue: *fanatic*, he'd call her. There was nothing worse than a fanatic. Moderation in all things, he'd say. How could we have driven cross-country if we'd been vegetarians? In the middle of winter? And then you're forever grubbing for protein, eating too many eggs, mixing this with that, drinking milk all the time. "We've talked about it, Ivan and I, plenty of times. We even tried it once or twice."

"And?"

She shrugged. "You know." She didn't go on. She had the feeling that Duke was waiting for her to confide in him, waiting for a word that would release them into a good gossip session about Ivan's unreasonableness, Ivan's temper, Ivan's irresponsibility. The thought, she had to admit, was like a cool wind—what a relief it would be, after all, to cry on someone's shoulder.

"You're a big girl, Susannah," Duke said gently after a minute. She wished he hadn't. People were always telling her—Carla, especially, and even her father—that she was a big girl now, that she didn't need to rely on Ivan for everything. "You don't need to rely on him for everything," said Duke.

"Oh, all *right*," she said suddenly, angrily. "It's not such a big deal, for heaven's sake. From this day forward I hereby swear never to eat another hamburger."

"You mean it?" Duke looked irrationally pleased, as if she'd announced delivery of the stove.

"Sure—why not? Let's go whole hog, ha ha."

An hour later, Ivan was at the door with a bag full of French fries and Big Macs, and pastry from Zakrzeski's. "I'm starving," he said, dumping everything on the table. "Let's pig out."

Oh hell, if only she didn't *love* him, didn't have so many *reasons* for loving him. She lay in bed while he breathed beside her, not quite snoring but breathing loudly enough so she could count each inhalation, each exhalation, and she thought of all the things she loved him for, even little ones like his annual planting of the vegetable garden in their Dimmick Street backyard, that afforded her the sight of his bent brown back with the sun on it, and his big hands poking in the tiny seeds and covering them tenderly, paternally. She smiled in the darkness. *In, out, in* he breathed, curiously fast, two breaths to each of her long slow ones. It used to worry her when they were first married, that quick breathing—she used to wake him up to make sure he was all right—but she'd become used to it, it was another thing to love. And she loved his body, always, and still considered it a blessing, too good to be true, when he turned to her in bed and with his warm hand drew her toward him. And she loved him because he had chosen her, had stuck with her, took care of her, believed in her, put up with her quirks. She forgave him his affairs, his sermonizing and nagging, not only because she believed him when he said that they were part of an attempt to perfect his life (something Susannah, in her own way, strove for herself) but because she felt they were a small price to pay for the benefits of marriage to Ivan, and because she didn't know what else to do. The alternative was unthinkable. She couldn't think it. It was a black hole, a nightmare.

But she wished, sometimes, in the dark as she lay beside him, with the cats tucked behind their knees and around their feet, that she had fallen in love with someone *easier*, someone kinder and more faithful and less picky. *You should get a dog if that's what you want*, she thought just before she fell asleep. She imagined a large, beautiful dog named Ivan romping among the affronted cats, and went to sleep smiling.

Sometimes, in the mornings after the twins left for school, Susannah walked down the road to Ginger Coleman's house. Ginger was a middle-aged divorcée with a son in business school in Boston and a daughter in nurse's training at Yale-New Haven Hospital. Her house was a five-year-old split level that had come to her in the divorce settlement, the details of which she told Susannah the first day she met her. The house had been built on a piece of the farmland that used to belong to the owner of Duke's house—a cantankerous truck farmer named Roswell whose heirs had sold off his property fast and cheaply at his death, as if to rid themselves of all memory of the old man. Ginger's house stood where the cornfield had been; unshaded by trees, it was hot from May to October, and Ginger—a large, frizzy-haired woman prone to cheerfulness—sat in her air-conditioned kitchen talking on the phone all day and entertaining visitors. She had staggering quantities of friends who called her up and dropped in on her, staying the night if they needed to, bringing her plants and homemade rolls and macramé wall hangings in exchange for her sympathy and good humor. She lived on substantial alimony checks; her husband had run off with a younger woman, and—as she admitted readily, crossing herself or knocking on wood for a continuation of her good fortune—she had profited handsomely from his guilt.

"That poor guy," she said to Susannah. "Saddled with a twenty-five-year-old tramp for a wife, a brother-in-law on drugs, a condominium with three bathrooms that don't work right, and a new baby that doesn't look anything like him. Plus a third of his salary every month for his ex-wife—not that he can't afford it. Don't think my heart doesn't bleed for him. But he made his bed, and if he's having trouble lying in it, that's his funeral."

Sometimes Ginger had a job. She was an intermittent Avon lady and Tupperware demonstrator, and she had looked after not only the twins but various offspring and grandchildren of her friends. She asked Duke if she could have a waitressing job at the Silvergate Café.

"Not that I go for that kind of food, normally," she said. "I can't eat salads, for one thing, because I have this hiatal hernia, and my doctor says too much roughage is a no-no, and if you ask me all that herb tea tastes like colored water and orange peel. I've got to have meat—a nice hamburger, a salami sandwich, a minute steak, and a nice Diet Pepsi to go with it. But I like you kids," she said to Susannah. "I'm real fond of Duke and those twins, and I'd like to help you all make good. And I'd be one hell of a waitress, that I'm sure of."

Ivan was dubious; he saw the restaurant staffed with young people—*girls*, Susannah knew, with healthy complexions and long legs—ads for the food. Ginger was fortyish and overweight, with unruly graying hair and thick, blue-tinted glasses.

"She's going to be perfect," Duke insisted stubbornly. "Homey and motherly. Everybody loves Ginger, and she's got more energy than all of us put together." Ivan sulked, but Ginger was hired, and she recommended a girl named Garnet, the daughter of a friend, as their second waitress. Garnet was a junior at the University of Connecticut, where she had waitressed in the dining hall for three years. But she couldn't start until school let out for the summer, and Susannah would fill in until then.

"I don't want you to be a permanent waitress, Susannah," Duke said. "Only while we get started, or if we should need extra help. You're a writer before anything."

For once, he and Ivan agreed. "You don't have the stamina, either, Susannah," Ivan said. "I don't want you to wear yourself out, especially now." He gave her the reverent look that he always did whenever he thought of her as the potential mother of his child. "And there's your writing to consider, of course. Hell, we didn't come east for you to give that up."

"Oh, I can always write," Susannah told them, trying to sound lighthearted. "I've got years. And I can write at night, you know, and on holidays." But she was beginning to feel hungry for her long, dreamy sessions with her notebook, though she didn't have a new idea for a story. Sometimes she sat with a pencil in her hand, looking at Ivan's painting and trying to summon back the urgency with which she had written "Cloud House," but the images and words that came to her were vague, and failed to coalesce. The delays at the restaurant were distracting her, she knew, and so was the tension, spun out of their failure to conceive, between Ivan and herself. Even her friendship with Duke, which she had fallen into naturally and spontaneously soon after their arrival, disturbed her; it seemed disloyal to get on so well with Duke just as Ivan's bond with him seemed to be weakening.

Now and then, though, a phrase in a book, or a face in the supermarket, or the look of the fuzzy-edged moon through the dirty kitchen window would unlock something in her brain and give her a glimpse into a time when she would write another story. Not quite yet, but before long. . . . Something about an enclosed space filled with light, something about a monstrous, horrifying springtime. She smiled to herself (her hands in the dishwater, the out-of-focus moon traveling slowly through the maple branches), wondering what would emerge from this moment.

She still spent hours and hours reading, oblivious to everything but the page before her. She took out a card at the Chiswick Public Library and brought home *Daniel Deronda, The Princess Casamassima*, and two Trollope novels she'd never read; they lasted her nine days, and she went back for more. At this rate she'd exhaust the tiny library in six months. She wished Peter would come back from the Cape so he could lend her books. He'd extended his stay to a month; she inferred a romantic entanglement. He called her from Truro one evening early in May, and though he admitted his writing wasn't going much better he sounded exuberant. She heard a male voice singing in the background above the clatter of dishes.

"Who's that?" she asked.

"That's Terry. Friend of mine." She could tell he had turned to Terry and smiled. "He's washing the dishes. We had mussels for dinner."

"Ah," she said. She knew Peter was gay, of course. How did she know? Had he told her that time he came to California, when they were all high? Or had she sensed it? She couldn't remember; the knowledge came out of that blurry period in her life.

"How's Dad doing?" Peter asked her. He pronounced *Dad* as self-consciously as she imagined she would say*Mom*, if she ever said it.

"He's exactly the same. Not very good but no worse. Dr. Strauss says it's miraculous, the way he hangs on. I talk to him every couple of days. I wish I could go out there and see him, but Ivan says it would be pointless."

"I thought he preferred it this way—Dad, I mean."

"Oh, he does, or so he says. No—he means it. And I suppose it's better." She sighed. "Peter?"

"What?" He chuckled as he spoke. The clatter of dishes had stopped, and his attention was half on Terry, who was singing in falsetto:

I'm called Little Buttercup, dear Little Buttercup,
Though I could never tell why.

She had been going to say that she was longing to see him, she wished he would come home, but she couldn't. She heard a crash, then muffled laughter.

"What, Suse?"

"I just wanted to remind you to come for dinner as soon as you get back."

"I will. I'll call you the instant I get in. Oh God, *Terry!*" There was another crash, and Peter said something to Terry that Susannah couldn't make out, then said into the phone, "Why don't you go over and see Mom before I get back? Just drop in. She'll probably be out in the yard. Just go around back and surprise her."

"But you said she didn't even want to see me!"

"I never said that. I just said she's still nursing a couple of old grudges. Hell, so are you. But five minutes would put everything right."

"It *would*? What makes you think—"

There was another crash, then the sound of a piano, and Terry's voice:

Then buy of your Buttercup, dear Little Buttercup,
Sailors should never be shy . . .

"Look, Susannah, I've got to get off the phone. Things are getting pretty wild here. I'll see you in a couple of weeks. Okay, sweetie pie?"

"Okay. Good-bye, Peter," she said quickly before he hung up, cutting off the laughter and the music. She stood on the landing, feeling irritable and left out, still holding the phone. She was home by herself, waiting for a loaf of cheese bread to rise; the others had gone out for Chinese food. What if she dialed Rosie's number? She had looked it up in the directory weeks ago, had memorized it without even meaning to. What if she called and asked if she could come over? Or what if she just hopped into the van and drove over there?

If she had paused to think she wouldn't have done it; recognizing that, she didn't stop, didn't let herself analyze. The call from Peter had made her lonely; the house seemed huge and empty. Without pondering further, she grabbed her keys and ran outside, leaving the door open behind her.

It wasn't quite dark. There were tatters of sunset over the trees down the road: rose madder, scarlet, ocher, carnelian. The night was cool. One of the cats, crouched on the porch railing, looked at her and meowed, and its eyes gleamed yellow and opaque. Susannah shivered in her denim skirt and cotton blouse, but she got into the van, reversed it down the driveway, and drove up Perkins Road to the highway. A wild exhilaration filled her. What nonsense it had been, these years of silent feuding. They were both grown women, she and Rosie. There might soon be a grandchild, for heaven's sake. And think how proud Ivan would be of her, if she came home and when he asked her where she'd been she could say, "I was over at my mother's."

She drove east out of Chiswick, past the restaurant, past Zakrzeski's, past the Chinese place—there was Duke's Volkswagen in the lot—past the turnoff for the school where she picked up the twins on gymnastics days, past the library, to East Chiswick with its grassy center and its quaint Main Street: the chic little seafood restaurant, the butcher shop with its gold-lettered window, the Town Market unchanged since her childhood. She turned left on Mott and right on Worth, her mother's dead-end street, and drove down to the house at the end. In the dusk, she could just make out that it was still painted a yellowish white, the front door was still flanked with rhododendrons, the walk still brick and winding. Little tan car in the driveway. Bright tulips along the fence. Lush grass, bordered with flower beds. She could glimpse the old playhouse out back; she knew from the TV shows that it was now a tool shed. Two windows in the house were lit, one downstairs where she remembered the living room was, and one upstairs. She sat in the van and peered out at the silent house—the same, precisely the same, as she'd imagined it hundreds of times in the sixteen years since she'd carried her bags down the brick walk and gotten into a taxicab. How strange it was, the house the same and herself so different.

A figure passed across the light upstairs, and passed back again—Rosie, of course. Susannah recognized the abundant hair and the thickening figure she'd seen on television. The light went out, and Susannah, panic rising in her throat, as if she'd seen a ghost, put the van in gear and turned into the driveway behind the little tan Audi, backed up and headed down Worth Street to Mott again. She didn't look back, afraid of what she'd see, and the van roared up Mott Street to Main and then Route One. Over its noise Susannah heard herself say *Nonononono* as she drove. She could never, never, never—how could she think it would be easy? And what was the point? Why stir things up? Rosie's silhouette in the window was enough to remind her—what a troublemaker her mother could be, what a vindictive, sharp-tongued woman. Nothing was ever pleasant with her, she was a villain. For no reason, Susannah recalled the time she flung her squash at the drapes in the dining room, and her mother's response. With Rosie, it was always slaps, insults, unchecked fury culminating in cold silence. *No*, Susannah said, speeding down Route One. The way to perfect your life was not to yank into it, against her will, a woman who never smiled, a woman with grudges, even if she was your mother.

Passing the darkened restaurant, she was reminded that she had left bread rising, the door unlocked, the house lit up like a jack-o'-lantern. Ivan would kill her if he got home first. But when she sped by Sun Luck she saw that Duke's car was still there. She pulled into her own driveway at last and ran into the lit-up house, the cats following her. The house was unburgled, intact, the bread still a heavy lump under its dishtowel. "Safe," she said to herself, aloud, and collapsed into a chair with Shelley in her arms. Her heart beat fast. *No*, its rhythm repeated. *Nonono*. But by then she felt slightly absurd, even ashamed of her flight. *Susannah, you jerk*, she said to herself. She wished Duke had a television. What she needed was a mindless comedy or an old movie to calm her down and cheer her up and keep her from wanting to cry into Shelley's striped fur. But Duke thought television was bad for the twins. Even "Sesame Street," he said, was passive entertainment; he'd rather see the kids out flying kites or playing with their magnetic ABCs. Susannah guessed she agreed, but she missed, some nights, the friendly presence of the old black and white set that used to keep her company when Ivan was out.

She looked through an old *Prevention*, and was absorbed in an article called "Overcome Fear Through Vitamin A" when Ivan and Duke and the twins returned. They brought her egg rolls and a paper container of vegetables, and she ate quickly while the twins watched her with attention. They thought she didn't eat enough. It concerned them that she didn't like ice cream, or carrot cake. "You live on tea," they accused her. To please them, she ate everything they'd brought her, and then she punched down her bread and put it in a pan to rise again.

"Promise you'll eat a piece when it's done."

"If it turns out okay," she said. Her bread had a tendency to bake into hard, impenetrable slabs.

"This looks good," said Mary Claire, poking the dough with one finger. "I think it'll work, Susannah."

For some reason, at those words, the desire came over Susannah to be pregnant, to have a child, so powerful and sudden it made her knees weak. She smiled blankly at the twins, who went off to give the cats their evening feed. Susannah steadied herself against the kitchen table. She wondered if she was already pregnant, if the quick bright flash of need she had felt was in fact a confirmation that the need would be filled.

She had a long-distance phone call a few days later, from a woman named Leslie Merwin, an editor at a publishing company in New York. Susannah had been so sure, when the operator asked for her, that the call was from St. Theodore's announcing her father's death, that it took her a few seconds to recover from her desolation, and to understand. Leslie Merwin had been shown Susannah's story, 'Cloud House,' by Otto Schenk at *SciFi Review*, and had wondered if Susannah was interested in doing a book of short stories.

"I want to use this one—'Cloud House'—and three or four of the others Otto has published, plus a couple of new ones. We're offering you a $5000 advance, half now and half on delivery of two new stories. And a December first deadline? Would that give you enough time? Want to think it over and call me back? I love your stuff, and our list is a little weak in the sci-fi category. I'll tell you what—think it over and call me back Monday."

"No—no!" Susannah gripped the phone with both hands. Duke was sitting on the kitchen floor repairing a toy truck; Ivan was at the sink washing dishes. The room was filled with sunlight. "No—I can tell you now. Yes. Yes, of course, it sounds wonderful. I'd love to. I mean, sure."

"That's just great," said Leslie Merwin. "That's fabulous, in fact. I like 'Cloud House' very much; it's so unusual, you have a real gift for the realistically eerie—do you know what I mean? At this point, I see it as the title story, unless one of the new ones turns out to be even better, or has a catchier title. I'll tell you what. Do you have a new story in the works?"

"Oh, sure," Susannah lied. "I always have a new story in the works." Ivan looked over his shoulder at her, and Duke put down his screwdriver. Susannah raised her eyebrows, nodded furiously, beamed extravagant smiles at them to indicate jubilation.

"Then why don't you send me an outline of it? Anything. Any ideas for the new stuff. In fact—" Leslie Merwin paused, and Susannah heard her take a drag on a cigarette. "I'd love to meet you, Susannah. Plan to come into the city and have lunch with me one of these days. But meanwhile I'll get your contract and your check in process, and you send me whatever you've got, and then I'll get back to you. Okay?"

They all had a beer to celebrate. Susannah felt stunned, and was almost inclined to think it was a hoax, a joke played on her by—whom? Otto Schenk? Peter and the wild Terry? Her mother? She suggested this, timidly, to Ivan and Duke, and when they laughed at her she expanded it into farce: "Suppose some sociologist or psychologist or someone is writing a book about, oh, I don't know—*gullibility*, people's reactions to improbable pieces of good news—and Otto Schenk gave them my name, and right now they're chortling over my reaction, saying they've never *seen* such pathetic gullibility."

She laughed along with Duke and Ivan, but even after Otto called to congratulate her she remained, deep down in her soul, skeptical—though she began, immediately, to turn over in her mind ideas for stories, trying to recall every illumination, no matter how vague, just in case.

She got her period the next morning, before she and Duke and the twins set off for a trip to the Aquarium at Mystic, and she tucked aspirin and tampons in her purse, feeling—as she did each month when her infertility was confirmed again—a mixture of disappointment and hope. Well, *next time*, she said to herself, and decided that June was a much better month to begin a pregnancy; the baby wouldn't be born in the dead of winter, it would be a spring baby. She pictured it surrounded by flowers. And it had been too much to expect, a pregnancy and a publisher (if it wasn't a hoax) in the same week.

They were going to drive along the coast, out to the eastern part of the state, for a holiday, a last fling. Delivery of the stove had been promised, at last, for the following Monday, and the restaurant would open on Wednesday. Meanwhile, Duke had heard of a man in Stonington who had an old-fashioned cash register for sale, just the kind of thing he'd been wanting for the restaurant. "They make that nice ringing sound when you pull the lever and the drawer opens," he said. "Reminds me of the store where I used to buy penny candy when I was a kid."

"And where was that?" Susannah asked him. They were driving up Route 95 in the Volkswagen, with the twins—playing hooky from school for educational purposes, Duke said—securely belted into the back seat. Susannah had braided their hair for them, and she looked back every once in a while to see the way the fat pigtails stuck out on either side of their identical faces. Their round greenish eyes were fixed on the back of their father's head while he talked, turning to Susannah when she swiveled around to smile at them, then back to Duke. They loved his stories of his childhood.

"Ashtabula, Ohio," he said. He wore a squashed-looking fishing hat pulled low on his forehead. "Great place to grow up. I went to Bunker Hill School, and on the first day the teacher, Miss Agnes, said to us—she talked real fast, like 'Take a piece of paper fold it into sixteen squares and draw a picture in each square.'" He raced through the sentence, making the twins squeal with laughter. "So I drew a dog in each square. Very painstakingly. The same dog, over and over. For some reason I thought that was what she wanted us to do. I can still see that dog—little barrel-shaped body, bullet head, stand-up ears, skinny little tail like a hook. *Brown* dog, with a red collar. Anyway, when I got done—and mighty proud of myself, too—Miss Agnes said to me, 'Ellington—'"

"*Ellington? That's* why you're called Duke?"

"Don't let it get around," Duke grinned at her. "'Ellington,' she said. '*Why* do you put such limits on your imagination?' And I looked around and saw that the other kids had drawn cats and houses and sunshines and apples, and they were all laughing at my sixteen brown dogs, and I burst into tears."

The twins' voices were shrill with delight. "Tell Susannah what happened then!"

"Well, I don't know if I should," said Duke. His eyes were smiling under his hat, and his round cheeks were pink with pleasure. "It's pretty embarrassing."

"Come on, Daddy. Tell her!"

"Well." He cleared his throat. "I'm ashamed to say I wet my pants." The twins squealed. "How I ever got through school I'll never know, after that beginning."

He talked all the way to Mystic, egged on by his daughters, telling Susannah stories of his childhood and the twins'. Susannah listened with amusement. It surprised her, the better she got to know Duke, what good company he was; shouldn't such a wholesome, uncomplicated, decent man—devoted dad, grieving widower, clever businessman, proponent of nuclear disarmament, solar heat, vegetarianism, and no television—be dull? Shouldn't—Susannah was being ruthlessly honest with herself, looking out the window at the fresh new greens of the landscape, listening to Duke with half her brain and thinking hard with the other half—shouldn't the *nice* man in her life, the man she was increasingly viewing as a contrast to Ivan's selfish whims, turn out to be colorless and flat? Ashley versus Rhett Butler, Linton versus Heathcliff? And yet it wasn't that way at all. Duke entertained her enormously, while she felt nothing but irritation and uneasiness, lately, with Ivan. And she blushed—chuckling, meanwhile, at Duke's description of the pathetic bunch of non-athletes he once got together for a baseball team—and chided herself for letting such a fantasy develop: that Duke would rescue her from Ivan, that she could solve her problems with Ivan by means of Duke, that if she didn't produce her own children she could be Mommy to the twins, that the faithful considerate husband she'd been wishing for years that Ivan would be, was sitting by her side, talking about sandlot baseball in Ashtabula, Ohio.

It frightened her, that she could have such thoughts, but she was angry with Ivan. He had seemed to blame her for getting her period, as if she'd done it deliberately to thwart him. "At least it shows everything is working, anyway," she had said, to cheer him up. "The fact that I'm so regular, every twenty-eight days, like a machine."

But that had been a mistake—he took it as blame, an insult to his own fertility. Why hadn't she seen he would? she had scolded herself, and the thought had immediately followed: *why do I always have to tiptoe with him*? She was sick of gauging his moods and weighing her words; and, God knew, he was heavy-footed enough with her. She lashed back at him and they had a full-fledged argument, and he had refused to go to Mystic with them. Later, getting ready to leave, she braided the twins' hair—then, at their insistence, braided her own as well—and wondered whether Ivan had started the quarrel in order to provide himself with an excuse to stay home. She suspected, though they left him out in the yard digging up the vegetable garden, that he had plans of his own that were more interesting than mucking around in the dirt. For once, his broad T-shirted back bent over a pitchfork failed to move her. He didn't look up to wave when they left, even though Duke honked and the twins yelled good-bye.

"He's still stewing over the stove business," Duke said.

"Let him," Susannah replied, and Duke looked at her in surprise.

With her hair in braids, Susannah felt years younger, not much older than the twins. She kept looking at her long face, reflected in the green Aquarium tanks, crisscrossed by stingrays, piranhas, and sharks. She made faces at her reflection, and hung on to the ends of her braids with her hands, enjoying the gentle tug of her hair against her scalp. The twins called her Rapunzel; they twirled the ends of her braids with their plump hands, and her hair whirred softly past her ears.

Mary Claire, the quieter twin, sat on her lap during the dolphin show, watching soberly while the dolphins jumped through hoops and fetched gold rings and played ball. Only when they barked for fish did she laugh. Mary Grace watched from Duke's shoulders, closer to the pool, and when the trainer asked for a volunteer to throw the animals a fish she cried, "I will! I will!" nearly falling from her perch, but a little boy in the front row was chosen.

"Boys get everything," she said over lunch in the cafeteria. "Girls don't have any luck."

"That's not always true," Duke said. "Look at Susannah. Not only is she a good writer but she has these pretty long pigtails." He reached out, shyly, to touch one. "I'd say she's mighty lucky."

"And three cats," said Mary Claire.

"That's not the same as getting picked to throw a fish," said Mary Grace, unconvinced.

"But it's pretty good," said Mary Claire, and took Susannah's hand.

Susannah and Duke were being vegetarians again, so they had salads for lunch, and afterwards they drove to Stonington, where they wandered up and down the quaint, narrow streets looking for the address of the man with the cash register.

"We could ask someone," Susannah suggested.

"Never!" said Duke.

"Daddy hates to ask directions," Mary Grace said.

"It's a nice day for a walk," Duke said firmly.

Susannah breathed in deeply. The air tasted clean and salty; the day was cool and full of promise, with a brisk little wind and plenty of sun—weather that was valueless unless it followed a cold winter. "It's just the kind of day I used to love, and that I missed out in Los Angeles," Susannah said.

The twins ran on ahead, and when they were out of earshot Duke said to Susannah, "I want to talk to you about something while I've got the chance."

"Oh God, Duke, what?" Not on this perfect day, she felt like saying. She looked desperately at the sun shining on a pink azalea bush, as if it was her last glimpse.

"I probably shouldn't even mention it," Duke said. "But I'm getting a little worried about Ivan."

"How come?" she asked, thinking how she really didn't want to know. When the wind wasn't blowing the sun was hot, and she and Duke stopped in the shade of a tree thick with shiny young leaves.

"I don't think his heart is in this—the restaurant." He looked at her, frowning in a way that made his pointed nose turn white at the tip. Susannah had on thin-soled sandals; in the hiking boots Duke habitually wore he was just her height. "It's my fault," he went on. "I talked him into it because it was what *I* wanted. What he wanted was to come east. It seemed the perfect setup, but—" He shrugged. "I have to admit now that I had my doubts, but I suppressed them. And I'm beginning to think I've gotten us all into something that isn't going to work out."

Susannah felt desolated. She remembered how she had doubted, and then become sure. Now here was doubt again. She looked for a place to sit; there was nothing but the curbstone, so she sat down on it, and Duke sat beside her. The twins were petting a cat on someone's front walk. In the yard was a plaster niche lined with shells, a statue of the Virgin, abundant hyacinths. "But he's never *said* he didn't want to go on with it, Duke. And he's worked so hard."

"I know he has, he's been great, you both have," Duke said quickly. "But his heart isn't in it," he said again. He sighed and looked down at his scarred hands. "He used to want to talk about it all the time—remember? Now he's not interested. It's you and I who talk about it—who hang around the place and make plans. Ivan's always out somewhere."

"It's the delay," Susannah said, but she wondered if she was right. Was it more than that? More than the stove, and restlessness, and wherever he went on his days off? She was scared. If they didn't run the restaurant with Duke, what would they do? She thought of her father, quietly dying back in California. For this she had left him there alone: for *what*?

"He hardly talks to us, Susannah. I keep getting the feeling it's you and me against Ivan, and that's not right." He touched her hand lightly. "You're his wife, I'm his best friend—used to be, anyway. We shouldn't be allied against him. But it keeps working out that way. Even today—here. Why isn't Ivan with us?"

"We had a fight."

"Oh. Well." Duke was silent. He looked up the street at the twins; they were squatted down on either side of the cat, talking to it. "But there are plenty of other times, Susannah. Almost *all* the time. Afternoons, nights, Ivan's out somewhere. You wait—we'll get home and he'll be out." He looked at her, troubled. "Ivan and I used to be such good friends. Even when you two were in California—maybe *especially* then. I suppose I should think about that. Maybe we get along better when we don't live in the same town—same house, at least."

There was another pause. Susannah wore a full black skirt; she looked down at her thin, white shins protruding from her skirt like crutches, covered with a fur of blonde hairs. She tucked her legs beneath her skirt. "Maybe if Ivan and I moved," she said. "Got an apartment."

"I'm not trying to get you to move out," Duke said. "Don't misunderstand me, Susannah. I don't really think that's the trouble. It's a lot more than that. But it's also simply that Ivan doesn't seem to be cut out for the restaurant business."

"But we're not even *in* the restaurant business yet, Duke."

The twins had moved off down the street, and they got up to follow. The cat accompanied them a way, then abandoned them and trotted off behind a house, tail up. Duke walked in silence, with his hands in his pockets, his eyes on the twins. "No, but . . ." He looked at Susannah and shook his head. "Hell, he doesn't even like food, he doesn't care what he eats or what he eats it off of, he just wants everything cheap and immediate—as if we were running a fast-food joint. He doesn't understand about quality. He actually suggested we use canned mushrooms when he saw the price of fresh ones." Susannah smiled, and Duke did too, after a minute. "Oh, I know it sounds ridiculous when you get down to canned mushrooms."

"No, it's not so ridiculous, Duke. I know what you mean. But—"

"I know," he interrupted her. "If I pulled out now, or you two did, I'd owe you a bundle. Don't think I'm not aware of that."

"That's not what I was going to say." She paused a moment, stopped walking, and put her hand on his arm. "I was going to say I think you're wrong about Ivan not being interested in the restaurant. I think he's as interested in it as he is in anything right now. But he's got two things on his mind." She felt herself blush, but she went on. "Getting me pregnant and chasing women." She laughed self-consciously and removed her hand from his arm, but they continued to stand still on the narrow sidewalk together. "And if you think those two things are incompatible, you don't know Ivan."

"Oh, I know Ivan," Duke said. "I know about the women, too, Susannah."

Her heart dropped—it was true, then, it was like old times, nothing had changed. Tears came to her eyes, and she became aware that she had cramps and a headache. "That bastard," she whispered, and Duke drew her to him briefly and let her head rest on his shoulder.

Yes, it was a relief, a release, an indulgence, a profound pleasure to stand supported by a trustworthy, sweetsouled man like Duke. The ugly thought that had been circling all these weeks articulated itself in her head: *he* does it, why shouldn't *I*? She imagined going to bed with Duke, his plump, comfortable body, his infinite tenderness. Desire stirred her but she realized, sorrowfully, that it was for Ivan. Infidelity didn't interest her any more than divorce did—Ivan's unceasing faithlessness, in fact, puzzled her as much as it hurt.

They stood there a moment on the quiet sidewalk, and then she pulled away with a laugh. "But that's nothing new. And God knows it doesn't concern you. I'm sorry I brought it up, Duke. I just wanted to make you understand about Ivan."

He looked at her with an expression she couldn't fathom: tenderness? pity? "I'm the one who ought to be sorry, Susannah—laying all this on you. Obviously, it's much worse for you than it is for me—his absences and all that. God, I'm an insensitive clod." An elderly couple walked by, hand in hand, and looked curiously at them. Duke tipped his hat and smiled; they smiled hesitantly back and passed on. "And you, on the other hand, are a good writer, and you have those pretty long pigtails. I still think things will come right for you."

"I hope that's true," she said. "I do love him, Duke." She felt she had to say it, to kill off her trashy fantasies right there. Rapunzel, indeed. She was no princess in a tower, she was a whiny woman married to a philanderer whom she had no intention of leaving—an old story, older than Rapunzel.

Duke nodded and hugged her briefly across the shoulders. She had a sudden whimsical impulse to tell him everything, the story of her life—not just amusing stories about her schools but the bitter, intimate tales she had stored up about her early childhood, her parents' enmity, her wasted years, her doubts about Ivan—up to and including her twilight drive to Rosie's and her distasteful fantasies. But she stayed silent, feeling pleasantly self-righteous. Her refusal to be tempted was a point scored off Ivan. She imagined him at that very moment unburdening himself to some nubile teenager. She looked up the street at the elderly, hand-holding couple, talking with their heads close together.

But *that's* what I want, she said to herself before she ducked out from under Duke's encircling arm.

They caught up with the twins, who had found an ice-cream parlor. The twins and Duke had cones, Susannah had ginger ale and an aspirin. They sat at a small round table, on wire chairs. Through the window Susannah could see straw poking from behind the grille on a lamppost. As she watched, a sparrow flew to the post, perched, disappeared behind the wire—it was a nest. She pointed it out to the twins, feeling depressed; every damn thing, every last little bird, had babies. She looked enviously at Duke, who ate ice cream with such perfect happiness because he had two—two!—adored children who hung on his words and said "Daddy" in that loving tone of voice. Her stomach hurt. She went to the ladies room to change her Tampax. "*I fall upon the thorns of life, I bleed*," she thought as she flushed the toilet, smiling grimly. She was thinking of Ivan. For a moment—she looked at her braids and her flushed face in the mirror—she felt the bitter desire to keep the pregnancy to herself when it came, not tell Ivan—to pretend to menstruate, cover up morning sickness, suck in her stomach and wear baggy dresses to hide an enlarging waist. The idea cheered her up.

"Rapunzel!" the twins cried when she returned, their round faces beaming, ice cream on their chins.

"Are you all right?" Duke asked.

"I'm fine," she said. "I was just thinking I might like a cone after all."

The twins were overjoyed; they seemed to have inherited from Duke a delight in feeding people, and they insisted on taking the money up to the counter and getting her ice cream themselves. "Pick me out a flavor," Susannah told them, and they brought back Rocky Road, a flavor she particularly loathed, but she ate it gamely while the twins finished her ginger ale. Ivan receded from her mind, like bad news on the radio. She felt perfectly happy. "Please don't worry," she said to Duke. "It's temporary, this thing with Ivan. Wait till we open, he'll be all over the place." He nodded, and took a sip of ginger ale.

The afternoon had clouded over by the time they found Virgil's Antiques, where the cash register reposed in a lightless back room. Susannah played the minuet from *Don Giovanni* on a rickety upright piano in one corner of the shop while Virgil and Duke dragged the cash register out where they could see it. Virgil dusted it off with an old undershirt, and they gathered around it. It was a turn-of-the-century brass-plated model, with a raised design of flowers and leaves; the keys were white porcelain with curly black numbers, and it did indeed ring musically when the drawer opened. It was so splendid Duke bought it immediately, without haggling, but it was too big to go into the Volkswagen's tiny trunk.

"Put it in the back seat," suggested Virgil. "Let the little ones sit either side of it."

They tried it, but Duke couldn't get the twins' seatbelts to fasten. He shook his head. "I'll have to come back for it. I don't let them go without seatbelts." The twins looked solemn; they knew their mother had died unbelted. "I'll drive back tomorrow and get it." He and Virgil lugged the cash register back into the shop.

"Maybe you could come with me, Susannah?" he asked her as they got back into the car.

"I don't think I'd better, Duke," she said, giving no reason, thinking of her head on his shoulder. Duke seemed to understand. She half-wished he would press her to go, but he nodded.

"I suppose not." And then, after a minute, "I didn't know you played the piano." He turned his head to give her a grin. "Is there no end to your talents?"

"I only know that one piece. One more relic of my variegated education." She was silent. It had begun to rain; drops fell from a dull white sky like bits of light. In the distance, farther than they were going, the sky was blue. "I suppose it's appropriate that I should remember that particular piece. From *Don Giovanni*." She had meant it as a joke, but it came out sounding querulous, and when she chuckled to indicate good humor the chuckle sounded forced. She closed her eyes; her cramps had returned, and the heavy, tugging feeling in her womb.

Duke's rough fingers patted the back of her hand. "Cheer up, Susannah. It's not that bad." She looked over at him. "Is it?" he asked. He had eyes the color of sidewalk, a curved scar like a scimitar on one cheek, the beginnings of a double chin. The brim of his squashed-in hat shaded his face.

"No," she said. "Don't mind me, Duke. I get melodramatic." The twins, in the back seat, began to sing "Home on the Range," their childish voices missing the high notes. Duke joined in—badly off key—with an apologetic smile, and so did Susannah. The happiness she had experienced at the ice-cream parlor returned to her, and she thought to herself—singing as loudly as she could, to keep the others on pitch—how nice she would be to Ivan, how she would overpower him with kindness when they returned. She would behave as if they'd never had their quarrel, as if she hadn't enjoyed quite so much her Ivanless day out, as if she hadn't called him a bastard to Duke, cried on Duke's shoulder, asked for pity in a thousand little ways, fancied herself a Rapunzel.

But he wasn't home, of course. He came in late, after she was in bed—but not asleep. She lay still while he undressed and got into bed. He turned his back to her and sighed deeply: a sigh of satisfaction? dejection? fatigue? She didn't want to know, didn't want him to discover her wakefulness, and speak to her, and tell lies. She heard him go to sleep—in, out, in—and she turned over, gingerly, feeling her womb nip sharply at her, pulled the sheet to her chin and tried to doze off. But she had nothing to think about, nothing to clear her mind after the miserable hour of waiting for Ivan. She had always, drowsy in bed, enjoyed looking ahead and planning, thinking: *next year, next month, on Wednesday I'll* . . . But that pleasure had been taken from her, or been lost en route from California to Connecticut, and with it her effortless sleep.

Somewhere, not far off, a train was passing. She could hear its hollow, eerie whistle in the dark, and, closer, the patter of rain. *Next year at this time* . . . She couldn't complete the sentence. It used to be the past that wouldn't bear thinking of; now it was the present as well, and the future. She closed her eyes tightly and thought of her story, of sunlight coming through glass to make a space filled with light that was as thick and frightening as darkness.

The Silvergate Café was jammed on opening day. It opened at 11:00 on Wednesday morning; by 11:15 people were trickling in, and by noon they were waiting in line for tables. Ginger and Ivan dashed from table to table, to the cash register, and back to the serving counter, while Susannah helped Duke in the kitchen. They had filled the long delays with speculations about every contingency and elaborate plans for super-efficiency, absorbing Duke's lode of learning from the restaurants he had worked in. They even practiced carrying trays and assembling salads. But nothing had prepared them for the chaos—for people who changed their minds, who had to have the menu explained to them, who wanted cucumbers left out of their salads or cream served with their rose hip tea, and who poked their heads into the kitchen with compliments and good-luck wishes. Ginger came into the kitchen at one point, sweaty and disheveled, her green and white checked apron spotted with spills, and said, "Who would have suspected such a craving for rabbit food in these parts? It looks like every vegetarian in southern Connecticut came out of the closet today." And Ivan burst in, kissed Susannah and clapped Duke on the back, and said, "Fame and fortune—I just hope there's some more of that broccoli soup in the fridge," and sprinted out again.

Duke heated more soup, sliced more red onions, chopped up more green peppers; Susannah cleared the trays Ivan and Ginger returned, and washed plates and teapots and forks. The old-fashioned cash register rang cheerily. Periodically, Susannah went out front to the blackboard menu posted over the counter and crossed something off: the quiches went first, then the mushroom caviare, the fresh strawberries and Carla's zucchini cake. When she looked around the room at the jaunty plants and green and white checked curtains and wood-topped tables filled with people eating Duke's food, she returned to the kitchen and said to Duke, "It looks exactly like a restaurant out there."

"What did you expect it to look like? A nursery school?" He was in high spirits, his face red and his fresh-cut hair sticking up, but he stayed calm, and moved without haste from stove to counter, keeping the orders miraculously straight, smiling his crooked smile. "An opera house? An animal shelter? Here," he said, holding out a big spoon. "Did I get this soup too salty?"

But nothing, it seemed, was too salty, or too anything. The hungry crowds left satisfied, and at 2:30 when the last customers departed and the green shade was rolled down over the front door and the CLOSED sign went up, the four of them sank into chairs, looked at each other, and burst into exuberant laughter.

"I can't believe it," Ivan said. "We're a hit. They were eating out of our hands." He took off his apron and wiped his face with it. "They cleaned us out. Right? What's left out there? I'm starved."

"Half a ricotta pie, a pile of sliced onions, and some cheese," said Duke.

They ate the cheese with some wheat crackers and finished the pie, and talked about what had gone wrong and how it could be put right—all except Ginger, who wouldn't admit there had been a single flaw in the afternoon. Even the speed with which they had run out of things she interpreted as a tribute to the food rather than the amateurish bungling Duke insisted on calling it.

"If you're an amateur bungler, Dukey dear, then I'm Reggie Jackson," Ginger said, taking a second hunk of pie. "You might even end up converting me to this stuff."

Duke smiled happily at her. "That would be the equivalent of St. Patrick converting the heathen tribes of Ireland."

After cleanup, and after they had helped Duke set things up for the next day—he already had a system, and already it was inflexible— Susannah and Ivan took him home and then went shopping. There were a few necessities they hadn't foreseen: paper towels, extra spatulas, a longer-handled ladle, more sponges—things they could pick up cheaply at one of the discount stores on the Post Road.

"Poor old Duke—he's dead beat," Ivan said as they were backing down the driveway. They watched Duke go slowly up the porch steps, hanging on to the railing. His T-shirt clung to his back, his hair was shiny with sweat. He stopped to pet Keats, who was sitting on the doormat, then unlocked the door and went in. "Our spent and exhausted artiste must renew himself through rest and meditation for the labors to come," said Ivan in a voice that had become, somewhere between triumph and cleanup, hard-edged with suppressed irritation. "Wearing himself out for his devoted followers, feeding the hungry, giving drink to the thirsty. In other words, he gets a shower and a beer while we browse through the housewares department at fucking K-Mart."

Susannah, detecting malice behind the joking, laughed anyway, then felt she had to say something in Duke's defense. "He does work like a madman," she said. "As if all the customers are starving and their lives depend on Duke getting food into them fast."

Ivan looked over at her, then braked at the corner, looked left, shifted, turned the wheel. "I didn't realize the restaurant biz was like the medical biz—the waitress falls for the chef the way nurses fall for the doctors."

"Oh, Ivan, for heaven's sake, I only meant—"

He put a hand on her knee, grinning. "I was kidding, honey. Joke." Susannah experienced one of her brief flashes of hatred for him; they were rare, always a shock, always quickly over, but against her will they stayed in her memory. This moment would come back to her, his hand on her, his blue shirt, the bug-specked windshield, the mockery in his voice. "Remember jokes, Susie? Ha-ha?"

"Jokes are supposed to be funny," she said. Her voice was prim and tight. I'm a humorless prune, she thought. He's made me that way. I will hate him forever. But even as she spoke and turned to glare at him, her anger was drying up, dying, he was so beautiful.

"Aw, Suse," he said. His fond angel-smile lit the van. "I'm sorry. It's been a long day." He touched her knee again, ran his hand up her thigh. "But I think we're going to make it—at the Café, I mean. If we can only keep our tempers." He grinned at her, in complicity, marking the quarrel's official end. "I suppose it's too early to tell," he said. "But it looks to me like we just might stay in business."

Susannah remembered Duke's prediction—hadn't, actually, forgotten it for long since their talk—but the tense knot of worry it had produced in her began to unwind. "I hope so," she said cautiously. "It certainly went well today."

He laughed suddenly. "It's like opening night at a play, isn't it? We ought to be sitting in Sardi's waiting for the reviews. 'The real star of the piece was Susannah Mortimer Cord in the small but eloquent role of the scullery maid....'"

Her laughter sounded shrill and childish; she felt giddy with hope. Ivan caught the sound and reached over to tousle her hair. "You're so cute when you're happy," he said.

"I *am* happy, Ivan. I'm just as contented as an old sheep in a nice sunny meadow."

He laughed at her, without mockery. She could see in his eyes that he loved her, that all was well. They pulled into the K-Mart parking lot. When they got out of the van the heat oozed up at them from the pavement like swamp gas, and inside the store the air conditioning blasted them, but Susannah noticed none of this. The cheap chrome and plastic in the kitchenwares department looked bright with promise.

By Sunday, when Peter came to dinner at the house on Perkins Road, they were all exhausted and had to order out for pizza.

Peter came in lugging a shopping bag, with a huge bunch of daisies under his arm. He set everything down on the kitchen table, amused at the boxes from Pizza Heaven. "I thought I was going to get something wholesome—nutritious—home-cooked, at least!" He laughed, hugged Susannah violently, and shook hands with Ivan and Duke. Susannah was amazed at his appearance. In the three years since she'd seen him, he had lost weight, acquired wrinkles, grown a mustache. His hair was cut very short except for long bangs that made his eyes look more mournfully dark, and his face was leaner, with hollows that reminded her—strangely, for there was no other resemblance—of Edwin.

"You look wonderful," he said to Susannah, stepping back to study her. She shook her head, smiling; she was wearing faded jeans, a black sweater that, she realized belatedly, was thick with cat hair, and a pair of Ivan's socks without shoes—her feet hurt. "You do," Peter insisted. "You look terrific. Your ears still stick out. Just a little. In a very nice way. And I like the braids, not to mention the rosy cheeks. All this junk food must be agreeing with you."

He hugged her again. His easy demonstrativeness surprised her pleasantly. All the ancient tensions between them, any legacy of childhood partisanship and long estrangements, seemed gone. Susannah took the daisy bouquet and buried her face in the familiar weedy smell before she put the flowers in water, thinking: We could be any old brother and sister.

Peter's shopping bag contained four bottles of champagne. "I'm impressed with this brother of yours," Ivan said, but he looked disappointed. He was passionately partial to beer. "Champagne's the only thing to drink with pizza," Peter said, winking at Susannah.

Duke stood frowning down at the two pizza boxes—one with pepperoni, and one without—while Susannah put the flowers, in their mason jar, in the center of the table and went to get plates. "Look," Duke said finally. "Maybe I could rustle up some omelets or something. We've got eggs, mushrooms, some onions, I think—"

"No, no," Peter said quickly. He looked horrified at the possibility of giving offense, or of causing anyone trouble. "I wasn't being sarcastic, Duke. I meant it, honestly." He opened a bottle as he spoke, and tipped the foaming champagne into a wine glass Ivan held out in the nick of time. "That's the great thing about champagne. It really does go with everything. Hell, you two must have drunk nothing *but* out there in California," he said to Ivan. "What a life—cheap champagne, fruit off the trees, and eternal sunshine."

"I like it here," Susannah said.

"I miss it sometimes," Ivan said; she looked at him in surprise, but he kept his eyes on the brimming glass and lowered it carefully to the table.

They sat down to eat. The pizza was cold and oily. Only Ivan and the twins ate with enthusiasm. Peter took a bite, set his piece down, and didn't pick it up again. Susannah sat beside him, still bemused by his presence. It seemed a miracle that he was there—her long-lost brother, with his hair falling over his forehead and his thin brown hand keeping everyone's glass filled, elegant even in khakis and a boring rugby shirt. He had Rosie's dog-brown eyes, but hers snarled and snapped, while his were warm with gold glints, and sad as a bloodhound's. She remembered him as a boy, dark and small, always tidily turned out and always bringing home good report cards. How I hated him, she thought with surprise, looking at him fondly. "She's so proud of her big brother": it was her mother's clipped voice, out of the past.

Peter talked about his writer's block as if it were flu. "I was fine until a couple of months ago, and then I came down with this. I think I've been in graduate school too long. Or maybe I'm just not cut out for this kind of life."

"Want a job at a terrific little café?" Ivan asked him. "We could use another waiter."

"I could wear an apron that says 'For this I spent seven years in grad school?'"

"What *do* you plan to do? Teach?"

"Teach and translate, I hope. I've taught my way through graduate school, and I've had a couple of translations published. But—" Peter fluttered his hands and shrugged in a deliberately over-elaborate Italianate gesture, and said in a thick accent, "Sometimes I justa want to *fongul* the whole thing and travel and be—how you say—a bum."

Susannah laughed. "You sound like Nonna Anna."

"Honey, Nonna Anna had an accent so thick you could make a sandwich out of it."

"Our maternal great-granny," Susannah said to Duke. "She was the most wonderful cook that ever lived. Present company excepted," she added, raising her glass.

"I wish she was here now, to take a turn in the kitchen when my feet start to give out," said Duke.

"Why do you call her Nonna Anna?" asked Mary Grace.

"*Nonna* means Grandma in Italian. She came from Italy. What do you call your Grandma?"

"We call our Ohio grandmother Ricky, and our Florida grandmother Mimi."

"And we have one grandpa," said Mary Claire. "In Ohio."

"What do you call him?"

"Grandpa."

"If I'm ever a grandfather," Duke said, "I want to be called Grandfather."

"Like in *Heidi*," said Mary Claire.

"Your grandchildren'll probably call you Pops," said Ivan. "Or Pappy."

"I just hope senior citizens are obsolete by the time I'm over the hill," said Peter. "I don't want to be a senior citizen. I want to be an old geezer."

"How about old fart?"

"Old fart would be just fine with me. I'd accept old fart. Also old fogy. My mother says she'll never consent to senior citizen. She says she wants to be a senior illegal alien."

Ivan laughed so hard he choked on his champagne, and coughed and pounded the table until he recovered.

Peter refilled his glass. "Have a little more cough medicine, old sock."

"Decent of you to offer, old chap. Don't mind if I do."

The four of them kept steadily at the champagne, and quickly fell into a tipsy intimacy, while the twins pounced on the corks and the gold paper and took them up to their room for one of their private games. Susannah was relieved to see Ivan and Peter getting along so well. Their only other meeting had been on that dreadful trip east for her grandmother's funeral, when they had stood outside the lawyer's office talking cursorily about—what? baseball?—while she had stood by in her hot nylon dress wanting to throw up, to sit down, to collapse, when millions of unsaid words had babbled at her until she thought she might go mad, when all she could think about was the little bottle of capsules she had left behind in California, wrapped up in an old pair of panty hose in her underwear drawer.

They were talking about baseball now, complaining about the strike that seemed imminent. "Hell, it's going to ruin baseball," Peter said.

Susannah broke into the conversation. "You'd probably strike, too, to keep the free-agent clause alive. I mean, who wants to be pushed around forever by creeps like Steinbrenner?" Peter and Duke looked at her in amazement.

"When did you get interested in baseball?" Peter demanded. "When you were a kid you wouldn't have known a baseball from a grapefruit."

"I keep telling you I had a very eclectic upbringing," Susannah said, smiling.

"And we thought you were totally committed to other-worldliness," said Duke. "Unsullied by such harsh reality as George Steinbrenner."

"She is," Ivan said. "But she has these quirks." He finished a piece of pizza, pushed back his chair, stood up, and shoved one hand into his pocket; Susannah heard the jingle of keys. *Oh no*, she thought. "And now, good people," Ivan said. "I must be off. Out on my nightly rounds. I get claustrophobic inside on a night like this. Peter—" He held out his free hand, and Peter shook it, looking puzzled. "Come and see us again soon," Ivan said. "I'll see the rest of you later." He headed

162

for the door, not looking at Susannah, and turned when he reached it. "Anyone want to come? Sure is a nice night." He seemed to be addressing the hanging lamp over the table.

They all said, "No, thanks," and the words rang hollowly in the quiet room. They heard Ivan go down the porch steps, and then the van started up. Peter cleared his throat. Susannah felt depression and humiliation grip her like teeth, and she swallowed a huge gulp of champagne that made her ears buzz. Duke, at the other end of the table, looked down at her, but she avoided his eyes. The silence lingered. She couldn't believe Ivan had done it, had actually walked out like that, with his flimsy excuse, embarrassing her in front of her brother. What if one of them had taken him up on his limp invitation—what if *she* had? Would he have driven her around for an hour, making insincere comments on the beauty of the evening? Would he have taken her with him while he screwed some teenybopper in the back of the van? Would he have strangled her and dumped her body in the pond? She would put nothing past him, the son of a bitch. She unclenched her teeth and drank more champagne. She realized she was getting drunk. From upstairs, she heard the twins' record player: "Rubber Duckie," over and over. Duke and Peter began a laboriously casual conversation about the best route to take to the Cape, but it dwindled away, and eventually Duke went to put the twins to bed. "Rubber Duckie" stopped abruptly, and Susannah heard the twins protest, Mary Claire's whine rising to a scream and then subsiding. Peter excused himself and went to the bathroom. She could hear him urinate, flush the toilet, wash his hands; it was awful how every sound carried in this old house.

"The Cape's a hell of a place," Peter said when he returned. Ah. He wasn't going to comment on Ivan's departure; she didn't know whether she was glad or sorry.

"I've never been," she said.

"I had a memorable time down there," Peter said. His face was impassive, and she wasn't sure how to take his statements. I don't really know him very well, she thought. "It rained a lot. I didn't get much work done."

"How about your friend Terry?"

"Oh—Terry." He rubbed the back of his neck with one hand. "Terry's all right." He let his hand fall to his lap; the gesture looked desolated. "He's a nothing. A nobody." Another silence fell, during which there was a squeaky meow at the back door. Susannah got up, unsteadily, to open it, and all three cats entered, tails up, expecting dinner. They rubbed themselves around Susannah's legs, getting in the way, while she shook Little Friskies from a sack into bowls. She stepped on a paw and there was a yelp, but when she stooped to pet the victim—it was Keats—he was already absorbed in the food, crouched over the bowl with his head on one side, crunching loudly.

"Jesus," Peter said. "Are they all yours?"

She nodded, not without pride. "They came from California with us. Aren't they gorgeous?"

"That must have been a cozy trip."

"Oh, it was. We loved it."

"Ivan, too?"

"Of course. He adores cats." She remembered suddenly what Ivan had said, that he missed California, and she felt chilled. She shivered and sat down again, feeling the champagne. She wished she hadn't brought up the cross-country trip, those long dull days with Ivan all to herself. "Remember how we always wanted pets?" she asked Peter. "And they wouldn't let us have any?"

"Did Dad ever get you one? After you went out west?"

"No. We moved so much. And I was always away at school. That woman he was married to—Pattijean? She had a couple of dogs, those little snappy ones. But they weren't my idea of pets."

"He was married to her—how long?"

Susannah smiled. "Six months. When I was in high school. They lived in Mexico."

"Some life, Susannah."

"It wasn't so bad. She was nice, Pattijean. I always hoped they'd get back together. The other one wasn't so nice."

"Cheryl?"

"Cheryl Ann Peters. She was really pretty awful. She used to get her hair done every morning. A *comb-out*, she called it. She used to put on high heels and get into her little white T-bird and go down to

André's for a comb-out. Her hair was sort of pinky red, and all ratted up. It didn't look like it was ever combed. But I guess combing isn't the same as a comb-out."

Peter tipped up the last of the champagne into his glass—a thimbleful. Susannah went to the refrigerator for two beers.

"This Mexican stuff must be all the rage," Peter said, looking at the label. "Mom gave me one last time I was over." He poured some into his glass and drank. "You haven't gone to see her yet."

"I did," Susannah said, feeling foolish. She wished she hadn't admitted it, wished she were as good an evader as Ivan. "I drove over one night and saw her through the window and drove back here like a bat out of hell." His laughter disconcerted her. "Peter! You won't *tell* her, I hope."

"Not if you promise to let me take you over there one day soon. You can't keep putting it off."

"Sure I can," said Susannah. The beer tasted peculiar, after champagne; she drank it anyway. "I'm scared to see her, Peter." She hadn't meant to say that, either. *It's the gin talking*, her father used to say when he rambled on—with an ironic smile, as if he was quoting something.

"Scared? Well, yes, I suppose you would be. She is, too."

"I don't mean just apprehensive after all these years. I mean—oh, Peter—she's always so arrogant on that TV show of hers. Always laying down the law. Do this, do that, don't bother with petunias, don't plant blue and red together, don't try to grow tomatoes from seed. She gets so fierce about it all."

Peter laughed. "That's her gimmick, Susannah. Everybody on television has to have a gimmick—a *handle*, it's called. To keep people alert. Ward off the old TV hypnosis. So Mom *scolds* her slavering fans."

"Like she used to scold me."

"She won't scold you now, Susannah. You're both grown-ups."

"That's what I keep telling myself. Then I remember Grandma's funeral. When I saw her through the window it all came back." Just thinking about it was like gasping for air—like being in the humid suffocation of a greenhouse. "She scares me, Peter. Really scares me. Makes me shake. Gives me the willies."

"She was distraught that day, Susannah. Don't go by that. You know how she felt about Grandma."

"I suppose." She took another drink of beer; it was tasting better.

"I'll tell you something, Susannah," Peter said. His face was very serious, and Susannah sat up straighter in her chair, alert. Now he would say something important, she would learn something. "I've lost a lot of things lately. Friends. A friend, to be exact."

"Someone you loved?"

He nodded. "My life fell apart. And then I went to the Cape, supposedly for peace and quiet because I couldn't work, and I couldn't think. I couldn't live with myself." He took a deep breath and paused, fiddling with the label on the bottle. "It was awful there, after a while. It was—disgusting. I drank too much, for one thing. And I couldn't make myself leave. Then one day I went out by myself for a walk on the dunes. It was raining. I was soggy, and miserable, and I was coming down with a cold, and all of a sudden I said to myself—or something said to me—Peter, you shmuck, why don't you get the hell out of here, go out to L.A. and see your father before he dies? Because I said to myself that if he died and I didn't see him first I'd never get over it properly. Do you know what I mean?"

She nodded, holding her breath, and laid her hand on his arm.

"Well, I'm not going to do it," he said. "The hell with not getting over it. There are a lot of things I'm not going to get over."

"Oh, Peter." Her disappointment was intense. Any day now—maybe this very minute, while his children got drunk together a continent away—Edwin would cease to be, would become a speck on the horizon. "It would be wonderful. If you went to see him. I wish you would."

He shook his head. "Nope. It's too late. He's *dying*, Susannah. What would be the point?"

She let go his arm, and he raised his hand and rubbed his neck again, making a face.

"Your neck hurts."

"It's the form my cold decided to take." He sighed, drank beer. "Don't you agree? That it would only upset him, at this point? Admit it. It's a hell of a thing to do to an old man on his deathbed."

"He's not old."

"But he's dying, Susannah. Peacefully, you said. The last thing the poor guy needs is me popping up at his bedside to remind him of what he's spent a lifetime trying to forget. What he's *killed* himself trying to forget."

"Her," Susannah said. "Rosie."

"Their marriage," he corrected her.

"Well. Whatever." She took little sips from her glass, thinking of what he had said. "You're right, of course," she said after a moment. "It would be a mistake to go and see him. And I think I'd murder you if you wrecked this for him."

He smiled at her. "So. The old teams choose up sides again."

"No." She smiled back at him. "Let's go on strike, like the ball players." Peter's smile broadened, then faded away, and she noticed again the thinness of his face, how it was shaped like Edwin's. "You know, it doesn't make sense that I always seem to be at war with someone," she continued. "I'm really a very peaceable person."

"I know, Susannah," Peter said. "And that's what I really wanted to say. When I was out on the dunes getting my stiff neck and deciding not to take off for L.A. after all, what *did* become clear to me was that you've got to make it up with Mom. It's pointless for him and me— Dad. It would just be soap opera. But you two have a lot of years left to be mother and daughter. I don't know if it's Hollis walking out or what—Hollis, the guy I lived with—" He paused, drank, closing his eyes so that his eyelashes made two thick curves. She remembered how she used to envy those lashes, her own were so short and sparse. She felt them with her finger; they still were.

"Tell me about Hollis." She wondered how many times he had walked out before he left for good, if he had roared away in a van and not returned until half the night was gone.

"You're changing the subject," Peter said, opening his eyes. He drank again, and drained his glass. They had each finished a beer. Susannah wondered if she should get two more. It seemed a long way to the refrigerator. Byron jumped to her lap, settling the question, and when she petted him his paws opened into stars, shut, open again. "I will tell you sometime," Peter said. "But what I wanted to say was that I think it's important not to just let things go. Not to let things get lost."

"Sometimes there's nothing you can do about it."

"True. But in this case there is something." He leaned forward. "Listen. She's a very nice woman. Getting old—sure. And crochety as hell sometimes. And she can be a little hyper, too. Hopped up. She can wear you out. Lately, I've got to admit she's been a real *strega*." Susannah grinned, recognizing the word—one of Nonna Anna's epithets. "But she's a great old girl, Susannah. Think of the fun we can have, the three of us."

Fun. She had lived with Rosie for ten years, and she couldn't recall ever having anything approaching fun with her. But she said, "Okay, Peter. One of these days you take me over there, and we'll all kiss and make up." She didn't want to think about it, the actual scene in which these events would take place. "But not quite yet."

"Whatever you say, kiddo."

She could tell he would be leaving soon, and she wished he wouldn't. She still expected him to tell her something, to give her a revelation of her own—at least to stay, tell her about Hollis, about *anything*, to be there when Ivan returned so she could look up with an abstracted air and say, "Oh—hi," when he came in the door. But Peter stood up, stretched, rubbed his neck again, and smiled at her, yawning. "Good old Sister Sue." It was an old nickname, taken from a book they'd had years ago.

"*Bunny Brown and his Sister Sue*," she said. "Mom used to call us that. And she always used to say 'She's so proud of her big brother.'"

"Well, weren't you?"

"Yes, I was. And don't grin that sly grin at me, Bunny Brown. I also hated you like poison." She caught his yawn, and laughed at the end of it. Byron jumped down.

"Ah, Susannah." They walked arm in arm to the door, and out. "I like this house," Peter said, looking back into it from the porch.

"So do I. I love it here. Next time you come I'll show you the vegetable garden, and the apple trees."

"Your mother's daughter."

"Hardly," she said. "It's all Duke's doing, and Ivan's. I have a purple thumb." She held it up. "Ink."

"Amazing," he said, "that here you are, living in this nice old house with a vegetable garden, and running a restaurant, and writing a book."

His eyes gleamed at her in the yellow porch light. "My very own little baby sister."

"I'm going to stay here, too, Peter. I don't ever want to leave."

"You look so solemn. Like you're about to swear a blood oath."

"I feel like it." For a moment she thought how it would be to do it—to cut open her purple thumb and dip a pen into the blood. She gave a brief laugh and kicked a pebble off the porch, stumbling a little. From down on Route One, like distant applause, came the sound of traffic. The twins' plastic kite, caught high in the maple tree, fluttered against the branches with a trapped, tearing sound. There was a slip of moon, and the air was cool, smelling faintly of something sweet. All the elements of the spring night had a ticklish familiarity, reminding her of the New England springtimes of her childhood, and she felt a thrill of happiness. How odd, she thought, that any memory of that miserable time should make her happy.

They stood looking up at the moon, picking out constellations, listening as a car turned down Perkins Road, passed the house, and stopped at Ginger's. Susannah recognized it: Ginger's sister Sheila, the one with the husband who drank.

"Old Ivan is out late," Peter said. "I thought that might be him."

"Old Ivan leads a very complex life," Susannah said shortly, and Peter didn't pursue it.

Her happiness didn't quite dissipate; it clung to her like the effects of the champagne. She stood by while Peter got into his Volkswagen and started the engine. Then she bent down and kissed his cheek through the open window. He reached out and tugged at one of her long braids. "It's good to have you home, honey pie."

Garnet, the second waitress, started work that week. Susannah knew immediately, from the way Ivan pretended not to look at her, that Garnet was what he'd been scouring Connecticut for, that he'd be sleeping with her before long if Garnet was willing—and she looked willing, a jolly, busty redhead with a premature tan, a dirty mouth, and a heart of gold.

In mid-June, Susannah stopped working at the restaurant and began writing a new story—"The Cage With Glass Walls," she called it. She worked on it with her usual slow, dreamy obsessiveness, staring out the bedroom window at the green tops of trees, the bright blue sky, the sudden black dart of a bird across the light. The story inched along, wearing her out, so that by early evening, when she had abandoned her notebook for the day, she used to walk down the road to Ginger's to be refreshed. Ginger, home from work, would be sitting in the air-conditioned kitchen with her feet up, drinking Tab. She always complained, first thing, about her feet.

"Have I got corns?" she would ask, rhetorically sticking one bare, bumpy foot into the air as evidence. "I've got corns the way your cats have fleas."

What refreshed Susannah was Ginger's way of achieving instant intimacy with people, by the simple expedient of baring her own soul, immediately and without reserve. In turn, Susannah found herself confiding in Ginger, and the sea of the personal, the *human* that embraced her in Ginger's kitchen was as cooling to her hot soul as the air conditioning was to her sweaty arms and face. She had never told anyone—only Duke, who already knew—about Ivan's infidelities, but she told Ginger, hoping for words of wisdom. All Ginger said was what Susannah had been telling herself for years, but when Ginger said them the words took on solidity, and universality, and inevitability.

"Life is full of choices," Ginger said. "You take the son of a bitch with his faults, or you leave him."

"Surely there are other choices," Susannah said timidly.

"What? Change him? Don't make me laugh. Love him or leave him," Ginger said, and added, "If he were mine—" She shrugged and raised one eyebrow. She liked Ivan, Susannah knew. Everyone liked Ivan, especially women. She couldn't recall ever meeting one who didn't. Even Margie—a devoted wife if anyone was—had flirted outrageously with Ivan during that visit. "If he were mine," Ginger said, "I'd take him, all right."

Susannah nodded. "I guess that's the choice I've made."

"Don't look so glum," Ginger said comfortably. She seemed to find such limitation of choice appropriate—agreeable, even. Her own options had been as sparse; the one she chose had worked out just fine. Ginger cut her way neatly through a life composed of crises made the best of—like a tried and true old knife, much-sharpened. "It could be worse," she said. "In his own way, he's devoted to you, and you know it. You lucky dog."

In Ginger's cool kitchen, Susannah became a lucky dog, a woman to be envied because her husband, though unfaithful, was Ivan. Ginger might commiserate with her, but she respected her, too, for landing such a man. This was soothing, and so was its corollary: though she was a lucky dog, she had problems, too, and Ginger's sympathy flowed out to her, gathered her in, calmed her. "That's life," Ginger was always saying. It was her philosophy, and Susannah adopted it eagerly: life, after all, was the whole point.

"I wouldn't be happy if I weren't so miserable," she said to Ginger. "Didn't someone famous say that?"

She could see she was becoming one of Ginger's magpie collection of crisis-ridden heroines, and she looked forward, during the long, full, feverish hours over her notebook, to the aimless talks in Ginger's kitchen—about other people's problems, or her own, about gruesome operations and soul-wrenching divorces and troubled children, about high prices and recipes and the Silvergate Café.

"I love that place," Ginger said. "I'd crawl on my knees waiting tables for Duke and Ivan. I consider it a privilege to be working there—really, I do, corns and all."

They hired another kitchen helper at the Café, a young black man named Simon who hustled from refrigerator to stove to counter as if he were on skates. The restaurant continued to thrive; they extended their hours, serving afternoon tea and light dinners; they talked of hiring a cashier. They even had a "regular"—a thin man with a white beard who came in every day for a bowl of soup and said he hadn't eaten meat in forty-nine years. Kiki Sheffield ate there and told Ivan, who waited on her, that the food was fabulous, not so wholesome that you couldn't eat it. The contract came from Susannah's publisher, and then the check; she bought the twins each a bicycle, with training wheels, and put the rest into a new bank account, in her own name. The twins went to stay with their grandparents in Ashtabula for the summer; Duke drove them out there, with the two new bicycles on a rack behind the car, then turned right around and came back so he could be at the restaurant bright and early the next morning. Susannah immediately missed the little girls—the warm, fat bundle of one or the other of them on her lap while she read a story.

Ivan's interest in procreation waned. The fertility chart slipped off the bedside table and stayed on the floor until Susannah, cleaning house, found it one day and threw it out. Her own desire to have a child increased. The more she missed the twins, the more real a baby of her own seemed. She imagined a sturdy boy with Ivan's eyes and smile, or a wispy little blonde girl with long pony legs. She took to waiting up for Ivan, sitting in bed reading, kept awake not by desire—not only—but by the need for the grown-up lovemaking Ivan used to talk about, the act that would ignite the miracle that nine months later would nuzzle blindly until it fastened on her breast, and sucked, and began to grow into a person to love. This anticipation kept her alert for the sound of the van turning into the driveway. Ivan, returning after midnight without comment, was always sleepy, sometimes distracted, but never unwilling, and there were tricks to cajole him into enthusiasm. After he fell asleep, Susannah would lie awake a while, clenched tight around her need, and hoping with a fervor that was strange to her.

She took to sleeping late. Often, Ivan and Duke were long gone, the day already hot, by the time she was finally urged from sleep by the rasping calls of the crows that lived in the fir trees behind the barn, or by one of the cats leaping to the bed to nudge her. She would dress in a hurry, breakfast on tea, and sit down with her notebook. She finished the story one humid July afternoon, read it over, put down the pages with a sigh, listening to the stillness of the empty house. It was too early to go down to Ginger's, too hot and sticky to do much of anything. She decided she would go out to the garden, pick lettuce, plunge it into a sinkful of cold, cold water to crisp it up, make herself a salad, maybe—in spite of the heat—make a loaf of some kind of new bread they could have with dinner later, and sit outside with her feet in the creek while it baked. She stretched her cramped fingers, closed her eyes for a moment, reached out a hand to pat Byron who purred on the bed beside her, and thought: *Now, this moment—this is what it is to be happy*. And all afternoon, while she ate her salad and baked bread and read outside by the creek, the words kept turning and tumbling in her mind: *This is happiness, this is life.*

Chapter Five

In the Mirror

Never (thought Rosie) had there been such a glorious May, a June so filled with delights: the climbing roses by the porch, the foxglove and daisies and Canterbury bells in the long border, the blaze of poppies against the white fence, the early lilies and the late tulips, and Ivan in her bed.

She had never had such a lover, never been so in love, never known anyone so miraculously beautiful. It was, she told him, as if her life had shifted from black and white into technicolor: "Like in *The Wizard of Oz*," she said. "When Dorothy enters the Land of Oz."

He laughed, and ran his hand down her bare arm to her wrist, and circled it. They were in bed: it was only there that she told him such things, in the half-dark. "And who am I?" he asked her. "The Wizard?"

"Oh, no—the Wizard was a sham. You're the tornado, Ivan. You're what makes things happen."

He put his lips against her neck. "Let's make something happen."

"Oh Lord, Ivan, I do love you." It was curiously thrilling to say it, to admit to him that she adored him. It had been years since she had loved anyone enough to be compelled to speak the words. The more she told him she loved him the more she loved him; the more she whispered it, when their bodies were joined, the happier the joining made her. "We're flower and stalk," she said, with him inside her, his chest against hers, his rough cheek on her face—feeling a bit foolish, carried away by the bliss of it, and yet believing it, feeling it true—that she couldn't live without him; that, like a flower plucked, she would die if she were taken from him.

"My blossom," he called her, and he would move his lips down her belly to what he called her rosebud, and find it with his tongue, making her tremble and cry out more words of love, more, until she had said them all, and was speechless.

He came to see her, after that first night, two or three times a week, and his presences and absences created in her a compressed cycle of preparation, bloom, decline, and renewal that was like the seasons: no wonder she was worn out and on edge; no wonder Peter called her "hyper"; and no wonder, either, that her book failed to progress.

Her garden, though, was the best she had ever produced. She spent her daytimes—the long, empty hours of sunshine when she knew Ivan was working and there was no chance of his showing up—toiling among her flowers. She tended the vegetables, too; and the snap peas climbed their screen in abundance, the six kinds of lettuce and the parsley and cress burst from the soil in their bright green rows, the hairy tomato stalks reached out to each other over the sides of their cages. She consulted her records—the vegetables had never done better. Everything was early, everything flourished, the weather was perfect, vegetables and flowers and fruits lifted themselves rapturously into the sun. Even the elusive sweet peas grew this year as if it was an English sun shining on them.

She rejoiced in the flowers, but the vegetables were a superfluity in her life. She was too keyed up to eat them, and her only delight in picking and washing and preparing was to offer them to Ivan. He was always hungry, and particularly after lovemaking. "You have the same effect on me marijuana used to," he told her, with the hesitant grin he always wore when he talked about his wilder days. "I'm starving. And ex-ta-*remely* high," he would say, rolling his eyes at her. Once, at two in the morning, she made him a salad, going out in the moonlight to pick fresh lettuce and peas, and thereafter she couldn't look at the vegetable garden without thinking of Ivan, without a shudder of joy, as if the hot breeze that blew on her, and the sun on her back, were his hands on her, his body pressed close to hers.

The flowers, though, assumed an importance that she recognized but couldn't define. She knew she was obsessed, and that her acre of ground was becoming crazy with blossoms, simultaneously a gardener's dream and a gardener's nightmare. The tasks she set herself were enormous—absurd and unnecessary projects she should have hired someone to carry out. She conceived the idea of digging up a stretch of lawn along the back border of her property, a scraggly, rocky area with a rotting rail fence, where she had never grown anything. She dug out the sod with a shovel, and down on her knees extricated every last root and weed before wheelbarrowing it all, in a dozen back-breaking trips, to a heap behind the compost bin. Then she pried out the rocks, and enough small stones to fill her wheelbarrow twice. It was such hard work she sometimes wept as she did it, and wished she'd never begun, and longed to quit, but she kept at it, knowing herself to be foolish, because it made the days go by and because in some way it made her happy. In the fall she would put in daffodil bulbs, and she imagined the long, even stretch of them, yellow and cream and white, bending at a gentle angle in the breezes of next spring. For the summer, she planted a long row of marigolds and ageratum—plants bought from a nursery—an unheard-of measure, but she had nothing in her greenhouse to fill such a space. The small plants looked anticlimactic in the huge border, but by late summer they would be a brushstroke of bright color against the old rail fence, blue yellow blue. . . . The spiky little ageratum were the blue of Ivan's eyes, she thought, pressing them tenderly into the earth. "There's no fool like an old fool," she said to herself, but with a smile—remembering how she had made that comment to Peter when she heard of Edwin's marriage to a woman young enough to be his daughter. Well, she wasn't, thank God, old enough to be Ivan's mother—quite. And what heights of bliss fools could reach, she thought. A cardinal began his piercing dog-whistle, and she squinted up to see one, high in a tree like a rose. *Perfect happiness*, she thought, smiling into the sun.

She supposed she should have waited and dug up her border for the cameras. Nothing like inspiring her fans to hard labor; God knows, gardening isn't supposed to be *easy*. But the cameras, her television show, Janice and the rest of them were another world, mere memories of some other, saner, duller existence. She thought: *I'll always remember this, no matter what, the summer I was fifty, and foolish, and beginning to live for the first time.*

She didn't feel fifty. She wasn't sure what "feeling fifty" meant. Of course, her feats in the garden exhausted her, but such exertion would have worn her out at thirty—would have put *him* in the hospital, Ivan told her. Maybe her back bothered her a little more than it used to—had she always so relished the slow sinking into a hot bath? And she rested, perhaps, oftener—involuntary pauses in her furious activity when she sat back on her heels and bent her head over her lap, waggling her shoulders to loosen them up, thinking dreamily of how Ivan would rub her back for her later, letting the sun beat down on her neck, listening to a cardinal calling and a woodpecker knocking out a tattoo. Had her legs and feet always gone to sleep so fast? She would rise, painfully, stamp over the lawn to get the needles out, and get back to work.

"You're an amazing woman," Ivan said. He repeated it often, referring to her body, her cooking, her garden. "Just amazing. I can't get *over* you." She hoped he didn't mean: *amazing for your age*. She didn't think he did. He never mentioned the fifteen years between them. He seemed not to notice wrinkles, the faint jowly droop to her chin, the dark pouches below her eyes, the stringy backs of her hands. He never told her she was beautiful, as Barney had done; but that was all right, she wasn't beautiful, she'd hated Barney's effusions. *Amazing* was all right with her. She knew it was her energy Ivan liked, her bounce, her zest for living.

So she interpreted his remarks and attitudes as she bent over her flowers out in the sun, for what she thought of out there, during the filling of all those long hours, was Ivan. Ivan.

What was curious was that he never spoke of Susannah. He never even acknowledged, really, that he had another life with a wife in it. Rosie began to wonder if they were separated. She knew he still lived with his friend Duke the chef. Ivan was full of stories about Duke—

their seminary days, Duke's wife's death, the precocity of his children. She knew, even, that Duke was worried about putting on weight, and that, since he lost his wife, he showed an unhealthy lack of interest in women that worried Ivan, and that he had bought his house and his four acres two years ago for a mere $68,000. Even when Ivan told her about the restaurant, there were Ginger and Garnet waiting on table, Duke and Simon in the kitchen, Ivan himself as waiter, cashier, busboy—the general practitioner, he called himself, doing a little of everything. But Susannah wasn't mentioned.

Rosie knew from Peter, who'd had dinner with them all, that Susannah had been there; surely he would know if she'd left her husband since, but if he did he said nothing. Rosie felt she couldn't ask Peter about it; she was terrified that he would begin nagging her again about a reunion. Rosie remembered that not two months ago she had seen that as inevitable, as a sort of gift to Peter, who seemed to want it so much—even as a relief. Now the idea horrified her. She had always told herself, rightly or not, that the scales on which she and Susannah balanced their relationship—their non-relationship, she corrected herself—were tipped heavily in her own favor. Susannah, after all, had left her mother; there was no getting around that cold fact. No matter what shared misunderstandings and antagonisms had prompted her, Susannah had done the leaving. But now the scales were incalculably askew: Rosie had appropriated her daughter's husband, her son-in-law. Something inside her sank like a stone whenever she put it to herself like that—he was her daughter's husband, her lover was her son-in-law. She tried to keep it from her mind, along with all thought of Susannah, as Ivan did from his conversation, but it kept returning. She would be feeding the roses, or arranging the hay mulch around the sweet peas, and the fact of Susannah would edge into her mind— the grown-up Susannah, a wronged woman, a victim. She felt no joy or triumph at her theft of her daughter's husband; her joy was all for Ivan himself, the pure and perfect Ivan who was her lover; and her triumph was over her fifty years. Toward Susannah, what she felt was a kind of pitying horror—that, and a wholly inappropriate curiosity.

She couldn't ask Peter for information, and she refused to ask Ivan, but one day she stripped off her gardening gloves early, took a fast shower instead of a long bath, and drove to Chiswick. She had been avoiding that stretch of Route One between Perkins Road and the Silvergate Café, doing her shopping in East Chiswick, putting off a visit to her hairdresser, even canceling a dentist appointment because her dentist was located uncomfortably close to the school where she knew Duke's daughters were in kindergarten—Susannah's old school, of which Rosie had a hundred humiliating memories.

But today—it was an afternoon in late June, warm and sunny, and exactly five weeks since Ivan had first come to her bed—today she drove purposefully, consciously putting on courage, talking to herself in the no-nonsense voice she used on television: *don't be absurd, there's nothing to be afraid of, you're just going to the liquor store for a bottle of gin, you have as much right as anyone to shop at the Liquor Boutique.*

She was sweating as she parked the car and got out. Her heart was doing its scary thudding routine. She clutched the shoulder strap of her purse, pushed her sunglasses up on her nose, and approached the liquor store. She hadn't yet seen the finished sign on the restaurant facade—THE SILVERGATE CAFÉ in elegant italic, white outlined in black on a grassy green background. *Nice*, Rosie thought, trying not to give in to the terror the sign created in her—the sign and the glimpse she had through the window of people at tables, green and white checked curtains, a waitress putting down a loaded plate; not Susannah, an older woman. Ginger? Her impression, before she ducked like a fugitive into the liquor store, was of bustling activity, of another life: Ivan's other life, shared with strangers—Duke, the waitresses, her own enigmatic daughter. She felt faint; a pleasant smell of cooking came to her briefly, then disappeared as she opened the door.

"What can we do for you today?" The fat man, rubbing his hands, looked at her breasts.

"Gin. I need a bottle of—" She looked around vaguely for the shelf of gin. A pudgy penguin waddled back and forth on a block of ice in a cardboard display; behind it, gin poured from a bottle into white plastic foam that sparkled when the light hit it. "I'll just see what's here."

He was ahead of her, smiling to show eerily perfect false teeth.

"Beefeater, Gilbey's, Seagrams, we've got a special on our house brand here—a good buy. What do you need? A fifth? Or bigger? What're you? Having a party?"

"No, I guess I'll just—" She hefted a bottle of Beefeater off the shelf and took it to the counter.

"Got enough tonic? Bitter lemon?" he asked, rubbing his hands. There could have been a melon, or a baby, under his waistband. She imagined the flabby little breasts, the tiny penis hanging like a toy under the melon.

"Yes, that's all, just the gin." Her hands were shaking as she handed him a twenty, waited for the change. He put the bottle into a narrow paper bag and handed it to her with a mock bow.

"Come in again, mademoiselle," he said. She realized he must be about her age. In that instant everything gathered around her: the abrupt decision to drive out there, the heat, the café sign, the liquor-store man, the lack of lunch—and breakfast, too? when had she eaten last?—and she felt faint. She reached out for the package, then dropped her hand. "Here—are you all right?" He moved out from behind the counter, took her arm, and led her to a chair beside a display of dai-quiri mix. "Sit down here. Want some water? Jesus." He laughed a little, seeing she had recovered. "Pardon my French, but I thought you were going to pass out for a minute there."

She managed a smile. "I'm sorry. I'm so hot. I've been out in the garden all day." She raised her hand to her head, pushed back her hair.

"I could tell," he said, and took her hand, lightly, in his. "See that? Dirt under the nails—ground in. I knew you were a gardener. My late wife's nails were like that all summer long." He kept her hand. "Rest in peace," he said.

She smiled again—inadequately, she knew, without sympathy or interest, and using his hand as a prop, she stood up. "I'm all right now. Just a passing thing." She walked over to the counter and picked up her package, still shaky but hiding it. She felt breathless, exhausted, and her voice came out little better than a whisper. She cleared her throat. "I'll go home and have a cold gin and tonic."

"That's the girl. Best remedy."

She started away from the counter. "By the way," she said, and paused, but she had to ask, and she went on, holding to the back of the chair where she had sat. "How are they doing next door? The vegetarians?"

He shrugged elaborately, slowly, half-closing his eyes. "What can I tell you? They're making a go of it. *I* can't explain it. I ate lunch over there one day. I ordered this pizza made out of zucchini squash." He chuckled. "I was lucky to get it down, I'll tell you. But the place is jammed every lunch hour. I hear they're expanding to dinners in the fall. Plus entertainment. Probably some tone-deaf beatnik with a guitar. Listen." He raised one hand, as if taking an oath. "There's one born every minute. You know what I mean?"

"They're young people running it?"

"*Nice* kids," he said, nodding. "A girl, looks like a hippie, and two guys. Now the girl is married to one of them, so I'm told—but I don't inquire too close." He shrugged again, but amiably. "What can I tell you? Nowadays you never know. All I know is that they're raking in the dough."

She nodded; her throat was dry. She would, actually, go home and have a drink. "The young woman," she said with effort. "Long blonde hair? Is that the one?"

"That's her. Not bad-looking, but *skinny*. What can you expect, though, with food like that?"

She gave a wan laugh. "Well."

"Here. Let me get that door for you. You sure you're okay? Have you got far to go?" He was beside her, opening the door to a rush of warm air, the cooking smell again.

"No—no, I'm fine," she said, took a deep breath, and walked toward her car. "Thanks—very much," she said, not looking back.

"Hey!" she heard him call. "Next time you come in I'll take you next door for some rabbit food." But she didn't answer. She got into her car and drove away without another glance at the Liquor Boutique or the Silvergate Café, going slowly, afraid to drive, afraid she would faint. Oh God Oh God, she thought. What am I doing?

Ivan came that night. She had drunk two gin and tonics, eaten a couple of boiled hot dogs and some strawberries for dinner, and spent some time looking at herself naked in the mirror (small waist just barely gone slack, big peasant hips, hard white thighs, a freckled triangle of tan pointing between large breasts no longer firm, grimy veined hands with permanent puckers at the fingertips, fit to be held only by the obese Liquor Boutique man). Then she had two more gins. Ivan found her in tears, leafing through a *Countryman* from Spring, 1933: "Do you realize that millions of rabbits are caught every year in the steel-toothed trap, and often linger for many hours with shattered or lacerated limbs?"

"What's this? what's this?" he asked, meaning her tears, taking the magazine from her, wiping her face with his hand. "What's this, my little blossom? What's wrong?" His voice was tender, but she could tell—how could she tell? something in his face? a narrowing of the eyes?—he didn't like it, didn't want tears from her, was even—was it something in the set of his head?—disgusted by them.

She smiled woozily, feeling the gin, holding out her arms to him. "I had a long, hard, hot day in the garden."

That was better. He knelt alongside her chair, put his arms around her, buried his face in her lap. "Those are mighty suggestive adjectives," he said, and she felt his smile against her thigh.

She conceived the idea of going to England with him. *Taking Ivan to England* was how it first came to her, swiftly amended: they could go to England together, visit Silvergate, rent a car and tour the south, maybe drive up to the Lakes. Neither of them had ever traveled abroad. Maybe what she needed was a vacation before she plowed into her book in earnest.

She had had a phone call from Joyce, her editor in New York—a friendly call, just to see how she was, with no mention of the book. Two weeks later there was a letter, gently reminding her that time was ticking away against her contract; Joyce couldn't wait to see a draft of the opening chapters, no matter how rough.

"I don't think it's writer's block any more," Rosie said to Peter on the phone. "You have to *be* a writer to have writer's block. And I haven't got the faintest notion how to write a book."

"Why don't you try talking into a tape recorder? You can certainly talk up a storm, God knows. And leave it to someone else to transcribe it and edit it."

"You mean 'as told to'? Like a movie star?"

"Why not? In fact, you should get Susannah to help." A silence. "Mom? Susannah—your daughter. I didn't tell you she's doing a book?"

"She's doing a book. What in hell does *doing a book* mean?"

"*Writing a* book. She has a contract. Science-fiction stories. I guess I never told you she's a writer. Or did I? Actually; I didn't even know it until recently."

The flicker of interest she had had in Ivan's Susannah, in the blonde waitress she had fled from seeing, flamed up again for this new daughter, the writing Susannah who was doing a book. She remembered, again, Susannah as a child, her flatness, her lack of shine—had that concealed, really, the empty, receptive soul of a writer? And how could it be that what eluded her so humiliatingly should come with ease to her daughter? But did it? Maybe it was damned difficult, maybe the girl sweated blood, wept, tore her hair, vomited, broke windows, kicked holes in the wall over her book. Fought with her husband, stormed out of the house. Humiliation faded in the flame of curiosity. "You mean she's been published already? Before?"

"Short stories. Millions of them—well, dozens. I don't know. A dozen, maybe. But now they want to collect some of them into a book."

She would go to the Chiswick Library and see if she could find anything—wouldn't it be odd, to read a story written by Susannah? Like hearing a ghost speak. She tried to remember her daughter's voice. A whine, that was all. Screams, yelling, tears, and then a whine.

"But, Peter, what about—?" She wanted to ask, couldn't. We should drop this subject right here, she thought, and looked out the window at the flowered patchwork of her backyard; if she squinted it blurred into blobs of rose, pink, violet, yellow, twenty shades of green, like a painting seen close up.

"She doesn't waitress any more. Just writes. They've hired a college girl."

Did that mean she still lived with Ivan? Would Peter forget to tell her they'd separated just as he'd forgotten about the book? *I see Ivan all the time,* she couldn't say, *and he never mentions her name. Why? Why?*

"The restaurant has really taken off," Peter was saying. "It's strange, too, with businesses failing right and left—restaurants, especially. Ivan told me"—her stomach lurched, she pressed the phone so hard to her ear it hurt; Ivan—"the failure rate for new restaurants is something like 95 percent. But you'd be amazed how good the food is. Vegetarian *nouvelle cuisine*. Not bean-sprout stuff. Heavy on the goat cheese, the braised endive, the sorbet—you listening, Mom? Why don't you let me take you to lunch there one of these days?"

"No."

"She won't even *be* there. Who will even know it's you? Hell, you met her husband once for five minutes—right?" Her husband. "I'll introduce you as one of my professors. My thesis advisor."

She had to laugh. "Peter, maybe you've never noticed, but you and I look rather obviously related."

"Okay. You wear a blonde wig, and I'll wear a false nose. Or wear a black veil over your face like Nonna Anna used to wear to church. With a hole in front so you can eat."

For a mad moment she was tempted; then she laughed and changed the subject. "Please. Be serious. I really need your advice. Should I get myself a tape recorder? I'll try anything. Maybe I could talk into it and have it transcribed and use it to work with, like the scripts from the show."

"I thought you'd already tried using the scripts."

"I've looked through them. I can use them for the later chapters— the specifics. But this is supposed to be half gardening tips and half autobiography, reminiscence—I don't know what-all. I thought I'd write about my father, about Silvergate." She hesitated. "I've thought of going over there. Going back to see what it's like and how it stacks up against my memory of it."

"That's a great, great idea. You need a vacation."

"I thought it might break this block or whatever it is." Said aloud, though, the idea seemed less attractive. Ivan was the point of it: Ivan. Not the book. Not hanging around England worrying about muttering her impressions into a tape recorder. "But I really couldn't leave my garden at this time of year," she said.

"*Hire* someone." Peter's voice was bordering on exasperation. Talking to her as she had to him when he was a teenager. "The damn flowers don't need you lurking out there every second. Any old anonymous arm can turn on the sprinkler and pull the weeds. Face it, Ma—they're not going to *miss* you. They're *plants*."

Absurd, how the words hurt. The pinks and greens and blues blazed more brightly than ever; she longed to be out there in the sun and the dirt. "I'll think about it," she said to get off the phone.

She did think about it, though. She let the book fade from her mind and thought about being in England with Ivan, alone, for a week, two weeks. She knew it was a rainy country, she'd even read that this particular spring and summer were the coldest and wettest ever in the British Isles, but she remembered nothing but sunshine, flowers, dusty garden paths, high blue skies with clouds like white roses. She would have Ivan all to herself. What fun it would be: they'd pay their £2 admission to see Silvergate—house and gardens, described in the National Trust booklet as "magnificent Palladian manor house, with extensive landscaped grounds; rose garden; topiary hedge . . ." And then dinner in a pub with Ivan, and a room in an inn with a big bed and an eiderdown and a little mullioned window to let the sun in. She felt a tremor of unease, imagining the morning sun lighting her unmade-up face, her mouth sagging in sleep. But she would train herself to rise early, she was used to rising early in the summer, and she would shower, fix her face, greet him fresh and energetic the way he liked her.

"Let's go to England sometime, Ivan." She tried it out one night.

"I'd love to," he said promptly. "I'd travel anywhere, any time. I love it. That trip cross-country—" He broke off, smiled at her duplicitously, as if that trip was their secret. "Name a place—anywhere. Pittsburgh. East Oshkosh Junction, Maine. England. I'll go—this minute."

"The south of England," she said. "We'd tour the southern counties. Kent and Sussex—there's an east and a west Sussex, we'd hit both—and Surrey and Dorset, and over to Devon and Cornwall." She didn't, after all, specify Silvergate. He would have heard of it from Susannah, and she didn't want to hear him say so—or not say so, either. "Wouldn't it be fun, Ivan? To get away?"

"It would be great, Rosie." He spoke with such fervor that she wondered what he needed to escape. Or was it enthusiasm for the idea of going away with her? Or both? She regarded him fondly, puzzling it out. They stood out in the garden. It was a cloudy night, nearly dark, and the light was slowly gathering up into the whitish sky. From the next street they could hear the shouts of children still playing ball. Ivan's blue eyes were colorless in this light—opaque and depthless.

"Could we, do you think? Could we really do it, Ivan? Just pack up and go?"

"I don't see why not. Later this summer? We could go to England. Or we could go to California. Let me take you to the Coast, Rosie. We could go up to San Francisco—it's pretty hot in Los Angeles right now, and it gets worse, but we could go up the coast a little bit, give you a look at the other ocean—the *real* ocean, not this tame little trout stream you've got over here."

"I thought you were a true blue New Englander, Ivan," she teased him, but she had to force a lightness of tone. She didn't want him to be missing California. "Weren't you born someplace like East Oshkosh Junction, Maine?"

"I'm homesick for the West Coast, Rosie." He was serious all of a sudden. He stood before her with his hands in his pockets, his face lifted away from her, up to the blank sky. "I don't know what it is. The weather, maybe. Everything outdoors. The space. I'll tell you, sometimes Duke's place really gets to me, all those little boxy rooms, all those doors to shut. And then the backyard. Except for a few scraggly apple trees and the vegetable garden, it's all bare ground. Grass won't grow, nothing grows but weeds. It's just old, worn-out dirt. And I stand out there and I feel as if I'm being pulled back, like a magnet. I miss the look of the place, Rosie. The look of it, the smell of it—I don't know. It's another world."

He stopped, and she stood silent too, possessed by the fear that he would hop into his van this minute, seduced by his own words to head back west where things grew and there was real ocean. It would be better, she thought to herself, if they haven't separated, if he has a wife to tie him here. *Don't go*, she thought. *Don't leave.* She squeezed her lips shut, afraid she would say the words aloud; better not to beg, she told herself, or to give orders.

He raised both his hands, suddenly, and ran them through his hair, scratching his scalp, rubbing his neck, running one hand down through his beard to his side and embracing her with the other. "But what the hell," he said in her ear. "Here I am, and I'm not going anywhere. Unless you and I take a trip out to the Coast. You say when, Rosie. Any time."

She leaned against him, amorous with relief. Her bear, her lovely, shaggy bear, with his bear hugs. But it was England she wanted to go to. California was for movie stars, for crackpot religions, for Edwin and his dreadful women. She and Ivan would go to England, maybe later in the summer after the royal wedding had absorbed the bulk of the tourists, maybe in August when England would be quieter, a paradise of gardens, a Garden of Eden. We'd have that, she thought, no matter what. (That refrain was beginning to figure prominently in her thoughts: *no matter what.)* We'd have those weeks together visiting gardens and drinking in pubs and walking in the lanes. And Silvergate: she imagined being there with Ivan at her side, and the more she thought about it the more certain it seemed that she could never visit Silvergate without him—the place all her memories ran back to, the place she would consider until she died to be her true home, the one she was exiled from. With Ivan, she could bear it. Even in the rose garden; even seeing how the ivy, with birds nesting in it, covered the side of the gardener's cottage; even going down the broad stone steps to the terrace where she used to run with the old dog— even there, detachment would be possible, but only with Ivan at her side. He was the one thing dearer to her than those memories. Ivan at her side—she'd have that, at least, no matter what.

She went to the library, and found one of Susannah's stories reprinted in something called *Sci-Fi Feast: Best Stories of 1979.* The cover was dark blue, printed with stars and, in silver, a row of names in alphabetical order down one side: *Susannah M. Cord* was there. The story was called "Songs Forever New." Rosie watched the librarian stamp the book and run it under a light that coded her card number and the book's number into a computer—the closest she and Susannah had come in years, she thought, first with mild amusement and then with an insane desire to laugh aloud. She carried the book gingerly to the parking lot, as if it were alive, or might explode.

Home, she got herself a cold beer and, sitting on the bench in the garden, opened the book immediately. Susannah's story began with an epigraph from a poem by Keats:

> Ah, happy, happy boughs: that cannot shed
> Your leaves, nor ever bid the Spring adieu;
> And, happy melodist, unwearied,
> For ever piping songs for ever new;
> More happy love! more happy, happy love!
> For ever warm and still to be enjoy'd,
> For ever panting and for ever young. . . .

She didn't recognize the lines, but she recalled, vaguely, having had to read the poem in high school. The lines reminded her of Ivan, and she wondered if Susannah had chosen them for that reason. She wondered if Susannah read poetry, if using poetry as an epigraph was a sign of pretentiousness, if Ivan had read the story, what he had thought of it, of the lines from Keats. It came to her, suddenly, that Ivan and Susannah must once have been in love, if they weren't now. She remembered how he had helped her out of the church that horrible day of the funeral, with his arm around her, protective, the two of them hunched together like old people, shuffling out the door. They took drugs, Ivan said—pills. Speed. But they must have done other things as well, laughed and made love and talked together as she and Ivan did. And other things? She wondered. Ivan might be a different person altogether, with Susannah. She pictured them—it must have been a scene from some movie, transposed—picnicking together by a picturesque river, Susannah all in white, Ivan with a crown of daisies in his hair, Susannah braiding daisies while Ivan read aloud from an old calf-bound volume of Keats.

She snapped the book shut, afraid that by reading Susannah's story she would learn more than she wanted to know. She sat in the heat drinking beer until the bright blossoms, and the bees traveling in and out of them with their metallic noise, and the sun beating on her head and arms, comforted her and made her drowsy. She was roused by Kiki Sheffield coming across from her yard with a plastic container.

"Pesto, Rose. I made you a batch." She set it down on the bench. "Don't you look comfortable. Isn't it hot?" She looked with admiration at the striped Rosa Mundi in full bloom against the fence, and put out one finger to touch a petal, a thorn. "Look at that. I've never seen anything like your roses. What's this one again? I can't keep them all straight."

"Rosa Mundi—rose of the world. It's supposed to have been Henry II's favorite rose. Henry II of England."

"Is that so?" Kiki's nut brown hands reached out again to cup a blossom, and she leaned forward to sniff it, then sighed and smiled at Rosie. "Your garden is amazing this year. I wish I had more time to put into ours. Margaret's having her baby, you know, in October, and I've just been on pins and needles."

"The first grandchild, Kiki," said Rosie, rising from her bench with the beer bottle in her hand. She took a swallow, emptied it. "You'll get used to it. Or so they tell me." She started toward the house; she didn't want to talk to Kiki.

"Lord, I hope so. I'm a bundle of nerves. And there's so much to get ready, I'm worn out. Margaret can't do much, she's just huge." There was pride in her voice, and a dash of triumph over Rosie's grand-childlessness. She put out a hand to keep Rosie there. "You know, I've been meaning to tell you, Rose. I ate at that restaurant—the one your daughter and her husband run? Twice, in fact. And it's *just fantastic*." She had a way of emphasizing and prolonging certain phrases: she got her lips into position for the *j* before she uttered it, and drew out the *a*'s in *fantastic*. "Truly a marvelous little place," and the *m* in *marvelous* buzzed like a bee.

"So I've heard," Rosie said shortly, continuing toward the house, then remembering the book and the pesto. She retrieved them from the bench while Kiki went on.

"And such a handsome waiter. Lord, a regular movie star. Is that your son-in-law, Rose? Or is he the cook? I saw another fellow out in the kitchen, just a glimpse through this sort of serving counter they have—really an ingenious arrangement, and so tastefully decorated. And a pale blonde woman? Would that be your daughter?"

"I don't think so, Kiki. I don't think she actually works there." Even that was more than she wanted to say, and she headed resolutely—rudely, probably—toward her back door again.

"Well, you're missing a treat if you don't eat there," Kiki said. "Try the soups. And they have the *creamiest quiche.*" The last word rose and fell on two notes as Rosie reached the door. "When can we get you over for Scrabble, Rose?" Kiki asked her as she turned to say good-bye. "Ralphie keeps asking for you." A mischievous grin across the peonies.

"Oh, one of these days," she said. "I'm really working well on my book, and I hate to commit myself. I never know when the mood will strike."

"Rose, that's wonderful." Kiki trotted with tiny steps up to the door. "You never told me that you'd conquered your writer's block."

"It comes and goes," Rosie said. She felt uneasy with any lie, even this tiny, necessary, wishful one.

Kiki was nodding, still smiling. "It comes and goes, I suppose, like the fellow in the van." Rosie started to say something—her chest tightening up, the sweat coming out on her forehead—but Kiki reached a hand out and touched her shoulder and said, "Oh, Rosie, you're blushing like a teenager. Listen, I'm glad you're happy. I don't want to butt in. When you get some free time you let us know. Meanwhile, I'll give Ralphie your love. No, not that." She laughed. "Your *regards.* Meanwhile, enjoy the pesto."

"Oh—yes—I will. *Thanks,*" Rosie called belatedly, but Kiki was already on her way to her own yard. She raised one mahogany arm in a jaunty wave.

Rosie went inside. The heat—the heat was getting to her. And she should never drink beer in the afternoon.

She wandered around the house, drowsy, agitated, hot. God, the place was getting shabby, she thought. The rose slipcovers were faded, the woodwork chipped, the windows grimy, there was a hole in the bathroom screen. She should hire someone—get the place properly cleaned, at least. Her cleaning lady had quit six months ago, and she hadn't bothered to find another. She hated having people come to do things. Peasant ancestry, she thought, smiling, straightening the old Redouté prints in the living room, thinking of her father, her grandparents. Miserliness: that was Peter's joke diagnosis; she'd rather do things herself than pay. Well, maybe. But whatever the reason, she disliked hiring people. Even the Chiswick Garden Center men who had been coming for years to mow, prune, spray for gypsy moths, made her uncomfortable. She stayed inside when they came, restless, watching through a window to see that they didn't trample her perennials. And when she had a cleaning lady, she followed her around, making nervous conversation, giving orders that came out either too brusque or too diffident: that was why Mrs. Wells had quit, she was sure—not because of her back.

Still, the house needed work. She was letting things go, she realized. Barney used to do a lot; he would have painted woodwork for her, they would have washed windows together one Saturday afternoon. *It's so hard when you're alone:* the whine of self-pity in the thought horrified her, and the pang of nostalgia for Barney was a surprise. She dragged out the vacuum cleaner and did the rugs, and she dusted the mantel and stuck a wad of paper into the hole in the screen to keep the bugs out. Then she swept the kitchen floor, stopping in the middle to recall Kiki's words, *the fellow in the van.* Did Kiki connect him with the handsome waiter at the Café? Did Kiki know the awful truth? Was the truth awful? Kiki would surely think so. Rosie was fond of Kiki, but now and then she reminded her of her cousin Debbie. Boring, conventional, conservative, dull—the words paraded through her head, but at the end of them there remained the suspicion that the truth was, in fact, awful.

What am I doing? she thought. She left the pile of crumbs and dust on the kitchen floor and went upstairs to look at herself again in the bathroom mirror. *I spend more time here than the wicked queen:* the half-hearted joke didn't cheer her up. Its implications, in fact, added to her depression. Susannah as Sleeping Beauty, herself the evil mother who wanted the handsome prince for herself—a new twist on the old story. She looked at her face—tanned, lightly freckled, not so wicked. Harmless, in fact. Old? She stretched the skin back on each side toward her ears. She looked younger, slightly Oriental, fish-mouthed. She let it go, and the furrows returned from nostrils to mouth, the skin on her cheeks showed its pores, the corners of her lips drooped. She felt, tentatively, with the backs of two fingers, the faint droopy thickening under her chin, and tears came to her eyes: *it's not fair*. But it was, of course; it came to everyone, this face. It was just that she wasn't ready: *not yet, please, not yet, not me, not* now. The tears ran down her cheeks, blurred her vision; she looked better, blurred. Too bad Ivan has 20-20 vision, she thought. Ha ha. But the tears continued.

She made an appointment for a haircut. Her hair was too long, wild, weedy, and the length, she decided, dragged her poor face down further.

"Short," she said to Sonya. "I don't care what you do. Just cut it off."

She kept her eyes closed during the operation. "You want a color rinse?" Sonya asked her.

"No," she said firmly. She refused to start *that*. She was proud of her few crisp gray hairs, considered them becoming. She kept her eyes squeezed tight, listening to Sonya snip while she told Rosie about her trip to Puerto Rico, her daughter's school triumphs, her puppy. *Concentrate on what you're doing*, Rosie said silently. Aloud, she told Sonya about her writer's block, her plans for a trip to England, her neighbor's pesto. The blow-dryer was hot on her neck; Sonya hummed over the noise.

"You can open your eyes now, Mrs. Mortimer."

She opened them, blinked: there she was, with hair too short, too trendy, too *done*-looking. She said nothing. Her face was red from the hot air.

"It looks real nice," Sonya said. "Come and look at Mrs. Mortimer, Frank," she said to a colleague. "Isn't this cute? For summer?"

Frank said it was nice and fresh, very becoming. "You look about twenty-one, Mrs. Mortimer," he said, patting her shoulder.

Rosie smiled rigidly. The combined ages of Frank and Sonya didn't equal her own.

"You don't have to do a thing to it, Mrs. Mortimer. Just wash it, run your fingers through like this, and let it dry. You don't even have to comb it. You might want to blow it dry if you're going out, just to tame it down a little."

"It's a little extreme," Rosie said at last.

"You'll get used to it," Sonya said cheerfully. Rosie tipped her, and Sonya kissed her cheek. "It really looks great."

She drove home, patting her hair, pulling it down over her ears—in vain. She looked in the rearview mirror at stoplights. She didn't want to get used to it. She was afraid she *would* get used to it and not see any more how unbecoming it was. Surely that was how some women got their terrible hairdos. No! She would let it grow out, at least a little, enough to get some wave back, some fullness around the face.

But in the meantime there was Ivan: would it put him off? Did men abandon their mistresses for a haircut? She studied him closely the next time he showed up, two nights later. She hadn't seen him in nearly a week, but his face beamed instantly into a smile. "Rosie! It looks terrific. I can *see* you now. Before, all I could see was hair. Hey—you've got eyebrows, just like everyone else. You've got ears!"

He kissed ears, eyebrows, exposed neck, hugged her close, chased her up the stairs to bed. So that was all right. And it wasn't her haircut that had kept him away for six nights. What was it? He offered no excuse; one of their silent understandings was that he needn't account for his time. After he left, Rosie lay awake until morning, watching the sky turn pink, then blue, and thinking: what does it matter what I do to my hair? The days were dwindling down, she thought, to a precious few. Precious. Few.

July was fiercely hot, but Rosie tried to stay busy in the garden nonetheless. The trouble was, there was very little to do. She divided the early iris and fertilized the annuals. She watered things in the evenings, with a complicated arrangement of drip-hoses and sprinklers to suit the special needs of each area; she had once devoted an entire program to the subject, giving the pros and cons of drip irrigation versus overhead, and instructing her viewers, whichever system they used, to get out there and do it in the early morning. And here she was, sleeping through the cool morning hours, until ten, until eleven—until noon one horrifying day—worn out from the late hours she spent with Ivan; or, increasingly, waiting for Ivan.

He visited her less—erratically, unrealiably less at first but finally, as July pushed on, his visits stabilized at one a week. Usually. Once he appeared two nights in a row and then didn't show up for ten days, the last three of which Rosie spent crying, drinking gin, sitting in the garden in the sun—just sitting, until she felt sick from the heat, and tired enough to fall into a miserable sleep.

She kept trying to pull herself together. She washed a few windows, she picked herbs and lettuce and forced herself to make huge salads which she then couldn't eat. She returned Susannah's book to the library and took out a stack of murder mysteries which she read voraciously, retaining nothing, and left heaped up in a stack, forgotten until an overdue notice came from the library. She got up at dawn to watch the royal wedding on television, and cried; she was glad she was alone, sniveling over the pretty bride, the coach, the English accents, St. James's Park in bloom—and then, unexpectedly, she wished Barney was with her. She played Scrabble with the Sheffields one night, and when Ralphie grabbed her in the kitchen and kissed her she kissed him back, at length, desperately, tears filling her eyes, and then barely spoke to him the rest of the evening. She couldn't even look at him across the table. His fat pink lower lip was like a slice of some tropical fruit; his blunt, soft fingers were like the slugs that plagued her vegetable garden; his jokes and his risqué compliments sickened her. When he phoned her a few days later she told him she couldn't have dinner with him because she had strep throat, and when she recovered she was going to England.

She did intend to go to England. She taped a map of the British Isles over the North America map Barney had put up, and she planned out their trip. They would rent a car at Heathrow and drive south and east to Kent, to Silvergate; that must come first. Then the inn-hopping, and the pubs. She visited a travel agent in Chiswick and got prices on air fare, car rental, hotels. She found a booklet listing historic inns, another with pubs and teashops: there they were, the leaded windows and down comforters and beamed ceilings, the funny pub signs, the high teas, scones and tarts, the bitter ales. "Now when shall we go to England?" she asked Ivan, but her tone must have been too playful, not serious enough, because he only laughed and said, "You must have a gypsy in your soul, Rosie. All you talk about lately is traveling."

"I do mean it, Ivan," she said another time. "I'd love to treat you to a trip to England. I need to go over and do some research for my book, and I'd really like some company." She turned to him in the dim light.

"*Your* company, love," she said. He lay on his back with his hands clasped behind his head, and she snuggled beside him, ran her fingers over his chest and down to his flat stomach. "I'd love to travel with you, Ivan. Just the two of us. We've never been out in the sunshine together—do you realize that? Wouldn't it be lovely?"

He sighed. "It would, Rosie." Her ear was against his cheek; the words reverberated. Then he turned his head to smile at her, and rose up on one elbow. "Hey—speaking of traveling, I've got to get going pretty soon. Do you know it's one o'clock in the morning? Are you going to lie there and talk about England, or—" He leaned down and kissed her, fiercely, covering her with himself. "Or are we going to do something else? Hmm? My little blossom?"

She didn't care what happened, whether they went to England or California or nowhere, so long as he kept coming to her bed, bringing her his body, his smile, his soft voice in the dark and what it said. But she thought about it still, those long hot August hours in the garden listening to the bees hum and the flowers grow and the Andrews kids play ball in their backyard: England, and Silvergate, and those two glorious weeks she'd mapped out for them. Lord, how she needed them, two weeks with Ivan to herself. She didn't see enough of him. *In two weeks*, she thought, *I'll get him out of my system*. She didn't believe it for a minute, but the notion seemed to justify the time he spent in her mind, the fantasies she spun out in the garden, the amount of gin she was drinking. This would be her last fling—England with Ivan. Once it was over she would buckle down, get seriously to work on the book, live on her memories. She smiled to herself. The Rosa Mundi had faded, she would fade, what did it matter? She would go to England with Ivan, and then—it didn't matter what then, not now, in the sun, with the memories still ahead of her, still prospects.

Peter went to Vermont. He had a cryptic postcard from Hollis: "I need to see you," with an address in a little town near Montpelier.

"I don't expect anything," Peter said. He had come for lunch; the next day he would drive north, to Hollis. He and Rosie sat on the porch eating salad, hard-boiled eggs, and the goat cheese Peter had brought. "I don't know what he wants, probably something totally unrelated to—you know—us. Probably wants to know what happened to his sweater." He smiled in a way that was meant to be ironic, but the smile was so full of hopeful joy it brought tears to Rosie's eyes.

"You still love him, Peter?"

He nodded slowly, the smile faded. "Oh yes," he said. "I most surely do."

"Maybe he'll come back with you," she said, and realized as she spoke that she had had, all those months, a glimmer of hope of her own, that with Hollis out of the picture Peter would, maybe—a foolish hope—but maybe he would settle down eventually with some woman. Grandchildren are all I have to hope for, she had said to herself in one of her tipsier, more melodramatic moments, thinking of her lost children. But she didn't communicate this futile, insane, insulting hope. She said, "I hope he will, Peter," and closed her eyes, resigned herself for the twentieth time, and meant what she said.

"I can't even think about that," Peter said. "It'll be good just to see him."

Oh, yes, Rosie thought. I know all about that.

She liked the goat cheese; it was the kind they used at the Café Peter told her. They were getting classier and classier, he said; they were trying to get a liquor license so they could serve wine, and they would be expanding in the fall, if things continued to go well. "They want to serve dinners, and have a piano player," Peter said. "I think they're going to make it. There's nothing else like the place around here. Though I think they'll need to move, eventually, out of that crummy shopping center."

She waited for him to say something about Ivan, but his name didn't come up. She longed to confess. "Peter, I'm having an affair with him, with Susannah's husband. Isn't that dreadful? Isn't it awful? Is it?" As if she could say such a thing to her son, or to anyone. A priest, that was what she needed—and smiled, thinking of Ivan.

She gave Peter some cash for his trip. "An early birthday present," she said, pressing it into his hand. He took it reluctantly. "Please," she said. "Buy yourself some new clothes, at least. You've been going around all summer looking like a house painter. Look at you!" He looked down at his faded jeans and worn moccasins. "Hollis won't know you in this getup. And if he does recognize you he will turn and flee in horror."

He grinned. "Ma."

"Go. Right now. Get yourself something to wear. And have a good trip. Give my love to Hollis." She hugged him, clinging tight.

"Are you all right, Ma?" he asked, hugging her back, patting her.

"Yes, yes," she said, teary-eyed. "I'm all right, I really am. I just want *you* to be all right."

"You look like you don't sleep enough," he said, holding her away from him and examining her face.

She raised a hand to her cheek. "Have I aged this summer, Peter, do you think? A lot?"

He regarded her with amusement. "What a question. You? You never change. You know that."

"But I'm fifty, Peter. I must *look* fifty." She blinked back her tears and ran her hands through her hair—Ivan's gesture. "Do I? Do I look old?"

"What does it matter? You look like yourself, Ma. You look terrific, you always do. You always will, too. You've got the right bones, kid. What is this? Why the tears?" He hugged her again. "Come on, Ma. You look great. What's the matter? You don't have a boyfriend this summer?"

She sighed, and kissed his cheek. "I'm just worried about you, I guess, Peter. It makes me generally sappy. Call me when you get back from Vermont? Whatever happens?"

He promised he would, and left, swinging jauntily into his little car, tooting his horn three times as he pulled away, happier than he had been in months. She tried to comfort herself with Peter's happiness, and when the sound of his car died away she returned upstairs to the bathroom mirror and inspected her face in it. Not so bad, really. The tan, the freckles were becoming. She rubbed cream into her cheeks and under her chin, and dotted it into the spiderwebs around her eyes. She thought suddenly of Barney, of making love with him on the hearth rug, and she smiled into the mirror. How long ago it seemed, what leaps her life had taken since that cold day she'd said no to Barney. And what if she hadn't? Would Ivan be visiting her and her old, bald husband? And Barney would pull Susannah into it, too. There they'd all be: Ivan and Barney trading funny stories out on the porch, herself and Susannah struggling to be chummy over the dinner dishes in the kitchen. Rosie's smile widened. Instead, Ivan was hers. *Mine*, she thought, and went downstairs to make herself a drink. It was while she was sitting in the garden, later, that curiosity fired up in her once more, so violently she almost got into her car, again, and drove down Route One to the Café: what *was* Susannah like? what *would* they talk about over the dinner dishes? where, in fact, was Susannah? and what was she doing? It was only with an effort that she stayed where she was, drinking gin under the maple tree instead of going off on a mad, mistaken search for her daughter.

Ivan came over the next night. "You're a day early," she said to him. She had heard the van—its own mild roar as it turned the corner, she'd know it anywhere—and had hurriedly combed her hair, pinked her cheeks, and run downstairs to meet him at the door. "It hasn't been a week."

"I didn't know you kept track." He held out a paper plate covered with plastic wrap. "Here's a piece of Duke's vegetable pâté I thought it was time you tried it."

Her first impulse was to recoil in distaste. She wanted no part of the pâté, Duke, the restaurant—Ivan's other life. But she took it and thanked him. "Let's have it later, for our snack." Their postcoital midnight snack—Ivan's, anyway—had become traditional.

"Just try a bite," he insisted. "Here." He reached under the plastic and broke off a piece. It crumbled in his fingers, and a stringy bit of spinach hung from it. She let him put it between her lips, and licked the last crumb from his fingertips with a smile, but she could hardly taste the pâté. The texture was slimy, and she thought it must contain pimento, which she didn't like. "Delicious." She set the plate down, and raised his fingers to her lips again.

"Do you keep track?" he asked as they went upstairs. "Somehow I wouldn't expect you to. You seem so self-sufficient."

He was behind her on the narrow staircase, and she turned and looked down at him. "I don't know about self-sufficient, Ivan. I used to be. I suppose I still would be if I had to." She sat down suddenly on the step; their eyes were level, and she took his face between her two hands and kissed him. "But I love you, Ivan. You know that. I'm crazy about you. I don't know how I ever got through my life before I had you to wait for." She kissed him again, fiercely, and ran her hands over his bearded cheeks. "Yes, I keep track," she said finally. "I live for the sound of that damned van, Ivan. You can't imagine how I love you."

He squeezed in beside her knees on the step below and whispered, "I love you, too, Rosie. My blossom. My rosebud. Just because I can't get here to see you, it doesn't mean I'm not thinking about you. Jesus, Rosie, you're on my mind all the time." He put his hand between her knees. She spread her legs apart and his hand reached higher, his fingers stroked her gently. She took a long, ragged breath. "Come on, honey," he said. "Let's go to bed."

Later, they drank Mexican beer and ate Duke's pâté. It wasn't bad, she decided. The pimento was bits of cooked red pepper. "And is this rice? Cold rice?" she asked, holding up her fork.

"I don't know what-all is in there," Ivan said. He was eating a tomato sandwich, thick ripe slices with cheese between slabs of rye bread. His appetite always astounded her. He would eat anything, in enormous quantities.

"I don't know how you do it," she said. "Not an ounce of flab on you."

He grinned and slapped his taut stomach. He was naked except for jeans. "It really bugs old Duke. He keeps trying to drop ten pounds. Keep busy, I tell him. Come on out and play some Softball." Ivan, Rosie knew, had found a softball team in Chiswick—the Chiswick Champs—and played with them twice a week. "But he'd rather sit around and drink beer and bitch about the strike."

"Ivan, *you* drink plenty of beer."

"Only after I've had some physical exercise." He touched her knee and winked at her lecherously. "If you know what I mean, baby."

She smiled at him: how beautiful he was in the dark kitchen, with the overhead light casting shadows on his face. "Tell me something about yourself," she said impulsively. "Something no one else knows."

He sobered instantly, removed his hand from her leg. "Why? What kind of a request is that?"

"You don't have to if you don't want to," she said. "It was just a thought."

He poured more beer into his glass. "But why? What made you ask me that?"

"Love," she said after a pause. "I love you, Ivan. And you have this whole life apart from me. Your daytime life. I just wanted some little secret, for myself."

"Hell, Rosie—you're my secret." His grin returned briefly. "You're the biggest secret I've got, honey. Just sitting here in this kitchen with you is like sitting on a time bomb. You know that?"

"Of course," she whispered. She put one hand to her throat like a movie heroine who has just escaped strangling. Her throat felt tight. "How could I not know it? I think about it all the time."

He gave her a sharp look, his eyes narrowed and his lips drawn back over his teeth. She hadn't known he could look like that. "Well, let me give you something else to think about," he said. "Since you ask." He drained his glass, tipping his head back. She watched his beard go up and down.

She clasped her hands tight together, tried to swallow, succeeded. "What is it?" It would be something terrible, something about Susannah: he was divorcing her, she had left him, he had left her, he had someone else, someone young.

"This." He wiped his mouth, with his odd fastidiousness, on a paper napkin and looked at her. "It's funny you should ask that, because this thing has been nagging at me. I've had this awful impulse to tell it to someone, but I didn't know who." She saw that he was desperately serious, and noticed for the first time that the whites of his eyes were mapped with thin red lines.

"Ivan." She put her hand over his. "You can tell me anything. Anything." It astonished her, it touched her heart, that Ivan—even he— could have his private agonies. And why shouldn't he? He was human, after all. It struck her that she had been unfair to him, assumed him perfect, unreachable by what touched common humanity, happy and uncomplicated and libidinous. And had wanted him that way. Just as he had wanted her—she remembered his displeasure at her tears. What a farce all this has been, she thought. She pressed his hand between hers. Her love for him, she believed for a moment, would kill her with its intensity, the way it made her heart tick fast.

"I miss being a priest. Sometimes."

She dropped his hand, shocked. It was not what she had expected. "That's incredible!" she exclaimed—the wrong thing to say.

He was irritated. "What's so incredible?" Or maybe it wasn't the wrong thing; maybe irritation was better for him than blank depression. "You mean that I could be so horny? I like sex so much? You think priests aren't horny? Shit," he said, and drummed his fingers on the table, his palm spread out. "I don't know what it is. I always thought I went in for all the wrong reasons. Now I think I came out for all the wrong reasons."

"What were they?"

"What was *it*. There was only one—*that* one. Sex, of course. I left so I could get laid."

"Only that?" *Only*, she thought.

"No," Ivan said. "I wanted to get married. Have a family. My own family, up in Maine . . ." He paused. All she could think was: this isn't enough for him, then. This body, this bed, all this waiting, this love, wife, mistress—*mistresses*, probably—women worshiping him, legs spread for him all over the place, wherever he goes, women wanting him, me—none of it enough. She would never understand, she thought. She didn't even want to hear it any more. It was beyond her. He was beyond her, he was lost to her, she was one of his wrong reasons. "My own family stinks, if you want to know. I've got a brother in jail for rape. My mother ran off with some Army jerk—years ago. My father's a drunk."

She didn't know what to say. If she couldn't touch him, stroke his cheek, take his hand, press her lips to his flat stomach, she had no response. A silence grew between them. She looked at the map of England on the wall: south from Heathrow, through Surrey, the Sussexes, east to Kent. Ivan sighed, and she looked at him: dark beard against tanned chest, brown face, long slanted eyes lit blue. "Well," he said. "None of that worked out so well, did it? The family bit?"

"I don't know. Didn't it?"

"Would I be here if it did?"

"I guess not."

"I think about going back. Not into the priesthood. I'm not—" *Worthy*, he was going to say. She closed her eyes. He went on. "There's a place out in California—up near Tahoe, the Nevada line. A haven for mixed-up ex-priests."

"And you think about it."

"That's all. Just think." He sighed again, picked up a bread crust from his plate and ate it absently. The silence grew so thick Rosie could hear the old clock tick in the living room. Ivan stood up, finally. "Well. I'd better go, Rosie."

She stood too, and embraced him hesitantly. "Remember, Ivan, I do love you." The words sounded as meaningless as the tick of the clock.

"Yeah, I do remember that, Rosie," Ivan said.

He didn't come back. Days and days went by, and she knew for sure he wouldn't come back again. It wasn't just the usual long interval. Something was missing from the way she waited. The quality of her waiting was changed, clued in by something in Ivan's face that night, or his voice, or his fingertips drumming on the table. Maybe it was her question that had done it, or the impulse that had made her ask it. But her waiting lacked hope, and was transformed, finally, from waiting to the purest, most deep and silent despondency. *No hope*, she said to herself. Even the flowers and vegetables seemed hopeless; so many of them had reached their peak and were on the decline, withering in the sun of mid-August, drooping, drying up, dying. The roses were long gone, the day lilies and daisies finished; the columbines and delphiniums and lupines had gone from purple to brown. All the lettuce had bolted, the ripening tomatoes would rot on the stem—she no longer picked anything. She watched the beans dry up, the peas curl and bleach in the heat. She hadn't the heart for the usual hot-weather tasks: dividing and replanting and extra watering. The change of seasons, summer already beginning to be transformed into autumn, wouldn't bear thinking of. Such futility, over and over until you think there's no end to it and then—wham!—there is. And what was the use of it all? Maybe she should move south, flee like the rest of them do if they can afford it, go someplace where the seasons slow down into one changeless, endless sunny summer. The leaves of the maple tree, the highest ones, that tapped at her bedroom window, were already turning scarlet; now and then one fell, a last beautiful gasp on the sidewalk.

She spent her time with *The Countryman*. "There is a custom still observed in some parts of Kent," she read, "of eating pancakes as soon as the first lamb is born." It told her to use a monkey jack for stump grubbing, to visit an ancient monastic guest house in the Cotswold Hills where she could hunt with the Heythrop, to use Ephedrol for catarrh, to send five guineas to the Cremation Society and they would take care of everything. The green cover for Winter, 1935, bore a public relations quote from "the late Thomas Hardy:" he said, "It makes one feel in the country." 1935, Rosie thought. She had *been* in the country then, running down the stone steps with her dog, brushing her baby teeth with Kolynos, growing flowers from seed in her own patch of garden. Ivan hadn't been born, Susannah was an egg floating somewhere in her little brown body, this issue of *The Countryman* was crisp and green as a new leaf, and her father was sitting in his favorite scratchy brown chair chuckling at it, nodding, reading bits aloud.

Peter returned from Vermont and called her up to say he and Hollis were thinking things over. Hollis had left the woman he had been living with. Hollis was by himself, in a rented summer cottage on a lake. Hollis would be coming back in the fall, if everything continued to work out. Peter was so happy his voice kept breaking, and he sounded on the verge of either tears or chuckles, reminding Rosie of his adolescent self. "Peter, I'm so glad," she said, aware that her voice sounded odd.

"What about you, Ma? When are you going to come out to dinner with me? Go to a flick?"

She went. It was a measure of her hopelessness that she gave up, went out, didn't sit in her house awaiting the sound of the van turning the corner. He's back in California by now, she thought. Or back with his family: Susannah. One or the other. Gone, anyway. She was silent with Peter.

"You okay, Ma?" he asked her in the restaurant. He kept his voice light—to mask worry, she knew. She was aware her silences worried him, but she didn't know what to do about it.

"I'm fine, honey. Tell me some more about Hollis." There was a plate of fish before her, and string beans, and tiny red potatoes. Somehow she had to eat it.

Peter talked; she encouraged him. She hoped he would be distracted by his own voice and his own delight from her hopelessness. "Aren't you going to eat?" he asked her.

"I had a huge lunch." She pushed her plate away. The fish sat in buttery stuff, gone cold. She drank her wine.

At the movie, she dozed off, and awoke to see a handsome man tied to a chair, shot to death.

"You want me to stay overnight?" Peter asked her when he dropped her off.

"Now why on earth would I want you to stay overnight?" she said. She opened the car door, and the light went on above her head.

"You don't look good, sweetie. Are you sure you feel all right?"

"You're worse than a spinster auntie," she said, forming her mouth into a smile. That wasn't enough, she knew; her eyes had to twinkle a little. "I am just fine, Peter. It's hot, and I'm an old lady."

He grinned and punched her lightly, twice, on the arm. "You may be old, sister, but you ain't no lady," he said, trying to make her laugh, but she felt her smile slipping down, and she stepped out of the car before Peter could see.

The next day there was a postcard from California: Lake Tahoe, looking blue. "I thought about it some more," it said on the other side. "And here I am. Sorry I didn't say good-bye. Love." After "love" there was a line drawn, a blank space where the name should be. She had never seen his handwriting before. It was angular and choppy, like the outline of a mountain range, and he didn't cross his t's. That seemed odd to her, that bit of carelessness; in California, perhaps Ivan was the sort of person who didn't cross his t's. A different person from the one who had walked like a god into her garden that day. She kept the card by her bed, to remind herself that he was a different person, that if he walked into her garden now she might not recognize him, possibly wouldn't even love him any more.

She stayed awake all night, walking up and down the stairs, into the living room, out to the porch, back upstairs. The moon shone through the stained-glass window on the landing, depositing ruby and blue petals at her feet. She considered going out into the garden, in the moonlight. It was a fine, clear night. But she decided that was mad, to roam in the dew at three in the morning. What if Kiki looked out and saw her? She drank a bottle of Ivan's Mexican beer. There was a whole six-pack left. She would drink a bottle a night until there was one left, and that one she would save.

The next day she decided she had to see Susannah—just *see* her. She would drive to the Silvergate Café again. It was Sunday; the place was open Sundays, she knew. And closed Mondays: Ivan had come over one Monday afternoon, rashly—had found her in the garden, and she had hustled him inside. He had promised to come another Monday, and they would drive out of town for a picnic, but he never had. Well, Sunday: she would at least avoid the Liquor Boutique man with the fat hands like Ralphie's. Maybe she would even have a meal at the Café. The idea made her smile; she would do it. And Susannah wouldn't be there, anyway. But she might be. Or she might come in. She would just look at her, just see what she looked like, how she was taking it, Ivan gone.

The weather had turned cool and rainy, the sky a uniform, washed-out gray. Rosie drove slowly down Route One to the little shopping center. This time she parked on the other side of the Café, by Wendell's Tropical Fish Paradise. The store was closed, but the fish tanks glowed green in the window. It was late, the Café was emptying out. She looked inside, standing chilled in the drizzle. Only a few people remained. She wondered if she was too late for lunch, but as she stood there two young women went in, sat down, were approached by a waitress who took their order and walked back toward the kitchen with it. Rosie went in and sat by herself at a table.

It was warm inside; the warmth spilled over from the kitchen and the food, and it smelled wonderful, good brown smells that suggested soup and bread. Sick people could get well here, Rosie thought. People could come here to be healed, fed with herbs, nourished. The word stuck in her mind—*nourished*—so that when the waitress came to take her order she couldn't think what to say.

"It's late," the waitress said with a smile. "I'd better tell you what we've run out of." It was the older waitress, the one with frizzy hair. Ginger? She rattled off a list of things, consulting a blackboard on the wall. "I should go up there and just cross all this off," she said. "But I haven't had a second."

"I'll just have the soup, if you have any left. Some nice hot soup," Rosie said. She smiled, shivering. "And bread with it, if you have any."

"How about a nice hunk of oatmeal bread? And the mushroom soup?"

"Fine. Anything. Soup and bread."

She looked around. It was all green and white, like a spring garden. In the kitchen, behind the serving counter, there was a red-cheeked man in an apron. She heard him laugh, and then a young black man appeared, grinning out at the waitress.

"Didn't you used to have another waitress?" she asked Ginger when she returned with her food. "A young girl?"

"Summer help," Ginger said shortly. "She didn't work out real well."

"No—I mean a blonde girl. A young woman."

"Oh—when we first opened. Sure. She's one of the partners, but she doesn't work here any more, actually. In fact—" Ginger set down a bowl of soup, gently; it was filled nearly to the top. "She's actually a writer. A good one, too. She writes science fiction." Ginger set down the bread, and a little crock of butter. Rosie couldn't speak. This was where she should ask questions, but she could only smile and pick up her spoon, nodding, ending the conversation. The reality of Susannah—*one of the partners, a writer and a good one*—silenced her; it made her throat close up again. She closed her eyes and inhaled; steam rose from the bowl: thyme, carrot, mushroom, butter, something elusive. "Careful—it's hot," said Ginger. "Blow on it a little." She opened her eyes—what kind of restaurant would have a waitress who told you to blow on your soup? She smiled, slid her spoon into the soup, and blew on it.

She hadn't thought she could eat, but she managed to get down half the bowl, and she ate a little bread. She heard Ginger call into the kitchen, "Duke? How's that quiche holding out?" and Duke answer, "It just gave up." There was another waitress, a colorless little woman in a long green-checked apron too big for her—must be the replacement for the one who didn't work out.

"How's everything here?" Ginger asked her.

"Delicious," Rosie said. "This is very good, nourishing food."

"I'll tell the chef."

Rosie felt the soup warm her as if it were alcohol. It loosened her throat, and calmed her. She felt that if she could just have soup like this three times a day she would feel less hopeless; she might even get out in the garden. "Sick people could come here and eat this and get well," she said to Ginger. Ginger looked at her curiously, then laughed. "I suppose they could," she said.

She was reluctant to leave, and she ordered a cup of mint tea. Two women at the next table were discussing gypsy moths. "Have you seen Swarthmore Street?" one of them asked. "It's just chewed to bits. Devastated."

"They make me sick," said the other, a tanned woman who looked like Kiki. "Literally. They make me want to vomit. I don't know which is worse, the caterpillars or the moths flying in your face or those filthy egg cases."

Rosie would have liked to join in, but she felt shy. "I don't mind them," she would have said. "Sure, they're disgusting, but I have faith in Mother Nature. They go in cycles. Wait—next year there won't be nearly so many. I did have my trees sprayed, but I had to. I'm a professional gardener. I can't take a chance on having my stuff destroyed. It has to look nice for the cameras." She said this long speech over to herself, then again. The women at the next table had fallen silent, looking at her. Had she spoken aloud? Did *look nice for the cameras* echo in the air? She didn't think so, but she wasn't sure, and she smiled vaguely and stood up. Time to go, like it or not. They'd be closing. Ginger was up at the blackboard, wiping it clean with a damp sponge. The black man from the kitchen came out with a tray and began picking up dishes. Rosie didn't see a cashier. "Do I pay you?" she called to Ginger, and Ginger came over with her check.

"I'll take it," she said. "Our cashier is off today. That's one reason things are so wild."

"They don't seem wild," Rosie said earnestly. "They seem quite nice." She left a large tip—three dollar bills under the butter crock—and headed for the door. As she reached it, Susannah opened it from outside. Susannah? Yes. A tall blonde woman, hair in braids, wearing a denim skirt and a pink polo shirt. Edwin's long nose and blue eyes. Susannah? The tight feeling came into Rosie's throat and chest again. She couldn't have spoken; she could hardly breathe. Susannah didn't speak, either. She held the door, and Rosie passed through it, and as she did so it seemed to her that Susannah gave her a look of miserable, unmistakable, profound comprehension.

Chapter Six

Ashes and Sparks

By the time Susannah ran into her mother outside the Café, Ivan and Garnet had been gone more than a week. She was, Susannah told herself, getting used to it. The empty bed, the painting taken down, the space in the closet, the shocked, rootless feeling—all that was easy enough to get used to, the way an invalid comes to accept the hospital, the nurses, the injections, the pain, as natural and proper. What was difficult wasn't the actual loss, or the lies, or even the dreadful truths the lies had masked, but the knowledge of her own capacity for foolishness. *This is life*, she had said contentedly to herself: *this is what it is to be happy*—and all the while the truth had been going on, picking away at her silly happiness like termites eating the heart out of a beam until it's nothing but a husk, and can crumble.

But Susannah refused to think in such melodramatic terms; she would not consider herself a husk, and she would not crumble. She knew what she was, it was simple enough, she'd known it for years—a silly, blind woman married to a philanderer. Even Ginger couldn't turn her into a heroine—but then Ginger didn't know the whole truth. "So you threw the bastard out," Ginger said, and sighed. "I suppose you know what you're doing." Susannah imagined Ginger saying to people—to her beleaguered sister Sheila—"She puts up with his goings-on for years, and then all of a sudden, wham! She's fed up, and she kicks him out. Not that I blame her, looks aren't everything, God knows, but it's a shame." And what would Ginger say if she knew all the truth? Would words fail even Ginger? Would the mechanics of coping grind to a halt? The Dear Abby wisdom run dry? The rueful laughter stick in her throat?

Garnet had come over and told Susannah. "I think you ought to know," she said. "Ivan is having an affair with your mother. She lives over in East Chiswick? On this dead-end street? He's over there all the time. They go upstairs, and a light goes on, and then a light goes off. He stays late."

The conversation took place one afternoon in the kitchen of Duke's house. Garnet stopped by after work. Susannah had made her a cup of tea, had commiserated with her about her sore feet, had asked about school, and then Garnet had said, "I think you ought to know."

"How did you find all this out, Garnet?" Susannah asked her. Oh yes, it was true, she had no doubt of that. It explained any number of things; they pounded at her temples, those things, giving her a headache. She felt like throwing up. But she sipped her tea calmly, keeping Garnet in her stern gaze. Garnet was a pretty thing—young, with smooth tanned skin, braless bouncy breasts, big brown eyes, muscular brown legs and dainty ankles. *Cow*, Susannah thought.

"I followed him," said Garnet. She didn't avoid Susannah's eyes, and her voice was defiant. "I had to know where he was. And then I asked him, and he told me."

"You asked him, and he told you." A light goes on, and a light goes off. "He actually told you he's sleeping with his mother-in-law."

A smile flickered around Garnet's lips. "Yeah."

"He's been sleeping with you, too, I suppose."

"No!"

"Come off it, Garnet." Susannah wondered at her own bravado. She had never actually seen one of Ivan's teenage tramps before. Garnet was precisely what she had expected—a pretty, stupid, sneaky cow.

"We've never done anything," said Garnet.

"Then why in hell did you follow him, you little bitch?"

She spoke the words with clenched teeth, gripping the edge of the table. Garnet recoiled, and then the sly suggestion of a smile returned to her face. "I have a crush on him," she said. "Of course. Who wouldn't?"

"Don't lie to me," Susannah said, but she spoke more coolly. Her mind was racing ahead. He was sleeping with this waitress, sleeping with *her*—Rosie—God knew who else he was seeing, what else he was capable of. It was as if a light clicked on, illuminating her life, and she could see for the first time how impossible it was. Who could live like this? *I must be crazy.* And *her:* she remembered the dead-end street, the house, the flowers, the figure passing the window. The light clicked on, and the light clicked off.

"Only once, then," Garnet was saying. "Once or twice, I forget."

"Get out of here, Garnet," Susannah said, but the girl was already on her feet, on her way to the door.

"Don't worry, he doesn't love me or anything," she said. "I mean, it's not anything like that. He doesn't love her, either. He wants to stay with you. That's why I thought you should know. I'm trying to do you a favor." Her voice rose at the end, approaching a wail.

"Just get out of here," Susannah said wearily. She didn't get up; Garnet's well-meant malice took all the strength out of her. Was she, then, to be grateful for Garnet's prying? For Ivan's failure to love all his women?

"I hate you," said Garnet, and sobbed once. "I just hate you so much. You never even go to his softball games. *I* go to his softball games. You don't even care about him."

"Go *away.*"

She did so, crying and muttering. Susannah imagined her sobbing behind the wheel of her little Datsun all the way to—where? Ivan? Ivan would still be busy at the restaurant, and then he would—supposedly—be home, unless Garnet waylaid him.

Susannah knew as she sat there drinking her tea that *something would happen.* It would be like Edwin, finally, dying; like Margie—something final, something horrible. She wondered for a moment if she would kill him. The light in her mind hadn't gone on for nothing. *All these years,* she thought, taking the cups to the sink. Garnet hadn't touched her tea. Susannah found it difficult to think straight, though she knew she needed to. Everything whirled in her mind: Garnet's bouncy bosom, Rosie's house lit up in the dark, mother-in-law jokes, Garnet's sly smile, Ivan going off in the van, the Silvergate Café, Duke. Standing by the sink, she looked out the window at the summer afternoon and tried to see a straight path through the maze. She had a quick vision of herself sticking one of Duke's sharp kitchen knives into Ivan's beautiful stomach. The sun shone brightly, equally, on everything, and she stood there a long time without the faintest idea as to what she should do.

In the end, though, she threw him out. He came home early, with Duke, and while he was out weeding in the garden she approached him and asked him to leave, and told him why. She hadn't known, until she looked out and saw him bent over, in shorts, pulling weeds, with his whole filthy secret life curled inside him, that what she wanted was for him to go. But of course that was what must happen. It didn't move her or impress her or flatter her that he begged her to change her mind, and that he professed to love her, and that tears even came to his eyes.

"I'm so mixed up right now, Susie," he said. "Can't you see me through this?" She said she couldn't. "I can change," he said, and she said he could change somewhere else, she wanted him to leave. He said it hadn't meant anything, and she said it had meant everything, and she would be very grateful if he would leave. He could have money, she didn't care if he took every cent out of the savings account, so long as he left.

They went over it and over it. "I don't care where you go," she said. "Or what you do any more. Eventually, I'll want a divorce."

She left him in the garden. She went inside, to the twins' playroom, and sat on one of their little chairs playing with a toy tool chest, hammering in wooden pegs and screwing in plastic screws. She heard Ivan come in, go upstairs, open drawers—how sounds carried in the old house—then come down and talk to Duke in the kitchen. She timed it on her watch; they talked for eight minutes, in low voices. It seemed a very long time. She tapped in a peg. The hammer was painted blue, the bench yellow, the pegs red. She turned the whole thing over and tapped the peg through the other side. Finally, she heard Ivan leave—

not banging the screen the way he usually did, but closing it quietly—and then the van started up, and crunched down the driveway, those familiar, depressing sounds. *I must be crazy*, she thought, *to have loved someone like him. To love a monster, to be content all these years*, and gave the red peg one last whack that sent it skittering to the floor.

"Susannah?" It was Duke, at the door. "Oh Jesus, honey, I'm sorry about all this." She stood up, the hot tears running down her face, and he put his arms around her. She cried, it seemed, for hours. Everything made her cry: every word of comfort, every thought that came to her, even the sound of her own sobs. They sat in the kitchen, in the rocking chairs by the cold woodstove. There was a plant on it now, a nice old sansevieria Duke had had for years; the sight of it made fresh tears come, and so did the cup of coffee Duke made for her after a while, and the plate of fruit and cheese he set out.

"It'll do you good to eat, Susannah," he said, and, sitting down at the table, he began to nibble cheese, looking over at her in a worried way. The late afternoon sun shone through the window in a stripe across his pink cheeks. "Come on. It's good Vermont cheddar and nice fresh grapes. Here. Have a peach, at least." He cut one in half and held part of it out to her, biting into the other half himself.

She couldn't help smiling. She took a fresh tissue from the box Duke had provided, wiped her eyes and blew her nose twice. He continued to watch her steadily, eating fruit. "Wait," he said, and got up to wet a dish towel with cold water from the sink and kneel beside her with it. "Wipe your face with this," he instructed, and then did it for her, gently, as if she was one of the twins and had fallen off her bike.

"Duke," she said, leaning her face against the rough cloth, inhaling the faint bleach odor, and the curious warm-bread smell that was Duke. "I'm sorry to be such a pain."

"You're not."

He patted her shoulder. She took the towel away and looked at him. "I don't know what I'm going to do. Can I stay here until I figure things out?"

"Susannah! Of course you can. How can you even ask?"

She gave a long, shuddering sigh, and stood up, leaning on him. She had a vague idea that she should do something, reject his hospitality or at least prove herself worthy of it: do the dishes? call a lawyer? get a job? "I suppose I had a nerve," she said. "Throwing him out of your house. He's your friend, after all."

"You're my friend, too, Susannah. You know that."

"I hope so."

"You *know* that," he said, and made her sit back down at the table and drink coffee.

"I must look a sight."

"You look all sort of flushed and pretty," he told her.

"Oh, stop."

"No—you do. Except your nose is kind of red. And your eyes are pink."

She laughed and drank more coffee. It was black and strong. She hardly ever drank coffee, and it seemed to go straight from her stomach to her brain, clearing it. She started to speak, but he stopped her.

"You don't need to think about what you're going to do yet. Don't worry about anything. Stay here and take it easy. Stay as long as you want. Hell, stay forever." She gave him a quick look, and touched one of her long braids. Rapunzel, she thought. "The twins'll be back in a couple of weeks," he said hurriedly. "It would be nice having you here. They'd sure miss you if you left."

"I could go to Ginger's," she said, feeling she must. She started to get up again. He put one finger on her wrist, and dropped a bunch of grapes into her palm.

"Stay here, Susannah. We're friends. This has been your home. Please."

"All right. I will, then." She ate a couple of grapes, to please him, and cut herself a piece of cheese. "And thanks, Duke," she added, taking pains to keep the disappointment out of her voice, and the fresh jolt of misery that choked her, so that the cheese stuck in her throat and she had to will more tears not to come.

Ivan left for California two days later. He phoned Duke at the restaurant, and Duke passed the news to Susannah, along with the fact that Garnet had gone with him. She took the news out to the porch, where she sat with her feet up on the rail, chewing her cuticles and contemplating the view of road, brook, trees, and beyond them the gently meandering smoke from the factory.

That was it, then—the black hole gaping, the nightmare come true. She had told him to get out, and he had gone, headed west with a teenage waitress—such docility, such last-minute regard for his wife's wishes. She imagined him and Garnet on the van's narrow bed, the fierce lovemaking when they stopped for the night at campsites in Tennessee, in Louisiana, in Texas. She hoped Garnet's raunchy good nature disguised the soul of an axe-murderess.

Duke stood in the doorway, keeping her silent company, and then he came out and sat on the railing facing her. "They're not going to L.A.," he said after a minute. "They're heading for someplace up near the Nevada border."

"Spare me the details," Susannah said, meaning to sound merely sardonic and detached, but her voice came out harsh, and Duke winced, mumbled "Sorry," and went back inside, leaving her feeling lost, and sad, with the urge to throw something.

She took down the "Cloud House" painting and carried it up to the attic, leaning it against a dusty pile of boxes. She wondered how long it would take for the painting to get its own dust covering, how long before it was just another old piece of attic junk, like the bushel basket full of spidery mason jars, or the stack of rotting leather suitcases. The wall in the bedroom looked huge and bare. Lying there at night waiting for sleep, with the cats stretched out, hot, on the floor or on the windowsills, she was conscious of the empty wall, and she decided she would, in time, get to like it better—far better—than the cheap prettiness of Ivan's painting.

But it didn't help her to sleep—that blankness, and the blankness all around. The old litanies, the beautiful words, the bits of poems, none of it helped: Sri Lanka, Sri Lanka, willow-wood, prairie, heliotrope, mallow pink, season of mists and mellow fruitfulness. . . . They no longer hypnotized her, conjuring up the visions that entered her dreams and, eventually, her stories. And her old reveries of Silvergate, plagiarized from her mother's memories, didn't help either: the roses, the hedge clipped into turrets, the goldfish pond and the lilies, all seemed irrelevant, more distant than Pemberley. She lay awake, crying sometimes, or trying to plot herself a future, more often simply lying with her eyes open and her mind numb. The house was so still she could hear, from down the hall, Duke turn in his sleep.

Duke became hesitant with her, and shy. He was, she knew, worried about the fate of the Café. She told him not to be, that the capital was hers, and that she still considered them partners. Ivan could fend for himself; as for her, she had bound herself up with the Silvergate Café and she would gladly, willingly, stay bound.

"The money is there," she said to Duke. "And I'm no business genius, but it's obvious that it's not going to be long before we start pulling in a profit—especially if we expand in the fall. I'm not worried."

"All the same," he said. "We should have a lawyer. Get it all put into writing."

"I don't really believe you're going to cheat me, Duke." Susannah wondered whether Duke had ever read *Bleak House*, and imagined him explaining earnestly to some Vholes, or Tulkinghorn, the tangled tale of Susannah and Ivan and Duke and the Silvergate Café.

"You never know," he said stubbornly.

"Yes, you do," she said, and smiled. "Sometimes you really do."

It struck her, talking to Duke, that she should tell Peter, and her father, about Ivan's departure. A broken marriage, like a death in the family, was an event that had to be communicated. Peter, however, had gone to Vermont to work on his dissertation; another friend, with another rustic cottage, had invited him. Not that she could have told him anything but the bare bones of the truth; how do you tell your brother that your mother has been sleeping with your husband? It was like that old song, "I'm My Own Grandpa." Edwin used to sing it to her; she had a vivid memory of him sitting in a camp chair somewhere—in Mexico?—with a drink in his hand and his head thrown back, singing.

That evening she telephoned Edwin, intending to tell him about the breakup, but he couldn't come to the phone, he was sedated, he was having a bad night.

"Nothing out of the ordinary," Mrs. Panza said. "Just pain."

Just pain. Susannah hung up, knowing she couldn't have told him and added to it. She remembered the tears in his eyes when she had promised to give him a grandchild, the slackness of his cheek when she wiped the tears with her finger. She was tempted, for one weak, perverse moment, to fly out to California, kneel by Edwin's bed, and cry—just cry into his shoulder, blubbering "Daddy," for the comfort of his trembly hand patting her back, his reedy voice breaking into some corny old song to cheer her up.

Duke hired a new waitress, a friend of Ginger's called Lois. "She's forty-one, and she's got three kids," Duke said.

"You're not going to run off to California with her?"

"I'm not going anywhere," he said, not smiling. She laughed, inappropriately, in confusion, and changed the subject. It was easy, now that they lived alone together, to stumble close to what wasn't going to be said.

The summer days went by, long, slow, hot, silent days that seemed to Susannah unreal, days that hovered like bees, tentative and waiting. The longer hours kept Duke later at the Café—that, or Susannah's desperately faked good humor—and when he did come home, at night, the house felt huge around them. Ginger kept inviting the two of them down to dinner at her place that first week, and they accepted each time, as if their crisis was so immense it precluded normal life. It was the house's silence they were fleeing from, and the awkward intimacies it pressed on them.

"You should marry Duke," Ginger said bluntly to Susannah after dinner one night. Duke was watching the Yankees on Ginger's color TV, and she and Susannah sat in the kitchen over second cups of tea. The joint grumblings of the dishwasher and the air conditioner enclosed their words.

Susannah flushed, and decided to be honest. "I think about it sometimes, Ginger," she said, and wished immediately that she hadn't. No: this was nobody's business; she briefly disliked Ginger's warm niceness that had dragged even that much out of her. "But it's absurd," she amended. "Duke and I are friends. I think about it only because I feel so lost. It's hard to be married so long and then all of a sudden be alone."

"Don't I know," Ginger said with feeling.

"But I'll get used to it."

"I'm sure you will. I did, in about three days. Got to like it a lot." Ginger grinned, leaned forward and said softly, "But I still think it's a good idea." She jerked her head toward the other room where Duke sat in front of the television.

She and Ginger went in to join him. The Red Sox beat the Yankees 4–2.

"Damn," said Duke, then got up to snap off the television. "But I can't complain. At least the strike is over."

He was getting paunchy, Susannah saw. She thought of Ivan's perfect movie-star body and couldn't tell whether the emotion she felt was revulsion or longing. The paunch made Duke seem genuine—not someone she'd made up. Her fantasies about Duke were all of comfort, ease, simple pleasure. She must have been crazy to love Ivan; how sane it would be to love Duke. And how right, of course, Ginger was. And yet there was Duke, as brotherly as Peter, patting her shoulder and making her tea, and going off to bed each night early, with a smile at her that was almost apologetic, faintly embarrassed, fond maybe, but certainly not inviting. The idea stuck in her mind, though, tempting her, affording a kind of comfort—assuring her, if nothing else, that she was sane, and capable of judgment. Sometimes she summoned up the fantasies herself; sometimes when they filled her head she tried to force them out, but they persisted no matter what she did, inventing themselves right along with scenes for her story.

Her story: it was another new one, about a science-fiction writer whose tales came true. It was called "Ashes and Sparks," a phrase from a poem she had read long ago. After the first few rough days, she was, incredibly, working well again, and the story filled her time, progressing with a logic of its own, originating from a part of her that was unaffected by events, a part that had its own life and its own emotion. She worked every day, with great concentration and very slowly, for hours. Then she went outside to sit, reading, on the ragged, shady grass by the pond or, sometimes, to work in the garden in the sun. She had to force herself, at first, into the garden. It was Ivan's job; she had driven him away, therefore it became her responsibility. But she was beginning to like it, at least in short stretches. She was getting a pinkish tan;

she had never had a tan in California, and she looked in amazement at the distinct white line on her wrist where her watchband went. She mulched the lettuce with straw to keep the moisture in; it seemed to flourish, and she was pleased when Duke said he'd never been able to keep it from bolting in August. She read somewhere that once a string bean is left to rot on the stem the whole plant withers and dies, and she inspected the beans daily, picking them before they got big and mealy.

The cats stayed near her, stretching themselves out between the rows and going to sleep on the warm straw. What a solace animals were, with their affections based on food and warmth, such simple, sensible creatures. She wondered whether Ivan missed them, driving across the country—into the sunset this time, how unpleasant it must be driving with the sun in your eyes—without the cats, without her, with only Garnet, a stranger; whether he thought of her weeding his garden back east, and of the cats looking up at her with their trusting yellow eyes. She patted them, murmuring their names, saying, "Hmm? Hmm, kitty-cats?" as if they might supply some sort of answer, but they only blinked at her, and when she squatted down to pull weeds they tried to climb into her lap.

She kept Ivan in her mind as she pulled weeds, dutifully, almost as though she was cramming for a test. It was vital, she thought, to comprehend Ivan, and what had happened. She wondered what he used to think about when he took himself out there to work in the garden. His deceptions, most likely; how to keep his stories straight and his women happy—all of the teenage tramps, the secretaries and hairdressers he picked up in bars, the idle housewives he amused after work or before dinner or whenever he could catch a free moment. She imagined him, during his five months in Connecticut, in a frenzy of lust, speeding from one assignation to another and then coming home to bury himself in his acquiescent wife. How she had loved him, that poor wife—years of stupid love. And then how quick the end had been—Garnet and her untouched tea, and herself crying in Duke's arms. She closed her eyes in the sun, and Ivan smiled at her, the tiny wrinkles fanning out from his blue, blue eyes. She remembered what a pleasure it was simply looking at him; he was like a god in the garden with his lean back bent in the sun. And probably, she told herself, he hadn't been thinking about any of them; the ultimate insult, that none of them—*us*, Susannah thought, *none of us*—mattered to him at all. Maybe he thought about baseball, or the California coast, or his childhood, or the day's take at the Café. *He doesn't love me, he doesn't love any of us*, Garnet had said. *It's you he loves.* Had she said that? If so, she had been wrong. Poor stupid Garnet. What would become of that poor cow? She hoped they drove each other crazy. *Your husband is sleeping with your mother*, she had said. A bombshell. Susannah told herself, from time to time, that she should talk about it with someone. Was it healthy to keep such a loaded fact to herself? Shouldn't she defuse it by spreading it thinner, collecting reactions and opinions and advice? Should she at least give Ginger a crack at it? But she kept thinking: not yet. She had never, she felt, needed so badly to spend time alone. She had never had so much thinking to do, so many threads to sort, and the most extravagantly tangled thread, the one that kept knotting itself in her mind, was the one Garnet had presented her with—the unthinkable fact of Ivan's affair with Rosie.

She thinned the lettuce and weeded the beans, and let that fact run through her consciousness until a coherent idea emerged: the reason she could tell no one about Garnet's revelation was that it had become a private matter—not between her and Garnet, or her and Ivan, but between her and Rosie. It was nobody's business but theirs, and—like it or not—it made a bond between them. Susannah looked up from the vegetables when this idea came to her, and squinted into the sun. For the third time in her life she felt an alien idea, even a monstrous one, take over her life and illuminate it: *something will happen.* She had, years ago, decided to leave her mother's house and follow Edwin, and she had thrown Ivan out, and now it was clear to her, there in the garden, that some sort of circle was on the verge of completion. Edwin would die, Ivan was gone, and Rosie and she were tangled tight together. Like it or not.

She recognized that an immense curiosity about her mother had been collecting in her for years, incorporating the remembered mother, the unreal television mother, the unknown woman in East Chiswick, the fun mom Peter described. What on earth kind of woman was she, who would seduce her daughter's husband? Or who *could* seduce a man fifteen, sixteen years younger? Not that Ivan was hard to seduce—and, in fact, Susannah wondered who had seduced whom. She could think about this more easily after her revelation in the garden, could speculate on the details of their affair without disgust. She remembered that Ivan had always liked Rosie. They had watched her television show together and seen that opinionated, funny, gypsy woman on their old black and white TV set, Ivan sitting beside her on the floor telling her what an incredible woman her mother was, how they should look the old girl up and surprise her. Recalling this, Susannah recognized that one part of her feeling about the whole mess was a sort of childish resentment at being left out. There they'd been, her husband and her mother, bound in whatever curious kinship they'd forged, and there had been no place for her. Had they discussed her? Had Rosie, triumphing over her daughter, made fun of her? She imagined Ivan detailing her sloppiness and dreaminess and incompetence, and Rosie coming up with all the old complaints. And she'd never had a chance either to defend herself or to join in their camaraderie—for they must have been comrades before they became lovers. She felt lonely, thinking of what she had missed. She was tempted to go and see her mother and tell her how she felt, but was half afraid that, face to face, the complicated emotions of curiosity and loneliness would be canceled out by pure jealous rage at the woman whose unnatural lusts had destroyed her marriage. Better to leave the bond unspoken, untested, though this didn't satisfy her either. The idea of Rosie replaced Ivan in her head, and with it came a great longing to see her mother, to have a look at the woman Ivan had risked their marriage for—because he must have known that would be the end. Who was Rosie, Susannah wondered—and what could she tell her? And what would it be like to clasp the hand of a woman like her? And what could they say to each other?

Then she did run into Rosie. There she was, a coincidence out of Thomas Hardy, walking out the door of the Café, looking old and confused and haggard, and Susannah was shocked to find that it wasn't contempt or anger or disgust or curiosity that filled her but plain pity. Surely this woman—it *was* Rosie, her mother, wasn't it? this tanned aging lady in a girlish sundress and too much rouge?—surely she had no power to hurt. She looked as if life had battered her so badly she had no powers left at all. Susannah held the door for her in silence and watched her walk past Wendell's and across the concrete to her little tan car, tottering slightly on her high heels, looking frail and run-down, like a person who has lost too much weight too quickly. If it had been anyone but Rosie, Susannah would have been tempted—only shyness would have prevented her—to go after her, touch her arm, and say, "What's the matter? Can I help?" and take her home and give her a shot of brandy and a shoulder to weep on. As it was, she only stood and watched, while this unexpected and futile pity invaded her, muddling everything worse than it was already muddled.

So she told everything to Duke that night. It was their first real dinner alone together—pasta with the fresh tomato sauce Susannah had made that afternoon when she returned from the encounter with Rosie too agitated and unhappy to read or to write—and afterwards they sat on the porch drinking beer.

"No, I didn't know," Duke said. "He didn't ever tell me much, Susannah. God. Your mother."

They sat side by side, in ancient, broad-armed wicker chairs that creaked, and looked at one another. There was a full moon, low in the sky, straight ahead of them like a piece of fruit. In its light Duke's glasses hid the expression in his eyes. "I don't even know what to *think* about that, much less what to say."

"Did you happen to see a woman in the Café this afternoon? Just before I came in?" She had gone over there for lunch—had looked up from her notebook and craved company all of a sudden, and food; she liked to get there late, and nibble on scraps. "A short woman, very tanned, middle-aged? in a sort of bare dress? curly black hair?"

"Long hair?" He gestured vaguely around his own neck.

"No. Short."

Duke shook his head. "I guess I didn't. Why? You don't mean that was *her*?"

"It was. She must have had lunch there."

"Pretty gutsy, considering."

"She was looking for him, maybe. She may not even know he's gone."

"Well, that's true," Duke said. "Ivan wouldn't waste much time on

222

good-byes, I don't think." They each drank a gulp of beer, looking at the moon. "So what did you say to her, Susannah?"

"Nothing. I couldn't say a word. Neither could she. She was mortified or horrified, I don't know what. Overcome. She was *suffering*, Duke. I've never seen such blatant suffering."

"Guilt. When she saw you. After all—" He held out one white hand and waggled it; it encompassed everything. "She's your *mother*," he said.

"Yes, but she's not only my mother, Duke. She hasn't even been my mother, not for years. And she's getting old. She's fifty, I think. Fifty."

"You mean Ivan was her last grab at it. Before she gives in."

"I suppose."

"And you're worried about what Ivan's done to her."

She looked out at the dark trees, darkening sky, bright moon, but what she saw was Edwin, a few years ago, before his illness halted him, at a swimming pool with one of his young women—his hair thinned, his face lined and jowly, his waist thickened, his legs spindly. He would be in swim trunks—it would be Mexico, this memory—and the girl-friend would be—who? It didn't matter. And why hadn't he been pathetic? While Rosie and Ivan . . .

"Yes," she said. "I guess that's it. That's exactly it. I'm afraid for her. She didn't look good, Duke."

"Call Peter."

"Peter's in Vermont."

"Maybe he got back. Call him."

"I will." Yes: Peter. It was the favorite son who was needed, not the errant daughter. Peter, she assumed, could handle Rosie—and she imagined Rosie in hysterics, Peter calming her, giving her brandy, saying, "Now, Ma, don't take it so hard," patting her shoulder; and Rosie gulping brandy, getting older and older, turning into a crone, a *strega*, an old lady bundled in shawls with a long sharp nose and bright eyes.

"My mother's almost seventy," Duke was saying. "I remember when I first noticed she was getting old. She didn't look any different, I didn't think, but she started calling everyone *dear*. Waitresses, clerks in stores—strangers. 'No, dear, that'll be all, we'll have the check, please.' That sort of thing. You have an awfully young mother, actually."

"She was a child bride."

They were silent again, but the quiet night seemed full of words, and what they said, the careless intimacy of it, seemed like the breaking of a long silence—even though in their week together there had been chatter enough whenever they met, Susannah's full of forced good humor, Duke's all encouraging facetiousness.

"I want you to tell me about yourself sometime, Susannah," Duke said in the darkness.

"Tell you what?" she asked, surprised.

"Anything. I want to know who writes those stories. I don't know how to say this, but I'm so grateful to you for letting me read them." He had read "The Cage With Glass Walls" just before the crisis and pronounced it *great*. "Our Dukey dear is a man of few words," Ivan had said. *Magnificently creepy*, Leslie Merwin had said of the story, and urged her again to come to New York and have lunch.

"I'm the one who's grateful," Susannah said. "Ivan would never read my stuff. My stories bored him silly."

"I really love them, Susannah," Duke said.

If only the pronoun was different, she thought, wondering if she could say this aloud—why she couldn't, why they got this far and no farther, this close.

"Let's go someplace tomorrow," Duke said. "You and me."

"What about the Café?"

"Monday tomorrow. We're closed."

"Monday. I forgot. Of course, today's Sunday." Early on Sunday mornings, if the wind was right, she could hear church bells as she lay in bed; she had heard them that morning, sleepily, and thought: *the holiness of the heart's affections*, and had worked on her story, and then had run into Rosie at the Café. All on a Sunday. Ivan used to hate Sundays; he was unsettled all day. "You're a shepherd without his flock," she had teased him, once, gently, years ago, and he had told her to leave him alone. Even lately, he was uneasy on Sunday mornings. At the sound of the distant bells he had pulled the pillow over his head, swearing. They had made love, once, awakened by the bells, and Ivan had taken a grim pleasure in the rhythm of their tolling. "Yes—let's," Susannah said. "Let's go somewhere—get away again for the day."

Get away *again*: the word stood out in the dark, recalling the conversation in Stonington, Ivan's hostility, Duke's fear, Susannah's sorrow, and the fun they had had in spite of everything. A wisp of cloud, like a dust-kitten, crossed the moon and was lost in the thick gray sky. Susannah waited for Duke to speak, and when he didn't she said, "You know, I used to think of Ivan as my savior. Maybe because he had just left the priesthood—I don't know. He seemed to take on that role—always trying to improve things." She could see Duke nod; his glasses glinted briefly in the moonlight, then went dark again. "And he did save me, Duke," she went on. "He really did. I can't tell you what a messed-up kid I was when I met him. And for a while we were both messed up. We just kept drifting along. But he finally got things together, and he did sort of save me, and I'll always owe him that. And now I've sent him away. There's something wrong with that—don't you think?"

"No," he said. "I can't see where it was wrong, what you did."

"I don't mean it was wrong. I just mean there's something wrong with it." She laughed briefly. "If you see what I mean."

"I suppose I do. But, Susannah—"

"No," she said, answering. "I would never, never, never take him back." She thought of all the resolutions she had broken; this one, she knew, was unbreakable. "Never."

They sat in silence. They had lived together a week. It was beginning to seem more natural. They had agreed, wordlessly, to go to bed and get up at different hours. It saved the awkwardness of meeting in the bathroom, of wishing each other good night at their bedroom doors, and the absurdity of parting there. And meals, too, would fall into their pattern: a late, simple dinner, followed by a companionable beer on the porch before Duke, who had to get up early, took himself off the bed and Susannah stayed up to read. Could people live that way, Susannah wondered—a man and a woman who were fond of each other live simply as roommates? She hadn't realized, while she was living it, how sexual her life with Ivan was—not just screwing, but how much day-to-day touching there had been. Could two people live without that? *Oh yes, of course,* she said calmly to herself in her head, and at the same time she felt a deep, damp depression, like fog, settle around her.

She spoke. "I've got to tell you, Duke—there's something else on my mind, and I need your advice." She was determined to make her way through the fog, now, quickly, before Duke yawned, stood up, stretched, said, "Well—" and headed for the stairs, calling back a goodnight.

"Oh, good," he said. "I love to give advice, and I hardly ever get asked for it."

She looked at him. He sat slouched, with his feet up on the porch railing. He waved away a bug. She could see, just, that in spite of his light tone he was frowning. "Well, I'm asking for it," she said. "Because I seem to be pregnant."

The frown smoothed out, and he closed his eyes and lifted his face to the moon. "Oh Jesus," he said. "Oh Jesus H. I. J. Christ, Susannah."

She touched his arm. "I don't even know what kind of advice I'm asking for, Duke. I want this child—that's the trouble, I suppose. I intend to have it. I never should have let it happen, of course, but I didn't think we'd actually break up. I swore I'd never let my marriage get so bad it would have to end. And a child would have helped us—it would."

"You don't have to apologize for it, Susannah." His voice was thick with emotion—but what emotion? She didn't know. "It's just—oh, Jesus, what a mess."

The fog swirled around her and she thought she might scream, smash her glass against the porch rail and with the jagged pieces slash something, anything—her wrist, her chair, the rolled-up awning. Duke stood up suddenly, and looked down at her, holding out a hand. "But you stay with me, of course. You stay right here."

She sighed deeply, set her beer glass down gently on the floor, and took his hand. He pulled her up to stand beside him, and took her in his arms. She felt his glasses against her temple. "You're always having to comfort me," she said. Her hands, in fists, pushed against his chest, resisting any more comfort beyond his words.

"Not enough," said Duke, holding her tight. "Not enough, Susannah. You go ahead and cry if you want to."

But she didn't cry. She unclenched her fists and put her arms around his neck. His hand on her shoulder blades moved down her back, pressing her closer, and he kissed her neck and her cheek, and when she turned her face toward him he kissed her lips, and she sank against him, circling his pudgy middle with her arms. After a while they went inside, locked up, fed the cats, and climbed the creaky stairs together to Duke's bedroom. Duke lit a candle. There was a copy of *Walden* on the table by his bed.

"I've imagined this so many times," said Duke.

For a moment astonishment overcame her, but all she said was, "So have I," and stepped out of her skirt, wondering what the catalyst had been—her abject need, or the simple passage of time, or the yellow moonlight, or the little fish of a baby swimming in her womb.

It began to rain in the night, and the sound woke Susannah. She got out of bed and tiptoed to the bathroom. When she returned, Keats and Byron were on the bed, and she removed them gently to the hall, closing the door on them; she didn't yet know if Duke minded cats on the bed. She curled up close to his back and pulled the sheet over them both, and, wide awake, listening to the rain tapping, she began patching together what she knew about him: he was gentle and humorous but he took life seriously; he wore glasses; he came from Ashtabula, Ohio; he was a good cook, good with his hands . . . Susannah smiled, with her cheek against his broad soft back. She liked him. He suited her. He smelled of sweat, soap, sleep. *A good man.* She wondered whether Edwin, who would never meet him, would have liked him; he had considered Ivan, she knew, a bum, but he'd half admired Ivan's coarse flamboyance, and she wondered whether he would find Duke dull by comparison—a bit too earnest, too self-effacing. And would he and Peter become friends? And the baby—the baby. Her period was two weeks late, the baby might not be real at all, she must go to a doctor. She wouldn't let herself hope, wouldn't even think about it until she had a test. She remembered when Carla thought she was pregnant. Susannah had gone to the clinic with her, sat in the waiting room while Carla went in, comforted her when she came out crying, gone through the months of waiting with her, visited her in the hospital with flowers, and there was Tyler, Carla's little son. It had all been worth it; Carla got along fine, taking in typing at home so Tyler wouldn't have to go to daycare, she thought children should be with their mothers, and there was always a man around, what Carla called a "father figure." It was all right; it worked. Even in the days when Susannah didn't want a child herself—refused to let herself want one—the sight of Carla and Tyler could bring a lump to her throat. She could still remember the time Tyler fell asleep on her lap and she laid her cheek against his soft yellow hair.

Duke stirred, mumbled something—half a groan. Often, before, as she lay awake down the hall, miserable over Ivan, she had heard Duke turn in his sleep, and once he had cried out, calling what sounded like "Hatchet!" and then sighed loudly, snored once or twice, and quiet returned. His bed squeaked horribly, an old metal thing with springs; they'd have to do something about it before the twins returned. The twins: what a good father he was. Better than a father figure: a father. She remembered Carla saying, "If I only had a father for my baby"—as if a father was some expensive baby gift, like an English pram. Susannah was half asleep. He's from Ashtabula, Ohio, she thought. He's chubby around the middle. His name is Ellington James Foster. He reads *Walden*. He imagined this. . . .

She didn't hear the phone. What woke her was Duke leaping out of bed and opening the door to the hall. "What—" But then she did hear it ring, and Duke answer it, and come back and say, "It's for you. It's Peter."

He put on the overhead light—the look of emergency, Susannah thought fleetingly, lights on in the middle of the night. She went naked to the landing, self-conscious, shivering a little. She could still hear the rain.

"Peter?"

"Susannah. Listen, this isn't serious—I mean, she's all right now, but she's in the hospital, and she wants to see you. I know it's early—"

Even though she knew perfectly well, she said, "You mean Mom?"

"Yes—I'm sorry. I'm probably incoherent. I've been here all night."

"Peter, what time is it?"

"Six-thirty. I don't even know why I'm calling you so early, it's just that she keeps asking for you. But she's asleep now, they gave her something. You can't even see her until eight or so, I think. Visiting hours start at eight, something like that. But it's been a long night, Susannah."

She rubbed her eyes and sat down on the top step, forcing herself awake. Duke came up behind her and put a bathrobe over her shoulders, and she thanked him with a smile. She could see dawn, now, through the window; it was the rain making it so dark. Duke went by her, down the stairs, touching her hair lightly as he passed.

"Peter? I'm sorry, I don't understand this. She's in the hospital and she wants to see me. What's she in the hospital *for*?"

"She shot herself, Susannah." The words hung in the air, distinct as bells. She put her head down on her knees. Her hand holding the phone went limp. The phone dropped to her lap, cool on her bare skin, but she could hear Peter's voice, high with the held-back hysteria she realized had been there all along. "She tried to kill herself."

"Oh God, Peter," she whispered. Distantly, she could hear Peter cough—she wondered if he was crying—then resume talking in a more controlled voice.

"Her neighbors heard the shot, and broke in, and called an ambulance and took her to the hospital. By the time I got here they were operating. She aimed for her heart but apparently she was holding the gun at an angle because it missed her heart and got her in the shoulder and tore some cartilage, and the bullet lodged in there. The surgeon said she was damned lucky." He paused, took a deep breath, and was silent.

Susannah could hear Duke in the kitchen, making coffee. She said, "Peter, why did she have a gun?"

"She won't tell me. She won't tell me anything. She wants to see you."

"Why *me*?" Susannah asked, but she knew; she remembered Rosie's sorry, defeated face, the look they had exchanged.

"I don't know. She just cries and says she has to see you. It was the first thing she said when she came to."

Susannah tried and failed to imagine this, her mother weak and

229

bloody, wrapped in white, groaning out her daughter's name. Oh God. "I can't come 'til eight?"

"I don't know, Suse, let me check. I know visiting hours are—wait. Let me go ask a nurse."

"You're calling from her room?"

"Yes. I got her a private room. She's asleep. Just a minute, I'll go find someone."

She heard him put the phone down, and imagined it lying on the stand beside the bed—tan metal, the stand would be, like Edwin's, with a box of tissues and a styrofoam pitcher of ice water. And her mother—white, withered, hollow-eyed—lying on the bed, the bed cranked up to an angle. Susannah strained to hear her breathe, but could hear nothing. Her arm would be in a sling, perhaps? or her shoulder bound round with bandages? Would she be hooked up to tubes? Susannah tried to picture Rosie peaceful and sleeping, but all she could see was her mother's ravaged face, too much makeup, the eyes looking straight at her and away, the mouth compressed by grief and shame and fatigue. Or did she imagine all that? And then to go home and shoot herself, aiming for the heart.

"Susannah? You can come any time, they said."

"I'll be there as soon as I can get dressed, Peter. She's at Yale-New Haven?"

"Yes—wait—let me—it's room 553, in the Trauma Unit."

"You'll be there?"

"I'll stay until you come, at least. I'll stay until she wakes up and I see how she is." He chuckled a little, and his voice lightened for the first time. "I thought we could all meet under slightly more pleasant conditions—over a drink somewhere, maybe." He sighed. "I'm sorry about this, Susannah. Dragging you in."

"I want to be dragged in, Peter. It's time I was." It seemed, as she said the words, as if all winter, and spring, and summer had existed to culminate in this.

Duke drove her into New Haven in his Volkswagen. They took their coffee with them in plastic "commuter cups" Ivan had picked up somewhere and Duke made her a piece of toast. She nibbled at it as they drove, absently, agitated. "I'm trying to imagine," she said, "putting the muzzle of a gun to your heart and pulling the trigger." The idea made her want to scream, wail, carry on somehow. It was a monstrous, vile idea, something to read about in books or see on the news. She remembered Kennedy shot, covered with blood; she had seen it on television, not long before her parents broke up, blood in the car, on his wife's pink suit. She had cried all that night—she and Peter. She felt she should be crying now, but she sat in the little car watching the cat's-paw raindrops and the half-moons left by the windshield wipers, trying to see her mother doing it: placing the gun, taking a breath, closing her eyes, thinking—what? this is the end, good-bye, good-bye, what does it all matter—and squeezing the trigger. And then oblivion, and blood, and coming to in the hospital asking for her daughter. "If she was a person in one of my stories I could understand perfectly," she said. "But my mother."

"You said she looked depressed, worse than depressed."

"She did. But then to do that, with a gun." She looked out the window. A gray curtain over everything: fog. "I think to shoot yourself takes a special kind of brave soul. It's different from pills or cutting your wrists or drowning."

"Violent, you mean."

"Yes, and reckless. There's no going back."

Duke leaned toward her slightly. "But in this case there was, thank goodness."

She looked away from the bleak landscape to Duke's gray eyes behind his glasses. In the little car they were very close together. "I'm sorry about wrecking your day off. First keeping you up so late, then dragging you out of bed at the crack of dawn." It was a brave speech, and she said it with difficulty; they had been brisk and busy since the phone call, dressing quickly, gulping coffee; he hadn't even kissed her. There had only been that touch on her hair, the bathrobe thrown over her.

Duke smiled, his face very distinct in the clear, unfogged morning light inside the car: the scar on his cheek, neat triangle of nose, soft hair, the wide thin mouth with its funny smile. "Don't you dare apologize for last night," he said. "Some things are a lot better than sleep."

Thinking, she didn't answer. Were his words a shy declaration?

And was she a heartless woman, to be pondering that instead of her mother's bloody deed? It was the baby, it was the maternal instinct, she told herself, then looked at Duke's oddly bony wrists, his square hands on the wheel, and knew it was something else besides that. Tenderness for Duke filled her heart, suddenly, and at the same moment she saw Ivan's face smiling at her, his teeth so white, his beard so dark—false smile, true smile, it had never mattered. She remembered how she had thought of sticking a knife into him, and thought of her mother in a pool of blood. "Duke," she said suddenly. "Will you marry me? After I divorce Ivan?"

There was a long pause, during which she considered opening the car door and throwing herself out on Route 95. She held back tears, and more words, waiting. *This is the end*, she thought wildly. *What does it all matter?*

Duke spoke finally. "I'm going to say something so sappy and awful it's going to make you sick, Susannah." *Don't say it*, she thought, and pressed her palms to her temples. "I'm still in love with my wife. She's been dead two years, and I still dream about her. I dream she's still alive, and when I wake up and she isn't I wish I were dead, and I think if it wasn't for the twins I would be, Susannah. I can understand the gun."

"I'm sorry," she whispered, and put her hands over her eyes and bent over and began to cry.

He touched her shoulder. "I'm sorry, too, Susannah. Don't cry. I'm sorry." The car swerved, and she looked up, rubbed at her eyes, but he had pulled over to the side, stopped the car, and he put his arms around her, awkwardly, in the bucket seats. There were tears in his eyes, too. "Stay with me, Susannah. You can stay as long as you want. Stay forever. I'll take care of you and the baby and everything. You can write your stories." Her ear was against his cheek; his voice buzzed like a radio. "It's just that I don't have a lot to give."

They sat in silence for a while. She stopped crying. It was very hot in the car with the windows closed against the rain. She imagined cars passing them, the commuter traffic beginning, people seeing them with their arms around each other, people smiling or envious thinking: *Lovers*. She sat up straight, ran her fingers through her hair, wiped her eyes with the backs of her hands. "Enough of this," she said.

He touched her cheek with his rough hand. "Susannah," he said, and it seemed to her that he looked at her with love. And yet he said he had nothing to give. *I'm always crying, and I'm always wrong*, she thought. She smiled, trying for jauntiness, and reached for her coffee. "For years I didn't cry," she said. "Ever. My father discouraged it. I got good at not crying."

"I thought the first thing everyone learned in California was not to repress things," Duke said, smiling back, and put the car in gear. They slipped back on the highway.

"Maybe I never had anything much to cry about before."

"I'm sorry, Susannah."

"Oh, don't keep *saying* it." He looked even sorrier, and she regretted her words. "Now *I'm* sorry," she said, and they both laughed. She looked at him, and saw Margie, with gold stars in her ears. "Life is but a paltry thing," she said. He glanced over at her, raising his eyebrows. "A tattered something, I forget. It's a quote." *You always forget*, came Ivan's voice. The coffee was lukewarm and tasted of the plastic mug.

At the hospital there was no place to park, even at that hour of the morning. There was a parking lot, not open yet. Duke drove around, swearing, and finally dropped her off at the entrance. "I'll find a spot and be back," he said.

"What a pain in the neck this is for you."

"Let's make a deal. I'll stop apologizing if you will."

Love means never having to say you're sorry, she thought; *that dumb movie*. She almost said it, a joke, but she couldn't say *love*. She wondered if he thought it, too, and kept it back. "Okay," she said, kissed his cheek, and got out.

At the main desk they gave her a pass, and she went upstairs in the elevator with a woman about her age in a wheelchair pushed by a man in a light blue suit—dressed up for the occasion. The woman smiled and smiled, as still as if she was sitting for her portrait, her hands limp in her lap. No one spoke.

On the fifth floor Peter was waiting in a chair by the elevators.

He hugged her tight. "Am I glad to see you," he said. He looked dapper and fresh except for brown circles under his eyes. "I've read all their *Time* magazines and drunk their wretched coffee and talked to their bloody psychiatrists all night. One of them keeps asking me about her childhood, and the other one thinks she might be allergic to dairy products. Dairy products! Jesus! She decided to shoot herself because she had a milkshake and a grilled cheese for lunch."

"How is she, Peter?"

"Sleeping like a baby. She's fine—physically, I mean. It really did scarcely any damage, considering." His buoyance drained away as he talked, and when they reached the door of Rosie's room, down a corridor where the chemical stink of medicine was strong, he stopped and looked at her with his mournful eyes. "But I'll tell you, Susannah—I don't look forward to her waking up. I mean—" He waved a hand. "Not that I don't want her to wake up, I just—"

"I know what you mean. I dread it, too. And I don't know what she wants from me." But I do, she thought as they went in: absolution, as if she were a priest. "You won't leave, will you, Peter?" she asked. "I know you're tired, but I don't want to be alone with her. I don't even *know* her."

He looked amused. "I'll stay, Sister Sue. Curiosity would keep me here if nothing else. And the chance to be in on a no-holds-barred emotional scene." He rubbed his hands expectantly, yawning through a grin.

"Oh, *Peter*," she said, glad he, at least, was his usual self. She felt exhausted already; it wasn't even eight o'clock in the morning, and she seemed to have gone through days and days of scenes and tears and sorriness.

And there in the room was Rosie, the woman at the Café, her arm in a sling resting outside the white blanket, her short unbrushed hair in snarls on the white pillow. She looked dead, unless you went close and saw the faint rise and fall of her chest, the blanket over it, the brown hand at the end of the cast draped over it as if for a left-handed pledge of allegiance.

Susannah shrugged and sat down in a chair by the bed. "I guess we can't do anything but wait." She looked at Rosie. At that instant her eyes opened and she and Susannah stared at each other. Susannah wondered if she should speak, and what. She had forgotten her mother's eyes were so brown, like dark bitter chocolate. Up close, her face free of makeup, she looked strangely young, she looked like Peter. "I'm here," Susannah said, almost involuntarily, and the heavy lids dropped over Rosie's eyes again, and she lay still.

Susannah glanced at Peter, who gazed back at her expressionless, then at her mother again. Was she still asleep, the brief awakening a false one? Or had she closed her eyes again as a sign—all she could manage in her weakened state—of rejection? Susannah felt a stab of panic just as she had the night she drove to Rosie's in the van. Maybe it wasn't forgiveness Rosie wanted. *I'm always wrong*, Susannah thought. Maybe it was more curses she wanted, more hate. Her right arm wasn't in a sling: maybe she would raise it, and slap her, hard, and disown her again, pour out the venom saved up all these years, Mount St. Helens; it would all come out, and it would kill not Rosie who had tried to die but Susannah who was trying to find a way to live. Good-bye, good-bye, this is the end. If she couldn't kill herself she would kill her daughter.

Peter spoke softly in her ear. "I'm going down to get some more coffee."

"No!" she burst out, too loud, and looked fearfully at the silent figure on the bed. "Don't you dare leave, Peter. You promised."

He sat back down, looking unhappy. A fat nurse looked in, brought a tray from a trolley, and left it without a word. Peter lifted the metal cover over a plate, grimaced, and put it back with a small *clank*. "No coffee," he said. Time passed. After a while, he whispered, "Where's Ivan?"

"Duke brought me," she whispered back. Later she would tell him.

They were silent again, and then Peter asked, "Where's Duke, then?"

"Parking the car. Then he'll be up."

Peter rolled his eyes, acknowledging the parking problem, and after a while whispered, "I think they only give out two passes at a time."

"What do you mean?"

"For visitors. Duke's probably down in the waiting room."

"Oh *hell.*"

"Shall I go see?"

"No! Peter—" Rosie's eyes were shut, her eyelashes two thick even lines on her cheeks, her mouth slack. She breathed evenly. Susannah didn't trust her. "Please stay here."

Peter was already up. "I'll be right back." He spoke with the exaggerated gestures and lip-movements people use when they whisper. "I'll just see if he's there and I'll tell him to get some coffee or something and then later he can use my pass and come up." He pointed—*down*, then *up.*

"Oh, *hell.*" She thought of Duke forlorn in the waiting room. "All right. But please hurry back." She put her palms together in a prayer. "Please."

He nodded and left, then stuck his head in the door. "Did you tell him what happened?" he asked in a stage whisper.

Susannah nodded, Peter disappeared, and immediately Rosie's eyes opened again. "Susannah," she said in a clear voice; Susannah, startled, said nothing; how strange it sounded, and familiar—her mother saying her name. "You don't need to be afraid of me," said Rosie. Her eyes filled with tears. "I'm your mother."

Susannah leaned forward, instinctively, and took Rosie's good hand. The tears spilled over and made a track down her cheeks, one on either side. Susannah thought of Edwin. "Don't cry," she said, and wiped first one side, then the other, with her finger. "It's all right."

"I went into the store and bought a gun. He asked me what I wanted it for." Her voice got weaker. "I said I wanted it to shoot myself with. He laughed."

"Ssh," Susannah said, and clasped her mother's hands tight. "It's all over now."

Rosie closed her eyes; tears seeped neatly out the corners, and her mouth tightened over a sob. Susannah stroked her hand. She could think of nothing to say. If it were Edwin, she could tell him she was pregnant; she didn't think that was what Rosie wanted to hear.

"They keep asking me questions," Rosie said finally. "They make me so tired. But I wanted to see you."

"I came right away. But we can talk later. They've given you something to make you sleep."

Rosie nodded, the tears still running without interruption down their tracks. Susannah took a tissue and wiped them again. Rosie kept her eyes closed, and before long Susannah could see she was sleeping, with a half-smile on her lips. Susannah took away her hand, and Peter returned.

"I was wrong," he whispered. "You can have as many passes as you want for a private room, but Duke thought he'd better not come up. He said this should be for relatives only. I left him in the cafeteria eating a cheese Danish." He looked at Rosie. "She moved."

"She woke up for a minute." Susannah put Duke out of her mind. She felt sick to her stomach: morning sickness? The medicinal smell didn't help, and the faint smell of egg from the breakfast tray. "She said she was tired."

"Is that all?"

"She told me not to be afraid of her."

Peter waggled his head and widened his eyes, an Eddie Cantor face. "Just what I've been telling you all along."

Chapter Seven

The Door in the Hedge

The first thing Rosie said, when they had parked the car and proceeded up the puddled slope to the house, was, "It's all wrong."

"What is?" Susannah asked her.

"Everything." She looked around at a flat plane ringed with hills;
behind her were the sparse, wet woods the road had wound through.
There were leathery yellow leaves among the green on the trees; they
fell to the car and stuck. There was a rank smell of pond, of not enough
sun. An unfamiliar bird cried *skreek* and flew up black against the
concrete sky. "Everything is," said Rosie.

What she wanted to do at that moment was get back in the car and
drive off, stop at a pub and have an early lunch with a couple of pints
of the thick, sweet ale she was getting used to. Forget the whole thing.
They could go to Knole, or Penshurst, or to the castle at Goudhurst. It
had been a mistake to come to Silvergate.

"It's the rain," said Susannah. "It's your shoulder hurting."

"No, it isn't," Rosie snapped. "It's everything. It looks so bleak and
desolate." She regretted her tone of voice, and she altered it. "There
used to be hops growing over there," she said, taking Susannah's arm.
"It was part of the farm, where they grew hops. And then the sheep

were—" She paused, confused, and looked around. *Was* that where the farm had been? This part of the grounds, in fact, didn't look familiar at all, at least not in this drizzle. It had been raining since they stepped off the plane at Heathrow. Of course, it must have rained when she was a child, but she couldn't remember it doing so; not, at least, like this—a relentless onslaught of chilly rain and fog. And the damp did make her shoulder throb, though she wouldn't admit it to Susannah. Susannah liked the rain, she said. She had gone out in it their first day, in Guildford, while Rosie collapsed into sleep at the inn. Susannah, armed with guidebooks, wanted to see the famous clock and the ruined castle. Jet lag didn't seem to affect her. *Youth*, Rosie thought, not without resentment, but Susannah attributed it to her pregnancy. "I've never felt better," she said. "I swear it's given me some kind of extra strength. And then," she added, teasing, "I did sleep on the plane, while you flirted with your fellow passengers."

True enough, or partly. Susannah had dropped off soon after they left Kennedy. She had awakened, obligingly, each time the steward-ess had brought sustenance—drinks, then dinner, then more drinks, then breakfast—too quickly, time out of joint, dawn outside the plane windows almost before the movie was over. But Susannah had dropped rapidly back to sleep between distractions, leaving Rosie to the movie—*Kramer vs. Kramer*, which she had already seen, with Peter—and to the attentions of the man in the third seat, a Nepalese economist from the International Monetary Fund who was going to a conference on Third World debt at the London School of Economics. "And to do a little swinging without my wife," he confessed to Rosie in a thick but not impenetrable accent. He smiled blandly at her and asked where she was staying in London.

"I'm not going to London."

"Not going to London! Your first trip to England, and you're not going to London? Then where *are* you going?"—as if the land sloped away from London, on all sides, into empty sea.

"I'm touring the countryside with my daughter," she said, indicat-ing Susannah, who slept sweetly on.

"Ah—that's your daughter," he said, rising in his seat a little to look at Susannah's legs. "Yes—but why the countryside? Excuse me for my nosiness, but I see that you, like me, can't abide movies and also find it difficult to sleep. So tell me—why in the world the countryside and not the joys of London?"

Rosie sighed, and chatted with him, let him buy her a drink but not put his hand on her knee, and watched Dustin Hoffman silently make French toast for his little boy, argue with his ex-wife, race through the streets of New York to the hospital with his son in his arms. She was tired, but she knew she couldn't sleep if she tried, and she was even grateful for the company of the economist. While he explained Britain's economic problems to her, she kept wondering why she wasn't thrilled to be on this plane, after all this time, heading for the land of her birth; why all she felt was fatigue, dejection, and the faint, tamed, but never wholly absent throb of pain in her left arm. When he asked, she told the economist she had broken her arm in an automobile accident.

She felt wiped out when they arrived at Heathrow. The economist disappeared, hustled through Customs, no doubt, by international officialdom. Rosie leaned on Susannah's arm as they waited in lines, and she was glad to sit on a bench while her daughter picked up their rental car. The crowds, the strangeness, tired her further—and the weather. It was ten in the morning, but England looked gray and dismal; it could have been dusk. Rosie watched an emotional reunion between a man in a UCLA sweatshirt and a woman wearing a paper pinned to her coat that read "*égaré*". They stood locked in a long embrace, and the woman uttered heedless sharp little moans at intervals, like a puppy. Then Susannah returned and left Rosie on another bench—outside, under a shelter, where she watched a group of students negotiate endless satchels and backpacks into a tiny car, joking in a language she didn't understand: Swedish? When Susannah finally brought the car around, Rosie didn't recognize her—a blonde woman with a wide, thin smile, driving a little red automobile.

"This is such fun," she said, holding the door and an umbrella for Rosie. "Everyone has the most wonderful accents. The rental-car lady actually called me *love*, and I am about to stow our luggage in the *boot!*" She did so, and drove through the airport maze to the main road, adapting with apparent ease to the wrong side of it. "I've never been such a great driver on the *right* side of the road," she said cheerfully. "So it's not that hard for me to switch."

Rosie struggled to stay awake, only vaguely aware that the gray dismalness of the airport had given way to lush, wet green. She fell quickly into the position of dependent, knew she was doing so, and decided not to care. She had been nearly a month with Susannah, almost since leaving the psychiatric ward. Susannah had come to stay with her, replacing Miss Poole, the nurse who had been hired to care for her at first. Rosie's house had been a refuge for Susannah, whose ambiguous life with Duke the chef had gone, somehow, mysteriously askew. Susannah had, to Rosie's grateful relief, substituted her own kind of comfortable, sloppy efficiency for Miss Poole's condescending and antiseptic vigilance—getting the meals, tending the gardens, washing Rosie's hair for her, tracking in grass clippings, keeping the house filled with slapdash arrangements of the flowers she cut every few mornings, and finishing her story upstairs in her old bedroom. Rosie had come to rely on her—this placid, messy, gifted, resurrected daughter—as she had never relied on anyone: not parents, husband, lovers, son. She didn't resist; it was, she figured, part of her recuperation, a treat she was entitled to because her arm hurt, and because she had just spent two indignant weeks being grilled by a psychiatrist with the brain of a turnip. And it was a gift she could give Susannah, who seemed to need someone to care for.

At the inn she went immediately to sleep, and awoke at teatime to find her shoulder hurting and Susannah combing out her wet hair in front of the mirror.

"England is the most beautiful place in the world," Susannah said. "It's all true, what everybody says. And those pictures in the guidebooks. It really *looks* like that. You should see the gardens—the flowers!"

"Oh, I know—I know," Rosie said, hoisting herself up in her bed, and, in spite of her aching shoulder and the rain blurring the window, the exhilaration she had anticipated took her over in a rush; she felt invigorated, and ready. The gardens of England, in all their autumn glory, were hers to see after all these years. And Silvergate, the loveliest of them all. She swung her feet over the side of the bed and went to the window. It looked out on the inn courtyard where, even in the rain, and with the daylight nearly gone, a border of coreopsis and purple loosestrife glowed with its own radiance. "Just look at those flowers," she said to Susannah. "I've spent my whole life in gardens, and I still can't get over them, how beautiful they are." Looking out, with Susannah at her side—was it something about the light? or the scent of the air coming through the crack of open window?—she was back for one brief trick of memory in the cottage with her parents and her grandparents, surrounded by flowers.

And now here she was at Silvergate, disoriented, peering through the drizzle at an alien landscape. Had she lost it, then? Her entire childhood? Would nothing come back to her? And how could memory be so fickle? "I don't know, I don't know," she said vaguely, looking around. Far beyond the wide flat stretch of patchy lawn, the low Kentish hills, yellow bordered with deep green and topped with a black fringe of trees, edged the gray horizon. In the distance she could just see a brick structure like a tower, with a cone-shaped roof: *an oast house*. The word came to her as if from underwater, and she clutched Susannah's arm, and pointed. "They dry the hops in those," she said excitedly. "Oast houses. That thing on the top is for ventilation—it turns in the wind. I haven't thought of them in years." It was a vision from her childhood, intact; it was like coming upon a photograph of an old, lost friend.

Susannah said, "That one seems to have been converted into a people-house. See? You can just make out curtains in the windows, and two cars."

"Oh, Lord, yes," Rosie said, and felt depressed again. It was all wrong, that the oast house, that eccentric-looking edifice, should be inhabited. She tried to remember the farm that used to be part of the estate. She should be able to recall the farmer, his family, there must have been children. But she could retrieve nothing, not even, for sure, where the fields had been—over there, surely, and stretching over toward the desecrated oast house? The right photograph refused to reveal itself.

"It must be fun to live in a place like that," Susannah was saying. "I'd love to have the room up in that tall tower part, to write in. It would be perfectly round, and the ceiling would slope up to a point—like living in an ice-cream cone. And I would make up mysterious, circular plots for my stories—but with a point to them." She laughed, and Rosie laughed with her, halfheartedly. Maybe it was Susannah's enthusiasm that was wearing her out. "And what a view!" Susannah swung around, in the rain, to look at the rest of the scene. Her hair hung down in a wet braid over the back of her yellow slicker. She refused to wear a hat. *She's such a child*, Rosie thought—though she was impressed with the way the child negotiated car rentals and maps and the perverse and narrow English roads. And she was pretty, too, Rosie thought, with her hair neatly braided and her eyes bright, and the damp weather obviously good for her complexion; her cheeks were pink, for once. She never would have predicted this fragile prettiness from her plain, whiny daughter—not to mention such relentless high spirits. What had happened to the sullen, grasping hippie whose arrival from California she had dreaded? And the deserted wife? The two of them had still, after all these weeks, not spoken Ivan's name.

Susannah faced her, beaming. "I'm so grateful to you for bringing me here, Rosie. And not just because I needed to get away. I love England—rain and all." She laughed again, her angular face becoming softer, her eyes crinkling with glee. *Like Edwin when I first met him*, Rosie thought, horrified. Memory engulfed her and made her weak. She took Susannah's arm again with her good right one, and Susannah squeezed it exuberantly. "Let's walk up to the house," Susannah said. "I'm dying to see the place."

"I'm not so sure I am," Rosie said. "It's like seeing a movie made from a book you liked. It's not the way you imagined."

"You were here a long time ago," Susannah said in her gentle voice. "It's bound to be different. But the house should be the same, at least."

"We'll see." She expected nothing. Or worse—the house turned into a Disneyland castle, all purple and pink and plastic, with gnomes. Nothing would surprise her.

They walked up the drive in their rubber boots, avoiding puddles. No one else seemed to be around; there had been only three other cars in the car park. "Not very good weather for tourists," Susannah said. "We'll have the place pretty much to ourselves."

The paved path was bordered on one side with trees, on the other with tree-studded lawn stretching out to the hills beyond. "I certainly don't remember it was so far," Rosie said. Her left arm pulled heavily against the sling.

"Well, you probably didn't come up this way much," Susannah pointed out. Rosie could see Susannah deliberately not referring to her mother's fatigue: she's *handling* me, Rosie thought; I've become someone who needs to be *handled*. But she was glad Susannah had developed tact—she was like Peter in that way. And she was relieved not to be coddled—not like that damned nurse, Miss Poole, whom she'd been forced to hire her first week home from the hospital and who had treated her like a demented child. At least Susannah helped her hide her weaknesses.

"I should think you would always have approached the main house from the back somewhere," Susannah went on. "From wherever your cottage was. Not up the main drive."

Of course. That was why it was all so wrong. Something buried deep in her mind turned over and half-revealed itself. Yes: that explained everything. How could she think the farm would be in *front*? That the main approach would have *hops* growing alongside it? She was completely turned around. She remembered now, distantly, the long back road in, a road lined with trees: evergreens? did she remember pine needles? or was that someplace else? were there rhododendrons, perhaps? But the road, she was sure, had divided, and one fork had curled around to the cottage.

"There!" Susannah said as they went around a bend, and Rosie looked up. There it was—Silvergate on its hill suddenly before them, with the mist still on it, the rosy brick glowing in the rain, and the massive chimneys and the little cupola and the steps widening out from the great front door to end in squat pillars topped with urns. The rain had let up a little, and they stopped to look at the house. Yes, this, at least, was right—the sober, tidy shape of it, the color of the brick, the soothing symmetry. It all matched up perfectly with something carved deep in her soul. Tears came to her eyes.

"It's lovely," Susannah said. "Just what you'd expect an English country house to be." She looked down at Rosie, still clinging to her arm. "Is it the way you remember it? It must be a strange feeling, to see it again."

"Very strange," Rosie said. "But it looks just the way it should look."

"Does it look smaller? The places you knew as a kid are supposed to seem smaller when you see them as an adult. I know your house did, at first—the inside, especially. My old room. And the tool shed—the old playhouse. I couldn't believe how low the roof was—I can't even stand upright inside it." She paused, as if uncertain whether to go on, then said, "It's funny, that you and I have both returned to the scenes of our childhood."

Rosie glanced away from the house to her daughter. She hadn't thought of that—of how disquieting it must have been for her, to return to live in a place she had left with such cold impatience, so many years ago. And yet Susannah had seemed, during all those weeks, placid and content. What had it cost her, Rosie wondered, belatedly.

The rain started up again, harder. "Oh, *hell*," said Susannah. "Shall we dash for it?"

"I'll try."

Her bad arm bounced painfully under her coat as they ran over the lawn and up the circular gravel drive, and she had to stop, panting, at the top of the steps in the shelter of the overhang.

"I'll wager that made the old arm smart a bit," Susannah said lightly in the exaggerated accent she had begun to affect as a joke. Her face was wet, her hair dripping, and her smile was replaced by an anxious squint Rosie was sure she wasn't aware of.

"No, it's fine," said Rosie, resisting the temptation to rub her shoulder, refusing even to grimace with the pain. She took off her rain hat and shook it free of the beaded drops. She would have liked to sit down. "It's been a while since I've run," she said.

"After we take the grand tour we'll stop for tea. There must be a nice cozy tea shop on the premises." Susannah's smile returned. "If there's one thing I've learned in my three days in England, it's that you're never far from a tea shop. There must be almost as many tea shops in England as there are McDonald's in Connecticut. *Almost*."

She pushed open the heavy door—oak, Rosie knew, weathered a silvery gray like the massive gate, centuries ago demolished, that had stood between the pillars at the foot of the drive and given the place its name. Inside, a woman in a blue National Trust blazer sat at a desk. Behind her, through a doorway, loomed the vast hall and the split staircase winding up on either side to a gallery. A discreet sign said: Admission £2. Susannah paid, and bought a brochure (50p). "It's a self-guided tour," the woman said. "You'll find everything you need to know in the brochure. Please remember that we keep the rooms rather dark to prevent further fading."

"It will probably be really dark in here on a day like this," Susannah chatted to her as she dug a five-pound note out of her pocket. "Though we keep being surprised by how quickly the weather changes. I mean, one minute it's pouring and the next the rain almost stops and the sun almost comes out." She grinned at the woman. "I'm sure that before we leave England we'll get some beautiful days."

"Feel free to ask any of the guides to illuminate the dark corners with a torch," said the woman imperturbably, "should there be anything you particularly wish to see," and she dropped the change into Susannah's hand.

Susannah thanked her, still cheerful, and said to Rosie as they passed through the antechamber and into the high, arched hall, "There's my first complaint against the old country. In America we replace our snooty ticket-takers with slot machines and computers." She began flipping through the pages of the brochure. Rosie was continually astonished by Susannah. She seemed to have lost not only the querulousness of childhood, but, now that they were abroad, her natural shyness and her air of detachment from the real world. Rosie surveyed her with affection as Susannah pulled her reading glasses out of her pocket—she never carried a purse—and set them on the end of her long nose. She squinted over the brochure in the gloom.

"I don't know how they expect you to read this thing in this light," she said. "This is a different one from the one you showed me at home." Her voice echoed in the huge room. *At home*, Rosie thought. She wished, impulsively, that she could hug Susannah there and then, in thanks for moving in and taking care of her, for not bringing up Ivan's name, for her willingness to let bygones be bygones. She hadn't, she realized, thanked her properly for anything; it was Susannah who was always thanking *her*. "Let's see—they haven't revised the bit about the gardens," said Susannah, peering. "Still no mention of the family." She flipped through the pages. "Nope—not a word." She looked with indignation at Rosie. "I'm going to write a letter to the *Times*."

Rosie smiled at her fondly, a look that seemed to surprise Susannah and disconcert her slightly. She dropped the brochure to the floor, and when she had retrieved it, she said, "Let's see the place, then—if we can in this gloom," and took Rosie's arm again to ascend the massive staircase.

They looked at the marble busts of the Elliott-Casson family in the Great Parlour, and the linenfold paneling and the glossy parquet floor, and they saw the Dining Chamber filled with the absurd glitter of its immense cut glass chandelier ("Installed in the eighteenth century," Susannah read from the brochure, and added, "Vulgar, if you ask me"), and they went into the bedchambers where the high, carved beds were hung with meticulously restored embroidered material—impossible to imagine anyone actually sleeping there. "Think of the dust!" Susannah said. "And how completely quiet and pitch dark it must have been at night, under all those hangings."

Rosie turned away. She couldn't, some days, see a bed without a grievous, vivid memory not so much of Ivan but of *other days*, another Rosie.

They moved on to the Long Gallery with its famous Reynolds portrait of the first Peter Elliott-Casson with his dog and his mistress. None of this was familiar; the only portion of the house that she knew was the servants' quarters in the basement, and these were closed to the public, used for storage.

"The really interesting parts," Susannah said, disappointed. "I'd love to see the kitchens, especially." Rosie thought of Duke, and of the thriving little restaurant back in Connecticut. Duke, she knew, had asked Susannah to live with him, and Susannah had refused. A *cohabitation de convenance*, she called it—a joke she didn't explain. Yet, Rosie knew, she had already written him a long letter. "I'd like to see a real butler's pantry," said Susannah. "The underside of all this magnificent overkill."

"You betray your lower-class origins," Rosie said, smiling.

"I adore my lower-class origins!" She fingered, gingerly, the metallic gold trim on a heavy velvet drape. "Did you used to envy all this as a kid? Wish you lived in the big house?"

"I must have been too young. I remember being completely pleased with our cottage."

"Your *'umble* cottage," Susannah corrected. "Where you ate porridge and was 'appy. Pardon my accent. I'll get it right after a couple of more days."

"You're doing fine," said Rosie. She tried to remember the Elliotts, vaguely recalled a jolly, overweight family who lived for their horses. She hadn't thought of them in years; Silvergate had always meant the Liliano family. Now she remembered the stables, and the whole bunch of them, children too, in red jackets for the hunt, and, once, a party— was it here, in the Gallery?—with a huge Christmas tree and a ribbon-tied package—paper dolls? "I wonder what happened to the family," she said. "I seem to recall they were down on their luck after the war. Something must have happened, anyway, for them to give all this up. They loved the place—that I remember."

"Just as well you left when you did," said Susannah. "They might have taken you down to ruin and perdition with them."

"Ruin and perdition—I doubt it. They probably just sold off a couple of their horses and got rid of this place and moved into their town house." A thought struck her. "I wonder if the weather vane is still on top of the house. A stork, standing on one leg. I used to love looking up at it from the gardens. I didn't notice it as we came in, though."

Susannah consulted the brochure. "It's still there, according to this. 'Set in place in 1650, when the house was finished, and miraculously preserved on the roof of the octagonal cupola to this day.' We'll have to look for it on the way out." She stopped to listen. "Can you still hear the rain? Or has it stopped? Look how green the light is in here—like the inside of an old bottle. I wonder if we could go out and see the gardens."

Rosie approached a guide—male this time, elderly, his chest sunk beneath his blue blazer, his hands shaky and ridged with veins. "How do we get to the gardens?"

"Oh—the gardens?" He touched her good arm and led her to

the window, and pushed back the drape. Dust motes attacked them. Through the old wavy glass, she could see that it was still raining, that clouds like old rags flew low over the hills. "You see?" said the guide. "Out there is the terrace, and down the steps is the rose garden. No roses now, of course, but just beyond is the yew hedge, and the little walled garden. Oh, that's a little beauty." His voice, faintly Irish, was proprietary. "There are still plenty of flowers in bloom—the chrysanthemums and the dahlias are especially fine just now, and the little autumn crocuses."

"Oh, I'm sure they are," said Rosie. "I know they are." She smiled down at the terrace, gray and wet, with its pots of gold chrysanthemums marking the steps. "I knew this garden as a girl—as a child. I used to live here. The gardener was my father, back in the Thirties."

The old man stood looking at her, frowning. His face was bright red, deeply wrinkled, with long creases in his cheeks and pendulous jowls above a skinny neck. "What's that?"

"I was born here at Silvergate," Rosie said. She glanced over at Susannah. Did the man even understand?

"The original gardener was her grandfather," Susannah put in. "My great-grandfather. The man who restored the gardens—who created all this." She spoke with restrained pride, and Rosie remembered Susannah at the funeral, claiming her grandmother, and her own anger. She bowed her head, looking out at the blurred greens, listening to Susannah's voice. "His name was Massimo Liliano; he came here from Italy to do this—*that*." She gestured toward the window. "He was responsible for it. He planned it out, he supervised the work, he saw that it was maintained. He was the head gardener here for years, and then his sons took over, my grandfather and my uncles. And my mother was born here, in the gardener's cottage."

The old man let the curtain fall. He seemed disoriented by Susannah's speech. In the gloom, he mumbled, "I don't know about that."

"Well, it's true," Susannah persisted, and Rosie marveled again at the confidence she seemed to have acquired simply by stepping onto English soil. Against the dark ancient wood, in the shadows, she looked regal—as if she belonged not in the cottage but in the manor. "I don't know how I could convince you," she said to the guide, "because our family doesn't even get a mention in this brochure." She flipped through it to the page on the gardens, and held it up. "Here: all it says is—"

The old man waved a hand, dismissed it, took a step back. "Get away with you," he said in his brogue, half bantering.

"But it's true," said Susannah.

"Well, but it's all irrelevant, isn't it? Because the gardens are closed today."

"Closed?"

"It says so in the book," he said, and his jowls shook as he nodded toward the brochure in Susannah's hand. "Clear as daylight. Open Tuesdays and Thursdays only after October first. So it doesn't matter whose daughter you claim to be, does it?" He was grinning, and he cackled; he'd decided to treat it all as a joke.

"But the gardens!" Rosie looked at Susannah in despair. She could have cried.

"We'll come back," said Susannah, and to the old man she said, "Is there a tea shop on the premises?"

He had stopped chuckling, and he looked at them kindly, sadly. "It's not your day, then, is it? Tea shop's same as the gardens. Tuesdays and Thursdays after October first."

They left, through the drawing room, down the grand staircase, past the woman at the desk. Susannah said good-bye to her; Rosie was too miserable to say anything.

"Come again," said the woman.

"As a matter of fact, we intend to," said Susannah. "We want to see the gardens."

"Oh, they're worth a visit." The woman smiled stiffly. "They're really quite lovely. Open Tuesdays and Thursdays."

"We have rather a special interest in them," Susannah began, but Rosie put her hand on her arm to stop her. She couldn't bear to go through it all again. She thought how the old man would tell the other guides about his crazy Americans.

"You might come back next week," the woman said politely. "Perhaps the rain will stop."

In the car Rosie gave way to tears. "It's as if I imagined it all. My whole childhood. None of it seems real any more. I never should have come, Susannah." She blew her nose awkwardly with one hand. "You can't go home again. It's true."

"But you have to try," Susannah said. Her own spirits seemed undampened. "We'll come back. It's what you've always wanted to do, and we're going to do it, dammit." She started the car. The windshield wipers cleared the view of the oast house in the distance. "Right now let's find a nice warm pub and have a good lunch. This rain's bound to stop by tomorrow, and we'll come back then and see the gardens. And the weather vane—the stork! We forgot!"

But Rosie was shaking her head—the first time she had felt vehement about something since she decided to put the gun to her heart. "No," she said. "It's all wrong. I've had enough." The tears started again. Her only consolation was Susannah; Susannah's thin competent ivory hands on the wheel, Susannah not insisting, heading the car down the drive, agreeable, content, her daughter.

And Peter, of course. In the pub she took out a postcard to write to him. "I don't know what to say. 'Silvergate was a flop. We miss you. Love from secondhand Rose.'" She sighed and put the postcard down: a view of a country lane. Sipping her ale, she did miss Peter. He had spent a lot of time with her and Susannah during her recuperation, making their odd reunion easier—sitting with them on the screened porch telling them funny stories, talking frankly about himself and Hollis, reminiscing about the good parts of his and Susannah's childhood. Rosie was grateful to him for reminding her that there had been good parts—not many, Lord knew, and quickly exhausted, but enough to cheer her up a little. She had cried, with Peter, and had tried to talk about what she had done—bought a gun and tried to shoot herself through the heart, for God's sake! Had she done that? When she came to in the hospital after the surgery her first thought had been that she was going to die—the pain was so great—and that she must be forgiven, must look into Susannah's face and find comfort. And when it became clear that she wouldn't, after all, die quite yet, her chief emotion had been relief. She didn't think of Ivan, and when Peter asked her, there on the porch, weeks later, on a hot September evening, over gin and tonics, "Why did you do it, Ma?", she was stumped for a moment, as empty of ideas (though not as hostile) as she had been with the psychiatrist; and then she remembered Ivan, and how she had listened and listened for the sound of his van coming up the street and stopping out front. That grinding noise when he pulled on the brake, that metallic thud of the door shutting, his quick footsteps on the brick path.

"It seems a million years ago," she said.

"But *why*, Ma?" he asked her again, gently, mercilessly. Susannah was inside, making spaghetti for dinner. If you looked toward the garage, you had to shade your eyes, the ball of the setting sun was so bright.

"I had nothing, Peter," she said. "And I was getting old. But not old enough. I saw my life stretching out for years and years and years. Empty. With nothing but gardens in it. Nothing but *plants*." She gave a bitter laugh, to hide the fact that all this was only half the truth, the Ivanless half. The lie was necessary; only to Susannah could she tell the whole truth—and not even yet to Susannah, who knew it anyway. To Peter she had to lie, for once—as he for years had kept from her that one vital thing.

But he was hurt, as she had known he would be, and she put out her right hand and touched his cheek with the back of her fingers; the effort pulled at the ripped muscle of her damaged left shoulder, and she winced with pain. But she stroked his cheek. "What about me?" he asked, as she had expected. "You say you had nothing. You had *me*, dammit."

"I know that, Peter. I couldn't have a better son." She paused, searching for words that would be both true and consoling. "It was something in *me* that was missing. The *nothing* I'm talking about. Things piled up on me and I sank. I dissolved. Like the Wicked Witch of the West." She frowned. *The Wizard of Oz*: it rang a bell somewhere.

"How could I have saved you?"

She looked up in surprise at his words. "Saved me?" The idea was absurd, and she shook her head. "I was unsalvageable, Peter." She remembered again the psychiatrist she had talked to in the hospital: *I think what you did was a cry for help*, she had said. A stupid woman. "What saved me," Rosie told Peter, "was—you know—what I did."

"And Susannah," he said.

She inspected his face, the strong eyebrows lowered, the eyes hidden in shadows. Was he jealous, then? Was that what made him keep probing? She shook her head. "I insist on taking all the credit. I saved myself. Like those villages in Vietnam—remember? That they had to destroy in order to save? Lord." The madness of the world, she thought. The world thick with death. "But Susannah came after," she said to Peter. "An old wound healed. And the new wound—" She touched her shoulder with a grimace. "That's healing, too."

"And now you're going to say that in ten years we'll all look back on this and laugh."

"No." She looked out to the garden, half brilliant color, half shadow, and then turned suddenly to smile at Peter. "I think we can laugh *now*. I'm very glad to be alive, Peter. I'm totally happy."

"Totally? That's pretty happy, Ma. That's unnatural." His brown eyes—affectionate, relieved—were laughing at her.

"Well, that's what I am," she insisted. It was true, she supposed, and she had finally convinced the psychiatrist of its truth, though it seemed strangely beside the point. The point was being alive—but how silly it seemed, merely to draw breath after breath, and have your blood race through your veins, happy or unhappy not mattering. And then there was the thing she perceived, now, every time she looked into the garden: that, having done it once, she could do it again, someday, when she was old, really old, or sick, or bereft, when the breathing and the racing blood became a bleak joke. She hoped it would never happen, but the knowledge made her feel calm and potent, made the late-summer garden more beautiful than ever and her children inexpressibly dear to her.

"I don't think English food is so awful," Susannah said. Rosie was having bread and cheese—ploughman's lunch—but Susannah was digging into the "combination special": a thick wedge of cheese and onion pie, two slices of fatty ham, and a salad, with pickled onions and plenty of wholemeal bread and butter on the side.

"I never much liked to eat," said Susannah, "until I became the owner of a restaurant. And now that I'm pregnant I can't seem to stop."

"I don't know where you put it," said Rosie.

"Into little Rosetta," Susannah said, patting her abdomen. There was the faintest of convexities. "Little Rosetta thinks gammon and pickled onions are the cat's meow." For the baby's sake, Susannah had abandoned her vegetarianism.

"I won't believe in her until I can see her," said Rosie. "You're as thin as a stick, Susannah. When I think how I'd begun to show at three months!"

"She's roughly the size of my thumb," Susannah said complacently. "And her heart is nearly completely formed, and it beats. And she's got little tiny fingers. She's just the cutest thing." She looked down fondly at her flat stomach. "The book says she's got eyelids, even."

"If it weren't for me she'd have a father, too," Rosie said. She hadn't meant to say it—not here, certainly, in a pub full of the noisy lunchtime crowd, with Susannah about to fork in a hunk of ham, with the pub cat on the windowsill looking out at the rain, the coils of an electric heater glowing in the fireplace, her shoulder throbbing. She hadn't meant to make this grotesque joke at all. She wished it unsaid.

Susannah was looking at her intently, with the dour frown that Rosie had come to realize meant merely that she was thinking hard. She set the forkful of ham down on her plate. The noise of the pub rose and fell around them, English-accented. "No," Susannah said finally, and her frown smoothed out. "My breaking up with Ivan was sort of a variation on what Peter told me you said about your shoulder. About trying to kill yourself," she said softly. "Destroying something in order to save something else. I couldn't have stuck with him much longer. I'm sure you know you were only the last of a long string. And not even the last." She didn't elaborate, and Rosie didn't ask. It was a million years ago, it was dead and gone, details didn't matter. "I'm not very good at open marriage," Susannah said. "It's much, much better that it happened. Not that I didn't love him, Rosie. I did. I adored that man."

"Yes," said Rosie in a choked voice.

"But I made a mistake. It's better this way."

Rosie looked at her. She seemed sincere, all the benevolence in her face for her mother, and the benevolence marked only with regret. Rosie could detect no bitterness. How could that be? But she put it from her mind. She wasn't ready for it. She nodded, and smiled a little. "All right. If you're sure."

"Oh, yes, I'm sure," said Susannah. They looked at each other and simultaneously shrugged, which made them laugh.

"Now," said Susannah. "'Dear Peter. We're sitting in a pub in Kent. It's been raining steadily for three days, and we're having the time of our lives.'"

The rain let up the next day, and the soft English landscape, cool in its autumn colors, was soothing to Rosie. She began to catch some of Susannah's knack of utter enjoyment—of throwing herself into the pleasures of the moment unencumbered by the past, by the future, by thoughts of home. Even the shadows cast by Silvergate were lightened, half-forgotten. Her shoulder stopped hurting for long stretches, and the tight feeling in her chest—*tension*, her doctor had said—let up altogether.

They traveled, slowly, across the south of England in an oval path: from Silvergate to the great houses of Knole and Penshurst and the gardens (open) at Sissinghurst, and then to Canterbury (where they came upon a church fête on the cathedral green) and south to Rye, to see Henry James's house. Then they drove on to Chichester, Winchester, Salisbury, and Wells, finding they liked cathedral towns, and they climbed to the ruined chapel on Glastonbury Tor, where Rosie felt a hint of her old strength returning. And then they headed north, in one grand, beautiful afternoon's drive, to Bath.

Susannah was reading *Under the Greenwood Tree* by Thomas Hardy and a book of Keats's letters along with her pregnancy book. She was keeping a journal, and she continued to write long, private letters to Duke—letters that must have amused her, because she sometimes broke into a chuckle as she wrote. Rosie devoured the local papers, especially the classified ads, finding in them what she found, at home, reading the old copies of *The Countryman:* human interest, humor, something to speculate about. She envied Susannah the need to write that seemed to be always with her; even reading, she held a pencil, underlined, made notes. On one afternoon, as they sat under the shedding plane tree on Abbey Green in Bath, eating rock cakes, Susannah suggested to Rosie that she help her write her gardening book—a suggestion that, once made, seemed so natural and inevitable that Rosie wondered why no one had thought of it before—then remembered that Peter had.

"I've wanted to ask you for a long time, actually," Susannah said. "But I wasn't sure if you were the kind of person one could make such an offer to. I didn't know if it might offend you." She paused and took a bite of her cake; there were crumbs all over the lap of her denim skirt. "I thought it was sort of presumptuous, offering to ghostwrite something you could probably jolly well do for yourself."

"Well, I can't seem to do it for myself," Rosie said. "I'm not a writer. I can't even do postcards. You write such witty messages, and all I can come up with is 'Having a great time, the weather is gorgeous.' Susannah, if you would help me write my book I'd pay you decently for the work. They've given me a huge sum already—for nothing. It still embarrasses me. How much do you think—?"

"I have no idea," said Susannah. "Make me an offer."

She waited, agreeable, eating, while Rosie considered. Rosie had no idea, either. She remembered her fears that Susannah was coming east to get money out of her, and thought of Peter's jokes about her stinginess: *Rosie Marner*, he called her. She didn't feel stingy, though. Her daughter's suggestion filled her with such glad relief she was ready to make over to Susannah her entire advance on the book. But she tried to think of a sensible figure.

"Suppose I pay you as much as your publisher is giving you for *Cloud House*. Then later we can make some arrangement about royalties. Would that be fair, do you think?"

"No," said Susannah. "It would be munificent."

"It's worth it to me," said Rosie. "I'm desperate."

Susannah sighed. "I must admit it would take a load off my mind, Rosie. I do need to support myself and little Rosetta, and I may never make another nickel from *Cloud House*. And the Café is an unknown quantity. That money would get me through the next year, and after that I could get a regular job."

The thought of Susannah working at a "regular job"—behind a desk in an office, selling things in a shop, teaching people to write—failed to take hold. Even in her efficient English reincarnation, there was something *wispy*about Susannah—something ungrounded, thought Rosie. The idea of Susannah as a single mother supporting her child—as she herself had done—was absurd. She wondered fleetingly about Edwin and his money, but didn't like to bring him up—another name they didn't mention. "You'll stay with me, of course," said Rosie. "Until you get on your feet. Until after the baby."

"I'll rent a room from you," Susannah said firmly.

"Nonsense," said Rosie, with equal firmness. "Your old bedroom is part of the deal."

Susannah shook her head. "I'll pay room and board, and if *Cloud House* gets a paperback sale or anything like that I'll get myself an apartment." She turned her stern profile away, intent on examining the little shops that ringed the green. "I'm not a sponger."

Rosie dropped it; she wasn't sure of her own motives, for one thing. Was she trying to buy Susannah's absolution—to make up for her betrayal, and Ivan's betrayal, and all those long-ago begging letters she had unmaternally ripped to bits without answering, and her years of anger at her lost daughter, with cold cash, with regular meals, with a stable home for her grandchild? With, in fact, this expensive English jaunt?

She shifted on the park bench. It had been a cold morning, but the afternoon was warm, and she was hot in her sweater. The rock cake sat heavily in her stomach. She had wanted to stop at a tea shop, but Susannah had been so hungry they had to go into a bakery and get a snack to eat outside on a bench. She had insisted on buying Rosie a rock cake, too—one of her little gestures toward independence. Rosie had finally figured out that Susannah felt just as dependent as she did, that while Rosie might be worn out and depressed and in pain, unable to drive or to cut up her own meat, she was paying for the trip. Money—Susannah's consciousness of her own financial limits compared to Rosie's largesse—was always coming into their relationship. It was an aspect of her reunion with her daughter that Rosie hadn't anticipated: she hadn't wanted to remember those letters; she preferred this new, serene, ungrasping Susannah. She wondered what Susannah retained from those days, whether she was embarrassed at the thought of her sly hints for cash, or grieved by her mother's lack of response.

What a pathetic pair we are, Rosie thought, looking at Susannah's set face. Even after weeks of togetherness they were still circling warily, glancing off each other, meeting now and then on common ground to share a laugh, some gossip, bits of their life stories, their pleasure in England, and then awkwardly stepping back behind their boundaries. Sometimes when their eyes met they looked away, then sometimes back, with rueful smiles. *And yet I like her*, Rosie thought. She was a good companion, she was sweet, she was putting up with a lot. Rosie wondered what she wrote in her journal, and what was in her letters to Duke.

She had to speak, and change the subject. "It's a funny tree, isn't it?" she said lamely, but Susannah looked with interest at the plane tree with its loose, shaggy bark and the globes of fruit, some dropped rotting on the ground.

"I've never seen one at home," said Susannah.

"They're all over New Haven," said Rosie, amused. "I'll have to take you on an expedition to the big city when we get back."

Susannah surveyed the tree, the green, the shops, the clear blue sky above the ancient rooftops, with her usual good humor. "I like it here in England so much, Rosie. I've always loved traveling, but I've never liked a place so well—except that little corner of Connecticut. *Your* corner." She laughed softly, and Rosie realized that Susannah's laugh, vaguely familiar all these weeks, was Edwin's. "Coming there from California woke me up," Susannah said. "I don't know how else to explain it."

Rosie had one of her brief, unbidden Ivan-memories: Ivan when she first met him telling her with such vehemence how he hated California, and two months later sitting half-naked in her kitchen homesick for it, for the blue wild ocean and the spaciousness. "I've always heard California is so beautiful," Rosie said. The remembered Ivan was so vivid before her she could have reached out and touched his warm, tanned chest.

"Beautiful," Susannah said thoughtfully. "Well, of course, it is, a lot of it. But it's inhuman. At least, that's how it seemed to me. *This*—" She gestured around the busy Bath street, at old stone and flower boxes. "This is human beauty—for people. And the countryside, Rosie—the hedges and the sheep and the hills." She turned to Rosie with Edwin's smile, wiping the last crumbs from her mouth, daintily, with a paper napkin. "Do you know the Los Angeles metropolitan area is as big as all of Connecticut?" She crumpled the napkin and stuffed it in her skirt pocket, took off her glasses—she wore them for eating as well as reading—and stowed them away, too. "He's gone back there, to California. I don't know if you were aware of that."

"Yes, I was," Rosie said. Susannah looked at her in surprise, as if Rosie's words had revealed something important. "I got a postcard," Rosie added, half-whispering.

Susannah took her hand, impulsively. You wouldn't expect Susannah to be a hand-taker, a toucher, but she always made contact. "Did you love him, Rosie? Tell me that."

Tears came to her eyes, blurring the little shops across the way. *He was so beautiful,* she thought. Without looking at Susannah she said, "Yes, I guess I did love him." The simple statement sounded false to her, though the words were true.

"But that was in another country," Susannah said softly, not letting go her hand, so that Rosie couldn't wipe her eyes, or cover her face when it contorted. Rosie thought: *I never would have done it if I'd known you first, Susannah,* but it wasn't something she could say aloud.

A woman passing, with a basket on her arm, pretended not to look at them. Rosie sobbed once, and Susannah retrieved the paper napkin from her pocket and gave it to Rosie. Rosie wiped her eyes. "Please don't feel bad," said Susannah. "I mean, feel bad about him if you need to—if you loved him—but not about me."

"But it's *only* you I feel bad about, Susannah." She gave her nose a rough, one-handed wipe, and crumpled the napkin in her fist. "Aren't you even angry? Don't you hate me? Are you a *saint*?"

Susannah looked down at her shoes: scuffed loafers, with knee socks forever falling down. She's a *child*, Rosie thought irritably. *A child. She knows nothing.*

"I hated you like poison at first," Susannah said. "I thought you were a monster. I felt sick whenever I thought of you." Tears burned behind Rosie's eyes. She breathed deeply through her nose. Her chest hurt. No saint, then, and possibly no wisp. Susannah went on, "But—and this may sound odd—I had my own problems. What happened with you and Ivan was just one more." Rosie felt diminished and resentful, and then, suddenly, relieved, as if she stood again at the top of Glastonbury Tor looking down at a tiny town, tiny people and cars, and then around at the vast sky. Susannah continued, in a voice that stopped and started, thinking aloud. "Then comes the really strange part, Rosie. Because I began to feel that it brought us together. Nothing else managed to—not Peter, not family feeling, not good will, not even curiosity. But that—" She looked at Rosie with frank affection. "That did it, Rosie. And so how could I stay angry? Look!" She gestured around, her slim hand taking in everything, then swooping to pick up a tawny leaf from the grass. She held it up, laughing. "Look! We wouldn't be here together, we wouldn't be friends, we wouldn't be planning to write your book. I wouldn't have a mother, Rosie."

A saint, after all, Rosie thought, and pondered it—that those nights with Ivan had led to this, an English city, a plane-tree leaf, Susannah's bright face smiling at her.

"Well, I'm still sorry," Rosie said. "I caused you pain." It was what she had wanted to tell Susannah, properly, all these weeks. A formal apology. Now, said, it hardly mattered.

"I'm sorry, too," said Susannah with a wry smile, and their two admissions wove together and officially blanked out years and years.

After that, they were at ease with each other. Their planned two weeks stretched to three. Rosie tried not to think about her garden; Kiki had promised to weed and water when she could. It would take Kiki's mind off her grandchild, due any minute. Rosie wondered whether the baby had come. She and Kiki had grown close. It was Kiki, after all, who had found her, Kiki and Jim, and she could vaguely recall Kiki cradling her, weeping, while Jim called the ambulance. She sent Kiki postcards: "Still having a great time, the weather is still perfect. How's the garden?"

They went south again, from Bath, into Dorset—Hardy country. They stayed two nights at an inn in Puddletown and went to the Hardy cottage. It was in Puddletown that Rosie took off her sling. It was too soon, Susannah said—against doctor's orders. But Rosie left it off, her shoulder didn't hurt at all, the sling was driving her crazy. "Look!" she said to Susannah, cutting up a piece of beef in a pub. "I'm a grown-up again."

She was very happy. She began reading the real estate columns in the newspapers with more than casual interest. "If my book makes any money, I just might buy a place over here," she said.

"Then you could jet back and forth between two gardens," Susannah said. "And we could write a book about it. *Transatlantic Gardening. Gardening for Jet-Setters. How My Pea Patch Contributes to International Understanding.*"

In the mornings, after breakfast—not every day, but most days—they settled down somewhere to work on the book, usually in a garden. They chose their inns for the gardens, and sitting there in the sun Rosie talked, and Susannah took notes. They were doing the biographical part, the personal bits, first. Rosie talked about her parents, her grandfather and her uncles, the gardens of her childhood, the strawberry bed she herself had planted at age five from runners snipped from the big kitchen garden at Silvergate. Susannah was amazed and gratified at how much she remembered, though to Rosie it seemed nearly everything was lost, or faded so badly by time that only trifles were left, details. But that was what she wanted, Susannah said. It was enough: not to worry. She would take those snippets and quilt them into something tangible.

"You're enjoying this?" Rosie would say, stopping in the midst of an attempt to get something right. "You don't mind?"

"I love it," Susannah assured her. "Quit fishing. I'm sure you've been told a zillion times that you're a very interesting talker."

"Well."

"Please. Go on."

Rosie told her, too, about her own babyhood, about the gardens in Boston, and Mr. McPherson, and her own hunger for the feel of soil and the sight of green shoots, and how they bought the house in East Chiswick. "I'll tell you when we get back how I began to garden there. I've got photographs of the various stages the yard went through over the years."

"I'm learning a lot," Susannah said, scribbling. "I feel like getting down on my knees in that border over there, and digging. Don't you think their dahlias need dividing?"

She wrote without looking, her eyes on Rosie, her ball-point pen skimming over the paper.

"How do you read it?" Rosie wanted to know.

Susannah showed Rosie her notes; they were perfectly legible. "What a talent," Rosie said. It made her strangely happy, that accurate, impersonal hand taking down her thoughts. She liked Susannah's competence.

"Is it interesting, Susannah?" Rosie wanted to know. "To people who don't know me, I mean? Will anyone want to read this?"

"Sure, if they like gardening. Why not?" Susannah grinned. "This is good stuff, Rosie. They were right to give you so much money. And it's going to be awfully well written. Wait."

In the evenings, Rosie sat up in bed reading newspapers, and Susannah wrote in her journal and read Keats's letters. Once, when her daughter was in the shower, Rosie flipped through the book. On one page was underlined, "I am certain of nothing but the holiness of the Heart's affections and the truth of the Imagination." Hesitantly, Rosie turned to the journal, a plain, blue spiral-bound notebook, and opened it at random: "We saw Jane Austen's grave set into the stones of Winchester Cathedral. Dignified, plain, no mention of her books, just devoted daughter and so on. I could have wept at the injustice and then thought it didn't matter after all. How many people see the grave? And how many read the books, which is where she really is. Then we sat by the river. River green, melancholy somehow, with yellow leaves floating on the surface, and I wondered if I'm a writer the way Jane Austen and Hardy and Keats were writers, and I didn't think so, and I managed to ruin the afternoon for myself."

Rosie closed the cover in confusion. She thought back to their day in Winchester, how cheerful and talkative Susannah had been, how she'd made some flippant comment about that Jane Austen memorial; how they had enjoyed the sunny riverbank (where Susannah had had a Cornish pasty and a can of 7-Up); how Susannah had read aloud from a book on cathedrals, comparing the three they had seen. Love for her daughter assaulted her, and when Susannah returned from the shower down the hall, with her hair bound up in a towel and her robe tied tight around little Rosetta, Rosie said, "I was looking through your Keats, I hope you don't mind. I like this line, about the holiness of the heart's affections."

"And the truth of the imagination," said Susannah. "Those are the words I live by—Mom," she added, shaking out her hair. She was trying to call Rosie *Mom;* it wasn't seemly, she felt, to call her mother by her first name. But the attempts were still forced, and either embarrassed or amused them both.

The peek into Susannah's journal bothered Rosie for a while. Then she forgot the snooping and remembered only what she had seen, and what it had revealed about Susannah. She regarded her daughter with curiosity, with care, with respect; for all her openness, her warm touches on the arm, her bubbly cheer, she was as secret as Edwin had been. So why do I love her, when I didn't love Edwin? Rosie wondered, but not for long. The years hadn't improved her ability to think without rancor of her ex-husband. The hell with him, she always thought when she thought of him at all. In Mexico with a wife younger than Susannah: that was all she needed to know. She could easily conjure the rest: Edwin fifty-five instead of forty, aging unbecomingly, loved for his money, a wasted life behind him and Susannah's laugh on his lips—a laugh too high, too giggly for a man.

They drove to Plymouth, to the sea, and climbed an ancient tower for the view from its railed balcony. The high salt wind whipped their hair, and sunlight, threatened by gray clouds far in the distance, gleamed a patternless gold on the dark blue water. Flags strung up for a boat race cracked like whips in the wind. "Over there is the Silvergate Café," Susannah said, looking out to sea.

A man standing beside them on the balcony grinned and nodded.

"Americans always get emotional at Plymouth," he said. "You go down to the quay there where the *Mayflower* left and have a good cry."

In a shop on the Crescent, Susannah bought a quilted whale and a quilted dolphin for Duke's twin daughters. Rosie bought one of the dolphins for herself and, half-ashamed of her childishness, presented it to Susannah for little Rosetta—then, when they had left Plymouth and were driving north and east again, regretted the impulse and wished for it back. It was the kind of gift Barney used to give her. She still thought of Barney now and then. Kiki had run into him and told him Rosie had been hurt in an automobile accident—Kiki, scrupulously, had told hordes of people this lie. Barney had sent flowers, with a card: "Coals to Newcastle, but get well soon. Barney." Tiny yellow roses— no *love, Barney*. Kiki told her he was seeing, seriously, some woman in New London, a teacher. Rosie regretted Barney as she regretted the quilted dolphin; no—*more*, she said to herself, being honest. Much more. She smiled to herself, amused at the comparison, imagining the dolphin in little Rosetta's crib.

She sent a postcard to her editor in New York: "Book going well. Weather perfect. Beautiful country." The sheep on the hillsides, Susannah said, were like fat brown sausages. The hedgerows were full of elderberries, black bryony, goose grass, old-man's beard. Rosie bought a book to identify them, and she and Susannah took long country walks and then pressed autumn wildflowers between the pages of their guidebooks. They watched the landscape change—but slowly, slowly—to an autumn with a hint of winter in it. There was snow, they heard on television, up north in the Lake District. Green was still the dominant color—it was greener than home, they were sure; autumn was later, more gradual, less dramatic—but the green was now well mixed with gold, and the oak trees were solid brown and dry, their leaves falling fast. Rosie and Susannah made plans to go home.

They had two days left when Susannah suggested they go back to Silvergate. From something in her voice Rosie was aware that the idea hadn't been dead in Susannah's mind but only dormant since that dismal day in the rain.

"Oh, Susannah—what for?" Even as she spoke, though, she knew they would go, and she was willing. She felt newly minted by their slow traveling, her shoulder nearly twinge-free, her soul refreshed. She dreamed of preparing a garden, working through the dirt with trowel and gloved fingers to pull out roots and rocks. In her one dream of Ivan he was as distant and untouchable as a priest; he was very tall, so tall she couldn't reach him, and he was dressed in black.

"For the gardens," Susannah said. "For your memories. For the hell of it."

"Oh—all right," Rosie said with a reluctance that fooled no one. Her heart was light.

They were in Somerset, and—the decision made—they proceeded east in the little red car, a day's trip through Wiltshire—across Salisbury Plain where they saw, in the distance, the familiar, awesome shapes of Stonehenge from the A344—and into Hampshire and the Sussexes to Kent, retracing their steps and reminiscing, now that it was coming to a close, about the high points of their trip.

"Cathedrals," Susannah said. "I would happily visit a dozen more. Next time I'm going north, to see the one at York." And then, without transition, "I miss my cats. I hope Duke's taking good care of them."

"We'll collect them first thing." The three cats—Rosie still couldn't tell them apart—had moved in with her when Susannah had, immediately taking over the yard and intimidating the Sheffield's tabby. "I sort of miss them myself."

"They seem to like Duke awfully well. I hope he hasn't alienated their affections."

Susannah, Rosie suspected, wanted to talk not about the cats but about Duke. "You've written him a lot of letters," she said tentatively.

"I'm trying to get him to fall in love with me," Susannah said.

"*What?*"

"By way of my glorious prose. I'm trying to win him with words."

Rosie studied her surprising daughter. They were driving through West Sussex in the late afternoon. The hills were dotted with sausage-sheep clustered together, the sun was low in the sky behind them. Susannah, pink-cheeked in a black turtleneck, smiled sideways at Rosie. *Pregnancy becomes her*, Rosie thought for the hundredth time.

"But why, Susannah? Are you in love with him?"

"Yes, I am," said Susannah. "It's one thing I've learned on this trip."

Her little smile broadened out. "I've learned to identify woundwort and goose grass and hawthorne. I can tell the apse from the transept from the choir. I've gotten to like ale and kidneys. And I've discovered I'm in love with Duke. Travel is so broadening."

"He's a nice fellow," Rosie said lamely. She had met Duke twice and had liked him—a quiet, self-possessed man with occasional flashes of impish humor. He had reminded her, in fact, of Susannah. She remembered that he was a touch shorter than her daughter, had grayish eyes and square, competent-looking hands. She remembered the pâté Ivan had brought her, and the meal she had eaten at Duke's restaurant. He and she and Susannah had sat on Rosie's back porch. She and Duke had talked about mulching. Later, she had been surprised to learn there was anything between him and Susannah; he had seemed so purely her friend. "I thought he already wanted you to come and live with him," she said.

"Oh, he does," said Susannah. "But he doesn't think he's in love with me. And I don't want to shack up with someone who isn't." She spoke lightly, almost as if mocking herself, but Rosie wondered what lay behind the casual words. She wondered what Susannah's journal said about it all, and what the letters to Duke contained. How could you make someone fall in love with you by writing him letters?

"Is it—" She looked for a word. "Is it fierceness you want?" Thinking she understood.

Susannah considered. "No," she said after a minute. "That's the last thing I want."

Oh, I do, thought Rosie, surprising herself. She was homesick all of a sudden—not for home so much (though she'd be glad to get back and relieve Kiki of her garden duties) as for her old self. She wanted to get dressed up and go out with a man who told her she looked good; she wanted to sit by her fire drinking with some man who would make her laugh; she wanted to climb the stairs to her big, welcoming bed with a man close behind her admiring her legs. She wanted the old game to begin again. *I'm only fifty*, she thought. Her shoulder was better, she had lost a few pounds walking the lanes of England, the ancient countryside stretched out in the sun around her, and she felt young, young.

They stayed at an inn just outside Chiddingstone, and had dinner there overlooking a garden that sloped to a silver rope of a stream banked with green, and beyond it deep green meadow.

"Does it stay green all year?" Rosie asked the innkeeper. "Doesn't it ever get brown and bare?"

He laughed, serving their fish. He was a thin, mustachioed man who had told them he was originally from up north, a Shropshire lad, but had moved to the mellower south where his wife's people were. "We get winter," he said. "We get our share of snow and cold, though it comes later here than some places." He asked where they were from, confused Connecticut with Cleveland, and had a cousin who had once been to California.

"That's where I'm from—sort of," said Susannah with a look at Rosie.

"That's where I'd like to go," said the innkeeper.

"Don't. Go to Connecticut." Susannah had already tucked into her dinner, and she spoke chewing. "Go to New England."

"Ah—New England. Now that's where I'm always told the autumn is so glorious." But he looked fondly out on his own green garden.

I'll come back, thought Rosie. I'll marry an inkeeper and grow an English garden and talk about the States with homesick American tourists. But at the moment she wanted to go home.

"I miss it," she said to Susannah the next morning. "I miss all the reds and golds and browns. Do you think we'll be back in time to catch some of it?"

"You're asking *me*?" Susannah laughed. "The expatriate? I haven't seen a New England fall since I was ten years old." They were on the road to Silvergate. "I think you're in just the right mood for this excursion, Rosie," Susannah added. Rosie had talked her into giving up on *Mom;* it had always sounded as if there were quotation marks around it. "If you're busy missing New England you won't get too upset about *old* England." She gave Rosie a quick smile, her small anxious one. "I hope it'll be better this time. At least we'll see the gardens. And we'll take notes for the book, and photographs. And tomorrow we'll be home."

They drove along the yellowing woods and into the car park. The sun was out, the brick manor house glowed pink, the octagonal cupola was there after all with its perching stork. The trees beyond the house were green and gold, and the gardens were open. Susannah and Rosie paid their admission again—to the same National Trust guide, who recognized them, smiled, said the gardens were especially lovely just now, before frost. They went straight through the house, feeling at home, out the double doors at the back of the Great Parlour to the terrace, and there before them, in a series of descending terraces, were the gardens of Silvergate: clipped and green, deserted, the turreted hedges blackish against blue sky.

They walked down to the formal rose beds—tidy and flowerless now, dotted with orange rose hips—and beyond them to the lily pond. The pond was perfectly clear, the colors of the trees reflected in it just as vivid in the water as on the shore, the surface ruffled by a light wind that gathered itself now and then into a gust. Rosie almost went up to the pond, knelt beside it and peered in to see her face, age fifty, where years ago her young eyes had looked back at her. But she refrained. It would be too much, somehow, of either ecstasy or pain, and the only logical culmination of such an act would be to throw herself into the water, and sink below the reflections of the trees.

The garden was perfectly quiet, not a guide was visible, or a gardener, or another tourist. Rosie and Susannah inspected all the little gardens, walking the graveled paths and admiring their neat regularity, their patterns, their variety.

"I remember them all," Rosie said, but she didn't say much more than that. Susannah was silent also, taking photographs and, eventually, wandering off by herself. *Tactful child*, thought Rosie to herself, turning down a path, and there before her was the battened green door in the yew hedge behind which, she knew—how could she have forgotten? it was as familiar, suddenly, as her own place back home— was the brick path that led to the gardener's cottage.

Rosie sat down on a stone bench and let the tears come to her eyes. Behind the door—and looking at the handle she recalled precisely the amount of pressure your thumb must exert, and the vigorous push it took to open it—behind the door the path curved to the right and then turned left, and there was the stone cottage with the tile roof, and the two squat chimneys, the heavy oak door, and the tiny-paned windows on either side. In this October sun the cottage would be tawny brown, and the Michaelmas daisies would still be in bloom by the door, and the Virginia creeper by the wall would be reddening. And her mother's gardening basket used to stand there, with her dirty blue gloves and the battered straw hat her father said belonged on a horse.

"Well? And how is it?" Susannah sat down beside her, camera around her neck; her blonde hair, unbraided, was tangled in her face, and she pushed it back and hung on to it.

"It's just fine," Rosie said, and blew her nose. "It's as it was. That's all I wanted from it."

Susannah nodded, and pointed to the birch trees behind the pond. The wind, blowing through them, flung their leaves into the water. "'*Goldengrove unleaving*,'" Susannah said.

"My mother used to say that," Rosie murmured, shyly but with delight. "Every fall." She smiled suddenly. "And '*worlds of wanwood leafmeal.*' That's what she called her compost heap. I'd forgotten."

"They're from a poem," Susannah said.

"Not Keats?"

"Gerard Manley Hopkins. 'Season of mists and mellow fruitfulness,' is Keats. And something something dum de dum '*the vines that round the thatch-eves run.*' And then something about apples and bees." Susannah let go her hair and rested her hands comfortably on her little stomach. "Why are you crying? Is it so sad?"

"I was missing my parents," said Rosie, her eyes wet again. Susannah's hair blew against her face. "And then you sat down and said that, just like my mother." *Wanwood leafmeal:* the crunch of leaves underfoot, and the bonfires of her youth, her mother with a square of red wool tied under her chin, her father heaping leaves with a rake, the woody smell of the smoke, the magical look of the smoke rising, thinning, disappearing. Her mother holding her hand.

"My grandmother," said Susannah. "I remember her so well. Her pretty English voice."

Rosie regretted, not for the first time, that because of her Susannah hadn't known her grandparents for so long. But there had been, she thought, enough regrets and apologies. She didn't speak of it, touched Susannah's arm. "Behind that door is the cottage where we

269

lived. Down a brick path lined with rhododendrons. A stone cottage with flowers out front, and a maple tree in back, and a wooden bench painted green, and my little strawberry patch."

"Let's open it," said Susannah, getting up. "Is it locked, do you think? Let's take a look."

But Rosie pulled her back. "No—please," she said. "I'd rather we didn't. I have it all in my head, Susannah, and we'll put it in the book. But I don't want to open the door. Unless—"

"I could look!" Susannah beamed at her, and stood up. "Great idea. You start back, up the path, and I'll open the door a crack and have a look, and I won't say a word. And if the National Trust swoops down on me with a paddy wagon you come and rescue me, and say it's part of our research for an important book." She paused, and looked closely into Rosie's face. "Okay? Or would you rather I didn't?"

"No—have a look." Rosie smiled, and put out a hand for Susannah to pull her up. "I'll head back to the terrace and meet you there."

The chrysanthemums were over, she could see that, and frost would come soon and cut down the loosestrife, the daisies that were left, the verbena in the stone urns. She stood on the terrace, not looking back down the garden path, looking up at the house rising above her in all its magnificence, and blew her nose. For a dozen reasons, it was time to go home.

Susannah came up behind her, light-footed, her hands in the pockets of her jacket. "It's getting chilly," she said.

They walked across the terrace together, but just before they went back through the double doors—through them they could see a party of tourists entering—Rosie turned to her daughter. "Just tell me," she said. "Is it the same, Susannah? Is it the way I remembered?"

Susannah impulsively hugged her. "I knew you'd want to know," she said with glee. "And yes," she told Rosie. "I couldn't see the back, so I don't know about the strawberry bed and the little green bench, but it's a stone cottage, with flowers out front—don't ask me what kind— and a chimney with smoke coming out of it, and not a soul around. Down a brick path lined with rhododendrons."

Rosie smiled, dug out her handkerchief and blew her nose for the last time. "All right, then," she said. "Let's go home."

Chapter Eight

Halloween

Dear Duke,

By the time you get this I will be home—this is our last night in England—but I'll write it anyway, for me as much as for you. I've often wished I had a double living in my brain, someone who could take part in all the thoughts that pass through it, some super-tolerant spirit with a high boredom threshold. For the moment you're its substitute. Lord knows, I've bombarded you with letters. It's only because, for all my pleasure in this beautiful country, I miss you.

Dear Duke, I look forward to coming home. It seems that we've been here a long time, though I know after I've been home a while I'll remember it as a painfully brief trip. I didn't begin missing things until just a few days ago. You, yes, I've missed steadily, and Peter, too, and the cats. But *things*. That just started. I miss your big front porch and my mother's little back screened one, and the Chiswick Public Library. I miss certain books, and everyday events like buying groceries, and I miss my old wool shirt that I considered too crummy to bring abroad. And I miss the look of it there. Rosie talks fervently about autumn in New England—the *foliage*, she calls it, and hopes we'll be home in time for a "foliage trip." Like the pilgrims going to Canterbury. Well, I want to see it, too. Maybe on one of your days off the three of us could drive to Massachusetts or Vermont or wherever one goes to worship foliage. We never took our trip, the one we would have taken had we not ended up at the hospital instead. Rosie and I didn't manage to get as far west as Cornwall, and Land's End, where I could have looked straight across the water at you, but the sea at Plymouth reminded me of our afternoon in Stonington. And that reminds me—please give my love to the twins and tell them I have various fripperies and doo-dads for them.

I'll return with a thicker waist than when I left. My favorite skirt is unbuttonable, and I bought a large safety pin in Rye to fasten it, a souvenir of Henry James's town. I feel great. The baby and I thrive in this clear air. Rosie also thrives. If I had known her old self I'd have to say she's her old self again. Her spirits have risen steadily. We did go back to Silvergate, to the gardens, on a sunny breezy perfect day, and she seemed overcome by her memories, which all returned to her, apparently, beside the lily pond, and in the rose garden, and at the sight of a little green door in the hedge (amazing hedges, thick and black and eight feet tall clipped into turrets and battlements) which she said led to the old cottage where she lived. And she wouldn't go through it. She keeps certain strongholds intact, hasn't mentioned my father, for example, not a word, and seems utterly without curiosity about Ivan. As if once people, or cottages, pass out of her life they lose existence, or hang on only in memory where they're kept within narrow bounds. Or they surface, I suppose, in dreams. I don't know how healthy it is, but I'm glad she didn't choose to go through the green door because I persuaded her to let me peek through (while she scurried off toward the main house as if pursued by demons) and behind it was a small-ish sort of modern building that evidently housed tools and garden equipment, including a tractor, and beyond that there was nothing. No brick path stone cottage flower beds, nothing. Just scruffy grass and what could have been a hayfield, all yellow, and the inevitable sheep in the distance. And I went back and told her, when she asked, and I knew she would ask, and was prepared, that it was just as she remembered, that her lovely magic childhood survived intact behind a little green door. And she shed another tear or two and that was that.

Was this whopper justified? And did she make it all up, she and my grandparents, out of *The Secret Garden* and Agatha Christie and those back issues of *The Countryman*?

Dear Duke, are you well? Does the Café flourish? I miss the smell of cooking, and the sight of you in your apron, and Ginger with her wild hair, and the twins. Scratch the cats behind the ears for me, except Byron who doesn't like it. I still have no answer to your question. For now, I'll go to Rosie's and help her write her book. And will you, I wonder, continue to ask me when I return? Will you even remember me after three weeks and a day and a dozen rambling letters? In a way I'm a different person, a thicker around the middle one with a tendency to put on a motley English accent from time to time, a person with a mother for the first time, a person whose soul has been bathed in these tender landscapes, and soothed. Will you remember me? I remember you, dear Duke, and our night together before its terrible end. I remember being so fond of your back when I curled up against it, and how for one night everything seemed settled. I realize now I'll never send this letter, and so I can say more: for instance that I do love you, Duke. I wish things were different, and that you didn't have your own little green door in a battlemented hedge. But that would be wishing you were a different person, one whose soul has been bathed and soothed by something or other, and everyone knows it's not real love if you don't accept the beloved *as is*. It feels like real love, though I do wish you were different, in just that one way. In every other way you're perfect, except that you won't love me. Your fatal flaw.

If I were still on the coast of England I would rip this letter to pieces and fling it into the Atlantic for you, and you would find it in the belly of a fish you buy at DeLuca's, a piece of paper softened and faded by its ocean voyage, on which you can just make out the words "I do love you, Duke." Or more cryptically, "tools and garden implements." Or "fripperies and doo-dads," or "the inevitable sheep." As it is, I'm in a posh hotel not far from Heathrow Airport, and I shall rip it to pieces and flush it down the last in our series of memorable English toilets— veritable geysers, they are, white-water rapids, hissing Niagara Falls explosions of water that will reduce my letter to limp pulp.

I'm homesick, that's my excuse for this drivel, but I'm not sure what home I'm sick for—your place, or Rosie's, or the Café, or someplace I've never been. Technically, I'm homeless, no less a wanderer than I've always been. I've tried to change your heart with these letters, because I can't accept what you said, that you have nothing to give. I know that's not true, but if you don't know it then my certainty isn't worth much.

Dear Duke, here in England my life has stood still for me so I can look at it, my life that I've dreamed my way through, half the time, like a cat—and I've turned it over carefully in my mind, with all the metamorphoses that have made it up: unloved daughter, spoiled daughter, dropout, reclaimed dropout, wife, betrayed wife, ex-wife, reclaimed daughter. All a mix-up, and that's not even the end of it, there's a part in there that has visions and arranges them into patterns and writes stories about them, and one that makes vows and after due deliberation breaks them when necessary, and one who loves animals, baseball, books, you. I've been looking at it, Duke—my life, myself—all over England, in these sleepy old narrow towns, behind crumbling stone walls, in fabulous gardens, in half a dozen cathedrals—especially in the cathedrals, looking up, and up, just as one is supposed to do—the spaces in them, the stillness, the height, the light coming through the colored windows, the sense of an inspired hand in all of it—what am I saying? That in the cathedrals, especially, I examined my life and asked questions and kept getting the same answer, this one: I will make Duke love me, I will raise our children, I will write my books. Beyond that I can't see, but I can see that far, and I write you this letter with those answers in my mind, and flush it down the toilet because none of my answers answer your question.

But I'm coming home, dear Duke, to do battle.

Coming up the Connecticut Turnpike in the back seat of Peter's little car, Susannah already missed the bright blue skies, the plump clouds, the green hedges and old stone walls of England. Route 95 was a scene of desolation, margined with dumps, wrecked buildings, waste stretches choked with weeds and strewn with parts of cars, cans, oil drums, garbage. The sides of abandoned warehouses and factories, and the concrete bridge abutments, were layered with graffiti: KILL SLADE, NO NUKES, FUCK WAR, FUCK YOU.

"We're romanticizing England, of course," Rosie said over her shoulder to Susannah. "We only saw the good parts. They have all this in England, too."

"I wonder where," Susannah said. She chewed dolefully at her cuticles, and narrowed her eyes to blur the passing scene. It didn't help.

Susannah was depressed and exhausted. She hadn't slept on the return flight—it had departed in the morning; and the red tape at Kennedy had taken, it seemed, hours; and a large man in a business suit had banged into her, nearly knocking her down, at the baggage claim, and he not only hadn't apologized but had glared at her as if it was her fault; and she had suddenly, irrationally, become consumed with fears for little Rosetta: what if she *had* fallen, what if she had miscarried there by the revolving baggage claim at Kennedy Airport, how could she have chanced a plane flight during her pregnancy, she must have been crazy.

While her mother and Peter claimed bags and chattered about the World Series and the beauties of England and the weather in Connecticut, Susannah's mind halted at the thought of her own fatigue, and it expanded, her tiredness, until she was tired of everything, and frightened at being home: *now what?* She should have stayed in England, she thought. Become an expatriate writer. Brought up her poor baby in a country where people don't knock you down and then look at you with hatred. She was amazed that they got out of the airport alive, and now here they were on this ugly stretch of road, and the ride was bumpy, making her vaguely carsick, and Rosie, of all people, was saying they romanticized England.

Susannah closed her eyes, returned to Rye, and entered the little glass-fronted pavilion in the garden of Lamb House, and Henry James got up from his table, where he was painstakingly putting together a wooden toy—a duck, maybe, with a bright yellow bill—and put an arm around her shoulder and said, "This is the real thing, old girl."

When she awoke they were on Route One, outside Chiswick. "I fell asleep," she said.

"And woke up just in time," Peter said. "How does the place look?"

They were passing the Café. *An omen*, Susannah thought, to wake up just then: an omen of what? The Café was lit up for dinner, cars massed in front. Peter slowed up.

"Want to stop?"

"No—we'd better not." She prayed they wouldn't overrule her. She needed time to prepare for meeting Duke; the idea filled her with dread. Here, home, what certainties she'd had were lost. "They must be horribly busy," she said.

"Still packing them in," Peter said.

It's mine, she thought as they went by. *Mine*—in surprise, comprehending it for the first time. She thought of novels, movies, in which a woman, usually a farm wife, suddenly bereft of her man, has to take over his role. She imagined herself presiding over the Café, arranging flowers on the tables—if they could ever afford flowers on the tables.

The image of the Café stayed in her mind—not Duke, not yet, just the Café. It was incongruous, she realized, with its crisp green and white checks and the classy sign and inside (she imagined it) the good smells and the beautiful food—and all of it sandwiched between Wendell's with its purple light in the window, and the Liquor Boutique with its usual dated and ungrammatical specials: OUR OWN HOUSE BRAND VODKA GIN SUMMER BARGAIN'S GALORE.

"I think we're going to have to find a new location," she said, liking the proprietary words. A little stone cottage—she imagined it—like an English tea shop.

"Duke's been making those noises, too," Peter said. "He's got his eye on a seafood place in East Chiswick that's just filed for bankruptcy."

"Seymour's?" Rosie asked. "Oh, my, Barney and I used to eat there."

"Not often enough to keep them in business."

"It's a nice little place—just right for the Café, Susannah." Rosie pointed out her window. "Just down there, as a matter of fact, where Hollander Street crosses. Remember that corner?" She sighed. "Oh dear. We should have just looked in on Duke and everybody."

"But I'm so tired," Susannah said quickly. "I don't know what's come over me." She forced out a yawn, which became genuine.

"Well, it can't be jet lag. She just doesn't get jet lag," Rosie said to Peter. "I've never seen such stamina." She turned to smile at Rosie. "It's pregnancy, that's what it is. At last you're beginning to behave like a pregnant woman." She reached back a hand, and Susannah grasped it. "We did have fun, didn't we?"

"I wish we were back there," said Susannah.

"We shall return," Rosie said. "We'll take Peter, and the baby."

"Duke says he'll bring the cats over tomorrow morning before work, Suse," Peter said. "If that's okay with you."

"Sure. Great."

"And he says to give him a call tonight if you're feeling up to it. He gets home around ten, he says."

"I know." He gets home around ten, she thought, and he takes a shower and has a beer and something to eat, and he sits on his porch thinking how he has nothing to give, no love at all, and then he goes to bed, alone. Tears gathered in her eyes. "But don't you wish we were back in Rye, Rosie? In the little garden at Lamb House? Remember how red the walls were? Remember the little gazebo?"

"I'm glad to be home," Rosie said firmly. They turned down her street, and she leaned forward to see her house. "I can't wait to get at my garden. Lord, what a list of chores I've got ahead of me."

Susannah had chewed her cuticle until it bled. She wished she had inherited Rosie's spunk and vigor. Here was Rosie, back from the dead and ready to smack the earth itself into shape—and here was Susannah, scared to death.

But how easy it was, after all, to settle into her old room again, to lie in the old maple bed propped on pillows, to drink the tea Peter brought her and read her accumulated mail. There was a letter from Carla, saying Tyler was taking Suzuki violin lessons. There was a note from Leslie Merwin saying her book was in production, and she would still love to meet her in New York one of these days, say when. There was a report from Mrs. Panza saying Edwin had received her two letters and her postcard, had enjoyed them, sent his love, said be good and be happy, continued as before, thank God. Nothing from Ivan, also thank God. No letter begging her to take him back: what she had feared since, in England, she dreamed it.

"It's not so bad, being home, is it?" Peter asked her when he brought the tea. He set the cup down, carefully, on Carla's letter. "Guess who's already out in the garden, hashing over the chrysanthemums with Mrs. Sheffield."

"And guess who's taken to her bed with the vapors."

"Enjoy it while you can. She'll have you out shredding cornstalks or some damn thing before you know it."

How easy it was, after all. She looked around the old shabby room—different from the room of her girlhood, but recognizable. Rosie had redecorated, of course; who wouldn't, on the departure of a wayward daughter? So it was yellow instead of blue, and there was wall-to-wall carpeting and wooden shutters at the windows and an oak dresser instead of the matching maple one that had been a present from her grandmother—Edwin's mother. But the bed was the same, even the too-soft mattress, and the light came in the windows just the same way—now, at twilight, with a soft pink glow. And the little pin-up lamp on the wall, with its pierced metal shade: for some reason, that hadn't been replaced, and the light shining through it, and the click it made when you turned it on, recalled her childhood as almost nothing else could—long hours reading on her bed in that circle of light—blissful, possessed escapes into books. She reached up and turned it on now, illuminating Peter, erasing the pale glow from the window.

"It's funny to be home," she said, but it was getting less funny all the time. It was beginning to seem almost normal, this room, this teacup, this pile of letters. The stack of manuscripts on the desk, accumulated during her six weeks tending Rosie, and a pile of books. The place between the windows where now there was a mirror but where, once, a painted-by-number sylvan scene had hung, done while she had the measles. She had stopped thinking, as she had those first days with Rosie: This is the house where my husband screwed my mother.

"We've missed you," Peter said. "I've seen Duke a couple of times, and we talked about you."

She closed her eyes. "Don't tell me."

"Only good things. He misses you, too. And Hollis wants to meet you."

She opened her eyes. "Hollis is here? With you?"

Peter smiled, with a look on his face she had never seen there. "He has a job with a solar architecture firm in Hartford," Peter said. "He commutes."

"And it's working out, Peter? It's for keeps?"

"Shh," he said, and put a finger to his lips. "I don't think in those terms. *Carpe diem*, Sister Sue. And gather ye rosebuds while ye may."

"What about Dante?"

"Dante." Peter stroked his mustache, still smiling. "You may not believe this, my sweet, but Dante—" He paused, for effect, crossed his legs, leaned back in his chair and grinned broadly. "Is done," he said. "*La commedia è finita.* Also typed, weighed and measured, and approved. I give my defense of the damn thing in January, and then I'm thrown to the wolves. A job." He pretended an elaborate shudder. "I'm too young to go to work."

They talked about his job prospects, about Susannah's book and Rosie's, about the solar summer house he and Hollis wanted to build, about England and the last excursion to Silvergate.

"And you think she's okay?" Peter asked Susannah. "You think she's the old Rosie?"

"The old Rosie *I* remember?" Susannah chuckled. "Not likely. She's a new improved Rosie."

"You've been good for her. And the trip, the book. The incipient heir."

As if to prove it, Rosie's voice sang up from downstairs. "Anybody home up there? Isn't anyone going to come down and appreciate my last mum before the frost gets it?"

Susannah hauled herself up from the bed—was it, really, little Rosetta that made her feel so heavy and slow?—and she and Peter went downstairs. They wandered through the garden in the cold twilight, the three of them, Rosie and Susannah in the heavy sweaters they had bought in Somerset. "It's coming," Rosie said, snapping off a blighted flower head. "Winter."

"You sound pretty happy about it," said Peter. "For a gardener."

"But winter's a gardener's best season," she said. "It's all anticipation. And *dreams.*" She took Susannah's arm. "I must remember that for the book. It's a good line. I don't know how you cured *your* writer's block, Peter," she went on. "But I just turned mine over to Susannah, and she's doing wonderful things with it. Making it into a silk purse."

They headed toward the house. "Oh, don't let's go in yet," Susannah said. There were three hours until ten o'clock. How to fill them, except with dread? "It's so nice out here in the dark. And you haven't told us yet if Mrs. Sheffield had her grandchild."

"It's cold, you silly girl. And you look like you're ready to drop over right there in my rose-bed. Come on inside and I'll tell you all about baby Jamie, six pounds five ounces. I'm so jealous." She squeezed Susannah's arm. "I can't wait for little Rosetta."

Inside, Peter had built a fire, and they gathered around it. Rosie yawned. "In England it's nearly midnight. Do you realize, Susannah, we'd probably be all tucked up into our feather beds by now? And remember the inn that gave us those lovely hot-water bottles for our feet? Covered in flowered flannel, Peter—all pink and white, like plump little babies."

Susannah laughed and then, yawning after her, was inspired. "I can't imagine why I thought I could stay up until ten," she said. "I can't possibly call Duke. Ten o'clock is going to be practically in the middle of the night."

She sounded to herself like a character in a play, but Peter looked at her with sympathy. "Why don't I give him a ring when I get home? You go to bed, and I'll tell him you'll see him tomorrow when he brings the cats."

Put off 'til tomorrow what you're too chicken to face today, she thought, and stood up, rubbing her eyes. "I think I will. Thanks, Peter." She stretched elaborately, feeling false, and vaguely guilty. "I *am* tired," she said with a touch of defiance.

"You look it—you look terrible," Rosie said helpfully. Susannah bent to kiss her cheek. "Sleep well," Rosie told her. "And little Rosetta, too. Get that child up to bed."

Susannah climbed the stairs, the extreme of her exhaustion momentarily lighted by the reprieve, but when she got to her room she nearly fell on her bed, and in one confused instant was asleep.

She awoke abruptly to pitch dark and the woolly smell of her Somerset sweater, disoriented for only a second before she recognized the particular silence of Rosie's house. She snapped on the light—10:30—and swung out of bed. She found an old nightgown in a drawer, put the sweater back on over it, and tiptoed downstairs. From Rosie's room came her dainty snore. In the cellar the furnace kicked on with a thump. There were still a few red coals in the fireplace, and the suitcases still stood in the hall. She missed the cats, good companions when she woke in the night, following softly downstairs at her heels, hoping for food, settling for her proximity.

She went into the kitchen and got a glass of milk—Peter had stocked the refrigerator, and she found bread and cheese for a sandwich. Then she sat down and dialed Duke's number; the longing to call him must have invaded her sleep and her dreams and, finally, awakened her. All dread was gone in this middle-of-the-night silence, 3:30 A.M. in England, the brown sheep probably beginning to stir in their pens—or out on the hillsides? Where did they go at night, those fat and ubiquitous sheep? When she returned, she would get up at 3:30 and drive out to see if they were there, like tiny hillocks in the moonlight.

"Hello?"

"It's me."

"Susannah." She had forgotten how deep and clear his voice was, how pretty her name sounded when he said it. "Welcome back."

"I missed you." For the moment, she could say nothing more.

"I missed you, too. And I'm glad you called. I was just making some chicken salad for the twins to have for lunch tomorrow, and then I was going to have a beer and listen to the radio for a while and go to bed. Peter said you'd gone to bed yourself. Why are you up?"

She swallowed. "I missed you, Duke," she said again. "I was afraid to talk to you or see you when I got here, I don't know why, just afraid of how I would feel or something, and then I woke up suddenly in the night, wide awake for no reason, and looked at the clock, and I wanted to call you all of a sudden. I couldn't wait."

"Susannah."

"It seemed weird to me, it seemed utterly bizarre, that I could have been afraid of you just because—well—oh, you know—and I just wanted to hear your voice to reassure myself that we could still be friends, at least, that you were still the same." She stopped. She hadn't meant to say so much, or to say it in this way. Why hadn't she rehearsed on the way to the phone instead of missing the cats, thinking of sheep on the hills, making a sandwich? But she hadn't known, when she woke in the dark needing to call, for what she had wanted to say—had known only that she wished for his voice. "I would have rehearsed this but I had no script," she said. "I probably sound crazy. Let's just forget this phone call, you go have your beer and I'll eat my sandwich and I'll see you tomorrow."

"You didn't tell me you made a sandwich."

"What? Oh. Well, I did. Just cheese."

"I like to think of you sitting there with your cheese sandwich. And are you in your nightgown?"

She sighed. "Yes. An old summer one, with my new sweater on over it, and a pair of black wool socks with a hole in one toe."

"What new sweater?"

"I got it in Somerset. There's a place that raises sheep and shears them and spins the wool and then the sweaters are hand-knit there by elves and fairies. Duke?"

"What?"

"Why are we having this conversation?"

"Because I'm so happy you're home, Susannah. I wish I could see you right now, in your English sweater, with the hole in your sock. Can't I come over and get you and bring you home with me?"

She thought for a minute, then said, "No. It's late. I need to sleep a lot more. And the twins—you can't leave them alone."

"Traveling has made you very practical, Susannah."

"Why do you keep laughing at me?" she asked, but happily—seeing his turned-down smile, his gray eyes: how different he looks without his glasses, she remembered. He had folded them up and put them on the table by the bed, with *Walden*.

"Because I'm so happy you're home."

"You said that already."

"But it's true. I want you to know that. I liked your letters."

"I wanted them to make you miss me more."

He laughed. "I missed you so much, anyway, that I can't tell whether or not they made it worse. Now that you're home I'll miss your letters."

"Should I go away again?"

"No, don't do that. Susannah? We need to talk—don't you think?

We need to get together and talk all this to death. There's a lot I want to say. I've been thinking, the whole time you've been gone, and I want to tell you what I've thought about. So why don't we do this—"

"What?"

"Well." He paused while she wondered. She had her own ideas, and she clutched the phone tight. Was this really love: this pure, embarrassing need?

"What?"

"Suppose I pick you up tomorrow night after work and you come home with me and stay the night, and then Monday is my day off and we could spend it together and get everything straightened out."

She smiled, pressed her lips with her fingers; it was so seldom in life that you heard exactly what you wanted to hear.

When they hung up, she ate her sandwich, breaking off small pieces and putting them into her mouth; it seemed too much effort to pick the whole thing up and bite into it. She was tired again, as if the talk with Duke had been equal to a six-hour plane ride, a trip through time zones. She got a glass of milk. There was beer in the refrigerator, the heavy Mexican kind Ivan always drank; but she didn't think about that, and noted only a small grateful rejoicing, a musical note somewhere in the back of her mind, that he was gone, a phenomenon—that music—that always astonished her. How could she have kept herself from knowing, while they were still together, how much she hated what he did? But she thought of Duke drinking his beer in the kitchen of his old house. Would the stove be going? If not, the kitchen would be cold, Duke would have on his lumberjack shirt, there would be either chamber music or bluegrass on the radio, and Duke would drink his Heineken out of a glass mug like the ones in English pubs. She remembered again their night together, and the shock of the morning, and the days following when she had stayed at Duke's because she had nowhere else to go, coming home from the hospital to flop, dead tired, on the bed in the room she and Ivan had shared. How she had kept her distance from Duke because he had said he had nothing to give; how she had thought to protect herself and had waked in the mornings, surrounded by the cats, certain that life held nothing for her except this, and maybe the baby, still unreal, that she carried in her womb. And then Rosie had asked her to come and care for her; and Duke had come to visit like a friend, or a shy formal suitor, or a caseworker checking up, had sat out on the porch with her and Rosie and Peter, sometimes, on the evenings of his days off, while they all talked baseball or vegetable gardening or English travel plans, never speaking a word to her in private or alluding to their night together or what was said afterward; until, the day before she and Rosie left for England, he had left the Café in Simon's hands, shown up in the middle of dinnertime, and kissed her in Rosie's living room, and asked her again, urgently, to come and live with him even though he didn't know, couldn't know what he could offer her in return except shelter, and friendship, and his desire for her; and she had said she didn't know, had no answer, kept thinking *life is too short*—but whether she meant too short to go through it without Duke or to settle for so little, she didn't know. And they had kissed and kissed, and she had promised to write and he had dashed back to the Café. Then, next day on the plane, while Rosie flirted with the man on the aisle, she had begun composing her first letter, and had resolved to fight.

Susannah went upstairs and turned on the radio by her bed, softly, to the public station—Bill Monroe and his Blue Grass Boys, that's what Duke would be listening to. She fell asleep during "Lonesome Road Blues," during the *accelerando* banjo solo.

She slept late, and then spent the day emptying suitcases: putting dirty clothes through the washer, reading over the journal she had kept, collecting into a manila envelope the pile of souvenirs Rosie had doggedly gathered—National Trust pamphlets, matchbooks, ticket stubs, postcards, a schedule of services from Winchester Cathedral—irrelevant now, absorbed into the past. Susannah worked inside while Rosie, out in the garden, spread compost and hay mulch. A huge box of bulbs had arrived, and Rosie talked of getting them all into the ground within the next few days.

"There are hundreds of them," Susannah protested on one of her trips to the backyard. She didn't understand bulbs: you planted them in the fall, they flowered in the spring if the squirrels didn't dig them up, then you pulled them out in the summer and put them back in again in the fall. Her mother's energy for this sort of thing astonished her; it was a Rosie she hadn't met before, except as a child. She dimly recalled a tight-lipped Rosie raging through her bedroom like a natural disaster in reverse, banging everything noisily into place.

"Don't worry about her," Mrs. Sheffield said. She was out working in her yard, too, though without Rosie's ferocity. They watched Rosie dump a barrowful of peat moss at the feet of the Rosa Mundi. "She's normal when she's being obsessive. Worry about her when she slows down and puts her feet up." But she called over, "Take it easy with that shoulder, Rose."

Susannah wandered back inside. She thought she should probably clean the place up—it was dusty after three weeks, not that she and Rosie had left it all that clean anyway. After she ran the vacuum cleaner in the bedrooms she sat down with her notebook to catch the thread of a story she'd begun to construct in England. She jotted down an idea, the image of a particularly grotesque gargoyle she'd seen somewhere, on the front of one of the cathedrals, and that led to a scrap of dialogue and the aimless doodling out of a plot line, and she forgot to finish the vacuuming. Rosie wouldn't notice anyway. Susannah had been reassured, when she came to stay at Rosie's, to find the place in a state of what appeared to be chronic untidiness—a surprise after the picture Ivan had built up, from her television image, of a woman formidably in control, someone Susannah should model herself on. Her own early memories were of a woman who valued glove boxes and silver polish. Seeing the shoes left under the table, the coffee cups on the windowsills, the old magazines stacked in corners, Susannah felt a real kinship with her mother, a real sense of daughterliness.

"Did you used to be neater when I was a kid?" Susannah had demanded.

"Aren't I neat now?" Rosie had asked.

Susannah took a bath after the washer stopped, and dressed carefully. She put on the blouse Carla had made for her when, briefly and intensely, she took up sewing during her pregnancy with Tyler. Susannah, whose only skill was putting words on paper, used to envy Carla the ease with which she mastered what she dabbled in—not just sewing and typing—which she did rapidly, errorlessly, giving it only half her attention—but knitting, basket-making, macramé; arts that involved the skillful weaving together of various elements, things that surrounded Carla in heaps on the floor, that she drew into her hands and, magically, transformed into useful objects. Carla said she would trade all her small talents to write like Susannah, but Susannah didn't believe her.

The blouse was heavy white cotton, meant to be worn unironed, with big sleeves that stood up at the shoulders, a high banded collar, a very small tomato stain on the front, and—most remarkably—tiny buttons marching down the front that were pea-sized faces, people's heads that Carla had clipped from old photographs and sealed, somehow, under plastic: a mustachioed man, and one with slicked-back patent-leather hair, a sweet-faced woman in a pompadour, a stern little girl whose round face filled the button precisely, another child with wispy ringlets and a big grin. Susannah loved these people. "What'll I do when the blouse wears out?" she had asked Carla, imagining all those wonderful faces banished away in a drawer full of old clothes. "Take the buttons off, and I'll make you something else to put them on," Carla had said. Susannah hadn't thought of that.

She put on her Chinese slippers and a shin-length denim skirt with an elastic waist, and arranged her hair in one long, frayed braid.

Rosie smiled when she saw her. "I'm glad you're going out with Duke."

"I'm not exactly going out." Susannah had told Rosie she'd be gone all night, had stuck her toothbrush in her skirt pocket.

"Well, whatever," Rosie said. "It makes me feel young, anyway, to sit here with you waiting for your date—as if I have a teenage daughter. I missed all that, with you. Oh, I know—" She raised both hands in playful protest. "It was my own fault."

"But it *wasn't*." They had been over that before: whose fault was it—who had deserted whom?

"And Peter's teenage years were so . . ." She looked for the right word. "Irregular," she said finally, and then frowned as if that wasn't quite it.

Duke arrived just before ten. He had rushed home to shower and change, and his hair was still wet. Susannah was touched by this, how he had hurried. He had on his squashed fishing hat. He looked thinner, she thought. He didn't kiss her at first, just took her hand, and they chatted for a few minutes with Rosie until—very much the teenager's mother—she said, "You two get along now, it's late," as if they had to catch a movie. They left her chuckling over a Monty Python rerun on television, and in the car Duke pulled Susannah close to him, and they kissed.

"I missed you."

"I missed you."

They drove straight to Duke's, fast. "Who's with the twins?" Susannah asked, happiness making her voice sound strange to her—higher, and fluttery.

"They have a new sitter, a friend of Ginger's named Estelle. She stays with them evenings and weekends, and there's a high school girl who fills in after school until Estelle gets there."

"That's a lot of sitters."

"I don't see the kids enough," Duke admitted. "I'm teaching Simon to cook so he can take over the lunch shift on weekends and school holidays. He's pretty good. He learns fast. I'd try to find a second cook, a professional, but I don't think we should spend that much. I'll give Simon a raise, of course, when I promote him."

"And the place is doing well? Still?"

"I can't believe how well, Susannah. We'll sit down and look at the books tomorrow." He stretched one hand out to touch her, and she leaned toward him. "Not tonight, though," he said. She traced with her finger the silky white scars on the back of his hand.

The twins were asleep, and Estelle left in a hurry. "I have a date," she said apologetically—a tiny woman in an upswept hairdo and dangling earrings. She looked as if she might be going dancing, but she said no, they were going bowling. "You've been away, I hear," she said to Susannah, making conversation while she gathered her things. "Welcome back from wherever."

"Thanks," said Susannah. She heard three thumps as the cats jumped down from beds and windowsills upstairs.

"Oh, those cats," said Estelle, sighed, hoisted her purse to her shoulder. "The twins were dolls," she said, and with a wave at the door was gone. The cats rubbed around Susannah's ankles, watching Duke. He shook cat food from a box into three bowls, and they bent over, crunching.

"They've forgotten me," Susannah said. She leaned down to pet Shelley, who continued to eat.

"At dinnertime they forget everything but Little Friskies," Duke said. "You remember that."

"They never change."

"Maybe that's why you're so fond of them."

"No," she said, watching him put the cat food away and fill their water bowls. "I have nothing against change."

Upstairs, Duke lit the candle in his bedroom. *Walden* was still by the bed, along with a book called *Root Cellaring* and one of Susannah's *New Yorkers*. She had to unbutton the little photo-buttons on her blouse—Duke couldn't manage them—and she stepped out of her skirt and left it where it fell. The candlelight threw giant, jumping shadows on the walls. "I've imagined this so many times," she said, smiling at Duke.

"So have I," he said, and put his arms around her. "Every single blasted day since last August fifteenth."

The candle eventually burned out, and the cats came in, one by one, and arranged themselves on the piles of clothes on the floor, waiting.

In the morning it was like old times. Susannah woke to hear Duke and the twins downstairs in the kitchen. The cats were gone, too, and pale sunlight came in around the sides of the green window shades and threw one fuzzy shaft across the foot of the bed. She stayed in bed a while, listening to the toast pop up, the refrigerator door close, Mary Grace ask for more oatmeal. She laid her head on Duke's pillow. "Here Keatsie," she heard one of the twins say. "Here Keatsie Weatsie, have some butter," and Duke say, "Don't feed the cat off your spoon, for Pete's sake."

Listening, she thought how she used to consider Duke and Ivan similar types, both forever vaguely aspiring to some shifting goal. But there was nothing vague about Duke; he was solid, sharp-focused. Her life with Ivan, the slippery texture of it, as fake as Ivan's Ancestor Heritage paintings, returned vividly to her as she lay in bed. *I'm happy enough*, she used to say in the flat on Dimmick Street—as if happiness was like pie, and a little could fill you up.

She dressed in her skirt—creased and cross-hatched with cathair—and a flannel shirt of Duke's she found hanging on the bedpost, and went downstairs. There was a fire in the stove. The kitchen smelled pleasantly of toast. Duke stood at the stove pouring boiling water into a coffee filter.

The twins jumped up to hug her. "Susannah! You slept over!"

"You've been gone so long."

"We took all your postcards to school, and Mrs. Curtis hung them up."

"I bought presents for you two," Susannah told them. "All kinds of little goodies." She looked at Duke, over the heads of the twins. "I must have left them in the car last night."

"We'll go get them," they said, and dashed for the door.

"A big green canvas bag in the back seat," Susannah called. The door slammed.

"Our mornings-after seem destined to be chaotic," she said to Duke.

He put down the teakettle and came over to the table to kiss her. "I was going to wake you when I got up but you looked so peaceful, with your hair all spread out." He kissed her again. "You looked so beautiful, Susannah."

"Ah, Duke." She leaned sleepily against him. "I'm glad to be here with you."

"Stay," he whispered.

Had it become, then, so simple, after all? *Stay.* And yet Susannah could sense swarms of unsaid words lurking at the borders of that simple one. "Later," she said. "We'll talk later."

The twins returned with the bag. "It *is* big," said Mary Grace.

"We were too polite to open it," Mary Claire said, handing it over, and Susannah laughed and hauled out the quilted whale and the dolphin, necklaces of blue beads, jars of jam with little cloth caps, dolls dressed like Queen Elizabeth I and Mary Queen of Scots, soap shaped like sheep, and *A Colouring Book of English Rural Life*.

"Look! They spelled *coloring* wrong," said Mary Claire, shocked.

"That's the English spelling," Duke said.

"We knew that," said Mary Grace. "Don't you remember in that mouse book? And *flavour*—remember they spelled that wrong, too."

"First grade seems to agree with you two," Susannah said. She was amazed all over again at how beautiful they were, with their curly light hair, their chubby tanned cheeks, their tiny hands, deft like Duke's. *If I stayed they would be mine—my children*, she thought, and folded her hands over the small swelling of her stomach. The twins hugged her, one on each side, and thanked her. She snapped the beads around their necks.

"Daddy says you're having a baby."

Susannah nodded. "Next spring."

"It's in there now?" Mary Claire spread her hand tentatively an inch above Susannah's abdomen.

"Sure. Go ahead. You can feel it."

Mary Claire lowered her hand. "It feels like you got fat."

"Let *me* feel." Mary Grace pushed her hand under her sister's. "It doesn't feel fat enough for a baby."

The school bus honked, and the twins flew around the kitchen gathering jackets and lunchboxes. They kissed Duke, kissed Susannah, ran for the door.

"Maybe he could sleep in that little teeny room next to our bedroom," Mary Grace called back, before the two of them clattered down the front steps. Susannah looked out the window to see them climb on the bus; two of the cats strolled idly down the path behind them and, when the bus left, sat down to wash in the sun.

"He could, you know," said Duke. "Or she. It's a nice little room."

"Duke—"

"Later," he said, and took her hand.

They stayed in bed until noon, and then they sat in the bright kitchen again, in the two rocking chairs, just as they used to. The sun had warmed the room, and Duke let the stove go out. Susannah made toast for them both, and Duke poured coffee. He picked up the quilted whale and stroked it, smiling. They sat in sunny silence until Susannah said, "Tell me—please. What you've been thinking all these weeks."

He looked up in mock surprise. "I thought you'd know by now."

"I mean—ultimately. About us. Tell me, Duke."

He frowned down at the whale. "Just that I was wrong, Susannah. It's you I love. You know that."

The silence returned, the sun continued to shine in, Duke traced the tail of the whale with his fingertip.

"But what else?" Susannah asked finally.

"Ivan," Duke said.

"Ivan?" It was like a hard blow to the head. She put down her coffee cup, pressed the bone between her eyes with two fingers. "Ivan seems about as relevant to this discussion as—I don't know—cat yummies."

"It's his baby you're pregnant with."

"Oh Lord, Duke. For heaven's sake." She stood up and walked to the door. The sun shone on Duke's apple trees. She could see red apples through the leaves. "For heaven's sake."

They went outside, not holding hands. How absurd, how *stupid* to be at war with the man she loved. *I'm a peaceable person*, she thought, not for the first time. "But it's *my* baby," Susannah said. They were on the path to the pond. A scrap of the twins' kite from April still flapped high in a tree, yellower than the leaves. Here, last summer, she had walked after her writing hours. She had sat with her bare feet in the pond and thought of the years she had wasted with Ivan, all those blind years. "He has no claim on it," she said to Duke. Leaves floated on the surface of the pond, and a dull green scum near their feet was laced all over with a tiny star pattern. "I don't intend for him ever to know about it. And I told you, Duke, I'll never take him back."

"You said *never never never never never*. If I recall."

"I meant it. I meant every one of those *nevers*."

Duke threw a stone into the pond; the ripples rocked the leaves, rippled the scum. "It feels like stealing to me, Susannah. That's all."

"Oh crap, Duke. Dammit." She didn't have much of a bad-language repertoire. "What do we do, then? You say you love me. You invite me into your bed. You make suggestive remarks about where the baby can sleep. You ask me to stay—what do you mean by all that? And now you tell me I belong to Ivan, as if this was fifteenth-century Italy. Or *Porgy and Bess*. What do you want us to do? Where do we go from here, Duke?"

Do I want this man? she thought. Why won't he just plunge in? *Fierceness*, Rosie had said. Maybe she was right.

He took her hands—fists—and held them to his chest. "Susannah. I want you to live with me. I want you to be a mother to my twins and I want to be a father to your baby. But I can't see how it's that easy, I don't see how we can look at it as a permanent thing. It's not because I don't love you. I just don't want to bind you down to anything yet."

"Duke, I'm getting divorced. Give me time, can't you? First there's this thing with Ivan, then there's my mother, then this trip. I'll call a lawyer right now." She pulled her hands away; he let her go. "Don't you *want* me to get a divorce?"

"Of course—God, yes, Susannah. You know I do. But I get everything out of this. Don't you see that? And I don't want to have it unless we're fair to Ivan."

"You mean tell him I'm pregnant."

"Well."

She sighed, turned away from him, and walked back up the path. He followed. "He'll *want* it, Duke," she said. "Joint custody or something. I don't want my child to grow up in California hanging around bars with Ivan while he picks up women."

"I really don't think that would be a problem, Susannah," Duke said mildly.

"Oh, *don't* you?" She walked fast, talking over her shoulder. "You don't know Ivan. When he's in the mood, what he wants more than anything is children. He'd get lawyers—Duke, in California they have lawyers who specialize in wangling custody for the wrong parent. Ivan always gets what he wants."

"It's a pretty hard secret to keep all your life, Susannah."

She stopped under an apple tree, and crushed a rotten apple on the ground with her foot. She remembered, that day in Stonington, telling herself she'd keep her pregnancy secret from Ivan. "I don't want him involved," she said, and kicked another apple away. One of the cats chased it briefly. What a child she had been that day—Rapunzel. As if life was something out of a book—magical and under control.

Duke, coming up beside her, picked an apple from the tree, polished it on his sleeve, and handed it to her with a courtly gesture.

"No, thanks," she said. "They look good, though," she added more amiably. Duke bit into the apple and chewed in silence, looking thoughtfully up into the tree. Oh, why couldn't they just go back to bed, forget Ivan? This was what she had dreaded, these complications of honor, these subtleties and barriers. First Margie, now Ivan—ghosts. She wanted only to lay her tangled life down beside Duke's and let them mingle, braid together like hair. She loved him because he was exactly what he seemed to be, and because he didn't want to change her; the only way he could disappoint her would be by deviousness, or by lecturing her about hanging up her clothes. And she liked his gentleness, his cleverness, the way he could make things, fix anything, the way he would take on a project and see it through. The garden was all dug under and mulched, the twins' playhouse freshly painted to protect it from the winter, the porch screens taken down. He never claimed he didn't have time for things, he didn't hang around bars and chase other men's women.

"I thought I saw him over in Chiswick yesterday," he said. "On the street. Then I thought I saw the van, I thought it passed me down by the turnpike entrance."

"Oh, *damn.*" She gripped his arm, pulling away the apple he had halfway to his mouth. He dropped it. "Damn Ivan. I really can't see how it affects us, Duke—where he goes or what he does."

"Don't you think he's here for a reason, Susannah? Don't you think he's here to see you, and talk things over?"

"I don't know, and I don't care," she said fiercely, but she could feel it sneaking up on her, like a monster in one of her old stories: the thing that would happen. How could she think it would be over so easily between her and Ivan? That she could slip from one man to another like a library book?

"Well," Duke said again, started to reach for another apple and thought better of it.

I'll have to put him in a story, Susannah thought. *The rescuer, the prince, the strong man. I'll just have to beef him up a bit.* And then, seeing the look in his gray eyes, the double crease between his eyebrows, the tense set of his head, as if his neck hurt—the way he was grappling with it, trying to incorporate her, his dead wife, his children, Ivan, the unborn baby, and God knew what else into his scheme of life—instantly she was full of love for him. She touched his sleeve again, rubbed her hand up and down the tweedy sweater. "You're right, Duke."

His face lost some of its tenseness. "I am?"

"I'll see Ivan. I'll search him out if he doesn't get in touch with me. It simply never occurred to me, Duke," she said, with a hesitant laugh. "You know me. I never—" She was afraid he would think her selfish, unrealistic; all the faults she knew Ivan had laid out for his old friend would come back to Duke and cancel out love. Who could love a dipshit, a dingbat, a woman who couldn't keep her mind on the situation at hand? "I was so busy forgetting him. I was so busy with the relief of it all finally happening. I didn't think it through." She looked closely at him, found nothing in his eyes but love and concern, and saw that she could tell him anything, be guilty of any number of faults, and the look in his eyes wouldn't substantially change. "I'll settle it with him," she said. "Tell him about the baby, work something out. I want him out of my life, Duke."

He drew her to him, and they stood a while under the apple trees, and then they walked arm in arm to the house. Duke pulled her down beside him on the step. "Talk to me, then," he said. "Be my Susannah." He kissed her and undid her shaggy braid, and pulled her hair around her shoulders. "*Carpe diem,*" he said, like Peter.

So they talked—talked on and on, there on the step, and not about Ivan. Susannah told Duke about the innkeeper in Chiddingstone who thought Connecticut was Cleveland, and Duke told Susannah about Simon's recipe for red chili muffins, and Susannah told Duke about the royal wedding panties she had seen in an English shop, on sale, and Duke told Susannah about a bar out on Route One that had opened and closed since she'd been gone, called Topless Towers, and Susannah told Duke about Jane Austen's grave, and Duke told Susannah about Seymour's, the ailing seafood restaurant he had his eye on. They went over the books for the Café and decided maybe they could think of moving the place after the first of the year—maybe in the spring. Duke told Susannah about the root cellar he wanted to dig out in the basement, and Susannah told Duke about a girl she and Rosie met at a country fair who was first runner-up for Miss Cheddar Cheese. After a while they went inside and ate bread with English jam on it, and Susannah made a phone call to California; Edwin's strong voice disconcerted her. "He's been doing well, Mrs. Cord," the nurse told her, "but it's nothing to hope on. Just be grateful for it while it lasts."

When the twins got home, bounding off the school bus like puppies from a kennel, they all went out and raked leaves and picked apples, and then Susannah took them to Pizza Heaven for dinner. As they passed a bar on Route One called Smokey José's Susannah saw a van like Ivan's parked in the lot, but she said nothing. The world was full of vans like Ivan's. The twins carried their stuffed dolphin and whale and wore their bead necklaces, and chattered to Susannah and Duke about Mrs. Curtis, their teacher, who was on a diet and who promised to take them all out to McDonald's when she lost twenty pounds. Over pizza, they asked again where the baby would sleep. In the little room next to theirs? So they would hear it if it cried?

"I think that would be a perfect place," Susannah said.

Duke smiled. Susannah pictured him with the baby, cradling it in his square hands, pinning on diapers as neatly as he eased pie crust into a pan.

She moved in on Halloween. "Do you mind, Rosie?" she asked. "Tell me honestly."

"A little," Rosie said, but smiled over at her. It was early evening, and they were in the car, hauling Susannah's things back to Duke's—a suitcase, the green canvas bag, and a grocery bag full of notebooks and papers. "I like to see my children happy, though."

These statements, Susannah felt, were literally true. Rosie would miss her a little, not a lot; and she did rejoice in her happiness, and Peter's; there was never a hint that she would have preferred more orthodox happinesses for them.

Rosie helped her haul her things into the kitchen, then kissed her and left. She was going to a Halloween party dressed as a gypsy. "At my age, you go as something glamorous," she said. "Lots of makeup and jewelry. No witches, no ghouls—too close to home." She had a date with a man she had bought a tape recorder from. "I'll see you bright and early Tuesday morning," she said to Susannah as she left. With the new tape recorder, and Susannah's pages of notes from England, and Rosie's scribbled inspirations, they were going to work on the book in earnest.

Susannah carried her bags up to Duke's room and then walked down the road, in the twilight, to Ginger's. The twins—dressed as witches—had gone to a sleep-over Halloween party. Susannah thought she might have a cup of tea with Ginger and then get Ginger to drive her over to the Café. She wanted to tell Ginger about her trip, about Rosie's recovery, about the progress of her pregnancy. Ginger had been out of town herself, Susannah knew—taken a week's vacation to see her harassed sister Sheila through a crisis. They had thought she would be home by now, but no one answered when she knocked, and there were no lights on. Susannah felt bereft. She had looked forward to an intimate, gossipy chat, to the latest word on Sheila, to talk of Ginger's likes, dislikes, friends, feuds. Walking by herself back up the road, she halfheartedly planned out an evening, resigned to a lonely Halloween until Duke got home at ten. She considered phoning him at the Café, asking if someone could come and get her. She'd gladly cashier or chop onions or simply sit in a corner and stay out of the way; it was company she wanted. But it seemed presumptuously wifely of her, somehow, to call Duke and beg a ride. She would turn on the radio, read old*Preventions* and *New Yorkers*, stay alert for any stray witch or gypsy who ventured down Perkins Road. She would call Edwin—later, between his dinner and his sleeping pill.

She leafed through two magazines. She ate a brownie and some sunflower seeds, and then, remembering little Rosetta, drank a glass of milk. She was playing the minuet from *Don Giovanni* on the old claw-foot piano in the living room when Duke called to ask her if she could come in to the Café and work. "Ginger was supposed to be back tonight," he said. "I don't know what's gotten into her. Or she must have told me tomorrow, not tonight, I don't know. I hate to ask a pregnant woman to come into this madhouse and actually *work*, but I've got Simon out there waiting on tables, and now I need someone to help me in the kitchen."

"I'd love to," she said, so promptly he laughed.

"You're lonely."

"Everyone's at a Halloween party but me."

"I wouldn't exactly call this a party, sweetie."

Simon picked her up. He was a tall, graceful black man, barely twenty, always in a shirt and tie, whose only interest seemed to be food. He made her tell him about English food all the way to the Café.

"It doesn't sound like much," he said when they pulled into the lot.

"They have fabulous bakeries, Simon."

"Oh—bakeries," he said scornfully. "Bakeries aren't *food*."

The Café was busy. "I don't know why all these people aren't out ringing doorbells and bobbing for apples," Duke said. "Who wants to eat out on Halloween?"

"I wouldn't mind," Lois, the part-time waitress, said. "Hi, Susannah. Good to have you back."

She found an apron and tied it around her middle, remembering her vision of herself arranging flowers, possibly in evening dress. She grinned, pulled her hair back tightly with string, and stuck it down the back of her shirt. "What do I do?" she asked Duke. She loved the kitchen, all stainless steel and shiny wood. Businesslike. She looked with affection at the big black stove; the fights over it seemed far, far away, years ago.

"Keep an eye on that soup, will you? And slice bread—that black bread. And I'm going to need some more tomatoes peeled. You know how? Take a slotted spoon and dunk them in that pan there—it should be boiling—and then peel them with a—here." He flung down a knife. "Hell, of course you know how to do it, don't mind me. And will you seed them, too? And when you get a chance we could use more walnuts chopped." He kissed her quickly. "Please."

"No kissing," she said, loving him in this role: how quickly he did everything, how he kept his good humor in the midst of the furor, how oddly handsome he looked in his white apron and his blue denim shirt. "Treat me like a regular employee or we'll never get through this," she said. "Pretend I'm Simon."

"Then I'll have to keep the jalapeno peppers out of your reach. Simon thinks hot pepper is some kind of religion."

"It cleans out your insides," Simon said, loading a tray. "It clears your brain. Also, it prevents colds."

"The Jalapeno Pepper Unification and Purification Church. Simon is the Reverend Moon of cold prevention."

Simon grinned and said, "You see how he can work and talk at the same time? He didn't used to be able to do that. He's coming along, this boy. One of these days he's going to be a fine cook."

After work, Susannah and Duke drove home. There was a sharp bit of moon in a clear sky, and they sat outside for a while, close together on the steps. "That was fun," Susannah said, though she was tired, and there was a very small ache, just beginning, at the base of her spine. "The craziness, the rushing around, the wonderful smells. And Simon—he's so funny. And I love to look out and watch people wolf it down."

"Oh well," Duke said, pleased. "I suppose it is. But this"—he put his arm around her; it was a cold night, with a wind—"this is more fun."

"It is," she said, and then, hugging him, suddenly sat up straight with a little cry.

"What is it?"

He drew back to look at her in alarm, but she smiled and moved close to him again. It was what she'd thought she had felt, earlier, while she was chopping walnuts at the Café—a dreamlike tug, a flutter like a bird. "The baby," she said. "Kicking. Here—feel."

They sat in silence, waiting, his hand warm on her stomach. "They never kick when you want them to," Duke said.

"Maybe she'd like a glass of milk."

"Try it."

They went inside, and Susannah drank a glass while Duke fed the cats. "It put her to sleep," Susannah said, wiping her milk mustache on the sleeve of her shirt. She watched Duke lock the back door, put away the cat food, draw the gingham curtains on the kitchen windows; and she thought of her father, sitting up in bed, maybe watching television, thousands of miles away where it wasn't even dark yet, at this hour, and where it wasn't beginning to get cold and leaves weren't falling. This must have been what he had in mind when he said *be good, be happy*—this dimly lit house, the baby curled asleep inside her, and Duke taking her hand to lead her upstairs.

They made love with drowsy slowness, then slept and woke in the middle of the night with their arms around each other. Susannah looked at the clock—three. Her stomach rumbled, not a kick this time but hunger. "Little Rosetta wants something good."

Duke yawned and sat up. "You've seen too many cartoons. What does she want? Pickles? Banana ice cream with tomato sauce?"

"Let's do something daring and wicked," Susannah said. He bent to kiss her, cupped her breasts in his two hands. "No, not that. I mean let's go over to the Café and finish up that mushroom quiche. And the bread pudding."

He squinted at the clock. "At three A.M.?"

"Wouldn't it be fun? To sit there on Halloween night all by ourselves having a meal? Think how spooky it'll be."

"Is your entire pregnancy going to be like this? Five more months of irrational behavior?" He got out of bed as he spoke, turned on a light, reached for a shirt. "Well? Come on. We'll go trick-or-treating at the Café."

But someone had beaten them to it. They went in the back door and, for one confused moment, Susannah thought they had forgotten to clean up, and then she took it in fully and saw that this was no ordinary mess, not even a salvageable mess. The place had been wrecked.

In the kitchen, pots and pans and implements had been pulled from their hooks, flung down, bent and dented. Food had been thrown at walls and in slimy heaps on the floor along with the shards of broken dishes. The trelliswork between kitchen and dining room was broken, jagged, pulled away from the walls and smashed, and the plants ripped apart and ground underfoot, dirt scattered everywhere. Even the black stove, indestructible, had been pelted with food, leftover quiche and whole-wheat flour and olive oil and melting butter running down its black sides, and one of the oven doors bent down and unhinged. In the dining room, chairs were smashed, tables overturned, the slate where the menu had been was broken to bits, the old cash register lay on its side, half its porcelain keys bent or cracked. Only the curtains at the windows and the door were intact, to hide what had happened.

"Oh, Duke," Susannah kept saying as they stood looking at the rubble. "Oh, God, Duke." She put her hands to her hot cheeks, too stunned to weep, or to say anything further. All around them, the destruction cried: *Hate*.

Duke walked around with his hands in his pockets, not speaking, a parody of his usual calm, kicking at things that had been broken and thrown to the floor. A pile of earthenware shards flew into the air, a bag of onions dropped with a loose thud. "You know who did this, don't you," he said at last in a quick tight voice.

She hadn't known until then, but she thought *of course*, and closed her eyes, dizzied.

Duke walked through the wreckage, kitchen to dining room and back, prodding piles of debris with his foot. She had never seen him angry before, hadn't realized at first that this quiet and controlled revulsion was anger. She felt a cold thrill, as if some dire, monumental fact had been revealed to her.

"I'm going to kill that son of a bitch," Duke said. "I'm going to find him and kill him."

She should protest, she was sure, but she stayed silent, and when, soon, he stopped pacing and turned to survey it all, and sighed harshly, she went to stand beside him. "That son of a bitch," he whispered. She touched his arm; it felt tense, electric. He looked at her, his eyes distant. "I know where he is," Duke said, and the muscles of his arm contracted sharply, as if he already had Ivan in his grip.

He was just coming out of Ginger's house when they pulled into the driveway: Ivan and Ginger, lit by the spotlight over the side door. Duke jerked his car to a stop beside Ivan's van, opened the door and jumped out. He leapt at Ivan and clung to him, hitting. "You son of a bitch," he kept saying. "You filthy bastard, you son of a bitch."

Ginger rushed forward and pulled him by the shoulders. "Stop it,

Duke. Stop it. He's going, he's leaving, let him go." Duke ignored her. Susannah got out of the car, slowly, feeling the baby's fluttery kick. The two men fighting were indistinct, badly lit, like an old movie. Duke hung on like an animal, as if with claws, pounding into Ivan wherever he could reach his fist—awkward, unpracticed blows that nevertheless caused harm. Ivan's nose began to bleed, and it was then that Susannah noticed Ivan wasn't trying to hit back. His struggles with Duke were attempts to get loose, and the look on his face was the look of St. Sebastian pierced by a hundred arrows.

"Duke!" Susannah cried, but he was already letting go, stepping back, panting, from Ivan's silent endurance. Ivan covered his face with his hands and leaned against the van. No one spoke. There was only the sound of Duke's hard breathing.

It was a long moment, like a play stopped because no one knew their lines, like the wait for a prompter who had momentarily dropped off to sleep. They stood, the four of them, in the chilly driveway, the open fan of light casting their shadows far ahead of them on the ground— all but Ivan, whose shadow was compressed between himself and the van. Ginger's frizzy hair looked transparent. A pair of tall oaks, not quite bare of leaves, reached across the road and almost obscured the sliver of moon. A small wind rustled invisible leaves over the ground. Susannah stood there, a long moment, but, still, a moment, during which Duke continued to pant beside her, Ginger continued to cross her two hands in horror over her mouth, Ivan to stand motionless against the bright blue van—and then Ginger walked over to where Ivan was and pulled his hands down from his face, first one, then the other. He had shaved off his beard, Susannah saw, and his face was bloody. He didn't look at anyone; he looked down at his hands, streaked with blood from his nosebleed.

"Ivan," Ginger said to his bent head, in a voice of such tenderness Susannah flinched. "Ivan? Are you all right?"

"Yeah," he said after a moment.

"Ivan?"

"Don't worry," he said. His voice sounded as if he had a bad cold. He raised the back of his hand to his nose, and tipped his head back. The bleeding had stopped. He turned his head, slightly, toward Susannah. "I'm leaving," he said. "And I won't be back."

"All right." She hesitated, felt she should say something further, but she had no words. She was still dazzled, even here in the near dark, by bright lights illuminating wood and chrome and clean white and the outrage and injury done to it all. He would lay his hand on anything, he would defile whatever came in his way. "Yes," she said. "All right. Good."

He turned then to look fully at her, but he didn't speak. The play stopped again. Ginger went into the house, and then, on impulse, Susannah left Duke's side and went up to Ivan—another long moment, while they stared at each other. She had meant to say something definitive, something beyond simple acquiescence in his plans, but again no words came. She stood beside him, but she felt miles and years away, and he seemed oddly unfamiliar, as if this wasn't the man she had lived with, just someone similar. Without the beard, he looked very young. She had never seen him beardless, and she thought *this is how he looked during his sad childhood.* The thought didn't make him any less unreal, or any less a stranger.

Ginger came back carrying two paper towels, one wet and one dry. "Here," she said, coming up to them. Her manner was brisk and motherly—put on, Susannah felt, for her benefit. "Wipe your face, Ivan," she said.

Ivan ignored her and held out his hand to Susannah. "Good-bye, Susannah."

She couldn't take his hand. She thought of the broken oven door on the big black stove; he must have climbed up and stamped down, hard, to injure it so. He must have raised casseroles and dishes and glass jars high over his head and hurled them down in a fury, like old prints of Zeus hurling thunderbolts. He must have thought of her, thought of Duke, as he smashed and kicked and threw things and made the little kitchen smell of hate and filth. She could wish him Godspeed, but she couldn't take his hand, couldn't touch him.

Ivan's lips pursed for a second in a grimace, and his hand dropped to his side. His clean-shaven face was strangely expressive and vulnerable. "I'm leaving, then," he said again, and Susannah was filled with pity for his empty hand, his naked face.

"That would be best," she whispered.

"Ivan?" Ginger held out the wet towel, and he turned to her and let her sponge his face. Susannah stepped back and went over to where Duke stood. He didn't appear to have moved. They waited, together, watching while Ginger wiped Ivan's face; he stood meekly, enduring it, Ginger whispering to him something Susannah couldn't hear, Ivan nodding. Then he got into the van and started it up. "Take care," Ginger said. Ivan backed the van past them out of the driveway, and turned up Perkins Road toward Route One. When the engine noise died away, they could hear Ginger sniffling. Susannah held Duke's hand.

"He's been with me all week," Ginger said. She looked worn out, her face subtly more ravaged than when Susannah had last seen her— or maybe it was just that she was a little drunk. "All week. Just drinking and talking. He kept the van hidden in my garage. He got drunk tonight—really drunk. He told me what he did at the Café. He just went crazy, Duke. I've been pouring coffee into him for the last two hours. He says he's going to drive all night." As she talked, she got hold of her voice, became brisk again. "He's on his way to Ottawa, Canada. Some kind of lay monastery. He went to a place out on the coast somewhere, a home for troubled priests or whatever, and they sent him back here, to this Canadian place, it's where they go to get their heads together. I just hope he drives carefully. I told him to pull over and sleep if he gets tired." She smoothed the paper towels in her hand. The wet one had become pinkish but not very; there hadn't, really, been much blood. Susannah wondered if Ginger would save it. "He'll be there—indefinitely, he says." Her voice broke on the last words and, whimpering, she bunched the towels together and raised them to her face.

Duke put a hand on Ginger's shoulder. She breathed deeply, calming herself. "Get some sleep, Ginger. Or do you want to come home with us? We'll put you up if you'd rather not stay alone."

"I'm all right," Ginger said. "I'm just *sad*, Duke."

"I know," he said. The three of them walked toward the car. "I'm sad, too."

Duke got into the car, and Ginger turned to look at Susannah. "You're not saying much, Susannah." She spoke with effort, as if the words caused her actual pain, in her throat or in her chest.

"Oh, Ginger—" Susannah put her arms around Ginger, breathed in the smells of hair spray and whiskey, said, "Ginger, I'm so sorry, I'm so sorry," and they both began to cry, taking comfort from the sound of their joint weeping until they laughed self-consciously and separated.

"God," Ginger said, and wiped her face again with Ivan's towels. "God, Susannah, what a life—isn't it?"

"It is," Susannah said, and sighed, and got into the car. "You're sure you're going to be okay alone?"

"I'm alone every night. What the hell." She went over to Duke's side and hung on to the half-open window. "Duke? You're going to reopen the place, aren't you? We can get it all cleaned up, we'll all pitch in."

Duke laughed shortly. "I don't know, Ginger. Talk to me tomorrow. I'm having a little trouble thinking constructively at the moment." He attempted a smile, unconvincingly. "Go to bed, Ginger."

She wiped her eyes. "Stay in touch, at least."

Duke's smile was genuine this time. "Ginger, we still live down the road from you. We're still *friends*. And when we reopen you'll be the first waitress we interview for a job."

He put the car in gear, and they drove back to their own dark house. It was four A.M. Duke built a fire, and they pulled their rocking chairs close together, their knees touching. Susannah had a glass of milk, Duke a beer. The three cats rubbed against their chairs, purring, hoping for food, gazing up at them with their round, surprised eyes, but eventually they gave up and, one after the other, fell asleep by the woodstove.

Epilogue

Peter and Hollis are building themselves a house, a wood frame, solar-heated four-room cottage on a hillside west of Hartford, in the Connecticut Berkshires. They are on the roof, nailing on shingles. If they look up from their work, they can see gentle green slopes, hills higher than theirs rising dark with trees, and the low hills below them to the west spread out, from this angle, almost flat. But Peter doesn't look up, doesn't like to be reminded he's twenty feet off the ground. He keeps his eyes on the shingles, pretending he's nailing them to an oddly pitched floor. Hollis respects Peter's fear, and moves carefully, talking in a low voice—no shouting, no sudden moves, no acrophobia jokes.

"What about Nelson's party?" Peter says.

"Forget Nelson's party. We're building this place so we can get away from parties like Nelson's, I thought."

"Just checking."

"Nelson's party appeals to me about as much as roofing this in gold lamé."

Peter gives a restrained chuckle, and moves in a crouch to a new spot. Hollis hands him a bag of nails. They have taken to dressing alike, when they're alone, and they both wear overalls, no shirts, white sweatbands, heavy work shoes. Taking the nails from Hollis, Peter feels as if he's taking them from his mirror image. If Hollis, who has

305

to watch what he eats, ever put on weight, Peter thinks how he would gain it too, matching him pound for pound.

"So we'll just go to Susannah's thing and then drive back here? Or will Susannah and Duke put us up?"

"Let's drive back. I don't relish being awakened by the cries of my nephew at six A.M."

"Maybe we could stay at your mother's."

"We could do that. Emmet will probably be there. I think she's taking him to Susannah's."

"Emmet is the English guy?"

"The one who looks like Leslie Howard. Not a bad chap. Hopelessly straight, in every sense of the word."

"Wouldn't Rosie be embarrassed if we stayed with her? With Emmet there? If he's so straight."

Peter laughs, not looking down. "It might embarrass Emmet, but it would take a lot more than that to embarrass my mother. Let's do that—then we won't have to worry about driving back here after the grand opening."

"It sounds like it's going to be some party."

"I just hope they do as well in this new place as they did at the old Café."

"Speaking of restaurants, what do you say we knock off and have some lunch?"

Peter pulls his hammer through the loop on his overalls, and wipes his sweaty hands. "*Andiamo*," he says gratefully, and heads with caution for the ladder. Hollis, as always, goes first, and holds the ladder while Peter descends. "Thanks, old buddy," Peter says.

It's cooler on the ground, even breezy. They both pause to look at their view. Green surrounds them, every shade of it, and above the hills and the line of trees the sky is perfectly blue, cloudless, shimmering. There is a smell of lumber and blossoms. Peter and Hollis reach out, simultaneously, and for an instant link their hands together.

From his bed, when he's propped on pillows, Edwin can see out the window to the garden where, months ago now, almost longer than he can recall, they used to wheel him in a chair. He can see the long red band of geraniums that stretches out along the gravel drive, and clumps of yellow that must be—what? Daffodils? Or marigolds? Or chrysanthemums? He can't remember, now, what blooms when, and it does no good to ask; he has asked, and he just forgets. It doesn't matter, anyway. There are the red flowers, the yellow ones, the green grass, the sky that is nearly always blue.

Sometimes he doesn't look out the window. There's the television: he has become very fond of a nature series that shows scorpions mating, lions dozing in the African bush, whales making their calm way through green, green water. And there is the photograph on his table of William, his grandson, a pink baby with an amazing quantity of fluffy yellow hair. He looks often at the photograph, attempting to find his daughter's face in that of her son; the baby is dimpled and roly-poly as Susannah never was, but the hair and the blue eyes are the same.

"He looks like a real little doll," Mrs. Panza says, when she comes with the pill. "A handsome boy, Mr. Mortimer. I'll bet he keeps his mother hopping."

"Looks like his mother," Edwin says with effort, and falls back panting on the pillows. When Susannah calls, later that evening, he is unable to talk.

"The new restaurant is doing just great," Mrs. Panza tells him. "And the baby is already turning over, she says."

"No," Edwin manages to say. He can't recall much about babies, at what age they do what, but he knows William is a remarkable child, a prodigy, and he smiles at Mrs. Panza, hoping he looks properly impressed.

She sits down on the chair by his bed—a solid, stout woman, big-bosomed. Edwin likes her big breasts, and the warm valley between them he can just glimpse when she bends over. Mrs. Panza smells of talcum powder, an innocent flowery scent.

"Your daughter says she wants to come out, soon, and bring the baby." She no longer calls Susannah "Mrs. Cord." She seems unsure, in fact, what to call her, and Edwin is no help; he can't remember her new husband's name, and isn't sure he's even her husband, as yet. It seems just a few days ago she told him she was divorcing one man and marrying another, but it must have been months ago: winter? "Mr.

Mortimer? What do you think? The baby is three months old, and she thinks he's ready to make the trip."

Edwin looks at the photograph. The baby is three months old. He imagines a three-month-old baby here, in this room. How big would a baby that age be? Did she say three months or three years? Months, of course, but—was it only three months ago that the baby was born? He thinks back to the baby, golden-haired, how he had loved her, had thought: *my salvation*—but that was Susannah, years and years ago. This was William, his grandson William.

"Here?" he says.

"Here," says Mrs. Panza, and she herself looks, he thinks, dubious. "Just a short visit. She'd like you to see the baby. But only if you're going to be up to it, Mr. Mortimer. I told her we'd talk it over, and discuss it with Dr. Strauss."

Edwin looks at the photograph. A nice baby, favors his side of the family, that yellow hair must be like silk, like Susannah's. Outside his window the flowers have dimmed, the green lawn has darkened. It won't be long before everything is dark, blank, black, and sleep comes. Mrs. Panza leaves, returns, props Edwin up so he can drink, turns on the light and the television.

"No," Edwin says, and feeling a little stronger he nods his head toward the photograph. "No, I don't think so," he says.

Ivan is working in the garden, weeding between the rows of lettuce, making his way toward the tomato plants. The sun beats hard on his bent back, and sweat drips down to the waistband of his khakis. He will finish the weeding, and then pick beans, and then in the raspberry patch he will drop berries into a basket and Japanese beetles into a coffee can filled with water, where they will drown. Drowning the beetles is the only chore he dislikes, but any fool can see they'd wreck the berry crop, so in they go, buzzing between his fingers and then flailing in the water before they stop, and float.

When he is finished in the garden, he will go inside and shower and put on clean khakis and a clean shirt and go down to the kitchen to snap beans for Brother Michael. Then he'll fill the water pitchers and wipe down the long tables before dinner, and he'll just have time to stop in the chapel before the bell. He needs to pause in the chapel three or four times a day, and he's happy there—though not so happy as he is in the garden. But the chapel drew him in over the long northern winter when the garden was unavailable, and the habit has persisted into summer. He stops only a few minutes, long enough for the stillness to sink into him, and he doesn't pray—only kneels, with his head in his hands, smelling candle wax and the curious musky smell of incense, though incense hasn't been used there in years. He thinks, sometimes, of William, his son whom he will never see, or of his two sisters in Maine whom he has, after all these years and against all odds, became close to again, but mostly he tries to keep his mind blank for these minutes—to become nothing, no one, pure existence, bodiless, without will or memory.

And it does no harm, of course, for Father Llewellyn or Father Seward to come in and see him there, head bowed. He has petitioned Rome for reentry into the priesthood, and both his superiors, he knows, will be required to evaluate him. He hasn't much hope: ex-priests are gladly welcomed back into the flock, but not as shepherds.

"It's a long shot, Ivan," Father Llewellyn has told him. "Don't be disappointed if it doesn't happen."

"I don't expect anything," Ivan always says.

"Good," says the priest.

After dinner, he goes again to the garden, and plays chess with the reformed alcoholic priest who has become his friend, or he works seriously at his sketching, doing pastel drawings of the other men—the portrait of old Father Aubrey with his head bent over his breviary is his best so far—and of the growing things in the garden: the heavy-laden arm of a tomato plant, the beans all in blossom climbing their pole, the rows of green lettuces like huge flowers, full of folds and shadows his pastels will never get to the heart of, Ivan thinks, even if he draws them every day for the rest of his life.